D0897243

Row House Days

Tales from a Southwest Philadelphia Childhood

Jack Myers

Copyright © 2005 by Jack Myers

All rights reserved. No part of this book shall be reproduced or transmitted in any form or by any means, electronic, mechanical, magnetic, photographic including photocopying, recording or by any information storage and retrieval system, without prior written permission of the publisher. No patent liability is assumed with respect to the use of the information contained herein. Although every precaution has been taken in the preparation of this book, the publisher and author assume no responsibility for errors or omissions. Neither is any liability assumed for damages resulting from the use of the information contained herein.

This is a work of fiction. Names, characters, places, and incidents either are the product of the author's imagination or are used fictitiously. Any resemblance to actual events or locales or persons, living or dead, is entirely coincidental.

ISBN 0-7414-2479-7

Published by:

INFINITY
PUBLISHING.COM

1094 New DeHaven Street, Suite 100
West Conshohocken, PA 19428-2713
Info@buybooksontheweb.com
www.buybooksontheweb.com
Toll-free (877) BUY BOOK
Local Phone (610) 941-9999
Fax (610) 941-9959

Printed in the United States of America

Printed on Recycled Paper

Published March 2005

This book is dedicated to my family, friends, classmates, teachers, neighbors, and all the former residents of the Kingsessing section of Southwest Philadelphia.

My story is your story.

Though our physical neighborhood is no more, our sense of community and shared spirit still survives through all the years.

Jack Myers
January, 2005

PROLOGUE

I was born in a dying city: Philadelphia, Pennsylvania—birthplace of the United States of America. William Penn, the Quaker visionary, mapped our streets in the seventeenth century. The brilliant Ben Franklin walked these same cobblestone byways in the eighteenth century, publishing *Poor Richard's Almanack* from his modest downtown print shop. Thomas Jefferson penned the Declaration of Independence here. The immortal George Washington led his colonial army from nearby Valley Forge. We were once the nation's largest city, as well as its proud capital. In days past, the revered Liberty Bell rang loudly across our great metropolis.

We were, at our zenith, a people of ideas and ideals. The very heart of a young and vibrant nation looking confidently toward a bright and promising future. A magnet for power, wonder, magic, and dreams. Home to legends, heroes, and giants. A happening place. The celebrated thousand points of light, that shining city upon the hill.

Philadelphia—a Greek word meaning City of Brotherly Love. At the dawn of its creation, the Founding Fathers envisioned not just another municipality but rather a grand experiment in the human condition. Theirs was the phoenix of a spirit that first sprang forth millennia ago in Athens. Those austere notions of Hellenic freedom and civic responsibility are embodied in much of the classical architecture that is our communal heritage.

So what went wrong? Why did we fail, and how have we fallen so far? As we begin the new millennium, time seems to have passed Philadelphia by. We find ourselves a second-rate stopover mired in the shadow of our nation's financial and media power, New York, and its seat of political power, Washington, D.C. The city's population is in steady decline. Factories have closed or moved elsewhere. Public schools attempt to warehouse and not to educate, and they fail miserably to achieve even this compromised goal. Yes, our downtown has benefited from a valiant and ambitious makeover, a

i

much-awaited attempt at a comeback—which is to be applauded. But the impoverished and battle-scarred neighborhoods that ring Center City with their derelict buildings, crack houses, brown fields, and collapsing infrastructure tell a different story. The old ideas and ideals have been steadily replaced by drugs, squalor, and despair. Crime, corruption, and apathy have become accepted ways of life, corroding and threatening our very existence. Life is cheapened, and the promise of a better tomorrow places a distant second to the meager spoils and base temptations available today. No future, no past—only the overwhelming demands of an increasingly desperate here and now. A sad end indeed to such a splendid, celebrated beginning.

At the downtown churchyard where Ben Franklin lies, passing tourists toss coins upon his grave for good luck. As Poor Richard long ago advised, a penny saved is a penny earned. Outside the churchyard, many of Philadelphia's hardened street people hover like vultures. They jockey for position, waiting for that right moment, perhaps a quick break in the action with no park guard in sight. Then quietly, quickly, they slip in, snatching up the scattered change, and make a clean getaway. The few coins left behind go into a fund to maintain this sacred and cherished site.

Is this to be our final legacy?

Ghettos aren't built, they are made. And once the malicious and destructive forces of the slum culture take hold, its death grip seizes with such power and fury that few who remain outside this insidious disease process seem capable of comprehending much less understanding it.

This is my tale, the story of a childhood spent growing up amid decline. Of life lived in a neighborhood that has long ceased to exist, except in the minds of former inhabitants spread far and wide. Names changed to protect the innocent—including my own. Some characters are composites, and certain events may not be told in strict chronological sequence. But these narratives are largely and fundamentally true, though they are filtered through the hazy and often imprecise device known as memory. And always they are told from the viewpoint of an imperfect child making his way in a changing world of increasing turbulence, conflict, and confusion.

Many of these tales are humorous, others sentimental, some poignant. More than a few could be considered disturbing. If you are offended or shocked by something you read here, I can empathize. But I don't apologize. Remember, I and many others had the experience of living through what you are merely reading. In other words, don't shoot the messenger. As you will soon discover, I've been through enough in one short lifetime and don't require any more excitement, thank you very much.

So I give you *Row House Days*, a book of overdue stories in dire need of telling, revealing events that have remained hidden for far too long.

Welcome to my world—or at least the world that I called mine not so many years ago. And now, let's go back in time. Back to the old neighborhood. . . .

City of Philadelphia

Bucks County

Far Northeast

Mt. Airy/ Germantown

Roxborough Manayunk

Olney/ Oak Lane

Near Northeast

Montgomery County

Upper North Phila

Frankford/ Kensington

West Philadelphia

Lower North Phila

University City

Center City

New Jersey

Cobbs Creek

Delaware County

Kingsessing

Paschall

South Philadelphia

The Meadows

Eastwick

Southwest Philly

Delaware River

Airport

Schuykill River

Philadelphia, PA

CHAPTER 1

The Stilt

It was time for my mother to put her foot down. Of course, she wasn't yet my mother, which was the reason for the ultimatum. No way was Pamela Kane going to get married, settle down, and start a family with my father-to-be cruising the high seas on an aging oil tanker. Gone ten months out of the year with the merchant marine, transporting that Texas tea from the Gulf of Mexico to the refineries of South Philadelphia, it just wasn't going to happen.

But I can't make this kind of money anywhere else, my future father reasoned.

And I can't raise children with a father who's never going to be home, Mom-to-be countered.

Obviously, Mom got her way. Dad said goodbye to his first love, the sea, quit the merchant marine, and came home to Philadelphia for good. Immediately he set about looking for new work. No easy task for an ex-merchant marine. He hits the pavement, knocks on doors, fills out dozens of applications, and sits through the occasional interview.

Comes the inevitable interviewer's question: So who're you with now?

Well, I was with the merchant marine . . . but I've quit that so I can find a local job and stay closer to home.

Merchant marine, huh? Doesn't that pay real good money? A lot better than *this* job?

Sure. But like I said, sir, what I'm looking for now's a job that's close to home. I'm getting married, and I don't want all that travel. . . .

A likely story. Pop-to-be soon realizes why he's not getting any offers. Every prospective employer simply figures he'll skip town for the bigger bucks next time a tanker is scheduled to leave port. Which is probably sometime in the middle of next week, if not sooner.

1

Desperate, my future Dad takes a job with the one outfit needy enough to hire him—the Milhouse Movie Theater up in West Philadelphia. They are looking for a new usher to start immediately, and my father needs a job. Any job. Has to start somewhere, even if at only mere fraction of his former seaman's pay.

So, night after night, under cover of darkness, my father-to-be faithfully patrols the aisles of the famed, legendary Milhouse Theater up on 52nd Street. Movie classics such as *Shane*, *The Day the Earth Stood Still*, and *Creature from the Black Lagoon* come and go. So do quite a few lesser films, including a few out-and-out stinkers. All in a hard day's night's work for up and coming usher James Morris.

It happens during one of the more highly forgettable flicks that a mini-disturbance erupts in a dark and remote corner just beyond one of the theater's two fire exits.

Rising to the occasion, my future father dutifully makes his presence felt, filling the entrance to the row in question with his fancy usher's uniform. Deftly he pulls his trusty flashlight, aims, and fires.

The beam falls on three colored boys, all high school age, all hunkered down and intensely pretending to be watching this particularly awful film.

Hey, guys, James soon to be James Sr. whispers. You have to keep it down over here. You're disturbing our other patrons.

Sorry, mister, one of the high-schoolers apologizes politely. It won't happen again.

My father nods, thanks the boys for their understanding, and returns to his post at the rear of the ancient art-deco theater. Not five minutes later, pandemonium breaks out again down by the fire exit. Laughter, shouting, general horseplay. Father-to-be hustles to the source of the disruption, snaps on his trusty light, and this time shines it rudely into the faces of the same three colored boys.

C'mon now, guys, usher James chides them. You've already had one warning. This makes two. Next time I have to come down here, you're out. . . . Understand?

2

Listen, we're really sorry, mister, the same teen spokesman answers. You see, my clumsy friend here spilled soda all down my leg. It was just an accident.

Satisfied by this explanation, young Jim Morris clicks off the beam and returns to his vantage point in the back. Not two minutes pass and comes another commotion. Popcorn flying, teens laughing, people *shooshing*. Sure enough, same spot, same culprits. Usher Morris has now witnessed enough. Striding down to the scene of the crime, he lights up the three suspects and, acting as judge, jury, and executioner, jerks his thumb toward the rear exit.

Okay, you three. Show's over tonight for you fellas. Time to go home.

Sorry, mister, the group leader says, attempting to be contrite. But he fails to suppress the muffled giggle. It really wasn't a very good movie anyway, he opines.

With that, the trio's mannerly mouthpiece gets up and files out into the dimly lit aisle. Then the second boy rises and does likewise. Usher James watches them, careful to light the way so no one trips and falls. Just one remaining still-seated miscreant . . . so my father-to-be points his light back down the nearly empty row of seats.

The third and final boy begins to get up. And up. And . . . UP. Future Dad does a double take. Possibly two more boys, one sitting on the other's shoulders? Some kind of trick? He shines the light up, down—then up again.

Nope, all one person. Seven feet tall and still growing. Now, a glimmer of recognition . . . my father has seen this face before. Philadelphia sports pages . . . basketball. It's none other than Overbrook High School front court phenom Wilt Chamberlain. Soon to be a member of the University of Kansas Jayhawks. Then on to the Harlem Globetrotters. Later, the NBA, Hall of Fame, and roundball immortality.

Yes, Wilt the Stilt. The Big Dipper. The budding legend who will one day score 100 points during a single professional game. Unrivaled. Unparalleled. Unmatched. Unstoppable.

A little-known fact about Chamberlain's career is that in some thirteen NBA seasons, in all those many games, he never gets ejected from a contest for unsportsmanlike conduct. Even more amazingly, he never fouls out of a single game. Not one . . . an astonishing statistic.

But on this night in early 1954, Wilton Norman Chamberlain is tossed from the historic Milhouse Theater on Merchant Street by my soon-to-be Old Man. Working as a temporary usher, just passing through on his way to more lucrative and steady employment. A memorable, cornball incident that's destined never to be inscribed in the colorful annals of Philadelphia sports history.

And now you know—as one famous contemporary commentator delivers his well-loved punch lines—the rest of the story.

Actually, for James Geoffrey "Little Jimmy" Morris, this is where my story first begins . . . for I am still waiting to be born.

Hot Box

Baby Morris is due in late February, 1955, but I decide to upset that careful timetable and arrive more than six weeks early. My parents don't have a car. Instead they hail a Yellow Cab for the emergency ride to Fitzpatrick Mercy Hospital in the nearby suburb of Derby. The only problem is the cabby mustn't be Catholic, doesn't know where the hospital is, and winds up driving us around in circles. What starts as an anxious ride now turns to near panic. Eventually, the flustered driver finds his way to Fitzpatrick before I am born in the backseat of his spotless vehicle rather than in the better suited, appropriately equipped maternity ward.

After a difficult and exhausting delivery, first-born James Geoffrey Morris weighs in at a less-than-strapping four pounds, fifteen ounces, and must be put in a special "hot box" bassinet almost immediately. Though premature, I am apparently healthy, except for an ugly purple bruise above my eye where the doctor's forceps inadvertently seized me. However, my inability to gain weight forces the medical staff to keep me under their special heating lamps for days on end.

4

Each day my anxious mother Pam is again promised that, yes, she will be allowed to see her baby very soon, once mother *and* child are both strong enough. But after three days of excuses Mom becomes hysterical, convinced I am either dead or horribly defective, and that Fitzpatrick Mercy Hospital is hiding some dark, terrible secret. Dad has been to see me, tries to convince Mom that everything is all right, I am fine, but Mom figures Dad is only protecting her from the awful news. Too horrible for Mom to contemplate.

At last, on the fifth day, I am finally reunited with my now despondent mother. My parents go home, relieved, where they wait expectantly for me to strengthen inside the hot box so that I may soon join them. More than a week later, Fitzpatrick Mercy finally gives them the A-OK, you can take your baby home now.

Our first family residence is Dad's mother's house on 61st Street. I arrive, the focus of Mom, Dad, and Gram's attention. My parents can't afford a crib just yet, but they make do just the same. With a dresser drawer as a makeshift baby bed, I never know the difference. They spend all their money on expensive goat's milk, which the pediatrician recommends for maximum nutrition and weight gain.

Hard to say whether it's the goat's milk or just Mother Nature taking her course, but soon I am beginning to thrive and put on some much-needed weight.

After months, the ugly purple bruise on my forehead fades, then vanishes. Eventually I'll be rolling over early, standing up early, talking early, walking early, and terrorizing adults early.

Seems Little Jimmy Morris is not one who likes to wait and take life as it comes. If I did, then I probably wouldn't be a Morris, and my folks would surely begin to suspect that someone at Fitzpatrick Mercy had taken home the wrong baby, pulled the old switcheroo.

But it soon becomes apparent this wasn't the case. Mom and Dad have the right baby. James Morris Jr.—regular chip off the old block.

And so now they're stuck with me: no refunds, no exchanges.

Alien Abduction

We swelter in the summer of 1956. Living in West Philadelphia, in our new apartment above a hardware store on 52nd Street several blocks south of Merchant. My father works the late shift at an Enco service station up on City Avenue. By the time he arrives home, it's usually well past one in the morning, and my mother and I are fast asleep in the bedroom. Before she goes to bed, Mom normally fixes Dad his supper plate and leaves it in the refrigerator.

On this particular night, a typical hot, steamy Philadelphia summer evening with little breeze, Mom prepares two bacon, lettuce, and tomato sandwiches and places a bottle of Coca Cola in the refrigerator door to cool.

When Dad gets home later, he washes up and strips right down to his undershorts and T-shirt. These are the "good old" days before air-conditioning, and the street hums with the sound of electric window fans droning like the sound of an ever-approaching prop plane.

It's far too hot to eat his late-night supper in the little window-less kitchen, so Dad quietly pulls up a chair at a card table by the open bedroom window, plops down the sandwiches and soda pop, and reaches for the Philco radio.

These old-time table-top radios aren't like the transistor radios of later years. They are bigger and bulkier, housed in boxy, wooden cases with grille cloth that makes them look like pieces of antique furniture. You twist a fat, round knob and wait. Wait for the faint, amber glow of dozens of magic vacuum tubes to warm up and get the radio going. Eventually.

Dad takes a bite of a BLT and a swig of carbonated beverage, then presses his ear up close to listen for the stations. Adjusting the volume knob to the lowest setting before OFF, my father then turns the opposing frequency knob to scan the dial's AM airwaves. New York, Baltimore, West Virginia . . . the air crackles with the sounds of distant late-night programming. But it isn't until my father picks up the faraway station in Iowa that he begins to zero in and fine tune the frequency. Something about aliens. Visitors from other planets. Starships. A guest panel of distinguished scientists and UFO experts.

By 1956, we are smack in the middle of the great '50s UFO "flap." Waves of UFO sightings are breaking out in various locations across our nation, spreading like attacks of the German measles. These serial sightings reach a crescendo, die down, then start up all over again. Large segments of the U.S. population seem certain that it's just a matter of time before the spacemen invade, or a crashed UFO is discovered. The great sci-fi movies of the time only serve to heighten these fantastic, grandiose expectations: *The Day the Earth Stood Still. The Thing. Forbidden Planet. War of the Worlds. It Came from Outer Space. Earth Versus the Flying Saucers. Invasion of the Body Snatchers.* Surely it is only a matter of time. By 1957, they will begin filming, in nearby Downingtown and Phoenixville, the movie that is to propel Steve McQueen to stardom: *The Blob*, about a space monster that hatches from a meteorite and swallows half a town.

Meanwhile, pressing ever closer to the radio, BLT in hand, stripped down to his shorts and undershirt, my father fine tunes that illuminated dial. A panelist from the Air Force is dismissing the entire UFO phenomenon as "hogwash." A little bit of swamp gas and way too much imagination. "Mass hysteria," he indignantly calls it. But a true believer on the panel quickly counters this argument. What about all the eyewitness sightings? All those "close encounters" by sober people who have nothing to gain and everything to lose by stepping forward to tell their spaceman stories? Such as the farmer in Indiana who is pulled from his field into a hovering UFO by some sort of tractor beam. The woman in Connecticut who wakes to see a small grey alien with almond eyes come floating through her bedroom window, levitating her from her bed, then floating her right out the window and into a waiting spaceship. The all-too-familiar stories of strange marks on the body, missing time, and nightmares of abduction. Surely something not of this Earth must be responsible.

My father sips his Coke in silence. Space ships that appear and then disappear. Inconclusive photographic evidence. Radar tracking by the military. Growing concern within the general public. Mass hysteria, Communist propaganda, or the beginnings of a mass invasion? Definitely food for thought on a very late, very dark, deathly quiet summer evening.

7

The curtain beside my father rustles. Relief from a slight breeze drifts in through the open window. Dad takes a quick bite from the BLT, fiddles again with the tuner, and leans ever closer to catch the faint signal from Des Moines. It's right at this moment that he sees it. Someone or *something's* foot! Poking downward through the curtains, reaching inside, quiet as a ghost. Silently it touches the floor just inches from my father's own bare feet. Then another foot coming his way. With a black boot, and a black pant leg. Floating right through the window. A body . . . an intruder.

A being from outer space? A robot assassin?? Gadzooks, has the alien invasion begun?

My father screams. AAAARRRRGGGHHHHH!

The body floating through the window flinches and screams. . . . AAAAARRRRRRGGGGGGHHHHH! Then the humanoid jerks and flops backward out the window. Lands on the iron fire escape with a sudden and loud CLANG!

Startled into action, Dad leaps from his chair, runs to the kitchen in darkness and grabs a butcher knife from the counter. My mother, now awakened by all the yelling and the clanging, reaches over and turns on the lamp by the bed. She blinks. The bedroom is empty.

Jim? Jim, is that you?

No answer. Then my father appears menacingly in the bedroom doorway, clad in only T-shirt and shorts, holding the butcher knife aloft. Dad sprints across the bedroom and jumps through the open window like some kind of caped superhero, flying out into the night onto the shadowy fire escape.

All right, buddy. I see you. Come out with your hands up. And don't try anything funny!

But it's far too late for this bluff. By now the infamous 52nd Street cat burglar, who has been terrorizing the neighborhood all year, is probably halfway to Merchant Street and long, long gone.

If there is any doubt as to our visitor's domestic origin, that doubt is erased the next day when my father discovers burglar tools scattered on the pavement beneath the metal ladder. Probably stole those as well, the sly devil. An offending screwdriver is plainly marked as coming from Sears & Roebuck, not from Alpha Centauri.

Just another ordinary, hot summer night in the city. Besides, with all the places in the world to pick, who on Earth would decide to invade West Philly? Even if they were from another planet? It just wouldn't happen. Not in a million years.

So we can rest easy knowing our neighborhood is safe from space aliens of all shapes, sizes, and varieties. But brazen second-story men, well, now they're an altogether different concern. . . .

The Face

For weeks the big searchlight has been brightening the night sky, sweeping around and around in a steady circle. Finally, today is the big day—the grand opening of the Food Fair supermarket over at 58th and Maryland, where they've got balloons and banners strung all over. Mom is pushing the grocery cart down the soup and canned vegetables aisle, and I'm riding shotgun as we roll though the land of plenty, my little feet dangling and kicking with excitement. Shelf after shelf, row after row of brightly colored cans, boxes, and packages in cellophane wrap. Sensory overload for a toddler, a cornucopia of tempting, eye-catching stuff just inches from my grubby little fingertips. So close yet so frustratingly far. Sooner or later Mom will get distracted, then I'll get my chance to grab hold of something good. Yell loud enough, refuse to turn it loose, and maybe Mom might even let me keep it.

Yes, going to the store with Mom is fun. Especially such a big store that stretches as far as the eye can see. You never know what you're going to bump into next. We turn down the cereal aisle, hundreds of boxes crammed full of sugar-coated goodies, including Frosted Flakes, my favorite with the grrrr tiger on the box, when I see another cart approach from the opposite direction. It's coming closer, closer. . . .

Another mom, another toddler riding shotgun on the cart just like me, feet dangling and kicking merrily.

But this little boy looks very different, as does his mother. I've seen an occasional face like theirs before, but not many. Once on a delivery man in a truck when Mom took me down the street for a walk before my nap. And another on a lady at the hospital where Mom takes me to have the doctors shine bright lights in my eyes.

Now the other cart with the other little boy pulls alongside us. The boy looks at me wide-eyed. He smiles, I smile. I take my finger, reach over, and point it in his strange, unusual face.

Look, Mom! Look! Black face!

Now I'm gazing up at Mom, waiting for her to explain what I'm seeing. But Mom isn't saying anything. Instead, her face is frozen in shock.

Look, Mom! Black face! Black face, Mom!

The other lady gives my mother a cold, hard stare—the kind that can curdle milk. She is a very large, very heavyset woman who towers over my barely five-foot mother.

Mom puts her hand on my shoulder, bends her head down next to mine.

Jimmy! Mom exclaims. Be a good boy. Don't say that, it's not nice.

But this turn of events is far too stimulating, far too novel for me to control myself. Again I point my finger in the direction of the little boy's exotic features.

Black face, Mom!

My mother quickly peels out, wheeling me and our cart over to the tea and coffee aisle—not that we really need any tea or coffee.

Once we're alone, Mom stops the cart to chastise me. Jimmy, you mustn't say bad things to other people. What you said was bad.

But Little Jimmy isn't really listening now. My attention is focused on the rows of identical blue cans, each with an identical white cup pouring out the exact same drop of brown liquid with the sparkle. Good till the last drop. I have already forgotten the little wide-eyed boy with the sunny smile, white teeth, and strange, dark face.

10

Out of sight, out of mind. Wonder what we'll see next today at this wonderfully exciting market.

Howie

I've got a little brother now, his name is Howard. But everyone calls him Howie. Mom says I need to be a big boy now. Stop trying to jam silverware and household tools into all the electrical outlets. Stop picking up the phone and bugging people who are trying to talk on the party line. Stop putting all the clean clothes from the dresser drawer into the washer. Stop putting all the dirty clothes from the hamper into the dresser drawers where the clean clothes used to be before I took them out. Eat my peas like a good little fella and stop hiding them under the dining room table. Little things like that.

Howie is round faced, chubby and grows fast; he's got no trouble gaining weight the way I did. Soon as he can, Howie is escaping his crib, getting into all sorts of mischief. Little brother doesn't take the scientific approach the way I used to, piling up the picture books and toys and stuffed animals, testing to see if they'll hold before I climbed out. No, Howie just grabs onto the rail, hauls himself up, and hurls his stubby body to the floor. Bam! No fear, no planning, just do it. That's my kid brother Howie Morris.

One day we're visiting Grandmom Kane's house near Dobbs Creek. Mom gives Howie his bottle, and little brother falls fast asleep in his crib on the enclosed porch. Should be out for some time, right? Wrong. Later, Mom and Grandmom are out in the kitchen, thinking Howie is still catching some ZZZs, when they hear the horrendous crash. They come running in time to see a terrible sight. Howie has woken up, hurled himself out of the crib, climbed up onto a rocking chair, tipped over the rocking chair, and rammed his hard little noggin clear through a pane of glass. Now Howie is screaming and covered in spurting blood from head to toe. Luckily Dad is elsewhere in the house, and my parents quickly scoop up bloody Howie, carry him to the car, and zoom off toward Fitzpatrick Mercy Hospital in nearby Derby to have the doctors pick out all the ground glass and sew little brother back together again.

Howie comes home looking like Baby Frankenstein, someone zippered his fat head, but otherwise he's as good as new. Meanwhile, poor Mom's nerves are shot, as are Grandmom Kane's. After a few weeks the stitches come out, and Howie's eyebrows, forehead, and scalp are covered with a crisscrossing maze of jagged white scars. Dad calls Howie his little Scarface, after the famous gangster from Chicago. But I can't pronounce Scarface, and when I try, it comes out more like "Shoelace." So now the inadvertent nickname sticks, and the whole family is calling Howie by the name "Shoelace."

Talk about stuff sticking, so does Howie's reckless act-first, think-later temperament. Over the coming years daredevil Howie will likewise put his hand through a window, get his lip caught on a chain-link fence playing touch football, slam his sled into a tree, fall out of a tree, step on broken glass, have a chunk taken out of his leg by a protruding spigot, get dragged through a river with a water-ski rope tangled around his ankle, and much, much more. Restless Howie, given time, will become a walking medical miracle.

Meanwhile, yours truly, look-before-you-leap James Morris Jr. won't even need a stitch. Maybe it's just good karma, a cautious approach, or both.

Just the same, it can be said that my motto is "Don't hurt the bod." Howie's motto is to heck with Jimmy's motto. Go for all the gusto life has to offer, both good and bad. And with little brother Howie, often the gusto is bad. Not that this is slowing him down any time soon.

So little brother is a happening kid in a happening neighborhood, and soon everyone knows Howie Morris. The boy's got thousands of friends and even more acquaintances. Knows more folks than some local politicians.

Me, I just cultivate a small circle of close friends and keep the world-at-large at a relatively safe distance. Live and let live, you go your way and I'll go mine.

But Howie's far too nosy for that. He's into everyone else's business and building his little network of known associates.

And as the years go by, Mom and Dad are going to have their hands full with baby brother Howie. Rogue, rascal, smooth talker, practical joker . . . always one of the boys, one of the gang.

Unfortunately, often the wrong group, the wrong gang.

A go-along-to-get-along type whose biggest problem is he's never learned how to just say no.

Sure thing, fellas. Sure thing. . . . Wait for me and count me in.

Candle Power

My mother's mother, Grandmom Kane, takes me one afternoon to her big church down on Lester Avenue. It's a grand, giant building, especially to a three-year old, made of huge blocks of heavy grey stone, rising high above 56th Street with the big golden metal cross way up on top glinting in the sunlight. Twin green domes reach into the hazy blue sky. Inside is all quiet and dark, and it takes a few moments for my eyes to adjust. Now I see the marble floors, the pretty white statues, all those rows and rows of shiny dark brown benches called pews. I like this strange place, with the spicy aroma of incense that fills my nostrils, the way the sunlight filters through the colored panes of glass high up on the distant walls. A few scattered people, mostly hunched old ladies covered in shawls, kneeling and praying and being very hush-hush. There's a kind of magic in this building I can feel, and it makes me smile.

Grandmom takes my hand and leads me to the far corner of the church, under the statue of a kind lady whom Grandmom calls the Blessed Mother. This is the best surprise of all, because beneath the statue of the lady with the sweet smile stand all these metal boxes filled with rows and rows of candles, some lit and some not. Dozens and dozens of flickering candles, far too many to count. Had my birthday months before and got three candles stuck in the middle of my chocolate cake. But I blew them all out, and everyone clapped.

Grandmom says we are going to light a candle, and I get to help. She takes some coins from her pocketbook, puts them in my hand, and lifts me up to where there's a hole in the box.

13

Drop them in, honey . . . it's to pay for the candle.

I slip the coins through the slot, and Grandmom reaches for a group of little sticks, pulls one out. Holding me firmly, she places the stick in my tiny hand, and guides my fingers with the stick toward an already lit candle. The stick touches the flame and, like magic, it catches fire. I smile, then giggle approvingly.

Shhhhhh, says Grandmom softly, now guiding my hand with the burning stick toward the first unlit candle. Steady, easy does it. The flame touches wick, shudders and wiggles, then the second candle grows a flame, too, burning as brightly as the first.

That's a good boy, says Grandmom, taking away the stick. Now that we've lit the candle, we get to say a prayer for someone. I'm saying a prayer for your great-grandmother.

Grandmom gets quiet again and prays, while I watch all the candles in their rows, dancing and glowing in the dark. I lean closer, closer.

She whispers, Don't touch, Jimmy.

Grandmom's mother died years before I was born. I don't know what to be dead means, except that adults know these other people you've never seen, who've never been around. So it must be something like going off to a very faraway place. But I don't think about it much—I'm too busy watching all the candles. Dancing, flickering, comforting, hypnotic. Getting lost in all these warm, wonderful lights—just like at Christmastime.

Grandmom is finished praying now. She puts me down, takes my hand, starts to lead me from the metal boxes with the candles. But I squirm and protest, try to pull away. I don't want to leave the candles. I'm not finished yet.

❧ What is it, Jimmy?

I point toward the candles, motion for Grandmom to pick me up again, bring me closer. She does.

We only have money for one candle, Jimmy. We can come back and light another one next week.

But I'm no longer interested in lighting candles—I want to do just the opposite. So I huff and I puff like the bad wolf in the story and start blowing out the little flames.

Jimmy . . . no!

I'm too busy huffing and puffing to listen. Grandmom turns me away, sets me down, but I immediately start to cry and fuss.

Jimmy, shhhhh! Be a good boy!

But I wanna blow, Grandmom.

No, you can't—that's not nice, Jimmy.

But Grandmom, I wanna BLOW!!

There's no consoling Little Jimmy now, I'm throwing a major-league tantrum right there under the watchful eyes of the Blessed Mother and perhaps a dozen of Grandmom's fellow parishioners. Some of the other ladies smile, but most just stare or shake their heads sadly.

I'm being a very naughty boy, and Grandmom has to take me outside where the sun is shining and hurts my eyes and the whole world is filled again with noise, traffic, and a multitude of other distractions.

That's enough of church today for little Jimmy Morris.

Cross-Eyes

I am going on four years old now, very outgoing, and increasingly cross-eyed. Mom blames it on the delivery doctor's forceps that left the big purple bruise on my forehead. The doctors call the lazy eye condition "strabismus" and say it is getting worse. My eye muscles are weak and I can't focus on objects properly. The doctors surmise that, if I don't have an operation, I may one day go blind. My father takes a second job to help pay for the operation. Meanwhile, the doctors give me more eye tests. They ask me to look at pictures of monkeys, giraffes, zebras, elephants, whales, and tigers in a little viewing machine. The tigers are my favorite, all fur-covered and black striped with bright orange, and I say, Grrrr . . . tiger! when I see them. The doctor says I am a very smart boy and my mother squeezes my shoulder. I tell the doctor I am a big boy now and have my own little stuffed tiger in my big person's bed at our apartment—don't need a crib any more, I'm not a baby.

Soon the big day comes, and my parents drive me to the hospital downtown with my pajamas and my little stuffed tiger. My mother says not to be afraid, I am a big boy now. The doctors prep me for surgery, put me under, and slice me open behind one of my eyeballs. To his surprise, the head surgeon finds lots of scar tissue and flies into a rage. Once they sew me back up, the head surgeon storms out into the waiting room yelling and screaming. This boy has been operated on before! Why didn't you tell me? My mother is crying because I have never been operated on before, never been out of her sight since the day I finally came home from Fitzpatrick Mercy, and she doesn't know what in the world the doctor is hollering about. The surgery is postponed until later in the week, because the doctors have to decide how to operate with all the scar tissue that's inside. Now I must stay an extra week in the hospital, my father has to stay longer at his second job to pay for two surgeries, and it's not until later that my mother realizes the doctor's forceps grabbing me at birth was what caused all the scar tissue behind my eye.

I wake up in a crib in the hospital and my swollen eye hurts very much. But I don't want to be in a crib—my mother and father promised that since I'm a big boy I can stay in a big person's bed, not in a baby's bed. Then I find out they have to make my eye hurt again and I can't go home when they promised. I see the little boy in the crib next to me and he is blind. This is a very scary place and they only let my mother and my father visit for a very short time. I want to get out of the crib and this hospital and go home with Mom, Dad, and my little grr tiger but I can't. I am afraid and I hug my tiger and cry a lot by myself, and then later they take me back to the operating room, put me under, and make my eye sore all over again.

When I finally go home I am not the same little boy who went into the hospital. I am frightened and suspicious and I don't trust anyone except my little tiger. Mom and Dad try to make me feel safe again and I can sleep in my big person's bed now, but I am no longer outgoing and the world is a very confusing place where people can be nice but later hurt you and don't do what they promise while they leave you all alone and scared.

Later my mother and father tell me I am going to have to wear glasses. I take more eye tests, get the glasses, but I don't like them and I don't want to wear the glasses. They feel funny on my nose but my mother and father tell me they make me look grown up. But if I am grown up, why did they make me stay in a baby's bed and are they going to take me back to the hospital again where they make my eye sore and leave me all alone and scared with just my little grrr tiger in a baby's crib and not a big person's bed?

Murphy's Law

Dad's got plans for a big Saturday. Night out with the boys. Problem is, the car won't start. No sweat, says his friend Harry from work. Borrow mine. So Dad takes Harry up on his offer.

Dad and his pals are cruising down Parkland Avenue in the borrowed wheels. They stop for a red light. Problem is, the car behind them doesn't. Next comes a terrible crunching sound, and Dad and his pals are bouncing around the borrowed car's interior, getting knocked silly. They all tumble out onto Parkland Avenue, dazed but unhurt. Walk back, check the car that hit them . . . looks empty, no one behind the steering wheel. They pry open the driver's door. Out falls one Leon Murphy.

No, not dead. Just dead drunk. What happened, he mumbles. What happened?

You fell asleep, drove right into us, nearly totaled our car.

Oh.

Dad exchanges insurance information with Leon Murphy. Mr. Murphy is a resident of North Philadelphia. Chances are he doesn't march in the annual St. Patrick's Day Parade.

Call the cops, say Dad's friends.

No, please don't, pleads Murphy. I already been in one accident last month. Now they gonna take my license, pull my insurance. Listen, don't call the cops, don't tell the insurance company. I got a good job. I'll pay, I'm good for it.

Dad's friends say, Don't listen to him, Jim. Call the cops.

Please, mister, says Murphy. Gimme a break. I'll pay, I swear.

Dad relents, promises not to get the cops involved. Takes Murphy's address and phone number.

17

I'll call you by Friday, Murphy promises.

Friday comes and goes. No call from Murphy. Meanwhile, Dad's got to reach into his own pocket to pay for repairs on friend Harry's wheels. That's a lot of body and fender work, none of it cheap.

Dad starts calling Murphy. No answer, no answer, no answer. Finally, he gets Mrs. Murphy on the line.

He ain't home, says Mrs. Murphy. Don't know where Leon is. Leon just comes and goes. Ain't none of my business.

Dad calls another dozen times. Finally gets Mrs. Murphy again.

Dad says to her, You tell Leon to be there Wednesday night at seven. Tell him to have the money. All of it. I'm coming up, and I won't take no for an answer. Then he hangs up.

Wednesday night comes around. Dad drives to North Philly. Alone. Finds the apartment building. People stare at him . . . what's a white man doin' around here at this hour in this neighborhood? Whatever it is, it must mean trouble. Cop, bill collector, parole officer, whatever. White man around here always means trouble.

Dad goes upstairs, finds the apartment. Knocks on the door. Mrs. Murphy answers. Leon in the living room, says Mrs. Murphy.

Murphy is indeed in the living room. Smiling. Along with three of his friends, playing cards, drinking beer.

Man, says Murphy, I don't think that accident was my fault. Why I gotta pay? I ain't gotta pay you nothin'. You just hasslin' me, that's all.

Now Murphy's three friends are all smiling, too. Crazy white man, all alone in North Philly, asking the brother for money. Ain't had this much fun in a long while.

But Dad has a couple of friends with him as well. He pulls them out, introduces them to all in attendance. World-famous friends. Mr. Murphy, meet Mr. Smith and Mr. Wesson.

Now no one is smiling. Dad warns everyone not to move. Instructs Mrs. Murphy to collect all the wallets, empty them on the table. Dad scoops up the money, then backs up toward the door.

In his best Bogart voice, Dad tells his captive audience to remain seated until they've counted to 100 . . . slowly. Then he's out the door, down the steps, in his car, and burning rubber for Southwest Philly, all in about two seconds.

Put out an APB. One lone white man. 5' 10", 160. Known associates are a Mr. Smith and a Mr. Wesson. Certainly armed, most likely dangerous, and most definitely crazy. Proceed with caution . . . anything could happen.

Murphy's Law.

The Peach

I am now five. Mom, Dad, little brother Howie, and I live in a second-floor apartment above a produce store on 55th Street. We are right beside the 55th Street bridge over which all the commuter and freight trains rumble. This street is a happening place for someone five years old. There's a supermarket, a barber shop, a luncheonette, a bicycle shop, a retail bakery, a beer distributor, a commercial bakery that makes loaves of bread, and especially the fruits and vegetables store downstairs. But mostly there's the constant trains that roar down the high tracks nearby. I eat Chunkies and Good 'N Plenty and wait for the next freight train to roll by on high. There are so many B&O cars I can't possibly count them all, even when I try. Coal cars, boxcars, refrigerated cars. So I give up and just wait for the caboose so I can wave to the trainman. Sometimes a hand reaches out of the caboose and waves back. That's what I want to do when I grow up. Be an engineer and ride the rails all day, from street-to-street, bridge-to-bridge, city-to-city. And I'll wave at every little boy I see, mile after mile after mile. Choo Choo Charlie was an engineer, and that's why I eat those Good 'N Plenties. So I can be an engineer, too, and have fun and licorice candy, just like Choo Choo.

Some nights Mom and I read a story about Sandtown, and a little black horse that I ride through the darkness. Mile after mile after mile under the trees and the stars. Riding the road to Sandtown. Riding, riding. Then sometimes the whistle blows and a freight rolls by the bedroom window, and I can see the lights in the cabin of that big diesel as it powers on by. And suddenly I'm in that cabin, too, riding that train into the blackness. Mile after mile on the endless ribbon of steel, lights flashing, horn blowing. Over the bridges and through the tunnels and around the bends. Riding, riding, over the rivers and through the mountains and past the cornfields waving in the breeze. I ask a grown-up how far the train goes in each direction, and they say it goes to Pittsburgh in one direction and Baltimore in the other. And so Pittsburgh and Baltimore become like magical, faraway places to me, and I can only imagine what they are like waiting for me at the end of the line. I just know that one day, like Choo Choo Charlie, I'll be in that train, up in that lighted cabin, riding, riding all through the night to Baltimore or Pittsburgh with a hundred or more freight cars behind me. Clickety, clackity, clickety, clackity all the way to Sandtown. When I'm big and all grown up.

During the days when the weather is nice my mother lets me ride my tricycle along the sidewalk. Riding, riding, back and forth, back and forth. Looking in the windows of the luncheonette, the barber shop, and the bicycle shop. Watching the cases of beer slide down the metal rollers into the beer store. The supermarket and Matt's Bakery are across the street, and I'm not allowed to cross the street. But whenever I get taken across, I run right up to the bakery window and press my nose against the glass until my mother or father or grandmother buys me a cookie or tells me, Next time, it'll spoil your supper to have a cookie now.

Mr. and Mrs. Lobb own the produce store below our apartment and they are very nice to me. Sometimes I stop riding my tricycle and walk in to say hello to their Irish setter named Rusty. Mr. Lobb is patient and teaches me about a new fruit or vegetable each day. Apples, I learn, grow on big trees. Tomatoes grow on tomato plants. Cucumbers grow on vines. Onions grow underground, and so on. I like all the colors and the neat rows and piled-high baskets of fresh produce. I like the lemon yellows, eggplant purples, lime greens, strawberry reds, potato browns, and the cool watermelon stripes. And I really like it when the big produce trucks pull up to the curb and deliver boxes and boxes of fresh fruits and vegetables straight from the farm in the countryside.

I have never been on a farm, and don't know anyone who lives on one. The nearest large patch of green is the park near the library three blocks away, but nothing much grows there except for trees, crabgrass, pigeons, and squirrels. But every day I learn something new from Mr. Lobb. Corn grows on tall rows of cornstalks. Pears grown on trees in big orchards. And pumpkins grow on vines in pumpkin patches.

Pretty soon I no longer want to grow up and ride the diesel engine. Instead, I want to ride a big tractor on a farm . . . just like Farmer Jones, the man who owns the farm way out in the country from which Mr. Lobb buys much of his produce.

Problem is, how does a little boy in a big city ever get to grow up to be a farmer like Farmer Jones? My world is a place of concrete, brick, asphalt, glass, and steel. Most farmers are born on a farm. I have never seen a farm, except maybe on TV. So I watch Mr. Green Jeans on *Captain Kangaroo* and also the *Real McCoys*. I can only hope that some day, some way I'll have a piece of land big enough to grow all the potatoes and corn and peas and string beans I could ever want. And then I'd sell them to Mr. Lobb and be a farmer, too.

Then one day, as luck would have it, while riding my tricycle back and forth in front of Lobb's Produce Store, I see something. A plant. Just a small plant, but a healthy, thriving green plant nevertheless. It's sprouting up from a crack between the store's foundation and the concrete slab beneath the fire escape. It's amazing that this little plant can even take root. The crack is so small, and there's not even any visible soil at the surface. I wonder what kind of plant this is, and if maybe it could've come from a seed that fell out of a broken fruit or vegetable that got carried into the Lobbs' store. So secretly, every day, I begin to carry a cupful of water around the side of the building to irrigate my crop. Then, while I'm across the street at the supermarket, I see a toy water pistol at the checkout counter and pester Mom into buying it. Now I squirt my plant every day, and it really starts to shoot up. Up, up, and away.

Finally, I ask Mr. Lobb to take a look at the plant. He assures me it's just a weed. But Mr. Lobb sells the produce, he doesn't grow it. Who knows, it still may be an apple or a pear tree or something like that. Mom and Dad agree with Mr. Lobb . . . it's nothing but a garden variety weed. But this doesn't deter me in the least. I'm determined to water this plant and hope for the best.

Jimmy and the Beanstalk, laughs Mr. Lobb. You're going to grow that thing right to the sky, and then a big giant is going to coming crawling down out of the clouds. Fee, fi, fo, fum. I watch the Green Giant commercials, and hope that maybe Mr. Lobb is right. Ho, ho, ho, I'd love to have my very own green giant from a green valley full of growing things. Wouldn't that be a hoot on 55th Street!

The grown-ups are convinced that my fixation with the plant on the side of the building is a passing fancy and that I'll get tired of watering it and forget all about it. Maybe then they can pull this ugly, growing eyesore out by its roots. But everyday I continue to sprinkle the plant with my water gun, and care is taken that my little project remain undisturbed.

Sometimes, before dinner, I'll be reminded of my daily duty. This is getting to be something of a Morris family joke.

Jimmy, did you wash up for supper?

Uh-huh.

And did you wash behind your ears?

Uh-huh.

And did you water your plant?

This sends me scurrying for my water pistol and the bathroom sink. Once loaded up with H2O I dash down the apartment steps, around the side of Lobb's Produce, give my plant a good soaking, then sprint back up and settle into my chair for dinner.

One early evening in August, upon seating myself at the supper table, Mom reminds me about my daily obligation.

Jimmy, aren't you forgetting something?

Umm . . . no, I washed up.

Maybe something else?

Umm . . . oh yeah, my plant!

My mother smiles. My father smiles. Little brother Howie just looks around clueless and wonders where the food is.

Sure enough, I jump up, get my water pistol, fill it up at the sink, dash down the stairs, and around to the side of the building. I'm about to level the squirt gun and squeeze the trigger when I stop. I blink, then blink again. No, my eyes aren't deceiving me. There it is, as big as life. A peach. Growing right smack in the middle of my plant, hanging from a green stem. Carefully, I reach out and touch it. I've done it! Success! I'm now a real farmer at last.

Mom calls down from the living room window. What's all the noise? What do you have there?

A peach! Excitedly, I pull it from the stem then hold it up high. A peach, a peach! Look everybody, I grew a peach! I race around and wave the peach in the window at Mr. Lobb. He gives me a big smile and a hearty thumbs-up. Then I run upstairs.

I can hardly wait for supper to be over. Meat loaf, mashed potatoes, and peas. I can hardly eat them fast enough. When dinner is done, Mom takes the peach I've grown, cuts it into slices, sprinkles on some sugar, pours on some milk, then serves it for dessert. My peach. Little Farmer Jimmy's peach.

That night, as the last freight train rumbles over the 55th Street bridge and on into distance, I dream I'm riding on my very own tractor. Wearing my own little pair of farmer's blue denim overalls. Riding, riding toward the horizon across endless fields of wheat and corn, on a farm that stretches as far as the eye can see. My farm, Little Jimmy's Farm.

Clickety, clackity, clickety, clackity goes that tractor all the way to Sandtown. All the way, all the way, all the zzzzz. . . .

The Reward

Dad gets a big promotion at Enco, the giant energy conglomerate. Instead of pumping gas, he's now the station's night manager. My old man is thrilled until my mother does the math . . . when she figures the hours he's putting in and converts his new salary to an hourly wage, she shows Dad he's really not making any more than when Enco had him pumping gas. Some promotion. You know Dad's gotta be missing the merchant marine and the big money he made sailing on those Texas-bound oil tankers. There's already me, Howie, and a third little one on the way. Gotta find a way to get his hands on some more dough.

One day Dad's going through the company bulletins they send down from headquarters. One in particular catches his eye. Be on the lookout for a white male, age thirty, wanted in eleven states on grand theft, theft by deception, and various bunko charges. Subject is one Curtis "Crafty Curt" Gorman, but goes by numerous aliases. Recently this individual was believed to have been the mastermind of a scam involving the sale of nonexistent Christmas trees to area hospitals and other organizations. His usual modus operandi is to enter an establishment, purchase a small item, then ask to pay with a large check, which later bounces. If you have any information please contact Special Agent John Warner of the FBI at the following number.

Dad files the information for future reference. Taking money from hospitals for Christmas trees you never intend to deliver . . . man, some people have all the nerve. No mention of a reward, but there's gotta be . . . it's a very big case. Hey—the FBI is involved, right?

A week later, a man comes into the Enco station. White male, age thirty. Hey Mac, I think the battery in my Chevy is dying. Can I get a new one? Pop pulls one from the shelf, twelve bucks. Say, Mac, you mind if I write you a check for fifty and get thirty-eight back? Gotta get to the hospital, the wife's havin' a baby, and I don't have time for no bank. Be a pal, huh?

The hair on the back of Dad's neck stands up. Sure, buddy, just gotta show me some ID first. Customer whips out his wallet, flashes a fake driver's license. Milton P. Hirschman. Yeah, sure. Dad knows in a heartbeat it's none other than Curtis Gorman live and in the flesh, a.k.a. Crafty Curt.

Crafty Curt whips out his trusty checkbook, starts writing. Make this out to Enco, pal?

Yeah, Enco. E-N-C-O. Say, um . . . Mr. Hirschman, I just remembered we got this new shipment of batteries in the back. Our new deluxe model. Last longer, has lots more get-up-and-go. It's on special . . . same price, twelve dollars. Let me get you one.

Don't trouble yourself, Mac. I'm sure this battery is fine.

Don't worry, won't take a minute. I insist.

Dad hustles from the counter, ducks into the storage room. Goes straight for the pay phone in the employees' lounge. Drops a dime to the cops. Stall him, say cops, we'll be there in five minutes.

Dad grabs any old battery, and a lug wrench for protection. Hides the wrench under his uniform and goes out to stall Crafty Curt.

Crafty Curt doesn't look so crafty any more. He's sweating bullets, knows something's up. Hey pal, can I get my change? I'm in kind of a hurry.

Dad gives him the battery, gets him the thirty-eight bucks from the register. The man starts to leave, and my father comes out from behind the counter, following him to the door. Crafty Curt drops the battery and runs. Pop pulls out the wrench, sprints across the lot, catches Curt, and tackles him from behind. Gets on top, cocks the wrench.

Don't move or I'll cave your face in, Gorman!

I give up. Just don't hurt me. I give up! Curt may be crafty but he certainly ain't crazy.

Sixty seconds later come the sirens and flashing lights. They cuff Crafty Curt, put him in the back seat of a squad car. You bastard! Gorman mutters through the open window. My Dad smiles. Yeah, that's what's known in law enforcement as a positive ID. But I sure had your number, didn't I, Crafty Curt?

The story makes next day's papers. "Enco Station Manager Nails Wanted Criminal." Lots of free publicity for Enco. Special Agent John Warner of the FBI drops by to thank my father personally. Curtis Gorman had been a one-man crime wave. Now he's off the streets, thanks to stand-up citizen James Morris.

They're calling my Dad a hero. But no one mentions anything about a reward. A trial date is scheduled, and my father will be called to testify. Maybe the FBI or Enco will pay a reward after the trial, Dad figures. He can sure use it with me, Howie, and another little one on the way.

Then the trial comes, and Dad is a star witness, giving a blow-by-blow account of Gorman's forgery, theft-by-deception, and

25

subsequent made-for-TV capture in the Enco station lot. The prosecutor thanks him. Special Agent Warner gives him the thumbs-up.

Next week Dad gets his pay envelope. Surely Enco will have included a little something extra. A token of their corporate appreciation. Heaven knows he sure could use it. Dad tears open the envelope, looks at the check, looks at the stub, and there it is. His big reward.

Enco has docked him for missing a day of work . . . the day he spent in court.

My House

I'm at Gram Morris's house on 61st Street, just Gram, my Aunt Tess, and me baking cookies in the kitchen. Gram decides we're running short of butter and chocolate chips, so she heads "Up the Avenue" to bolster our supplies. This leaves my little five-year-old self in charge of cookie production along with my visiting Aunt Tess. While I'm busy using the available cookie-cutter patterns to stamp out some ready-to-bake dough, Aunt Tess takes it upon herself to whip up a few cookies on the side without using the proper shapes. Naturally I take exception, tell Aunt Tess she's not preparing our cookies up to code, and begin removing the dough mixture from her workspace. Don't want her ruining the entire batch, you see.

Aunt Tess says, Hey, you, give that back.

I say, No, Aunt Tess, you're not doing it right. That's not the way we make cookies around here.

Aunt Tess insists, and so I begin hollering and ordering her from the kitchen.

Befuddled, Aunt Tess leaves the room in a huff, walking through the house and out to the enclosed front porch. There Aunt Tess sits on a glider to wait for Gram. Gram will surely fix this little brat's wagon.

I follow my aunt, and when she's comfortably seated and awaiting the return of my grandmother, I reach up and turn the latch on the living room door. Pop!

26

Mr. Jimmy, Aunt Tess calls out, Did you just lock me out?

Yes, Aunt Tess.

You open that door this minute, Mr. Jimmy.

No, Aunt Tess. No until you promise to make the cookies right.

Now Aunt Tess comes to the door and looks through the glass. When she begins knocking on the door I retreat to the living room steps, climb the stairs part way, and peer down at this angry grown-up from over the banister. Again, Aunt Tess demands that I open the door at once.

No, Aunt Tess. This is *my* house and I won't let you in. Not until you do things right.

Aunt Tess finally gives up and returns to her seat on the front porch, resigned to waiting for my grandmother to right this terrible wrong. The nerve—a petulant child giving orders and locking adults out of the house on a whim!

After a few minutes I grow mellow at the sad sight of my good-natured aunt marooned on Gram's front porch. So I pop the lock, swing open the door, and motion for Aunt Tess to come inside.

I'm sorry I got mad, Aunt Tess. You can come in my house and make cookies.

When Gram returns from "Up the Avenue" with the butter and the chocolate chips, Aunt Tess immediately begins complaining about being locked on the porch by her mother's temperamental five-year old grandchild.

Astonished, Gram seeks to confirm Aunt Tess' incredible story.

Gram asks, You say Mr. Jimmy *locked* you on the porch and wouldn't let you back inside?

Aunt Tess vigorously nods to the affirmative, pointing at me for emphasis. No mistake about it, it was Mr. Jimmy, locking his poor Aunt Tess on the front porch.

Well, says Gram, her hands on hips and staring at her daughter, *What did you do to the boy, Tess?*

CHAPTER 2

First Day in School

Because I am supposed to be a bright little child, the School District of Philadelphia allows my mother to enroll me early in first grade and skip kindergarten altogether. They say that, although I am only five, I have the intellectual capacity of a seven-year-old. Despite this, I look four and act like two. One problem I have is taking instructions too literally. I guess my mother should be proud, but there's a limit to following things to the letter. Sometimes it can put you in a very stupid situation, such as on my very first day at school.

Mom preps me for the big day. I am going off to Longstreet Elementary School to begin my illustrious academic career. I am told to behave in class, be nice to the other children, wait my turn, and always do what the teacher says. I must always obey the teacher. School, I am assured, is going to be fun, and I am going to be like a big boy now. This is what big people do all day. They leave home and go somewhere to have an exciting adventure.

Most important, my mother emphasizes, is what is going to happen at lunchtime. The bell will ring. The teacher will take all of the children back out into the schoolyard. I will be right there waiting, my mother explains. But if I am not, you must wait right on the school steps and don't move for anybody.

Mom quizzes me. Now, what happens when school lets out for lunch? The bell rings, I say. The teacher takes all the children into the schoolyard. You should be there waiting for me. If you aren't there, then I go and sit on the school steps and wait. You'll be along any minute. And don't move for anybody.

Very good.

All right, so there I am, first day of school and all is going well. The teacher is nice, the other kids are noisy but OK, and there's always something going on to hold my interest. I get picked first in one of the games because I put my hand up quicker and higher than anyone in the class. I think I can really get used to this school thing. Before I started, I wasn't so sure. That's why I asked if I couldn't just retire and stay home, the way Gram does on 61st Street. But now I think I'll keep going to school instead. Story time is my favorite, quiet time makes me sleepy, and I really like the way the crayons smell.

The bell rings. Sure enough the teacher takes us all outside, just as Mom said would happen. I walk out into the schoolyard, then out the side entrance and go around to the front steps. Mom isn't there. No problem. I sit down on the steps and wait. And wait. Just as I was told. Then after a while I hear the bell ring again, and the schoolyard grows quiet. What I can't see from the front of the school is that all of the children, along with our teacher, have gone back into the building and returned to our classroom.

Nobody ever mentioned anything to me about recess.

So I wait, and I wait. Our teacher doesn't realize that one little boy never returned from the playground. Finally, after nearly an hour, an alert neighbor sees me sitting there all alone and calls the school.

Hello, is this Longstreet Elementary School? Do you know you have a child sitting out on the front steps all alone? He's been sitting there for nearly an hour.

Mrs. Glass the school principal walks out of her office and over to the front steps. There I am, waiting. What is your name, little boy?

Jimmy Morris.

And why are you sitting on the steps?

I'm waiting for my mother.

Well, your mother won't be along until later when school lets out for lunch. You need to come back inside with me.

I shrug, shake my head politely, and stay on the steps. After all, I was told not to move for anyone.

It's all right, Jimmy. You can come inside with me. I'm the principal.

I remain seated on the steps. I was told to obey my teacher. I don't know anything about any principal person.

Mrs. Glass has her secretary wait with me on the school steps while she returns to her office to call my mother. My mother now has to come all the way back to school so I can be told it is OK to return to my classroom, and that this principal person is really like another teacher, only she's the boss of the teachers and I must obey her, too.

Confused, I return to my classroom, and all of the other children stare and giggle. The teacher is mortified. Already, on my first day at Longstreet School, I am earning a reputation. Instead of James Morris I will soon become known as Dizzy Morris. And I have only some eleven years and nine months to go before I earn my high school diploma.

Well, at least my mother *is* waiting for me when that lunch bell finally rings at noontime. Perhaps I should consider retiring after all and just keep Gram and all her cats company. I already know all the rules at Gram's house, and I needn't worry about doing things according to the schedule of some stupid bell.

Hey, works for me.

Bloody Murder

After the first few weeks of school my parents buy a row house just a few blocks past Longstreet Elementary, which means we move from our apartment. I must say goodbye to Mr. Lobb, Mrs. Lobb, Rusty the Irish setter, Lobb's Produce Market, and the 55th Street bridge with all the trains rumbling on high. I don't want to move, but Mom says it'll be another big adventure, just like starting first grade. And there'll be lots more kids to play with because of all the houses, Howie and I will have a bigger room, and of course we'll be much closer to school so I can walk to first grade all by myself. No more waiting on the steps for Mom after school lets out.

Besides, with this summer's arrival of baby sister Laura, the Morris family has finally outgrown our little apartment.

So one weekend we rent a little truck, and Dad, Mom, and Uncle Joe fill it with our furniture and clothes and other things. With the rooms emptied out and the carpet rolled up, I sneak a rubber ball into the living room and bounce it off the walls when everyone else is outside with the truck. But soon it's time to go for good and we drive on down to our new home on Littlefield Street between Wennington and Venice, just off 56th. Dad makes several trips, and on one I get to ride up in the truck cab, which sits high above the street. I imagine this is what the cab of those big diesel engines must feel like, so already I feel like I'm having a pretty good adventure.

We make the final trip to our new house around dusk, a fixer-upper end-of-row next to a long driveway that connects to Beaufort Avenue, another narrow residential street that parallels us between 56th and 57th. The house looks like hundreds and hundreds of other row homes in the Kings Cross neighborhood. Two stories, long and narrow, postage-stamp lawn, concrete stoop, high porch with balustrade, white trim around the windows in the second-story bedroom up front, and a flat roof. But this house is different from all the others in one way . . . it is our very first real home, the Morris family home.

Grandmom Kane has already given notice to her landlord for the house she rents up on Dobbs Creek Avenue in West Philly. She plans on renting another house just across the street from us on Littlefield. We had the apartment above the produce store near the 55th Street bridge so we could be around the corner from Grandmom. Now it's her turn to move down the street from us.

In a few days, after I've gotten used to my new home and my new school, Mom takes me aside for an important lesson. Now, you would think that after the first-day-of-school incident with skipping recess and sitting on the steps and not listening to the principal that I might have learned something. No, not really.

Jimmy, says Mom, you're getting to be a big boy now, and I want to be able to send you across the street and around the corner to the store for groceries. Now I'm going to explain something to you first and I want you to do exactly as I say. All right?

Yes, Mom.

Good. Now Jimmy, you must understand, there are some people in this world who aren't very nice. I mean grown-up people. Most people are nice people, but a few aren't. The problem is, you can't always tell the bad people from the good, because the bad people pretend to be nice when they really aren't.

I know this is a little confusing, but there are a few simple rules to follow, and they should keep you out of trouble. Okay?

Uh-huh, I say, more than a little confused.

All right, says Mom. Just do what I tell you, and you shouldn't ever have any problem with bad people pretending to be good people. Now, Jimmy, if any stranger ever offers you candy or money, just say no thank you. And if they offer it to you again, tell them you aren't allowed to take it. And if they still insist, you stop whatever you're doing, drop whatever you have in your hands, scream as loud as you can, and run straight for home. Is that clear?

Yes.

All right, now pretend I'm a stranger, and I hold out a Hershey's chocolate bar for you, or a dollar bill, and I say, Here Jimmy, this is for you. What do you say, Jimmy?

No, thank you.

But Jimmy, I really want you to have it. Don't you like chocolate? Wouldn't you like a dollar?? It's for you—take it!

No, I'm not allowed to take it.

But Jimmy, I really, really *insist*. Here, have some chocolate! Take the money. It's yours!

NO! I scream.

Good, Jimmy—very good. Now what else do you do?

I turn and begin to run out of the room. My mother calls me back.

That's a good boy, Jimmy. Very good. That's just what you do. You scream *bloody murder* and run all the way home. I'll be right here.

Okay, Mom.

Sure enough, I'm soon running regular errands around the corner to Nolan's Grocery Store. Across Littlefield Street, up the driveway behind 56th street, turn, go up the driveway behind Wennington Avenue, and around to Nolan's.

One day Mom sends me to Nolan's for a quart of milk. No problem. I skip along up one driveway, turn, and make my way through the second driveway. But just before I reach 56th and Wennington, I meet an old lady who is sweeping the driveway behind her house near the entranceway from 56th.

Little boy, she says, are you going around the corner to the store?

Yes, I am. I'm buying milk for my mother.

Well, would you mind doing me a favor? If I give you this dollar, could you buy a loaf of bread and drop it off on your way home?

Sure, I can do that.

Here's the dollar, Little Boy. Thank you very much.

I take the dollar, very proud to run an important errand for an adult. Head over to Nolan's where I purchase both the bread and the milk. On my way home I see the old lady who's still sweeping the concrete clean behind her garage.

Lady, here's your bread, and here's your change.

The woman takes the bread, takes the change, smiles, and holds out a dime for my troubles. I look at the shiny new dime, start to reach for it, then remember my mother's words. *Jimmy, if any stranger ever offers you candy or money, you say no thank you. Sometimes bad people just pretend to be nice when what they really want to do is be mean.*

No thank you, I apologize, and pull my hand back.

Oh, but Little Boy, I really want you to have this dime. It's yours.

But I'm not allowed to take it.

But I *must* pay you for going to the store. Here, please, take this dime. I *insist!*

Warning bells are going off in my five-year old head. There, she said it. *Insist!* The magic word. I must now scream and run, scream and run. A sudden jolt of adrenaline surges through my tiny body. I toss the glass bottle full of milk up into the air, end over end. It crashes with a shatter and a splat at the old lady's feet. White liquid and shards of glass fly every which way. The woman's jaw drops as if she's seen a ghost. I take another step back, out of reach, turn, and run for home. Now I must scream for all I'm worth.

Bloody murder! I yell. BLOOODY MURDER!!

I bolt down the driveway behind Wennington, make the hard right turn, and sprint for home down the driveway behind 56th. Bloody murder! Help! *BLOODY MURDER!!*

A man is washing his Ford station wagon behind his 56th Street home. He watches, mouth open, garden hose spilling water all over the ground, as I come screaming by. I look at him, he looks at me. He is expecting blood. Lots of blood. But there is nothing, and then I am by him and heading into the home stretch toward our front door.

I see Mom now, she's on the porch washing windows. She hears the yelling and drops her sponge. I see her already pale face go snow white, staring at me as I approach.

Mom, Mom . . . . Bloody murder! *Aaaaahhhhhhh . . .* *BLOODY MURDER!!*

My mother comes running off the porch and down the steps. She intercepts me as I reach the sidewalk in front of our postage stamp lawn.

Jimmy, what is it? What's wrong? Where are you hurt?

Bloody murder. Lady. Bread. Dime. Bloody murder. . . .

I am crying now from the excitement, upsetment, and shortness of breath. But Mom is here with me now, and I am safe. It takes several minutes for my mother to piece together the story of the lady from Wennington Avenue, the bread errand, and the dime she tried to give me as payment.

It's OK, Jimmy, she assures me. What the lady tried to give you was a tip.

A tip? Nobody every mentioned anything to me about a tip.

When I fully understand what has happened, I get very angry. Not only have I ruined our quart of milk for no good reason, but I've also run in the opposite direction from an easy 10 cents.

Translated into kids' language, that means two Chunky bars or a can of bubbly sweet root beer. All because I simply did exactly what I had been told to do.

I was just following orders, I'm not the general in this army.

This puts Mom on my bad list for the rest of the entire day. Dimes are not all that easy to come by when you're five years old.

And you know for sure this lady's never going to ask me to go to Nolan's again. Not in a million years. So not only can I forget this dime, but all the other dimes as well. And that's got me seeing red.

Bloody murder, if you ask me.

Fit 'em wit Nixum

Dad's a Richard Nixon man. Mom's for John Kennedy.

We're having supper at the dining room table in our new fixer-upper on Littlefield Street. Our parents are talking politics, which is unusual, and disagreeing, which isn't unusual. The presidential election is less than a month away, and it's got all the signs of going right down to the wire. Nixon and Kennedy are crisscrossing the country, campaigning nearly nonstop. Emotions are running high, even at the Morris household.

Face it, Dad tells Mom. You're just voting for Kennedy *because* he's Irish and he's Catholic.

I am not.

You are too, Pam.

Mom says, And the only reasons you're *not* voting for Kennedy are *because* he's Irish and he's Catholic.

Not true.

Is so.

I'm not voting for him, explains my father, because he's a rich boy whose rum-running father is out there trying to buy the election. These people think they can buy anything—including the White House.

And I'm not voting for Nixon, Mom observes, referring to our Vice-President, because even President Eisenhower doesn't trust him.

That's ridiculous, Dad smirks. Ike's for Nixon.

I agree it's ridiculous, Mom quips. The President ought to be able to trust his own VP.

Dad laughs, then winks. Tell you what . . . let's ask the kids. Jimmy, who do *you* want to be the President?

Silence . . . all eyes on me. I've seen both Kennedy and Nixon on television. Kennedy has a handsome face, nice smile. But Nixon looks a tad on the grouchy side.

Kennedy! I announce, siding with my mother.

Dad scowls. Pam, you're gonna turn him into an Irisher yet.

Mom smiles. All right, Howie . . . what about you?

Three year-old Howie blinks, not comprehending.

C'mon, Shoelace, says Dad, using Howie's pet nickname. We're gonna fix 'em with Nixon, right? Dad pumps his fist in the air and repeats. C'mon, let's fix 'em with Nixon, right?

Howie's big eyes twinkle and his face lights up like a Christmas tree. Ear-to-ear grin.

Yeah! Howie cheers. Fit 'em wit Nixum!

We all laugh, including Howie. Now Howie's pumping his little fist in the air just like Pop.

Fit 'em wit Nixum, fit 'em wit Nixum!

Baby sister Laura is the tie-breaker, but she's asleep in her crib. Not yet three months old. Even at the Morris house this one's way too close to call. Meanwhile, the fate of our beloved nation hangs in the balance. . . .

Still, times are good. America marches optimistically toward the future.

Streetcar Suburb

Our new house sits right smack in the middle of the Kings Cross section of Philadelphia. It's what they call a streetcar suburb—thousands of nearly identical two-story row houses, red brick and white trim. Built after the turn of the century, just before the Great War, way out at the far-flung edge of the city. Seems the opening of the elevated train or "El" up on Merchant Street jump-started a major development boom. Following the row houses came the trolley lines, spreading westward like spokes from the hub of Center City—the Maryland Line bordering West Philly to the north, Lester Avenue through the heart of Kings Cross, then Parkland to the south. Miles of trolley tracks embedded in a carpet of grey Belgian blocks. In the early days they had streetcar lines running north and south on the numbered streets, completing the grid. But later, after the Second World War, these lines were removed in favor of bus routes.

The original inhabitants of once-trendy Kings Cross were mostly of English, German, and Scotch–Irish stock. Plenty of Episcopalians, Lutherans, Methodists, and Presbyterians—many of their churches still stand. But sometime during the 1930s and early '40s a subtle change begins to take place. Jews start moving in, just trickle at first, while the first owners begin selling out and moving on. Then, scarcely a decade after the Jews have gained a majority, a second wave of neighborhood immigrants washes over Kings Cross—the Catholics: Irish mostly, some Italians, the occasional German and Pole. Throughout the 1950s, and now into the '60s. By the middle of the decade, the grade school at Our Lady of Perpetual Peace will have become the largest Catholic elementary school in the United States.

Us Morrises are on the 5600 block of Littlefield, a tiny one-way side street. Our sister street is Beaufort, with which we share a narrow alleyway. You're supposed to pronounce it "*Bow*fort" but the locals all call it "*Bew*fort." Below us, separated from Littlefield by a driveway with basement garages, is shady, two-way Wennington Avenue. Two-way Venice Avenue runs above Beaufort. Mom-and-pop stores dot nearly every intersection. In the bigger scheme of things, this puts us just a few blocks north of the commercial district on Lester Avenue, where our busy trolley line heads to and from downtown, and the imposing twin green domes of OLPP ring the angelus bell far and wide.

There's a rhythm to this tiny corner of our great city, as regular as the ocean tide coming in and going out. The men leaving home early in the morning in their blue-collar work clothes, lunch pails swinging and thermos bottles full of coffee, heading for the factories down by the river, the repair shops, construction sites, the distribution centers, and the loading docks. The women preparing breakfast, seeing the men off to work, then children off to school. Kids in younger grades walking home at noon for lunch, time enough for a quick sandwich and glass of milk, then returning hurriedly to class. The predictable tide of humanity returning in the afternoon, school kids lugging book bags first, followed by the men in overalls and work shirts toting their empty metal boxes and vacuum containers.

Although Kings Cross is overwhelmingly residential, not everyone leaves the neighborhood for work. Besides the mom-and-pop store owners there's the Milk Man, Bread Man, Mail Man, and Insurance Man, the latter going door-to-door with policies and important papers wrapped in a fat rubber band. Mustn't forget blind Broom Man in dark glasses, hawking his homemade wares. And Fuller Brush Man, case full of cleaning supplies so cleverly packed and organized. Knife-sharpening Man, coming around the back way with his foot-operated wheel and handy welding kit for quick household tool repairs. Rag Man combing the narrow streets, turning trash into treasure. Leather-lunged hucksters, backing their fruit and vegetable trucks into the driveway entrances, singing *Jer-sey to-ma-toes! Freestone pea-ches!* And *Hey, hey . . . cherry, cherry wa-ter-mel-oan . . . buy 'em up, I wanna go home!*

Summertime brings a profusion of seasonal vendors and assorted characters. There's Serenade Man, singing show tunes for quarters, hustling corner-to-corner for a paying audience. Pony Man with rides for the little ones, complete with leather chaps and a ten-gallon hat for galloping high in the saddle. Carousel Man, his colorful, caged-in mini-Merry-Go-Round housed on a flat-bed truck. Organ Grinder Man, with a spunky little monkey doing flips, tipping its tiny cap for your pennies. And everyone's favorites in the hot weather, Mr. Softee in the musical white truck that glows after dusk, and his competition, the traveling Water Ice Man, flavored snow cones so cold they 'cause the dreaded brain freeze when you slurp too fast.

Unlike our little apartment on top of Lobb's Produce Store there are many kids my own age to play with on Littlefield. Husky, serious Bobby Schaeffer next door. Sandy-haired, freckled faced, buck-toothed Jackie "Bugs Bunny" O'Hanlon just down the street. Lanky, dark-haired, studious Davey Cutler farther down the block. Wiry, quick-tempered Frankie "Tutti Frutti" Pellegrino across the way, got his nickname throwing a fit and chasing after Water Ice Man's truck, gotta have that Italian ice. And round-faced, apple-cheeked, sweet-toothed Donnie Fahey from just around the corner, our unofficial leader, you can always count on him to flash a quick smile and say something goofy.

The older boys all look after us, teach us how to play the time-honored street games and hang out on the corner stoop telling stories. Tough-looking, tough-talking Sal "Cuz" Cusumano, who's really a fun-loving, likable guy once you get past all the muscles and bravado. Sal's brooding sidekick is Bruce Cutler, Davey's older brother and the tallest, biggest kid for several blocks in all directions. Funny man Billy "Con" Connelly, sporting a dopey grin and an Alfalfa-like cowlick. Skinny Sammy Shapiro, a curly-haired bundle of nerves who can't sit still, so jumpy he's scared of his own shadow. Tall, blonde-haired, All-American Tommy O'Hanlon, Jackie's older brother and probably the best athlete in all Kings Cross. And finally happy-go-lucky Steve Anderson, withered right arm on account of polio, but he can play boxball, halfball, and sock-it-out with the best of them using one good hand . . . sometimes Steve even carries me on his broad shoulders, I hope one day I'll be that tall.

The start of the 1960s are the halcyon days in Southwest. A time of relative prosperity—war and depression a fast-fading memory. The thriving, teeming, bustling land of hula hoops, Duncan yo-yos, Keds, PF Flyers, dungarees, T-shirts with horizontal stripes, short-shorts, crew cuts, DAs, Brylcreem, Vitalis, Schwinn bikes, Radio Flyer wagons, roller skates with keys, cars with fins, pinball machines, juke boxes, drive-ins, burgers, fountain sodas, penny candy, rock-and-roll on 45s, hoagies, Philly cheesesteaks, and milk shakes with real milk. . . .

On the black-and-white television—which takes minutes to warm up, clear glass vacuum tubes glowing orange—we watch *Gunsmoke, Bonanza, The Honeymooners, Dragnet, Highway*

Patrol, I Love Lucy, The Ed Sullivan Show, Clutch Cargo, Captain Kangaroo, Perry Mason, Car 54, Where Are You?, My Three Sons, Dennis the Menace, The Fugitive, The Flintstones, Lassie, What's My Line?, The Wonderful World of Disney, The Mickey Mouse Club, The Real McCoys, The Andy Griffith Show, and Leave-It-to-Beaver.

Rock-and-roll has reached an awkward stage, suffering and sputtering through temporary growing pains. The harmonizing doo-wop wave of the late-1950s has run its course, and the transitional, teen-idol, bubble-gum sound of the early '60s is now in full swing. The radio plays Frankie Avalon, Connie Francis, The Orlons, Chubby Checker, Bobby Vinton, The Shirelles, Bobby Darin, Fabian, Dion, Neil Sedaka, Paul Anka, Bobby Vee, Brenda Lee, and Bobby Rydell. Somewhere just outside the fringe of this adolescent mix thrive Elvis Presley, Roy Orbison, Chuck Berry, and Ray Charles.

Dick Clark's *American Bandstand* broadcasts its immensely popular television dance show to a waiting young nation—from a West Philly studio near the El and just a short bus ride north from Kings Cross. Meanwhile, the Beatles are but a struggling young band of mop-haired mods from across the Pond, laboring in obscurity while doing their Liverpool imitation of American rhythm and blues. Sudden stardom for the Fab Four remains years away.

On child-saturated Littlefield and over at Longstreet Elementary, the younger Baby Boom kids like myself go for such novelty sounds as *The Purple People Eater, The Wah Watusi, Oo ee the Witch Doctor, Mashed Potato Time, The Twist, The Chipmunk Song, The Loco Motion, The Bristol Stomp, South Street,* where all the hippies meet, *Alley Oop,* and *Itsy Bitsy Teenie Weenie Yellow Polka Dot Bikini.*

For a time it seems this innocent, teeny-bopper, milk-and-cookies culture will last forever. The streets are safe and graffiti-free. The music relatively harmless, the TV and picture shows squeaky clean. Children appear well-scrubbed and for the most part well-mannered. The parents, teachers, and proper authorities are firmly in charge.

But our extended state of grace is not meant to be. By 1970 the neighborhood will be grooving to an altogether different beat, with a whole new set of recently arrived occupants. No one coming out of the conformist 1950s can possibly envision the approaching chaos and turbulence of the middle and latter '60s. The JFK assassination. Vietnam. Johnson's Not-So-Great Society. Forced busing. Martin Luther King, Jr. Bobby Kennedy. The Manson Murders. Illegal drugs. Psychedelic acid rock. Long hair. Woodstock. Intergenerational warfare. Tuning in and dropping out. Civil unrest. Race riots. White flight.

Total, complete, catastrophic collapse in Kings Cross in less than ten years. A time for growing up fast, and for growing old and hardened far too soon. A time for moving up, moving out, and moving on. To the suburbs, to Northeast Philly, to South Jersey, to anywhere but Kings Cross, for better or worse.

But all of this turmoil lies in our unsuspected future. For now, at this moment, we are young, confident, happy, and carefree. At home, living a modest version of the American dream in our comfortable streetcar suburb.

Meanwhile the pressure slowly builds, still largely unnoticed and undetected, along the fault lines of society's tectonic plates. Waiting for the day when the Earth will rumble, a giant crack will appear, Kings Cross will stare into the abyss, then slide down into the mighty crevice and be swallowed up whole.

Gone for all eternity.

Learning the Ropes

I'm playing in the driveway next to our house when the two DeLuca brothers, Vince and Tony, come out the back door from their place on 56th Street. It's a shared driveway, but the DeLuca boys don't see it that way. The driveway is DeLuca turf, and they don't want some little crumb-grabber taking up space and getting comfortable in their domain. So when they see me bouncing a ball there, the DeLuca duo comes over, calling me Four Eyes and Sissy, and knock me to the ground.

I cry, get up, run inside my house, tell Mom. She patches up my scraped knee, gives me a hug.

The DeLuca brothers are older than me, bigger than me, and there's two of them. Little Howie is too young to help.

41

Next day I go out to play, and the same thing happens. Bam. One thing leads to another, and now the DeLuca brothers are using me for a punching bag, calling me a little dirt ball and a retard. Knock me onto the cement driveway, kick me when I'm down.

Now I'm really bawling and scrambling for home. Again Mom cleans me up, wipes my tears, gives me a big hug and a kiss. I don't understand why these boys are so mean, I just know I'm scared and I hate them.

Mom goes out to the porch, yells at the DeLuca boys who temporarily retreat though the cubbyhole to their 56th Street basement.

The third day the DeLuca brothers laugh at me, call me Fairy and Mama's Boy. Look around, don't see my mother rushing to the rescue, so they smack me a few times and throw me to the ground. I run inside, tell Mom, but the boys have run and hidden before Mom can go out and give them a piece of her mind.

That weekend we're all in the car, Dad driving, Mom with baby Laura up front, and me and little Howie in back. Mom tells Dad all about my problems with those neighbor bullies Vince and Tony.

Good, I figure. Now maybe Dad will march straight over to 56th Street and smack those DeLuca brothers silly, put an end to all their meanness.

But to my surprise, Dad gets testy with Mom.

Dad says, You can't baby the boy, Pam. He's got to learn to stick up for himself, to fight his own battles. You keep protecting him like that, he's never going to be able to play outside. Is that what you want?

Now Mom is upset, she doesn't want her little Jimmy being roughed up by a couple of budding JDs. Besides, they're bigger and older. And there's *two* of them.

Dad says, Stay out of it, Pam. Let Jimmy handle it himself.

Then he turns to me in the back seat, points his finger. Jimmy, these kids do this to you again, I want you to fight them back . . . you hear me?

I drop my head, stare at my shoes.

Jimmy, Dad repeats, I'm telling you to fight them back. Yell at them, punch them, kick them, do whatever you have to do. But it's your driveway too—you understand?

I barely look up, nod my head, look down again. In my little mind's eye I can see Vince and Tony coming at me again, laughing and taunting and slapping and punching. These mean kids are going to keep it up and there's nothing I can do—I'm too tiny—and now my last chance for help has just gone up in smoke.

It's a big, bad, cold world out there, and now suddenly I'm on my own.

Sure enough, next chance they get, here come Vince and Tony. Shoving, grabbing, hitting. I go down, pull myself up, start to run for home, then remember Dad's instructions. So I stop, turn, and half-heartedly take a swing at Tony, the younger DeLuca brother. I miss, but Tony gets a surprised look on his face. A punching bag swinging back is not supposed to be part of the script. So while little brother Anthony, a.k.a. Antny or Little Tone, is standing there momentarily confused, trying to process this new wrinkle of information, I kick him squarely in the shin. Then I take off again, make a beeline for our front door, dive headfirst into the living room.

I don't know it, but Mom has been secretly watching from the porch, peeking around the corner of the house.

Next weekend we're all in the car again, and Mom gives Dad the report card on my DeLuca brothers situation. Mom's laying it on thick, too. Jimmy stood right up to them, she says. Looked them right in the eye. Punched and kicked and hollered for all he was worth. Didn't you, Jimmy?

To hear Mom tell it I'm a tiger, a regular Jack Dempsey.

I just nod from the back seat. Dad turns, gives me a big grin of approval.

Attaboy, Jimmy. You did good.

Mom smiles, too, and now all's right with the world.

Dad leans over, whispers to Mom. . . . *To tell you the truth, I'd like to smack the snot outta those two little guineas myself.*

Eventually, the DeLuca brothers grow bored, gradually leave me alone, and I can play in the driveway whenever I want. I make friends with Bobby Schaeffer, the boy next door, and Jackie O'Hanlon, the toothy, freckled-faced kid from down the street. Having friends around is good. Vince and Tony only seem to bother smaller kids who play by themselves and don't fight back.

Easy pickings. Little Jimmy Morris doesn't want to be easy pickings.

The Werewolf of Longstreet

The roughhouse DeLuca brothers aren't my only headache. Getting picked on is something that must come with the territory in first grade, too. But I think the fifth-and sixth-grade girls who hang around the corner of 57th and Venice after school are taking the harassment a bit too far. These kids stop at this particular corner because they all live on different streets in various directions, and it's the last spot they're together before having to go their separate ways.

Problem is, I've also got to cross at 57th and Venice. Now these older girls are picking on me. It's mostly just name-calling, but sometimes they shove and trip us little kids when they think no one's looking.

One girl is worse than the others. Far worse. Shari is the biggest, fattest, ugliest, and meanest of the bunch. She frightens me, and some days I don't like walking home very much.

It's a Friday afternoon and school has let out for the weekend. Sure enough, Shari and the other sixth-grade mooses are lounging by the corner at 57th and Venice. I mind my own business, try to slip by unnoticed, and then they start.

Hey, where ya think you're goin', ya little squirt?

Yeah, can't you even say 'excuse me'?

Rookie first-grader walking the daily gauntlet. I keep walking, keep my big trap shut. But just when I think I'm in the clear, Shari the Main Moose sticks her big, fat foot out and trips me. The ground rushes up. I throw my arms out, hands facing forward, and break my fall. But I get concrete burns across my palm and it stings. Holding my sore hand I try not to cry. But it keeps stinging, and I feel the tears start to flow. I'm getting up, looking at my tormentors, and they're all laughing back at me.

Aw, mocks one big girl. Is the little baby gonna cry now?

More laughter and merriment at my expense. Then Shari stops laughing and gets that nasty look in her eye. Main Moose hisses, Hey—who do you think you're lookin' at? Run along, ya little brat.

I'm unable to endure their shameless bullying any longer. Quit it! I yell at Shari the Slob. Leave me alone, you fat cow!

In the schoolyard I have recently heard a boy call some girl a fat cow. She cried. But that's not the response I get from Shari. Instead, the huge girl's face contorts into a mask of fiendish rage. The transformation is so horrifying that Lon Chaney would've been impressed.

Shari looses her cool and starts screaming. What did you call me? *What did you call me?*

She charges like a blitzing linebacker. Fat Cow is as tall as a grown woman. Certainly taller than my petite mother, and much, much heavier. Three times the weight of a pip-squeak first-grader like me. Next thing I know I'm being body-slammed against the cinder-block retaining wall that encloses the lawn of the corner property. The back of my head conks into the hard, rough surface. I see stars and feel dizzy.

Panic! Gotta run, gotta escape. But before I can react, it's too late. Shari is grabbing me and shoving me against the wall. She pins my arms, my hands. Pushing harder and harder. It hurts and I'm scared.

I try to struggle, but it's no use. Shari is a giant. Catch my breath, deep breath, then I start screaming.

HEEEELLLLLPPPP!

Shari starts leaning her massive body against me. With both hands she reaches up and grabs hold of the wall's ledge just above my head. Uses leverage. Pull, push, PULL, PUSH. Fat Cow is smothering my screams. Squashing me against the sandpaper-rough cinder blocks. God she's a monster! I can hardly move an inch. Her open coat drapes over my head. My face squishes against her striped blouse. Darker, darker . . . pressing, pressing.

Can't breathe. Need air. Try to move my head, turn sideways for oxygen. Can't.

Terror. She's trying to kill me. I'm going to die. . . .

Instinctively I do the only thing left. Close my eyes, open my mouth wide, clamp down with every ounce of strength my little frame can muster. Biting hard. Growling like a crazed terrier, shaking my jaws left, right, left.

Loud screaming. Only this time it's not coming from me. Suddenly it's light outside again, and I can breathe. I gulp and look.

More screaming, louder hysterical terrifying screaming. Fat Cow has collapsed to the sidewalk, clutching her enormous belly.

Frozen in place, Shari's rotten girlfriends stare in disbelief. In shock, they gaze down upon their horizontal ringleader, then over at me. Looking at me as if I'm some kind of freak, some sort of killer. Now it's my turn to play Lon Chaney Jr. . . . as the Werewolf.

Hey, kid, one finally blurts out. Hey!

I turn to flee, arms and legs pumping into action, leaving all the screaming and the crying behind. I sprint across Venice as fast as my little feet will carry me. Out of oxygen by Beaufort, I'm going on pure adrenaline by the time I cut into the alleyway behind Littlefield. Stumbling down the narrow passageway between rusty iron fences, I gasp for breath and try to clear my head.

Seeking shelter, I empty into the driveway behind 56th and duck into a dark cubbyhole across from the rear of my house. Curl up, knees to chin. Breathing hard, collecting myself. Finally, when I'm a little calmer, I somehow get the courage to go inside.

All weekend long my parents know something is wrong. They ask, but I won't tell. I want to tell, but I'm scared. Biting someone in the belly is a very bad thing.

My father's mother visits for the weekend. Immediately she realizes that her little Mr. Jimmy is acting very strangely.

I overhear Gram inquire, What's the matter with the boy? Is he sick?

Frightened of something, Mom replies. But about what he won't say.

I spend an hour cradled in my grandmother's lap, then gently drift into sleep. Maybe by Monday morning my troubles will all go away. Away, away, away.

The weekend passes, and now it's Monday morning. I must face the terrifying walk to school. Coming to 57th and Venice, I survey the scene of the crime. Look around. No sign of Fat Cow, none of Shari's friends. I start to breathe a bit easier and continue on.

As I reach the driveway behind Venice, a figure emerges. It's a woman. Large, strange woman with heavy black-framed glasses, a beehive hairdo, and a flowery print dress.

You! the woman shrieks, pointing an accusatory finger.

I freeze. A second figure now emerges from under a stairway. Fat Cow. Immediately she starts sobbing, as if on command.

That's him, Mommy. That's the one.

You little *animal*! Strange Lady hisses, grasping my arm and wrenching my slender shoulder. You should be locked away where you can't hurt anyone else.

Shivering, I try to pull away. But Strange Lady yanks my arm roughly, pulling me closer. I don't want closer.

Want to see what you did, little animal? Strange Lady rumbles. Show him, Shari. Let him see the bite mark. Let him see what he did to you.

Shari pulls up her blouse and a roll of fat comes hanging out. I don't want to look, but Strange Lady makes me. Shari steps forward, sniveling, gazing down upon her own enormous belly. Ugly purple and red teeth marks. Some kind of brownish medicine spread across the wound. Not a pretty sight.

Poor girl had to get a tetanus shot, you little *monster* you!

But the full moon is no longer out, I've lost my fangs, and I'm just one scrawny little boy scared senseless.

Strange Lady says little else. She proceeds to drag me the remaining block-and-a-half to school, with simpering Fat Cow in tow. I'm herded into the school office where Strange Lady loudly demands to see Longstreet's principal—right this very minute. Again, as if on cue, Fat Cow commences with the bawling and the whimpering.

A secretary whisks me into a small back office, seats me in a chair. Mrs. Glass, the principal, arrives. Here come the school psychologist as well as other administrative personnel. They all cram into this tiny little room, along with Strange Lady and Fat Cow, who's still doing her show-and-tell with the bite mark. The school officials are all gawking, shaking their heads in disbelief, giving disapproving looks to me—the Feral Boy from Trannsylvania.

Strange Lady bellows, This animal must be removed from our school! I've since learned that Strange Lady's name is Mrs. Tannenbaum. Mrs. Glass asks Mrs. Tannenbaum and Fat Cow to wait in the main office. Once I'm alone with Mrs. Glass and the school psychologist, the grilling starts.

James, did you bite Shari on Friday?

Nod yes.

James, why did you bite Shari?

I try opening my mouth to explain, but no words can come out. All I can do is look down at my little shoes and tremble. I did a bad thing, now I'm in trouble.

Perhaps we made a mistake when we admitted him at five, I hear Mrs. Glass tell the psychologist.

He tested at seven years, intellectually.

Sure, but that's hardly the issue if he's only three emotionally.

True. A biting episode of this magnitude certainly points toward infantile regression.

Mrs. Glass briefly steps into the other office. I hear her ask, Has his mother been called?

Yes, she's on her way, the secretary's voice replies.

Our principal returns, and the interrogation resumes. After what seems like infinity but is actually twenty minutes, my mother appears in the doorway.

Mom!

I'm crying and my mother is hugging me, squeezing my hand. I'm here, Jimmy. I'm here.

Then the fireworks begin. I look up at tall Mrs. Glass. Hulking Mrs. Tannenbaum. School psychologist with her pinched face and studied look of extreme gravity. My diminutive mother, barely five feet, coming to my defense, battling them all, face dancing with freckles. This is what Mom calls getting her Irish up.

This child is a menace, Mrs. Tannenbaum is shouting. If he is not removed from this school at once, I am bringing a lawsuit against the school district!

Please, Mrs. Tannenbaum, Mrs. Glass intercedes. We must have all the facts before any decisions are made. We mustn't act imprudently.

My daughter was viciously bitten! What other facts do you need? This is an outrage. I demand action!

My mother says, I'd like to get at least one fact straight, if I may. What did your sixth-grade daughter do to my little boy? If he did bite her, it certainly didn't happen without provocation.

My daughter called him a name, shrieks Mrs. Tannenbaum. And for that she deserves *this* kind of savagery? Not to mention enduring a very painful tetanus shot. Show them, Shari.

Again, Fat Cow hikes up her blouse, accompanied by the mandatory boohooing. Mrs. Glass says, All right, Mrs. Tannenbaum. Please calm down. Mrs. Morris, I'm afraid she may have a point. If James presents a danger to other children, perhaps we'll have to discuss making other arrangements.

As my mother begins to reply, the office phone rings. The secretary motions for Mrs. Glass to take the call.

Please, Edna—not now. Can you take a message?

It's about Friday's incident, Mrs. Glass. A neighbor says she saw the whole thing from her porch window.

Mrs. Glass quickly changes her mind, decides to take the call. Soon it becomes apparent the lady isn't calling school to complain about Crazy James. No. She's calling to complain about the tall, heavyset girl who's been pounding the daylights out of little kids. She could've hurt that boy on Friday, pushing him and smothering him the way she did. Disgraceful. He's not much more than a baby. Doesn't the school watch what's going on out here? The woman was ready to go outside and yell at the girl before the munchkin defended himself.

Neighbor lady says Fat Cow Shari should be removed from school before some little tyke gets hurt . . . and somebody gets sued.

Now it's Mrs. Tannenbaum's turn to backpedal, trying to defend her precious angel.

But. . . . but . . . he bit my child! You all saw the bite marks!

My mother erupts. Listen, you! If this fat tub of lard ever so much as gets near my child again, I'm going to bite the both of you myself!

Please, ladies . . . control yourselves, pleads our embattled principal.

You're still lucky we don't sue, Strange Lady has the nerve to reply. My baby is the one with the marks!

Now it's time for my mother to use her ace in the hole.

Fine, go ahead—sue, Mom explains. The witness will testify on our behalf. Meanwhile, I'm seriously thinking about pressing criminal charges.

Mrs. Tannenbaum laughs. Criminal charges? Don't be ridiculous. You can't have my daughter charged with anything . . . she's just a minor.

My mother smiles. I'm not talking about your daughter, you imbecile—I'm talking about *you*.

Me? What on Earth for??

I believe the charge is kidnapping, Mrs. Tannenbaum. You did, after all, accost my son on the street—and forcibly dragged him to this office, did you not?

Strange Lady appears stunned. A pained look of realization also crosses the principal's face. My mother doesn't miss it.

And you, Mrs. Glass. I'm surprised at you . . . permitting this woman to manhandle James without so much as a peep out of you. Heaven knows what you were thinking . . . both of you. You ought to be ashamed.

It's shaping up to be a long and tiring Monday for Principal Dorothy Glass. And this is only just the beginning. Mrs. Glass will be earning her pay for some time. James Morris still has most of six long years to go at Longstreet Elementary School.

It promises to be most interesting.

CHAPTER 3

The Taboo

I have survived the first grade. Somehow. Despite my shaky first day not knowing about recess. Despite having to do the Werewolf thing so I don't get crushed by Fat Cow. Despite wanting to go home and "retire" like my father's mother, or elderly Mr. Lerner across the street, I have muddled through. I've been made to stand in the corner, come after school, been scolded as a "bad" child, and been forced to courier notes home to my bedraggled mother. Several parent–teacher conferences were deemed necessary. But now here I am, graduated, looking forward to my first summer vacation. And also on my way to second grade. No doubt I'm looking at more of the same.

Jimmy's a nice boy, Mrs. Anson comments on my year-end report card. *If he can work more on paying attention and concentrating on the task at hand he will go far.*

This is very a big "if" considering the numerous scoldings, punishments, and after-school parent-teacher conferences that highlight my first year. Seems my little mind has a mind of its own.

To celebrate this auspicious occasion, my Gram and Uncle Joe treat me to a celebratory dinner at The Parkland Restaurant. Big booths, air conditioning, mini-jukeboxes on the booth walls that play all the latest tunes. Not to mention soda pop, giant hamburgers, and trolley cars rolling past the front window. Feels as if I've died and gone to schoolboy heaven. After all, first grade nearly killed me . . . not to mention my long-suffering teacher, Mrs. Anson, with her hair up in a bun and old-fashioned glasses with their thick, black frames.

Once we're all seated, the owner's wife pulls a pencil from behind her ear and takes our orders. Not the slightest bit of hesitation on my part: One hamburger well done with fried onions and ketchup. Cole slaw. Side dish of corn. A root-beer soda. No problem because this is exactly what I order at every restaurant . . . except for the Szechuan Palace up on Merchant Street where they serve only Chinese food.

Maybe later, to top things off, I'll have a dish of chocolate ice cream. The perfect meal to start off my very first summer vacation.

Gram, Uncle Joe, and I sip our glasses of water while our meal is prepared. I, of course, must chew on the ice. Someone feeds coins into their booth's mini-jukebox, and the mellow, soothing sounds of Percy Faith's *A Summer Place* drift through the busy eatery.

I like The Parkland almost as much as the Chinese place on Merchant. Gram, Uncle Joe, and I have been to the Szechuan Palace more than once, and for a while there I had come under the impression that Chinese food is magic. Quite literally supernatural. Sure, the sweet and sour chicken tastes great all right, but that's not what makes it "magic." I'm talking about real magic— like potions, spells, and pulling rabbits out of top hats. You see, whenever my plate gets a little low on fried rice and moo goo gai pan, I inevitably start watching the hustle and bustle of the Chinese wait staff as they move from table to table. My father's older brother Sam had been a military adviser in China during World War II, and Gram's house on 61st is stocked with oriental paintings, vases, and knickknacks brought back from the Far East. Dragons, tigers, ceremonial swords, ornate temples. . . my favorite painting, hanging above the landing on the stairway, features an idyllic farm scene with a half-dozen workers wearing coolie hats laboring in an expansive rice field under a golden, glowing sun. Stylized and exotic, China fascinates me. Whenever I dig holes in Gram's back yard for my Tonka trucks, I wonder if it's really true that, if you could dig your way straight through the Earth, you'd pop out somewhere in China. I know my uncle went the easy way, across the ocean by ship.

Then, I look down at my plate, and . . . Presto! Abracadabra! As if it's materialized out of thin air, I have a heaping refill of more fried rice and lo mein chicken. Maybe even half an egg roll. It's not until I catch my grandmother sliding food from her plate onto mine that the mystery of the self-replacing Chinese cuisine is solved.

But perhaps The Parkland is the most fun, after all. No fortune cookies, but how can you beat good old-fashioned American hamburgers? No novel, mysterious Chinese people to watch, but the owners *are* from Greece. Or at least that's what I overhear my grandmother say.

In the booth across from us, a little boy my age is playing with his mashed potatoes and acting rammy. I watch as his folks quietly read their little monster the riot act, but to no avail. Junior just keeps at it and at it. He sucks loudly on his straw even though there are only ice cubes left in his glass. He squirms in his seat like a worm on a hook. He looks up, down, around—everywhere.

Then he sees me. I keep staring. Junior makes a funny face at me. Then another. I stick out my tongue. Bad blood is quickly developing between The Parkland's two munchkin diners.

Our war of menacing expressions is conveniently interrupted when the owner's wife brings us our plates. A tuck of the napkin, a big draw of root beer through the straw, and I dig in.

Someone feeds a mini-jukebox again, and Frank Sinatra begins to croon the spirited song *High Hopes*. All about those "high-in-the-sky apple pie" hopes. The melody is upbeat, the words uplifting. You can do anything you want to if you put your mind to it. I am inspired. Now I know just how I am going to get some payback with funny-faced Junior in the other booth.

Gram and Uncle Joe want to know all about first grade. About Mrs. Anson. About the corner safety patrol kids I am learning to resent. The storybooks we read. The songs we sing. How we learn our ABCs. Details about Sherman Sykes, my one classmate who manages to get into more trouble than even I do. Between bites of hamburger and mouthfuls of corn, I manage to tell them.

Now Junior's family is getting ready to leave. His dad pays the bill, leaves a tip, and they all roll out of the booth. As I expect, the chump turns and gives me one last goofy face, then sticks out his tongue for good measure. I glance sideways. Gram and Uncle Joe are talking now and not paying attention to me. I grab a stray kernel of corn from my side dish and place it between finger and thumb. Junior smugly files past, completely unaware. I take aim and flick the corn expertly, nailing him on the side of his thick skull. He wheels around, face turning red, and begins to shout incoherently . . . all the while gesturing and pointing in my direction.

I immediately pretend total ignorance, and munch my burger blissfully. Junior begins foaming at the mouth and speaking in tongues. All dining ceases, and the other patrons stare in bewilderment. The departing family hustles Junior out the door, where he gets roughly yanked and mistreated, all the while continuing to protest and point back inside the restaurant.

Uncle Joe gives me that suspicious, *I know you've been up to something* look. My grandmother just smiles at what a perfect little gentleman I am, not acting out like the rude little child who just caused such a dreadful scene.

♫ ♫ ♫ ♫

Whoops there goes a billion kilowatt dam!

He's got them . . . hi-igh hopes, Oh them . . . hi-igh hopes!

Big finish. Thank you, Frankie.

Now The Parkland goes quiet again, and I settle down to enjoy the rest of my hamburger, corn, cole slaw, and root beer. Conversation shifts toward Uncle Joe's day at work. My uncle is employed as a research assistant for a big scientific company downtown, also known as "Center City." He does chemistry experiments on things such as leather, vinyl, and various textiles. "Little Joe" is the only person in our whole family to go to college, even if he didn't finish. But now he goes to special night classes above a pizza shop uptown for something called "computer science." Joe is convinced that one day these "computer" machines will run the world. It's the wave of the future, Joe says.

I've seen one of these computers in a black-and-white movie on late-night TV at Gram's house. The computer had the voice of a person, and thousands of lights and dials on its control panel lit up when it spoke. After the movie gets going, the computer goes insane and kills the scientist who invented it. Pretty soon the vacuum-tube sociopath is taking control of the brains of other machines and robots. Power-hungry and maniacal, it seeks to destroy all humans and rule the world. But the U.S. Army saves the day in the end, and some good-looking, leading-man type gets to pull the plug on the Brainiac monster. All's well that ends well, especially on late-night creature-features. But anyway, Uncle Joe is a smart guy, so who knows? Maybe one day he'll be right about computers. And if so, does that mean kids like me will have to stay in school? What with all the computers doing the thinking, who needs brains?

Someone feeds another table-top jukebox, and now *Never on a Sunday* is playing. Maybe the owners of The Parkland put this song on, because this music's from Greece, too, just as they are.

♫　♫　♫　♫

Oh, you can kiss me on a Monday, a Tuesday, a Wednesday.

Joe is talking about his boss, and how their one experiment with tanning leather isn't going right. Joe wants to increase the "PH" level, or something like that, but his boss and a coworker say no. Joe says, if they'll just listen to his idea, they can make the leather softer, which is better for making seat covers and wallets. Gram agrees, because Joe is so smart. Joe went to college.

Seems I may go to college too some day . . . if only I can learn to concentrate.

♫　♫　♫　♫

Oh you can kiss me on a payday, a weekday . . . but never on a Sunday 'cause that's my day of rest . . .

This is a funny song, this song from Greece. All about how you can do something on one day, but not on another. Strange, but also somehow oddly familiar.

Well, concludes Joe, at least today's Friday, and that means I don't have to worry about it again until Monday.

Friday. . . .

Oh no! Friday. You can't eat meat on Friday—it's a sin. God will know. My mother will know. She'll have a conniption and ground me for the entire summer. Then I'll probably have to go to Hell . . . even though I'm still only six years old.

Partially chewed hamburger, bun, and onion lodges in my mouth. I can't swallow and I can't spit out. Now I'm not breathing, and I begin to choke. Paralyzed and frightened, my little eyes grow big.

Gram sees my distress, tries patting me on the back. Quick, Joe, she motions for my uncle. He's got something stuck in his throat.

Now Uncle Joe is slapping me on the back, only much harder. People stop eating. The whole restaurant watches, concerned. The owner's wife comes running over with a glass of water.

Jimmy, are you all right? Gram says.

No I'm not all right, but it's not what she thinks. My mother's family, the Kanes, are Catholic. My father's family, the Morrises, are Protestant. I don't know all the ins and outs, but the Morrises don't seem to understand the seriousness of not eating meat on Fridays. But at my mother's supper table, it's macaroni & cheese with fish sticks and stewed tomatoes most Friday nights. If we're lucky, maybe the occasional pizza—no pepperoni, of course. No exceptions. No if, ands, or buts. It's a sin, period, and it's my mother's number-one rule . . . not to mention that head guy the Pope.

I'm crying now and pointing at my mouth. At least Joe's back slapping has dislodged the burger bits. Ashamed and not knowing what else to do, I begin to spit the food onto my plate. This causes quite a stir, and Gram and Joe are horrified. The other diners are whispering and straining to look. Putting the glass of water on our table, the owner's wife frowns and takes a step backwards.

Now The Parkland's owner comes rushing to our table. He wears a look of monumental concern, the creases on his tanned forehead lengthening. He is afraid there may be something wrong with our dinner.

To me: Are you all right, little boy? To Joe and Gram: Is there anything I can do?

I wash my mouth out with the water and drop my head in humiliation.

I did a bad thing, I confess to Gram, Joe, and the Greek restaurateur. It's a sin. The owner blinks, then looks at Gram and Joe as if he's seen a little green man from one of those late-night sci-fi movies I love to watch . . . the kind that Roland the Vampire hosts on Saturday nights.

Quickly the owner removes my plate and whisks it off to the kitchen.

Jimmy, what's wrong? Uncle Joe asks. What sin? What's going on?

I ate meat on Friday, I mumble. Maybe I'll have to go to Hell. . . .

A momentary pause. Uncle Joe rolls his eyes in disbelief. Relieved, Gram laughs and shakes her head in amusement.

Jimmy, she assures me, patting my arm, It wasn't your fault. You forgot it was Friday. Besides, it's not going to hurt just this one time.

Yes, it will, I disagree. Because then I remembered, and I still had the hamburger in my mouth.

Don't worry, my grandmother reasons, there are lots of starving children in China who'll never get to eat a hamburger. It would've been all right if you finished it.

I wonder about this. It would definitely be a sin to eat the hamburger, because it's a Friday. But it would also be a sin to waste the hamburger. Gram has a point. But starving children in China? How can there be starving children in China when the Szechuan Palace has all that pork-fried rice, egg roll, and wonton soup? Besides, I thought Mom told me all those starving children were in Africa. Maybe I've got my geography mixed up, but it seems to me Africa is in a different place from China. So what's the story?

Gram says, Eat your corn, Jimmy.

I look at Gram, then Uncle Joe. Don't tell my Mom, okay?

Don't worry, they reply, smiling and nodding. It's our little secret.

I gladly finish my side dish of buttered corn. After all is quiet and calmed down, Uncle Joe pays the bill and we leave. The Greek couple smile painfully, they look very relieved to see us go.

Never do get my chocolate ice cream. Guess maybe that's God's little way of paying me back for my sin. Or Gram's way of letting me know not to waste a perfectly good hamburger.

Being Protestant must be lots easier than being Catholic. How come it's not a sin for Uncle Joe and Gram to eat meat on Fridays? And how did Mom and the Catholics ever get stuck with such a hard rule?

Maybe my mother could explain. But if I asked her, she'd want to know why I was asking. Then she'd find out about my well-done Friday hamburger at The Parkland for sure. So I decide not to bring up the subject. Oh well, maybe that's why God made Saturdays . . . so Catholics can enjoy burgers, hoagies, and cheesesteaks on the weekend once Friday is over.

Board of Education

It really just comes down to a difference in perspective: I am an anarchist. The members of the Longstreet School Safety Patrol are fascists. Every day they feel they must tell me what to do, and I in turn feel compelled to tell them to get lost. I'm the little rebel without a clue, let alone a cause.

Wait . . . stay there!

Okay, now you can cross.

Ridiculous! The endless rules in school are bad enough. Tacking on more rules outside is intolerable. I simply won't stand for it. I am in second grade, plenty old enough to cross the street without needing the slightest bit of help. As a rookie first-grader I had put up with this nonsense. Now enough is enough. Who needs goofy, space-cadet kids in safety belts and yellow rain slickers telling them when to walk and when not to walk? Even if the Safety Patrol is staffed by fourth-, fifth-, and sixth-graders? They're just a bunch of losers, suck-ups, and apple polishers . . . all of them.

You're reported, James Morris!

Big deal! See me shaking?

Sometimes I even dance out into the street when I see a car coming . . . just to make the safety scream. Kinda makes my long, boring, second-grade day.

One tries to grab me, but I tear off his safety belt and run away with it. It makes an awfully nice memento—not unlike some-

59

body's bowling trophy, or the STOP signs that older kids steal and hang up in their bedrooms.

Now you're *really* reported, James Morris!

Oh, no . . . please, not that. I'll do anything you want. Anything. But don't REPORT me! Snicker, snicker.

Safety reports are dutifully filed with the appropriate administrative authority. James Morris, James Morris, James Morris. . . . They pile up higher and deeper.

I hate how they have to call me James and never Jimmy.

Eventually I get called to the office and warned. Next, I have to stay after school. Finally, a note is sent to my mother and I get punished on the home front. Is there no fairness in this sham of an educational system?

They slow me down but don't stop me. This is guerrilla warfare, and I must offer stern resistance. Can't let them get me down, can't let the system beat me. Whenever a safety says STOP! I'm compelled to say GO! It's as if I'm preprogrammed and I'm just following the steps as they've already been laid out. This is my destiny.

Question authority will eventually become a well-known counterculture slogan, a battle cry that will command and ignite my generation. But rather than question authority, I'm just thumbing my second-grade nose at it. Seems like a mighty good idea to me . . . on principle.

However, authority often has a long reach, and the powers-that-be sometimes feel the need to strike back. One afternoon a sixth-grade messenger suddenly appears in Mrs. Weinstein's second-grade class and hands our teacher a note. It's a summons. From Mr. Rumpstle, up on the third floor. He's the sixth-grade teacher in charge of the Safety Patrol. Seems patrol morale has reached an all-time low. Mr. Rumpstle plans to change that.

Mrs. Weinstein motions for me to come to her desk. I'm instructed to follow the message courier upstairs.

Oooooouuuuuu . . . James is in trouble now! someone in the third row announces gleefully.

Quiet! Mrs. Weinstein orders. This is the teacher whose favorite pet name for me is Dizzy.

Rumplestiltskin's gonna whip Jimmy's backside, I hear someone whisper.

Fear grips me. I try to maintain a modicum of cool while smiling nonchalantly at my classmates. All eyes are on Dizzy Jimmy Morris.

I follow the sixth-grader out into the empty hallway and up the stairs to the third floor. It now occurs to me I've never been on the third floor. Never had a reason to be, since it's where the fifth- and sixth-grade classes are taught. Didn't expect an invite for another three years, at least.

The door to Mr. Rumpstle's class swings open. Reluctantly I walk in, not much choice. Some thirty pairs of sixth-grade eyes stare back at me. A desk creaks loudly, no doubt someone rubbernecking to get a better look. One of the nearly grown girls lets out a sheepish giggle.

Aw, he's so cute!

That's enough, says Mr. Rumpstle from behind his imposing teacher's desk. Now he stands . . . he's a tall man. The only man in our entire school besides the janitor. His voice booms like thunder on high from a summer cloudburst.

So *you're* the famous James Morris, huh?

Yes, I answer softly, avoiding eye contact.

You mean the same James Morris who's been reported fourteen times in the month of October alone? Longstreet's own little Jesse James?

I shrug. How are you supposed to answer a knuckleball of a question like that?

Well? thunders Mr. Rumpstle. C'mon, now . . . don't tell us you're *shy*!

My knees knock together. I begin to stammer. I–I guess so.

Very well, then. Come over here, Mr. Big Shot James Morris.

Nervously I comply. Mr. Rumpstle towers over me looking quite perturbed. He reaches over, starts tugging and sliding an empty student's desk until it comes to rest at the head of the class . . . right between the front-row kids and his chalky blackboard. Confused, I simply look on without the vaguest notion. It certainly seems an odd time to be rearranging the furniture.

Now Mr. Rumpstle reaches down next to the radiator and grabs a wooden paddle.

Drop your pants, James, he commands. Bend over the desk here.

I'm no longer confused—I'm in disbelief. Seeking guidance, I shoot our sixth-grade audience a quick glance. The girls look frightened; the boys can't wait.

Let's go, James, Mr. Rumpstle prods. Drop 'em.

As instructed, I drop my pants. I feel my undersized body shaking involuntarily. At least my underpants are clean . . . for now.

Slowly, awkwardly, I lean over and stretch my full weight across the smooth desktop. Thirty mesmerized faces look back at me sideways. I always thought teachers in the public schools weren't allowed to hit students. In the Catholic schools anything goes, but not in the public ones. Guess I thought wrong. My mistake.

Now one of the girls begins to cry.

Please, Mr. Rumpstle, pleads another . . . don't hit him.

You can't, Mr. Rumpstle, explains my original female admirer. He's so cute!

The boys aren't nearly so charitable.

Let the little sucker have it! encourages one smiling lad.

Yeah, show 'im who's the boss, Mr. Rumpstle, encourages another.

Mr. Rumpstle starts fiddling with his handy-dandy Board of Education. Rubbing it gently as if it were an old friend . . . one he's had to use many, many times. Posturing. Making sure he positions himself where I can see the paddle. Then, with a THWACK! he smacks it loudly across the palm of his left hand.

The girls all gasp in horror. I tremble ever more violently.

Go ahead, hit him! shouts one of the biggest boys.

I look up. My eyes beg for mercy. Mr. Rumpstle looks down at me and smiles sadly. I'm very sorry, James . . . but this is for your own good, you know.

Mr. Rumpstle then circles behind me, out of sight. My unprotected backside is sticking out, an inviting can't-miss target. I close my eyes.

SMACK!

I flinch, expecting pain. Instead, nothing. Mr. Rumpstle has brought the paddle down across his teacher's desk. A heavyset girl with stringy blonde hair and thick glasses starts to boo hoo. Her myopic little eyes grow red behind foggy lenses.

Okay, here we go! booms Mr. Rumpstle's megaphone voice from somewhere above and behind. Are you ready, James?

I tense, hold my breath. Still nothing happens. The suspense is starting to get to me worse than any paddling. I almost wish Rumplestiltskin would just paddle my backside and be done with it already. Skip this humiliation part, thank you. Just hurry up and send me back downstairs with a well-deserved sore hiney.

Now, James, this is probably going to me hurt me more than it hurts you, Teacher explains. But we *really* can't tolerate this sort of behavior—now can we, James?

Something in Mr. Rumpstle's voice has just given him away. He's overplayed his hand. Realization comes to me in a flash—Rumpstle's got no intention whatsoever of hitting me. It's all just a fake, a con job, some calculated bluff. The Safety Patrol chief wants me to break down and blubber like a baby. Then he'll tell me to pull my pants up, because *this* time he's giving me a break and letting me go. But first tell everyone how very sorry you are.

It's not going to happen.

The tension in my body subsides. The thirty sideways faces continue their staring. The pause grows longer, more uncomfortable. Rumpstle waits, not sure of his next move. I certainly don't have the foggiest.

Suddenly I begin laughing. Small, nervous, tension-filled laughs. I can't help it. It's as if some giant, unseen hand is tickling my body. Under my arms, in my sides, on my stomach. A shudder, some muffled giggles, and now I'm bursting into full belly laughter.

The sixth-graders are shocked. I chance a peek over my shoulder. Mr. Rumpstle is backing away, red-faced, and he's now leaning the paddle back against the radiator.

All right, you may pull your pants up now, teacher barks, desperately trying to save face. But remember, James . . . next time you won't be so lucky. You've had your last warning, young man.

Hollow threats. Rumpstle knows it, and I know it. This posturing windbag is only trying to preserve his precious dignity.

The girls are all smiling. Cute, spunky little four-eyed James has been spared. The boys, meanwhile, frown and shake their collective heads in disappointment. They wanted some action. Serious, heavy-duty action.

Aw, c'mon Mr. Rumpstle, complains one husky youth. Let me hit him for ya.

But my mother hasn't raised herself a fool—my pants are already pulled up and hitched. Just in case Rumpstle gets any ideas and decides to change his mind.

But Mr. Rumpstle wants nothing more to do with me . . . just wants me out of his sight ASAP. Nancy, would you escort this boy back to his class, please?

Mr. Rumpstle never summons me to his third-floor classroom again. I've got a free pass to do whatever I want with the hapless Safeties in their nerdy white belts and nerdier yellow rain slickers. Serves them all right, too. Gonna be open season on the space cadets.

And so the legend of Longstreet's "Bad" James Morris is born. I resume tormenting the Safety Patrol for another month or two, but this soon ceases to hold any challenge. My brain with a mind of its own is soon drawn toward other, more interesting diversions.

Yes, do question authority. But just to be on the safe side, better come prepared with a thick hide. And always, always, wear clean underwear.

Take it from me, "Dizzy" James Geoffrey Morris—I should know.

The Right Stuff

Mrs. Weinstein's second-grade class crowds around the television set in anticipation. Today is America's big day, February 20, 1962, the first attempt by a United States astronaut to orbit the Earth. It's part of President Kennedy's ambitious goal of putting a man on the moon by 1970. Millions watch in anticipation, including all the kids at Longstreet Elementary School. But I am not with my classmates on this historic morning. I am home, having been up all night with a high fever and a serious case of the measles. Now the fever has finally begun to break, and my little body is demanding sleep. But I refuse to sleep, and make Mom promise to let me see the lift-off.

Mom says, You're very sick and need your rest, Jimmy.

After I see the spaceman, Mom. After I see the spaceman.

So my mother carries me downstairs to the television set in my weakened condition, lays me on the floor. Gets my pillow and blanket, some juice, and makes me as comfortable as possible, which is not very. The launch is delayed, and I fight the Sandman.

Promise you'll wake me, Mom. Promise.

I promise.

Finally, it is time. The "A-OK" is given. Mom gives me a shake, sits down right next to me on the living room floor, up close near the tube. She squeezes my hand as the countdown begins . . . .

"Ten . . . nine . . . eight . . . ."

I have some vague idea of the danger the spaceman faces. The other day, in the grocery store, two older men were talking about the Mercury mission and the awesome power of the rockets. Mister, says one, you wouldn't catch me in one of them things for all the tea in China. No, sir. They're flyin' gas cans is what they are. Nothin' but a flyin' bomb. The other man just nods in absolute agreement.

"Six . . . five . . . four. . . ."

The voice of the astronaut's backup pilot crackles over the spaceman's radio. . . .

Godspeed, John Glenn.

Now my mother is making the sign of the cross, and I know that Grandmom has lit a candle this morning in the big church down on Lester Avenue.

"Three . . . two . . . one . . . ."

The mighty Atlas rocket engines erupt, building thousands of pounds of pressure under a space capsule smaller than Uncle Joe's Studebaker. Then, after a few tense moments, the hold-down clamps release, and we have liftoff.

Mom squeezes my hand again and we smile. John Glenn climbs higher and higher, reaching for the stars. Within minutes he's a hundred miles above Earth, traveling at 17,000 miles per hour. He will orbit the globe three times in some four and a half hours. But by the time Glenn is making his first pass over Africa and zooming toward Australia, I am already fast asleep. Her promise fulfilled, Mom carries me up to my bed and tucks me in where I'll lie sleeping until long after John Glenn has splashed down in the Atlantic Ocean, and they're already making plans for the ticker-tape parade.

At supper I am feeling better, and I tell Dad how I stayed awake to watch the spaceman. He flew faster than a speeding bullet, Dad. Maybe even faster than Superman. Dad says it took guts to do what John Glenn did, and he may not be Superman, be he certainly is a *super* man. This is high praise coming from the man I know to be the bravest person in the world. Dad says he takes his hat off to John Glenn, and it's a proud day to be an American. And this makes me feel special because I know that I, too, am an American, and being American is a very good thing.

After all, we have the right stuff.

Days later I return to Mrs. Weinstein's class all better, and the other kids tease me—James, James, you missed the spaceman! Mrs. Weinstein let us watch it right here on TV. And I say, No, I didn't miss a thing. Had the best seat in the house and watched it all the way from liftoff to splashdown. So knock off your stuff and just shut your traps.

The Pigeon

Sure, it starts out as merely a baseball thing, but then progresses to something else altogether. It's the summer of '62, and I've discovered America's favorite pastime: baseball. Or, more specifically, baseball-card collecting. The Philadelphia Phillies, Connie Mack Stadium, hot July afternoons, the crack of the bat. By mid-summer I own cards for half of the Major League players, and most of our hometown Phillies. And I spend hours relentlessly scouring the neighborhood for cards I haven't collected. Spend my change, swap, flip, beg, bargain . . . whatever I have to do. Jim Bunning, Johnny Callison, Richie Ashburn, Whitey Ford, Roger Maris, Stan Musial . . . the pile in the shoebox keeps getting bigger and bigger.

Then, the cold winds of autumn come, and baseball season grinds to its inevitable end. But my passion for collecting continues. Coins, monster cards, Superman comics, prizes from Cracker Jack boxes. Okay, so maybe I will never really become an honest-to-goodness football fan. Football, for me, just doesn't spark the same kind of magic. But I can still, nevertheless, pursue my penchant for collecting with the same dogged determination. So when the Mom-and-Pop stores switch from selling baseball cards to football cards, I start a new pile. Soon I'm trading, flipping, and spending my allowance with gusto for the pigskin packs. There's something special about the aroma of Topps bubble gum, the crinkling of the wrapper being opened, the joy of fanning through brand new cards in mint condition. . . .

In 1962 Philadelphia, there is one football card cherished above all others: the elusive and quite valuable Chuck Bednarik. Now at the end of his storied Hall-of-Fame career, "Concrete Charlie" is a Tyrannosaurus Rex in football pads. Born in the hard-scrabble coal fields of upstate Pennsylvania, Bednarik has menaced running backs, quarterbacks, and tight ends with unrivaled ferocity. Bednarik doesn't just tackle opponents, he crushes them. Future television sportscaster Frank Gifford's career gets violently cut short courtesy of a typically vicious Bednarik hit. As the last of the two-way, 60-minute legends, Concrete Charlie is a man's man. A throwback to the days of leather helmets, the flying wing, and the drop kick. Neighborhood fathers routinely recount and embellish Bednarik's gridiron exploits. They use the highest of superlatives, and speak in tones of hushed reverence. When God made this Hunky, He broke the mold . . . there'd never be another one like him. Chuck is one mean coal-cracker, a football player's kind of football player.

Hero of the Philadelphia Eagles' miraculous 1960 championship season, Bednarik previously played his collegiate ball at the University of Pennsylvania, just a short trolley ride from our neighborhood. Franklin Field doubles as home for both the Penn Quakers and the Eagles, so the Concrete One is truly a native son. No local athlete, with the possible exception of Wilt the Stilt, is more revered and idolized.

For some inexplicable reason, this NFL season's Bednarik card is such a rarity it seems hardly more than a rumor . . . which makes this already highly sought-after prize all the more valuable. No one on our block owns a Bednarik. No one on Wennington Avenue or Beaufort Street either. I hear talk in the schoolyard of a boy whose cousin's next-door neighbor's got a Bednarik, but no one's actually *seen* a Bednarik. You'd think we were discussing priceless Rembrandts or van Goghs instead of a measly football card.

Scarcity, I'm learning, increases value. Exponentially.

Considering the demand for Bednariks, you'd think the manufacturers would be salting the packs with them . . . at least in the Philly area. But just the opposite is taking place. It's almost as if the Bednariks are being yanked from the packs before they reach the corner stores. Do the card makers know how feverishly kids in our city are searching for the Concrete Charlies? Have they created an artificial shortage to spark an artificial Chuck Bednarik mania? Do we have a conspiracy in our midst to extract the maximum amount of children's allowance money in pursuit of a basically nonexistent bubble gum card?

These are hard questions, and I don't have any answers. All I know is I've gotten some allowance money on this cold, breezy, autumn evening and I'm heading straight for Sperling's Drug Store at the corner of 56th and Venice. On arrival, I recognize a few of the boys camped out on the ledge underneath the pharmacy's neon-lit window. Some additional light falls in a circle from the store's sign suspended directly above.

These are older boys, nine and ten, from over on Windermere Avenue. I know maybe one or two by name, but the Windermere Boys' reputation precedes them. They're roughhouse boys—bullies—who go to parochial school at Our Lady of Perpetual Peace. Huddled against the November wind, they've got football cards spread across the ground under the smallish ring of fluorescent light. Obvious wheeling and dealing is under way. One of the kids spots me and speaks before I can go through the door.

Hey, kid! You buyin' any football cards in there?

Uh-huh, I reply cautiously.

Yeah? Whatchu lookin' to get?

Chuck Bednarik, I answer without hesitation.

Oh yeah? Hey—I got a Chuck Bednarik, the boy says helpfully.

My eyes widen, my pulse quickens. You do? Really?

Yeah, sure. Got 'im right here.

I watch as the older boy fans through a pile of cards and plucks out a Bednarik. He holds it out briefly for me to see, his pals all the while watching. Yes, this lucky stiff owns the Holy Grail of 1962 NFL football-card collecting. There's the familiar green uniform, the ferocious crouched pose with the three-point stance, stylish Eagles wing on the helmet. The name CHUCK BEDNARIK jumps at me from the bottom of the card. It's the real Concrete Charlie deal, and this Windermere boy's got it. And I've just *gotta* have it. Somehow, some way.

Wow! I react excitedly. What do you want for it?

I don't know, he shoots back. Whaddaya got?

I reach deep into my jacket pocket and pull out dozens of football cards wrapped tightly in a rubber band. Always ready to trade, I've got my cards organized by team, with duplicates at the bottom of the pile. So immediately I start pulling and reading.

Um, I got three Eagles here, four Bears, a couple of Redskins, some—

Nope. No deal, the kid says curtly.

All right . . . how 'bout I add this Giant, and maybe a Green Bay Packer too?

Nah, nothin' doin' . . . I ain't interested.

Well, why don't you just tell me what you want?

Okay. Let me see your cards.

Reluctantly I fan my dozens of cards across the sidewalk. My potential buyer scans them with only mild interest. In fact, he looks downright bored.

I don't know, the boy shrugs. Not all that many great cards here. Tell you what I'm gonna do . . . you give me *all* these cards, I'll give you Chuck Bednarik.

What? I protest. I have fifty cards here at least. Maybe sixty.

So? comes the irritated response. You don't have Chuck Bednarik, do you? But I do. . . .

Now I'm angry, but I want that Bednarik card so bad I can just feel it in my grubby little hand. All mine. I want it more than any baseball card, football card, comic book, or old coin I've ever collected. If there's such a thing as Bednarikitis, I've got it.

I scoop up my cards, then stand. I'm going inside to buy more cards, I announce. Maybe I'll get lucky this time and get a Chuck Bednarik myself.

Go ahead, taunts the Windermere boy. But I've got the only Chuck Bednarik around here I know of. You can't get Bednarik. They ain't puttin' any more in the packs.

I march right into the store and buy two packs instead of my customary one. Now I've blown every last cent of my allowance money. Once back outside, I grab some space on the ledge under the other, unoccupied window and rip open my first pack of cards. A Cleveland Brown, two Steelers, another Bear, a Cardinal, and even a Philadelphia Eagle. But no Chuck Bednarik.

So, I take a breath, pop the pink rectangle of chewing gum in my mouth, and tear the wrapper off the second pack. A Detroit Lion, a Redskin, a Baltimore Colt, a Green Bay Packer . . . two more Eagles! . . . but definitely no Chuck Bednarik. Just great. Bye, bye allowance and still no Concrete Charlie. Jeez. . . .

Hey, kid! You get Chuck Bednarik yet?

No, I admit dejectedly.

Too bad. Still wanna trade?

My little mind races. I *really* want Chuck Bednarik. If I trade my cards, then keep buying more cards the rest of the season, I might be able to build my collection back up. And I could trade or flip for most of the Eagles. But Chuck Bednarik? There was no guarantee I'd ever get a Concrete Charlie. Especially if they really have pulled them out of circulation as rumor has it. Maybe it's now or never, do or die.

All right, I hear myself saying. Deal. I'll give you all the cards I showed you for Bednarik.

Hey, did you get any more Eagles in them new cards you bought just now?

Yeah, two. Why?

I want them, too.

WHAT? I balk, turning to walk home. No way! . . . Forget it.

Okay, he agrees. Tell you what—keep the new cards you bought. Just give me all your others.

We've struck a deal. I step back toward the circle of light. The Windermere boy steps forward, facing away from the drug store. He intercepts me along the shadowy edge of the circle, blocking my light. I reach into my pocket and remove my stack of cards I've carefully rewrapped in the rubber band. The boy reaches for my cards.

Nuh uh, I pull back. Let me see the Chuck Bednarik, I demand. Considering the rep the Windermere Boys have, I half

71

expect he's going to make a grab for my cards and keep the Bednarik. He's bigger than me, older . . . plus all his buddies are there. I'm more than a little nervous.

What's the matter, kid? Don't you trust me? I'll give you the card.

He holds the card out. There's not enough light, I'm looking at it upside down, and I only get a few split seconds for a fast glimpse. Green football uniform, crouched position, Eagles wing on the helmet. Yep, looks like the Bednarik. I take the card quickly, shove it in my pocket, and fork over my entire deck of fifty NFL cards.

See ya, I say immediately. I gotta get home.

Sure. See ya around, kid. Nice doin' business with ya.

I wheel around, walk briskly up 56th Street, and cut through the driveway between Venice and Beaufort. I'm heading home, and I'm thrilled. My season-long quest for the coveted Bednarik has been fulfilled. Success!

I let out a squeal of delight. Yes! Now I'm skipping along the concrete, autumn leaves swirling around. I'm singing, I've got Chuck Bed-*nar-ik*! . . . I've got Chuck Bed-*nar-ik*!

Turning, I follow the driveway behind 56th, crossing Beaufort. Dancing, congratulating myself. I can't wait to show the Bednarik to my friends on Littlefield Street, and to all those doubters in the schoolyard. A collector's dream-come-true. I did it!

Bounding up our stoop, I cross the porch, rush through the front door, head straight for the dining room table, and pull out my card. I sit . . . my heart is racing, the excitement building. . . .

Green uniform, crouched position, Eagles wing on the helmet. . . .

JIM TAYLOR C

Philadelphia Eagles

This can't be. I blink. I stare. I rub my eyes. I stop breathing. Blink yet again. The card remains the same.

JIM TAYLOR C

Philadelphia Eagles

I can blink all I want. It's not going to change what the card says. I kick back the dining room chair, jump to my feet, throw the Jim Taylor card on the table.

Aaaaahhhhhh! I begin screaming. Aaahhhhhhhhhh!!

My mother rushes in from the kitchen expecting blood and major trauma. Instead, all she sees is a seven-year old boy in tears. Shaking, sobbing, looking at a dumb football card.

Jimmy, what is it? What's wrong, what's the matter?

I point at the card accusingly, as if it's tried to bite me. I cry, It's J-J-Jim Taylor! Jim Taylor!! It's supposed to be *Chuck Bednarik*, I explain. The boy told me it was Chuck Bednarik, and he gave me *Jim Taylor*! He took all my cards!

Now I'm getting hysterical. Mom picks up the Taylor, glances at the stats on the back. Says this guy Jim Taylor's a pretty good player. He's an All-Pro center.

Nice try, Mom, but it ain't gonna work. No way a Jim Taylor card can touch a Bednarik. Not even in a million years. Moms just don't understand about things like Chuck Bednarik. And now I'm inconsolable.

I put on my jacket, walk back through the darkness to Sperling's Drug Store. The corner is empty. No doubt the Windermere Boys laughed themselves silly all the way home. Nothing left to do but turn around, shuffle back to Littlefield, head down. Fell for the old switcheroo, I did. What a stupid moron.

They've stolen my cards, my pride, and a little bit of faith I had in other people.

Jimmy, you'll have to learn to be more careful, my mother advises. Let this be a lesson to you. Just because someone tells you something doesn't mean it's true.

Right, Mom. Soon I'm rebuilding my NFL collection. I never do track down that elusive Bednarik card, however. Not to worry. I'll be fine. Baseball spring training will be coming around in a few months. That's my real passion, baseball. . . .

No, what really bothers me are the taunts. The whispers. The things said behind my back . . . but just loud enough for me to hear. From down the street, around the corner, across the playground. Whenever I see a group of those Windermere Boys. . . .

I've got Chuck Bed-nar-ik. For months afterward I'll see them and wince, because I know I'm going to hear it. *I've got Chuck Bed-nar-ik.* Of course I pretend not to hear. Ignore them, play it cool. But deep down inside it really, really hurts. For months I get the taunts, but it seems like years. Even today, the memory of those words still ring in my ears.

I've got Chuck Bed-nar-ik.

How could I have possibly been *that* gullible and trusting?

A week after my football cards are boosted, I'm still smarting over the theft. No way to get them back from the bigger Windermere Boys, so I have to come up with some other plan. When Mom gives me a nickel for spending money, I go to the drug store to restart my collection. On the way over I get an idea. . . .

Buy one, get one free.

So I pick up a pack of football cards and, when the druggist is busy with a customer, slip a second pack in my jacket pocket. It's a big store, and they sell a lot of medicines. Surely the moneybags owner will never miss a lousy pack of football cards here and there. Maybe by the end of the season I'll have replenished most of my purloined collection.

Back home in my room I open both packs. Some Cardinals, Packers, Bears, and Giants. One Steeler, one Redskin, and only one lousy Philadelphia Eagle. No, not Chuck Bednarik. . . .

I leave the cards on my dresser drawer. Later, when Mom is dusting, she comes across my football cards. Knows the cards are new, two packs worth, but I only had money for one pack. Calls me upstairs for an explanation.

Umm, umm . . . it was some kinda bonus pack, or something. Guess I got lucky, huh?

Nope, Mom's not buying that weak story, not for a second. Asks me, Jimmy, did you steal a pack of football cards?

Yes, I confess . . . lowering my head, ashamed.

Okay, put you coat on. We're going around the corner.

We reach Sperling's Drug Store, and Mom gives me another nickel, which is coming out of my next week's allowance. But then she stands just inside the entrance, arms folded.

Mom, aren't you coming up with me?

Why, Jimmy? I'm not the one who's been stealing. This is on you. *You* handle it.

I gulp, shuffle up to the counter, manage to mumble to the store owner about what I've done. Hand him his nickel. The man glares at me, gets all red-faced, gives me a lecture about how hard he works. All the hours he puts in, his small profits, the many nice things he does for his customers and for the whole neighborhood. A real blowhard. Makes me feel lower than low, and now I'm really sorry I ever got the idea to take that pack of baseball cards.

I tell the man I'm sorry, I won't do it again, but he asks me to leave his store anyway. Mom walks me back home, and little is said. There's nothing much to say. All I can hope for now is that Mom won't tell Dad. This whole situation's bad enough already.

Eventually, weeks later, I dare to return to the drug store. But now every time I go in the owner watches me like a hawk. Doesn't trust me any more—not for a second. Guess I can't blame him, although he doesn't have to be so nasty about it. Probably figures once a thief, always a thief, or something like that.

Fool me once, shame on you. Fool me twice, shame on me.

Now I've shamed the entire Morris family. All for a lousy pack of football cards . . . and I don't even like football that much, anyway. I remember something Dad said about the Depression, how despite everyone being poor, almost no one would steal. People still had their pride. People wouldn't stoop so low as to steal. Just wasn't done.

Not like today, Dad says . . . today when people are bold and brazen and don't seem to care what other people think. Or don't have a conscience to bother them.

I promise myself I'll never steal anything again. Ever. I don't ever want anybody looking at me again the way Drug Store Man looks at me. The way Dad would look at me if he knew. It's not worth it, not even for that one-in-a-million Chuck Bednarik card.

Birthday Boy

Howie's favorite television show is *Bertie the Bunyip*, where the host carries around this puppet that's supposed to be some mythical, furry animal from Australia and entertains all the little kiddies with his stories. Mom decides to treat Howie and take him downtown to the television studio to watch an episode of *Bertie the Bunyip* . . . live and in person. Brother Howie is all excited, can't wait, can't eat, can't sleep.

Halfway through the show the host and his puppet sidekick, Bertie, come to one of the most popular features of the program— the birthday celebration. Any boy or girl in the audience who's celebrating a birthday is invited up on stage for ice cream, cake, and a small birthday gift, courtesy of our friend Bertie. Howie watches all the kids marching up to get their ice cream, cake, and presents, and temptation gets the better of him. Soon he's on camera, under false pretenses, with the legitimate birthday kids. It's January, his birthday's in June, but who's going to know? Mom sees Howie on stage, shakes her head, and figures to quietly reimburse the studio for the gift once the show has concluded. Too risky to cause a scene with all the lights, camera, and action.

Kids are gulping down the cake and licking ice cream. The man and Bertie put the mike in each child's face, asks some simple questions. Now it's Howie's turn. Mom can only hold her breath and pray.

Bertie says, Hello, little boy. What's your name?

Howie Morris.

How do you like the ice cream and cake, Howie?

Fine, says Howie, vanilla ice cream and chocolate cake smeared all over his guilty kisser.

And is today your birthday, Howie?

Uh-huh, Howie fibs.

The man hands Howie a smartly wrapped birthday gift. Bertie the Bunyip inquires, And how old might you be today?

Howie smiles for Bertie, smiles for the camera. All Philadelphia is watching. . . .

Four and a half, says Howie proudly, chest puffing up.

It's not hard to tell who Howie's mother is. She's the small, red-faced woman in the audience who's just hidden underneath her chair. Oh, dear God! What will the neighbors think?

Ask a simple question, get a simple answer. And as the Morris family will tell you, that's the one thing you can say about Howie with certainty. He's simple.

CHAPTER 4

Snow Job

Money, money, money. There's dough to be made when the snow comes falling down. The bigger kids are out earning the bucks, so why not me? Once I help my mother to clear our sidewalk, the shovel is mine to use.

I'm off in search of my first customer. Knocking on doors, giving them my pitch.

Lady, may I shovel your sidewalk? Mister, can I clear the sidewalk for you? I've got a good shovel. . . .

Everyone thinks I'm cute. Such a fine, ambitious little fellow. But I'm still getting no takers.

Thanks, honey, but my husband will do it when he gets home.

Sorry, little boy, but Bobby Collins always does our sidewalk.

No thanks, little man—I was just about to do it myself.

Up one side of Littlefield and down the other. No luck. Frustrated, I decide to try some houses on 56th Street, just around the corner. Fewer kids on 56th Street, more old people.

Second door I try, I get a customer. Success! An old lady named Mrs. Rosenberg. She says, Certainly, young man. You may shovel the front of my property, steps included.

Proudly I begin the job. Lots of steep, high steps on 56th Street houses. Sizeable landings. And those lower front stoops, too. Long, sloping sidewalks. For such a tiny boy like me and six inches of precipitation, this is a ninety-minute job—easily. Maybe two hours.

So I put my head down, keep going. Shovel and scrape, shovel and scrape. The high steps, the landing, the lower steps, the sloping sidewalk. I do each section meticulously and thoroughly. After all, this is my first customer. I want to make a very good impression. Perhaps Mrs. Rosenberg will tell the neighbors what a good job I've done . . . then I'll have more customers next time it snows.

Whistling while I work, I'm already counting my money. I know from the bigger boys that a job like this is worth 50 cents at a minimum, 75 cents with any luck, and a whole dollar if Mrs. Rosenberg is a soft touch.

Wow, a whole dollar!

Shovel and scrape, shovel and scrape. Looking good, looking better. No cutting corners, no half-hearted scooping. Every step, every square is wiped clean and neat. Absolute perfection. I'm out to prove that little Jimmy Morris can shovel sidewalks with the biggest and best of them.

An hour and forty minutes later I step back, survey my work one last time, then knock on Mrs. Rosenberg's door. Proudly display my handiwork. Very nice, very nice, says the old lady. You do excellent work. I beam from ear to ear. Mrs. Rosenberg invites me inside. Now it's time to be paid, time for my big reward.

My first customer retrieves something from the kitchen, then fetches her pocketbook. She comes back. Smiles. Hands me a supermarket-brand can of ginger ale, and one thin silver dime.

Thank you very much, young man, says Mrs. Rosenberg. You can do my property whenever it snows.

You're welcome, I mumble, nearly in shock. A dime? This can't be. And a measly store-brand can of ginger ale?

I hate ginger ale. . . . too tart. Not sweet, like root beer.

Leaving Mrs. Rosenberg's house, I begin to cry, then run for home. Mom will straighten this out. I'm telling Mom.

Seated at our dining room table, I sob, tell Mom my whole sad story. How I worked for almost two hours. Did a good job. Only got paid a lousy dime and a generic can of awful ginger ale. Mom listens, waits for me to finish.

Mom asks, How much did the lady agree to pay you before you started the job?

I shrug. She didn't. . . . But it's not fair, Mom. Other people pay a lot more. Some even pay a dollar. It's worth a lot more than a dime.

That may be true, my mother agrees. But you can't blame Mrs. Rosenberg if you didn't set a price before you started shoveling. I'm sorry, Jimmy, but let this be a lesson to you. A smart little businessman knows how much he's getting paid before he does the work.

I am dumbfounded. This is an outrage! Mom should be making Mrs. Rosenberg pay me what's fair. It's not right to take advantage of a little kid. I'll show that Mrs. Rosenberg. . . .

I have an announcement. Mom, I'm going right over to Mrs. Rosenberg's house and giving her the dime back—and the ginger ale too.

Mom starts to stop me. Says, Now wait a minute, Jimmy—

But I'm not having any of this nonsense. It's simply not going to stand. I say, No, Mom . . . I'm giving the lady her dime back—and her stinking ginger ale, too. And then I'm going to put all her snow right back where I found it. Every single snowflake!

True to my word, I march right up to Mrs. Rosenberg's door with the dime and the can of soda. Knock on the door. Mrs. Rosenberg, I'm sorry, but I can't accept your dime and here's the can of soda, too.

Puzzled, the old lady takes them back.

Then, shovelful by shovelful, I start returning the snow . . . all of it. Back on the high steps, back on the landing, back onto the stoop, and back across her spacious sidewalk. Take that, lady!

Little Howie had previously shown absolutely no interest when Mom and I had cleared our sidewalk. Ditto when I went to shovel out Mrs. Rosenberg's property. But this is different. This is fun! Putting snow *back* onto a sidewalk? Hey, that's neat! So little brother Howie gleefully joins me in my mad mission to re-cover the Rosenberg property in all the fluffy white stuff. He's jumping around and kicking and flinging snow all over the joint, having a grand old time.

Meanwhile, Mrs. Rosenberg, arms folded, frowns down upon me from her high window. I frown right back, keep on going. Scoop, dump, scoop, dump. A little over an hour later, Howie and I have returned all the snow to more or less its original location.

News of my bizarre confrontation with Mrs. Rosenberg spreads quickly through the neighborhood. Lots of laughter and merriment. What a spunky kid! Suddenly I have the most famous, most talked about snow-removal service on Littlefield Street, perhaps in all of Southwest Philly.

The ones who have the biggest laugh are the older boys on my street and Wennington Avenue—my competitors.

Hey, you shoulda known better than to take Mrs. Rosenberg for a customer, one of the neighbor kids chides me.

Why?

Because she's Jewish, the older boy explains. Them Jews don't pay for nothin'.

Oh.

Yeah. Just stay away from all the Jews' houses, and stick with the other ones.

Okay, I answer. But how do I tell which houses have the Jewish people?

My question sends the older boy into an hysterical fit of laughter. He grins, Boy, you sure got a lot to learn. Shakes his head in amusement.

Well, I may be slow to learn, but the Jimmy Morris snow-removal business survives nevertheless. Through the remainder of that first winter and into the winters that follow, I slowly pick up a small but loyal handful of regular customers.

My very best, very favorite customers are Mr. and Mrs. Lerner, an old couple who live next to Grandmom Kane just across and down the block from us. Even though Mr. Lerner is elderly, he always comes out and gives me a hand with clearing the steps. That's especially nice when you consider the Lerners pay a whole dollar.

When I stop by Grandmom's house in the summertime, Mr. and Mrs. Lerner give me cookies and iced tea, and sometimes I sit with Mr. Lerner on their porch and listen to the Phillies game. My grandmother says the Lerners are wonderful neighbors. Salt of the Earth, she explains—whatever that's supposed to mean.

Next Christmas I happen to notice that the Lerner house has a special set of candles in their window . . . not like the regular multicolored Christmas lights most folks string up on their porches.

It's a menorah, Grandmom explains—for Hanukah. The Lerners don't celebrate Christmas . . . they're Jewish.

Jewish? My best customers?? How is *that* possible?

Now I'm really confused. Hey, maybe I should give some of the Jewish houses another try.

But forget Mrs. Rosenberg. . . never again.

Where's Herman?

Gram has had cats for as long as I can remember. Mostly alley cats with iffy dispositions, so I learn to keep a respectful distance. But one big tom, Herman, is different. Herman looks to be half-raccoon, half-house cat, with no-neck, a shredded ear, and an agreeable personality. Herman spends hours every day in his private hunting preserve, the sloped railroad embankment that falls away from the side yard of the house on 61st Street, just below the stone retaining wall. It's a place infested with thick, thorny sticker bushes. By the time Herman comes home from the hunt his fur is usually matted and tangled with sticky burrs that have hitched a ride. Dad and Uncle Joe are always removing the burrs from Herman's coat—a thankless, never-ending job.

Once, while we were still living on 55th Street in the apartment above Lobb's Produce Store, Uncle Joe brought Herman for a visit. Put Herman in a cardboard box on the back seat of the Studebaker. But by the time Uncle Joe had driven from 61st and Parkland to 55th near Maryland, my buddy Herman was stressed to say the least. Jumped out the car door and ran away the second Uncle Joe opened the box. We looked for Herman for hours, calling and calling, certain he was lost. I stayed up late, worried that my pal Herman was gone forever.

But Herman knew his way home. Slinked the nearly two miles through Southwest Philly and showed up bright and early the next morning on 61st Street, waiting for his breakfast as if nothing unusual had happened.

That Herman's a sly one, says Gram. Not much on looks, but smart.

Whenever I'm around and Herman's not hunting, Herman prefers to hang out with me. Watching television, reading on the porch, napping, building miniature houses with my Lincoln Logs set. My buddy sits right there, rarely more than an arm's length away. Gentle enough so I can pick him up, carry him. Purrs the moment I stroke his wiry, matted fur.

Gram lets me help feed Herman when it's chow time for the felines. Over the years an understanding has developed . . . Herman is Little Jimmy's cat. One day when I'm older, I figure I'll be the one pulling out all the burrs.

Then, one weekend, Dad and Mom drop me off to visit Gram and Uncle Joe. We have dinner, sit on the porch, later watch TV. Then it hits me . . . where's my buddy Herman?

Gram, Uncle Joe . . . where's Herman?

Uncle Joe looks at Gram. Gram looks at Uncle Joe. Gram clears her throat, says Jimmy, we have some bad news for you. Herman is lost, and we can't seem to find him.

I say, Lost? How can Herman be lost? He walked home all the way from 55th Street the time Uncle Joe brought him to visit. Herman's a smart cat. He knows where he lives.

But we can't find him, says Gram. I'm sorry, Jimmy.

So I look and look and look. But no Herman. Not on 61st, not on Slocum Avenue, not on Greenwood Avenue, not down by the railroad. Herman seems to have vanished. And nobody knows anything.

Lady, have you seen a big tabby cat, looks like a raccoon, missing a piece of his ear? Mister, have you seen a striped cat around here with a bunch of burrs in his fur?

For months, whenever I'm around 61st Street, I keep an eye out for my Herman. Nothing. If I'm in the Studebaker with Uncle Joe and Gram I remind them to keep an eye out. They do, but only for a minute or two. Then they go right back to talking, and I realize they aren't really looking.

I know Herman is never coming back. He knows where he lives. Herman is too smart to be lost. Something has happened.

It's back-to-school time, and the weather starts turning colder. Halloween soon comes around, and Uncle Joe stops by to visit some cousins who live down by the airport, Philly's unofficial dumping ground for unwanted pets. Later, near the parked Studebaker, Uncle Joe spots a calico kitten. Lost, all alone, unwanted. Big green eyes, beautiful orange, black, and white fur. Puts the kitten in his jacket pocket. It's a fierce one, nearly feral, and proceeds to claw and bite Uncle Joe's hand.

Joe brings the new cat home to 61st Street. I try to feed it, pet it. But it hisses and scratches at me, too. Definitely nothing like Herman.

All I want is my old buddy back safe and sound.

Tell me—have you seen my Herman?

Rusher in the Rye

Jackie O'Hanlon is going to the movies. Double creature-feature up on Lester Avenue. So is Bobby Schaeffer, and Donnie Fahey, too.

Mom, Mom . . . can I go with Jackie and Donnie and Bobby?

Mom gives in, lets me have 35 cents. Now little brother Howie gets wise and starts a ruckus. Uh, oh . . . he wants to go with us.

Mom says, Take your brother along and watch him.

But I don't want to take him, Mom.

And why not?

Because . . . he's just a *kid*!

Take him with you or you can give me the 35 cents back right this minute.

Aw, Mom!

Oh well, so we're off to the movies . . . all of us. Heading for the old Lawton Theater. Me, Jackie, Bobby, Donnie—and Howie, too. Not fair me being the one who gets stuck dragging along his little brother. So I read Howie the riot act . . . tell him to keep his trap shut, stay out of our way, and don't be a pest—or *else*.

Howie says, Knock it off, leave me alone, or I'll tell Mom.

I roll my eyes. *Just great, just what I need.*

The first movie is a stinker. *Plan 9 from Outer Space* with Bela Lugosi as, who else, Dracula. Dracula's somehow mixed up with heavies from this flying saucer that looks like a pie plate. Naturally, they're trying to conquer Earth for their evil purposes. It's lame, hokey, and corny all at the same time. Predictably, by the end of the doubleheader's first feature, the place is pretty restless. Kids are cutting up, running around, throwing popcorn. The usher, a young fat guy named Kyle, is earning his money today. Kyle prefers better movies so we kids don't act up and he can snooze away the afternoon in his aisle seat at the back of the theater. But not this afternoon, because today there is no rest for the weary. Fat Kyle is getting a very sorely needed workout.

As unlikely as this sounds, the second film manages to be even worse than *Plan 9*. It's called *Monster Beach Party*, and it's about some sea creature that comes out of the ocean to feast on all these stupid teenagers strumming guitars at a campfire on the sand. Only the monster looks like a couple of guys inside some dumb paper-mache´ costume—one guy for the head and the other for the tail—and it moves at the glacial speed of about three miles per hour. The beachgoers only get eaten because they fall down, scream a lot, thrash around, close their eyes, and wait to be gobbled up like so many burgers and fries at The Parkland Restaurant. It's pathetic, and before long Kyle has a medium-sized mutiny on his hands.

Kids scream, Fake, fake! We want our money back!

Kyle says sit down and be quiet. But c'mon, Kyle, this is an outrage. Thirty-five cents for two cheesy movies with fake-looking monsters and nonexistent plots. Yeah, we may be punk kids, but we're consumers, too, and we demand decent entertainment for the hefty price of admission. Certainly not this embarrassing slop after suffering through another dreary week in the local public and parochial schools dreaming about Saturday afternoon at The Lawton. Jeez, what a letdown.

Howie doesn't seem to mind, though. Good movie, bad movie . . . just as long as he's out with us bigger kids. All those mutineers now throwing popcorn and goofing off only add to his pleasure. So Howie gets with the program, and pretty soon he's booing and getting rowdy along with everyone else.

Jackie, Bobby, Donnie, and I pretend to go back for more refreshments, instead sneak around behind Kyle the zoo keeper, pelt him with some Juicy Fruits, then a quick escape down the other aisle. Over the seats, under the seats, along the rows . . . uh oh, here comes hefty Kyle with his flashlight. But he'll never catch us, we're too smart, too quick—except for little Howie, who jumps up and zigs when he should've zagged. Falls right into Kyle's grubby hands, the first miscreant Kyle's probably caught all month. Now Howie, all of six years old, is being rudely escorted to the exit and kicked out of the old Lawton Theater in disgrace.

Aw, jeez! *Now* what am I supposed to do?

Don't worry, says Jackie. He'll be sittin' on the curb outside when the movie's over. Enjoy the rest of the movie, such as it is.

But I know I can't be leaving my baby brother all alone out on the sidewalk. Hey, after all it's *my* turn to watch him. And besides, he might run home and tell Mom about our extracurricular activities, then I'll be grounded for weeks. So I say so long to Jackie, Bobby, and Donnie, and voluntarily head for the exit to fulfill my brotherly duties.

Howie is standing alone outside the door, crying—looking lost and helpless. I tell him, What's the matter with you, ya little moron? Why'd you let yourself get caught?

Howie is crestfallen. He's been nabbed by porky Kyle the usher, separated from the gang, tossed from the theater, and now scolded by his big brother. This has definitely rocked his severely-limited world.

Listen, forget it, I tell Howie. Let's go home. On the way I coach the little blabbermouth on what to say, what not to say. Tell him, The first movie was about Dracula and some aliens in a flying saucer, okay? The other about some weird-looking sea monster eating swimmers at the beach. We had popcorn, soda, sat with Donnie, Bobby, and Jackie, behaved ourselves, and had a great time. Don't say anything about running from the usher, diving under the seats, throwing Juicy Fruits, and getting thrown out of the movies. You got that?

Uh-huh, says Howie. I got it.

We arrive home. I help Howie with his coat. Mom comes in from the kitchen, wiping her hands on her apron, big smile.

Well, you're home early, boys. How were the movies?

Blabbermouth Howie lights up, starts talking. It was great, Mom! The first picture had a flying saucer with vampires, the second one a dragon monster on the beach, and we had lots of popcorn. Then we booed and yelled, threw some stuff and hid, climbed all over the seats, and then, and then. . . .

Mom gets a funny look on her face, and I'm trying to give Howie the high sign. But little brother Howie's in the zone and on a roll.

. . . . and then, and then—the RUSHER GOT ME! The *rusher* got me by the shirt and took me outside, and I wasn't allowed back in!

Now I'm looking for a place to hide, but it's too late, the damage has been done, I'm definitely toast.

Mom turns to me, barks . . . James Geoffrey Morris! What's this all about?

But by the time I'm done trying to tap dance, I'm in even deeper. Lose my movie privileges for two precious weekends. Being stuck with your kid brother at the Saturday movies is bad enough. But when they report on everything you and your buddies do, that's the absolute worst. Dirty pool, if you ask me.

Maybe these movie-maker guys ought to make a horror picture about Howie, the little brother who follows you every-where, reports on everything, has a photographic memory, and a great big motor mouth. The blood-curdling power to bring you down at any moment.

Scary, huh?

Anyway, this is the last time I ever get to watch a movie at the old Lawton Theater on Lester Avenue. By the time my movie privileges are restored, the Lawton has closed its doors, gone out of business for all eternity.

From now on we must hike all the way to The Parkland Theater at 63rd over in the Haskell neighborhood. I hear some of the grown-ups talking, and they're blaming television for so many movie theaters closing. It's not like the old days, they say, when there wasn't any TV, only radio, and everything you watched was at the movies, including the newsreels about the war. Now there are no more contests, no more special promotions, no more free dishes, no serials. Just overpriced popcorn, fountain soda, and no Humphrey Bogart, Tyrone Power, or James Cagney. Today, with people staying home and watching the boob tube, pretty soon we won't have any movie theaters at all. A sad state of affairs, indeed.

Looks like movie theaters are going the way of the buggy whip and gas street lamps. Guess that's progress, such as it is.

Me?—I like movie theaters. I'm for keeping the good old days.

And I for sure wish they didn't have to go and close The Lawton.

In All Sizes

We're driving to the supermarket, with me and Howie in the back seat, and Mom, Grandmom Kane, and baby Laura up in front. Grandmom is driving because Mom doesn't know how, and Grandmom only learned last year. In the streetcar neighborhoods, many people go an entire lifetime without learning to drive. There's no real need with all the trolleys, your relatives just around the corner, and the stores so close by. Everything in walking distance.

Grandmom is driving at a snail's pace, white knuckling it because there's still snow on the streets from yesterday's storm. She's nothing like Dad, who, as he says, can drive the crates they come in. Mom warns Howie and me about tormenting Grandmom and breaking her delicate concentration, so we keep quiet.

We come to a halt at an intersection, and this delivery truck comes zooming through, left to right, and when it passes by we see three boys barely older than me hitching a ride on the back bumper. The boys cling tightly, their boots sliding across the snow, white powder kicking up. Howie laughs, points, and you know what he'll be up to in a few short years. Wee, that looks like great fun! I just gawk and think to myself, wow, these kids are really gonna catch it when their folks find out . . . probably get the strap and be grounded for an entire month.

Mom screams, Jesus, Mary, and Joseph! Are those kids crazy?

Grandmom shakes her head in disbelief, too upset to continue with crossing the intersection. She's squeezing the steering wheel so tightly not a drop of blood is reaching her fingers, and her hands are all white like ghost hands.

Mom turns, glares back at Howie and me. Swears, with dead seriousness, that if she ever catches either one of us riding the trucks through the snow, she'll break both our legs. A kid could fall off a bumper and in an instant be run over by a car following close behind. No time to stop, and once is all it takes. Mark my words, I'll break both your legs.

Now Grandmom decides to add to the gloom. She warns, You know, boys, those coffins come in all sizes. Do you understand what I'm trying to tell you? They make them in all sizes. . . .

I appreciate Grandmom's concern, and I don't plan on hanging from the back of a speeding truck any time in the near future. But Grandmom grew up in the olden days and doesn't seem to realize things are much different now. Grandmom and her sister suffered diphtheria as children, and both nearly died. Gram, my father's mother, lost her little brother Charles who was only four. And Grandmom has told us about those days long ago when the influenza came to Philadelphia and killed thousands. She was still a girl, barely nine, when the disease swept through the neighborhoods like wildfire. People died so fast there was no time for proper burial. Then the men with the carts came down the streets, calling out at all hours, *Bring out your dead! Bring out your dead!* And pretty soon the carts would be filled up, and they'd be wheeling the bodies away to the big hole where they dropped the corpses in one on top of the other and covered them quickly so maybe more people wouldn't be catching the sickness.

But today is a new day with doctors and vaccines and medicines and serums and all their tests. Kids don't even get polio any more like Steve Anderson did, the one with the withered arm. So I appreciate Grandmom's concern, but kids are very safe today, and Howie and me don't know any kids who ever died, or even came close. That's just something for old people to do nowadays. So thanks, Grandmom, but everything's really okay, and there's certainly no need for you to worry.

Sometimes grown-ups can be such worrywarts.

Dogs vs. Cats

Mrs. Byers is trying to teach our third-grade class the difference between the Soviet system and the American system. One side prizes the group, while the other favors the individual. She wants us to choose the system we think is better.

For example, says Mrs. Byers, let's take Row Three here. In Row Three, we have Shirley, Kenneth, Sarah, James, and Steven. Now, let's say everyone hands in today's homework assignment—except Steven. Who should get a bad mark?

Blank stares from the class. What kind of dumb question is this?

Come on, class, urges Mrs. Byers. Who should get a bad mark if Steven doesn't hand in his homework?

Hands go up. Mrs. Byers picks one. Claire, who should get the bad mark?

Steven, of course, Claire Miller answers. Claire, never one to miss an opportunity, makes a face at Steven. Most heads nod in agreement. Mrs. Byers smiles.

Well, that's the way it's done here in America, Mrs. Byers explains. But in the Soviet Union, everyone in Row Three would get a bad mark—just because one person forgot his homework. Because *one* team member let Row Three down, *everyone* in Row Three gets punished. That's how Communism works. Think that's fair?

No! someone shouts out. That's stupid! Again, heads nod in agreement.

Another sly smile from Mrs. Byers. Class, any comments?

Something is bothering me here, and suddenly I feel my hand reaching up. My little mind with a mind of its own.

Yes, James?

I ask, Well, what about football? Or baseball, Mrs. Byers? If a player fumbles the ball, or strikes out, then his whole team can lose. Are football and baseball sort of like Communism?

The whole class laughs. Crazy James is asking funny questions again. And Mrs. Byers has that funny kind of look on her face.

Well, says Mrs. Byers slowly, you make a good point, James. But we're mixing apples and oranges here. The American way versus the Soviet way is much more important than football or baseball. We're talking about whether it's better to reward people for what they do as individuals rather than as members of a group. I think most people would agree that it's more fair to be treated as an individual . . . isn't that right, class?

Nods of agreement.

Yeah, that's *right*, James, Claire chastises me.

I'd like to raise my hand and mention how just last month we had been watching a film in the screening room in the basement, special treat, when two kids began to talk with the lights down low. Mrs. Byers stopped the projector, warned the class to be quiet, and then resumed the film. But then the two kids started yacking again, and Mrs. Byers snapped. She stopped the film, sent us all upstairs, made everyone write 100 times, I WILL NOT MAKE NOISE WHEN WATCHING THE MOVIE. I didn't think this was very fair, because I had been quiet and wanted to watch the movie. But I got punished anyway along with everyone else. So I wonder if maybe Mrs. Byers acts like a Communist sometimes just because a few kids get under her wrinkly skin.

But I decide not to say anything about this because, if Mrs. Byers is really a Communist, she might get mad and send me to this cold, dark place the Soviets have called Siberia, where they sentence all the people who have minds with minds of their own.

Now Mrs. Byers has another idea how the American system is better than the Soviet system. It's called the vote. Democracy. The freedom for the majority of people to decide what's best for the country.

In the Soviet Union, notes Mrs. Byers, they've got the vote, too. But it's not the same. Let me show you. Let's say this is Russia, and the school decides we're going to have a class pet. But the only kind of pet we're allowed is a snake. So you can have a vote, but you can only vote yes or no to having a snake, no other kind of pet. Is that a good way to do it?

No! many of my classmates call out.

Why not?

Because, says Ruthie, what if we don't want a snake? What if we want some other kind of pet, like a dog or a cat?

That's right, Mrs. Byers agrees. And in the American system, you'd get a vote for the kind of pet you wanted. Like this. . . .

Mrs. Byers writes on the blackboard:

SNAKE   CAT   DOG

All right, class. Now let's have an American-style vote. Who says we should have a snake?

One hand goes up. It's Sherman Sykes, who's half-asleep. Everybody laughs. I can just see Sherman now, feeding mice to our pet snake. He'd have himself a ball. Maybe gobble up a mouse or two himself just to watch all the girls turn green.

Mrs. Byers puts a **1** under SNAKE.

Now it's down to dogs vs. cats. In my mind this is a no contest. Cats are clean, quiet, use the litter box, purr, catch mice, and go to sleep on your lap. Like Gram's cat, my good buddy Herman, the giant, raccoonlike Chuck Bednarik of felines who's been missing for months now. I'd give anything to have Herman back safe and sound on 61st Street. I still haven't given up hope. Maybe one day my buddy will come back.

And dogs? Well, Donnie Fahey's older brother Skip can tell you about dogs. When Skip was five, he bent over to pet a boxer.

The boxer bit him on the face, and Skip had to have special surgery. Donnie tells me that Skip is still afraid of dogs and wakes up all the time with nightmares about being bitten. To my mind, dogs bark a lot, growl, smell funny, do their business all over the place, and are liable to bite you for no good reason. Who would choose to have a dog when they could have a cat? This is silly.

All right, class . . . who votes to have a cat?

I raise my hand immediately. Look around. To my astonishment, only two other hands are up. Both are girls. One is Rachel Moskowitz, and the other is Jill Simmons, who is very shy and sits way in the back. But when Jill sees only two other hands except her own, down her arm goes in a jiffy. Coward.

I stick my hand up even higher. Look around in defiance.

Anybody else? asks Mrs. Byers. Nobody else. Mrs. Byers puts a **2** under CAT.

All right, class . . . and how many votes for a dog?

Hands all around. It's unanimous . . . well, almost.

SNAKE	CAT	DOG
1	**2**	**24**

If this were the Soviet Union, says Mrs. Byers, we would get a snake. But in America, we'd get a dog.

I still want a snake, says Sherman. I think snakes are cool.

Everyone laughs at bull-necked Sherman, but I don't think this is very funny. If this were the Soviet Union and I were running the class, I think I'd ship everybody off to Siberia, maybe teach them a lesson. Besides, how come if the Soviet Union is so bad, it put a man into space before John Glenn? I don't think they'd be dumb enough to stick us with a snake in the Soviet Union.

Choosing a pet from among snakes, cats, and dogs. Not even close. How is this vote thing supposed to work if so many kids are retards? What numbskulls! I hope when grown-ups vote they use better sense.

We do arts and crafts for the next hour, and I sulk and make some half-hearted scribbles across the drawing paper. My mind is a mile away, on 61st Street, sitting on Gram's front porch, my long-lost buddy Herman the raccoon cat purring away at my side.

I know in my heart that no matter what anybody ever tells me, cats are better than dogs. Way better. Just like root beer is better than ginger ale. No contest.

Come back, Mr. Herman. I sure do miss you.

Coleman and Sarah

We have a new pupil in our third-grade class. He is shy, soft-spoken, looks at the ground when he speaks, but has a big, infectious smile. His name is Coleman James, and he sits way across the room from where I am. Coleman is colored. He's the first black child in any of my classes since I've been attending Longstreet. And since no black children live on Littlefield Street or anywhere really close, this makes Coleman somewhat special. I wish I sat closer so I could talk to Coleman, and maybe we could be friends. But after a while the novelty of Coleman fades, and Coleman is just another friendly, familiar face. Coleman is simply Coleman, and except for the fact that he inexplicably seems to have gotten his first name and last name jumbled around, I don't pay him much mind.

That all changes the day Mrs. Byers gives us a group assignment.

Mrs. Byers makes us split into several small circles, desks facing inward like covered Conestoga wagons. My group of five includes my buddy Dale, Sarah Webber who is very nice, horse-faced Claire Miller whom I can't stand, and a blabbermouth girl named Rose who is Claire's nutty sidekick. Claire is group leader, and Mrs. Byers wants us to make a list of all the kinds of things we like and don't like. But Claire, our leader, changes this slightly to the kinds of *people* we like and don't like. Claire doesn't like fat people, short people, rude people, dumb people, noisy people, ugly people, most boys . . . the list goes on and on. But she likes Rose, her three other girlfriends, and her grandmother, who gives Claire lots of money to spend. Rose, the sidekick, adds that she doesn't like people who are stuck up or snore a lot. Then it's my turn.

I say I like people who are nice to me, don't like people who are mean to me, and let everyone else pretty much go about their own business. Dale seconds my motion, and now it's Sarah's turn.

I like *everybody*, says Sarah meekly.

Sarah, you can't like everybody, snaps group leader Claire. That's impossible! Sarah says no, God made all people, and her parents have taught her that every person in the whole world is special. Every person should be loved.

Loved? Horse Face laughs and says you can't love *everyone*, that's crazy talk.

Yes, I love everybody, Sarah says sweetly but firmly.

Exasperated, Claire looks around the room, spots a boy named Girard. This character Girard is probably the weirdest kid in all of third grade. He's small, odd-looking in a sort of Peter Lorre way, throws temper tantrums, and smells bad. He smells bad because he still makes in his pants and wets himself. The school has to call Girard's mother when this happens, and she stops by with a whole new set of clothes. Meanwhile, we've got to act cool, pretend not to notice, and keep everything hush-hush, else Mrs. Byers will jump down our throats. Kids give Girard a lot of room, like he's some kind of human porcupine—or worse.

Claire points in Girard's direction . . . Sarah, do you love Girard?

Yes, Sarah answers quietly.

Now Claire looks around, spots Physical Phil Buckley. Phil is the class weakling, a lowly doormat, and picks his nose to boot. Phil's Mom makes him carry a ridiculous briefcase to school, and the poor kid takes more abuse than any three kids I know put together.

Sarah, do you love Phillip, too?

Yes, whispers Sarah, growing more uncomfortable by the minute.

Horse Face is in disbelief. Now she looks over to the far side of the room. Spots Coleman, and her eyes grow wide.

Sarah, what about Coleman? Do you love even *Coleman*?

Sarah drops her head, stares at her table. Yes, I love Coleman, too.

But Coleman is, you know, *black*. . . .

I love everybody the same, Coleman, too.

Sarah verges on tears, but Horse Face and Rose are in hysterics. Claire races to another table. Pass the word, Sarah loves Coleman. Like wildfire, the news leaps from one cluster to the next. Soon the whole room knows. Kids look, point, giggle, and snicker. By recess the whole third grade is in on the rumor. Sarah loves Coleman, Sarah loves Coleman. Pass it around. Soon the chants start.

Sarah and Coleman, sittin' in a tree,

K-I-S-S-I-N-G.

First comes love, then comes marriage,

Then comes Sarah with a baby carriage!

Later, when I see Claire on the stairwell, I tell her that's not what Sarah meant. Bug off, Four Eyes, Claire sneers.

Horse Face!

Four Eyes!

Horse Face!

Did I mention that Claire also hates people with glasses?

I don't love everyone, not by a long shot. I could maybe love Sarah, since she's very sweet and has the guts to tell people what she believes, even if they make fun. I don't love Coleman, but I do think I like him. And I know I hate Claire. I'd like to slap her ugly horse face silly until she whinnied like a mare and begged me to stop. If anyone deserves a good, hard smack it's Horse-Face Claire Miller.

But you can't win with the girls. If I pick a fight with Claire and beat her up, then I'll be the laughing stock of Longstreet for hitting a girl. And if I lose? I'd have to curl up under a blanket in my bedroom closet and never show my face again in school or anywhere else for as long as I lived. Life as I know it would be over.

So what am I supposed to do about Claire Miller?

And why is it that the nicest kids, both boys and girls, always have to take the most guff? I wonder if it works the same for Communist kids over in the Soviet Union, or if there's some rule there about everyone having to share the grief equally.

I don't know—sure beats the heck outta me. Maybe next time Mrs. Byers has us do the circle thing, I'll be in a group with Coleman, and then I can get a line on what he thinks.

Just don't team me up again with old Horse Face Miller and Rose her blabbermouth sidekick who hates stuck-up people.

Hey, it takes one to know one, Motor Mouth.

CHAPTER FIVE

Twelfth Man

I fall in love with baseball the first day of Little League try-outs. Love at first sight, forever and ever. How could anyone resist the bright-green diamond, warm sunshine, a hundred other kids eager to play, and that distinctive crack of the bat?

Jackie O'Hanlon's big brother Tom takes us all down to the Dobbs Creek practice field for the big opening day. Me, Jackie, Tutti Frutti Pelligrino, and Chuckie Long from Beaufort Street. It's great going to the ballpark with minor Kings Cross celebrity Tommy O'Hanlon. He's the star of the Honus Wagner League, ages 13 to 15, and everybody knows Tommy on sight. We four little eight-year-old rookie scrubs are lucky to be in his company. Tommy is boss, and everyone knows it.

Hey, Tommy! Put some linseed oil on that glove over the winter, did ya?

Yo, Tommy! How's the MVP doin' this spring, huh? Got that bat of yours all ready?

Tommy O! You back to win another championship this year again, buddy?

Me, I've got to be the runtiest eight-year-old kid there, with Coke-bottle glasses to boot. But I want to be a baseball player just like Tommy . . . even if I am scared of playing "hardball" for the very first time. I may not be the league's next "Hammerin" Tommy O'Hanlon, but I've got my new glove from Christmas, the Pee Wee Reese model, and I'm ready to roll. The good news is I get drafted by the two-time defending 8-12 years-old champs, the mighty Knights of Kings Cross. The bad news is they pick me dead last, only kid left standing on the field. Everyone looking, everyone smiling.

It sure is lonely standing out there all alone, being last.

Soon I'm attending practice, then suiting up for games. Our black and gold shirts look so cool, and I wear mine everywhere—proudly. Doesn't take long to figure out why The Knights are two-time champs. Not only do we have the biggest and best players, but Coach DeLuca is driven to win. Coach is from the Vince Lombardi school of athletics—winning isn't the most important thing, it's the *only* thing. . . . Except of course when it comes to starting Coach DeLuca's two sons, Vince and Tony, no matter how bad they stink—every single game. Same two Bozos who used to bounce me around in the driveway when we first moved to Littlefield. Can't hit, can't field, but their dad's the coach. So they've got it made in the shade, the lucky devils.

Wish *my* dad was the coach. But he's always fixing cars down at the Brimstone shop, even on Saturdays. No time to come to the games, let alone be the manager.

The league rule is you have to suit at least twelve kids and also play twelve . . . a minimum of two innings each. Our squad numbers seventeen. So five of us munchkins, including fellow Longstreet classmate Chuckie Long, sit on the bench while we win game after game. The Kights rule, most teams can't even touch us.

Grandmom Kane works as a waitress, and attends as many Kights' games as her schedule permits. She's a familiar fixture at the 49th Street ball field, usually seated at the end of the bleachers, often still in her waitress uniform, politely cheering for my juggernaut Knights. Game after game I sit, watching, never playing an inning, and game after game she comes. Always faithful, always smiling, always rooting for The Knights. The warm summer evenings become a blur, one six o'clock contest after the other.

One week a boy quits. Now we are sixteen. Next week, another quits, and then another. Fifteen, fourteen, and counting. Someone's family goes on vacation. Down to thirteen. But now the end of the season is fast approaching. Only one more game remains in this memorable summer . . . for the championship against our arch rivals, the blue- and gold-shirted Bisons.

On championship night my grandmother takes her usual place in the bleachers. The teams take the customary fielding practice, batting practice. Tension builds. The umpire appears, adjusts his bulky, navy blue chest pad, snaps on the mask, and soon it's game time. But Ryan Mullen, our left-fielder, is nowhere to be found. His parents are supposed to be driving him back from the seashore for the game, but they haven't shown.

Now we are twelve. The magic number. By the rule book Coach D *has* to play me tonight—in the championship game no less! And for at least two innings. Holy smokes! No doubt he'll try to get a lead, then sneak me in for innings six and seven. Excited, I run to the bleachers to tell Grandmom the big news. I just hope I don't blow my big chance. My *only* chance of the summer.

Our Mighty Knights jump to a lead, but The Bisons hang tough. Inning after inning, the game remains stubbornly close. The Bisons' pitcher throws hard, and I doubt I'd ever be able to get a hit. But in practice I've noticed something . . . since I'm so small, it's easier for me to get walks. Tiny strike zone, tough pitching target. So I imagine myself up at bat. I'll crouch down even lower, beg a walk. Then I'll move up to second base, maybe on a fielder's choice. Someone will smack a line drive to the outfield, and there I'll be, rounding third and sliding into home in a cloud of dust with the winning run. Amazing.

Talk about Heaven!

Then, during the top of the fifth, one inning before Coach has to play me in my very first game, we spot a familiar station wagon rolling into the adjoining parking lot. The Mullen Family and Ryan, our AWOL left-fielder. Coach smiles with obvious relief upon seeing Ryan's freckled face and black and gold Knights shirt. Next inning Coach D puts Ryan in left field, and I remain on the bench, like the usual bump on a log, for the rest of the game and season—crestfallen. Grandmom continues to smile, still claps, still cheers on my Mighty Knights. Finally, our big third-baseman Keith Stillman booms a deep one into the gap for a triple, and Knights base runners are cruising home one after the other. We win the game . . . and an unprecedented third straight championship. Coach is so happy he buys us all Italian water ices to celebrate. I'll never forget our winners' order: twelve tutti frutti, one root beer.

Later that week, in a packed clubhouse auditorium, I accept my championship trophy just like all my teammates. Grandmom, still smiling as proudly as ever, asks to see it. I hand over the shiny, golden trophy, majestic metal batter on top, and lower my head in shame. Confess to Grandmom how embarrassed I am with the award. How could I possibly deserve such a marvelous trophy never having played even a single inning? I feel like peeling off my prized black and gold Knights jersey right there on the spot . . . forever. I'm tired of baseball, humiliated with sitting.

But you were the most important player on the team, Grandmom explains. Don't you understand? Without you, The Knights wouldn't be champs.

I don't understand. How's that possible? I hadn't gotten a single base hit, or made a single play.

Jimmy, she continues, without you, the Knights would've forfeited the championship. You can't start the game without twelve players. Ryan didn't come until later. If you had quit, or didn't show, The Bisons would've been champs, not The Knights. Your coach even took me aside and told me so. . . .

I guess Grandmom is right, and begin to feel better about the situation. But still, it's embarrassing sitting there all summer like a bump on a log, never playing an inning. Not a swing, not a catch, not even a single try. Coach just takes me for granted, and so do all the other kids. I'm the league's Invisible Boy.

I'd rather have people mad at me than be ignored. Nothing is worse than nothing.

Jackie O'Hanlon gets runner-up mention as Rookie-of-the-Year playing shortstop for the .500 Hawks. He's going to be just like his big brother, "Hammerin" Tommy O'Hanlon. Budding neighborhood star athlete at everything . . . baseball, basketball, the works.

Question is, what's better? Being on the championship team, the Knights? Or being runner-up rookie of the year with the .500 Hawks? I know Jackie had a whole lot more fun than I did, getting to play every game at shortstop. But isn't the main idea of baseball to be a winner? To have the best win–loss record, to take that championship title?

Coach DeLuca sure thinks so.

Me, maybe I'm not so sure. But I don't tell anybody that. Most of all I don't tell Coach DeLuca.

I put the shiny championship trophy on top of the dresser in me and Howie's room. Don't look at it much, and soon it becomes invisible, too. Just like me.

I don't ever want to get another trophy as long as I live for just sitting and watching. Win or lose, I want to play. Let Jimmy Morris play, too. Even if I do drop the ball, strike out, make my usual mess of things.

Maybe next year Coach will remember how I stuck it out on the bench. Didn't quit. How for five innings I was the all-important twelfth man, saving us from automatic defeat. Gave us his coveted, all-season-long, sought-after repeat.

Made Mr. DeLuca the Coach of the Year.

Yes, maybe Coach will remember and give me some playing time. Perhaps just an inning or two here and there—when we're shellacking the other team, and I can't do any real damage because we're ahead by, like, eight runs. Nobody can mess up so bad the other team scores eight runs.

So maybe Coach DeLuca will have a change of heart.

Just maybe. . . .

The Boogeyman

It's after dark and some of the younger guys are hanging around on Davey Cutler's stoop. Me, Jackie, Donnie Fahey, Bobby Schaeffer, Frankie the Fruit, Davey, and little brother Howie. Halloween is fast approaching, the leaves are turning bright yellow and red, and the air is cool and crisp. Cuz is there too . . . Salvatore J. Cusumano. Our favorite oldhead. Leather jacket, white cotton muscle shirt stretched tight, tiny gold cross on a chain around his thick neck, black hair slicked back into a DA. Cuz is talking about monsters. Specifically, the monster that stalks Southwest Philly. Our neighborhood Boogeyman.

Happened about ten years ago, Cuz explains. Back in the early 1950s—before some of you squirts were even born. There was this guy, just a regular guy, nobody even remembers his name . . . doesn't matter, anyway. Well, one day this guy's crossing the street, and POW! He gets run over by this speeding

Cadillac, see. Nearly rips his face off, blood all over the place. But listen up, 'cause this is where it really gets weird. The guy shoulda died right on the spot—but he doesn't die, see. He's hurt real bad, brain damage and all, and so he crawls off the street and down into the sewer. Next day the guy wakes up down there and he's still alive, but he ain't right. Doesn't know who he is, where he is, or nothin'. So after a while he starts to get hungry, but he ain't got no mouth 'cause the grille on the Caddy bashed it all in.

So you know what he does?

No, Cuz . . . what's he do? Tell us.

He waits just inside the sewer entrance . . . you know, up at street level. Waits for the first little kid to walk by, then WHAM! He reaches up, grabs the poor kid by the legs, and drags him down into the sewer. Nobody sets eyes on the little squirt ever again.

What happened to him, Cuz?

Well, nobody knew what happened at first, see. It was a mystery, 'cause no one saw what went down. They figured the kid maybe got lost, somebody snatched him, whatever. Nobody had a clue.

So then what happened, Cuz?

Well, then another kid went missing, and another and another. . . .

Wow, Cuz. Really?

Yeah, but then there was this kid named Kenny Jeter. Ever hear of him?

No, Cuz.

Guess not . . . he was before your time. Anyway, Kenny lived up near Maryland Avenue, just a few blocks from Dobbs Creek Park. One day Kenny's walking home from school, same as usual, when he's standing at the corner, minding his own business, just waiting for the light. Suddenly, WHAM! Outta nowhere this arm reaches up from the sewer and starts to drag Kenny down. Well, Kenny's not gonna go quietly, see . . . he starts kicking and screamin' his head off. Just before Kenny disappears down the sewer, this lady comes by and sees what's happenin', so she runs to a pay phone and calls the cops.

Did they save Kenny? Did the police catch the Boogeyman, Cuz?

Well, by the time the cops got there and put a man in the sewer, there wasn't much left of Kenny. They saved the kid—barely, but the Boogeyman crawled away through the tunnels when he saw the flashlights comin'. Never did catch him.

So what happened to the kid, Cuz?

Kenny's still in the hospital, says Sal. He'll be there the rest of his life, however long that is. He was a hundred pounds or so before the Boogeyman pulled him into the sewer. Now he's only fifty or sixty pounds, tops. Poor kid's a vegetable, hooked up to all these IVs and tubes and whatnot. The Boogeyman sucked all his blood, drained all the fluids outta the kid. That's how he eats, how he survives. Doesn't know any better, and he can't eat nothin' else 'cause of all the damage to his face. The few people who've seen him say his face is right out of a horror movie—like five pounds of ground hamburger with two beady eyes starin' back at you. No nose, no mouth . . . just this raggedy hole through which he sucks all the blood.

Is the Boogeyman still alive, Cuz?

Yeah, as far as anyone knows he is, says Sal. They haven't caught him, and nobody's too anxious to go down into the sewers and try. There's miles and miles of sewers down there, fifty, seventy-five, maybe even a hundred years old. Who knows? Goin' every which way, in all directions, eventually emptying down at the creek. I doubt anyone could catch the Boogeyman, even if they tried. It's his turf down there—he's the boss. Under the streets, the Boogeyman rules. . . .

Jackie says, I haven't heard about any kids missin'.

Cuz looks at Jackie, then smiles. No kiddin', Sherlock. The grown-ups keep it quiet, cause they don't wanna start no panic. You really don't think your parents tell you *everything*, now do you??

We all laugh at Jackie for being so naïve, for doubting Cuz's story. We believe. Jackie looks embarrassed, decides to shut his mouth.

Watch out for the sewers, Cuz warns. Especially after dark. Don't get too close. Remember, he goes for the ankles. The Boogeyman can last almost an entire year feeding on just one or two kids—but you don't wanna be his next meal, do you?

No, Cuz . . . not us.

Good. Be careful. I'll see ya around, guys.

Wow. See ya, Cuz.

For the next two weeks, Cuz, Bruce Cutler, Billy "Con" Connelly, one-armed Steve Anderson, and Tommy O'Hanlon delight in hiding in alleyways and cubbyholes after dark, jumping out at us with jackets pulled over their heads. Moaning, groaning, making idiotic slurping sounds. Very funny. After a while I'm no longer amused, and begin to think that Cuz just made the whole thing up to scare us. But I'm not gonna be scared, not me. Nobody is gonna play with my mind.

Then one night I'm sleeping and have this terrible nightmare—the Boogeyman is coming up the back alley for me. He's crossing our tiny yard, grabbing onto the down spout, climbing up the wall like a giant spider. Now he's peering in our second-story bedroom window, face like a pepperoni pizza with a cavernous hole for sucking the blood of innocent children. Sliding open the window, coming in our room, just me and little brother Howie . . . closer, closer. . . .

I wake up, sweating and panting. It's just a bad dream, there's no Boogeyman, not really. But I can't get back to sleep because I keep looking at the window into the blackness, into the unknown. And I suddenly realize it's true—that nobody knows what's under our streets in those old rusted pipes and miles of buried storm drains all leading down to Dobbs Creek.

And so I keep watching the bedroom window, and listen for sounds coming from the alleyway, just in case. . . .

Camelot

We're doing math problems at our desks when a messenger enters Mrs. O'Shaughnessy's fourth-grade classroom, hands her a note. I glance up, happen to see our teacher's expression . . . she looks as if someone's smacked her with the yardstick. Something strange is definitely up. A few minutes later Mrs. Stivers, Mrs. O'Shaughnessy's friend and a fifth-grade teacher, comes to the doorway and beckons our teacher out into the hallway.

I listen, can't make out all the whole conversation. But the teachers are animated enough that some of the words carry back into the classroom.

SHOT . . . DALLAS . . . DEAD . . . OH, NO! . . . ON THE NEWS . . .

Other kids catch on fast, and soon we're all on the alert.

Mrs. O'Shaughnessy returns, ashen-faced, tries to maintain self-control. Clears her throat, makes an announcement to the class.

Children, the President has been shot. Please do as I say, remain in your seats, and be quiet until the bell rings. This is no time to be acting up.

We remain quiet, fidgeting all the while with nervous energy, heads bowed in silence. Mrs. Stivers returns, beckons Mrs. O'Shaughnessy once more into the hallway just outside the cloakroom. More loud whispering, sighs of utter disbelief.

When our teacher returns, Ruthie Cohen gets up the nerve to raise her hand.

Yes, Ruth?

Mrs. O'Shaughnessy, is the President dead?

Shhhhh, cautions Mrs. O'Shaughnessy. Yes, the President is dead.

Collective gasp from all us students. We ask no more questions. After what seems like eternity, the bell finally rings. Three o'clock. Our teachers lead their classes solemnly outside, like one giant funeral procession.

Bedlam erupts in the schoolyard. Kids running, talking, gesturing, screaming. All that bottled, pent-up, nervous energy released in the same instant. Eddie Winkler, Luke Peterson, and I race off school grounds toward 57th Street. A cold gust of wind swirls a pile of crinkly, brown leaves, and Eddie kicks at them excitedly.

Eddie says, Hey guys, guess what—I know who shot the President!

You do? Who, Eddie, who?

Sure, Eddie says—I know. John Wilkes Booth, that's who!

Instinctively I realize the person who has shot the President will go down in history . . . forever. A hundred years after Booth shot president Lincoln, every schoolboy knows his name by heart. I don't know yet who shot President Kennedy, but I know he is about to become one of the most famous persons in the entire world. Who is this man, and why did he shoot our President?

I arrive home to find my mother in a state of shock. She voted for Kennedy. Thinks he is a terrific president, one of the best ever, even better than Eisenhower. How could someone do something so horrible? How could this happen?

Maybe Dad will have some answers. But when he comes home from Brimstone, to my surprise he's every bit in as much shock as my mother. Dad voted for Nixon, but he's angry . . . very angry. Perhaps in his own way he's even more upset than Mom. After all, this is The United States of America. Things like this don't happen here.

On the news they're saying the man who shot our President is named Lee Harvey Oswald. Just 24 years old, around Uncle Joe's age. He's supposed to be a Communist, lived in the Soviet Union once, but that doesn't mean much to me. Doesn't tell me why he went and shot the President.

One thing I do learn about Oswald—he looks just like the neighbor kids, the Schaeffers. Big, little, young, old, boy, girl . . . doesn't matter. All the Schaeffers look like the picture they're showing of the assassin. Same silly pout, cocky know-it-all grin, and dimpled chin. For years to come, whenever I look at a Schaeffer, I'll think of the Texas School Book Depository. Automatic, can't help it. The resemblance is uncanny.

Come Saturday, the neighborhood is eerily quiet. Kids aren't allowed to run and play as on normal Saturdays. We dress up, sit on front steps, speak in low tones. All of the Kings Cross section of Philadelphia resembles one giant funeral parlor, hushed and in mourning.

On Sunday Mom begins to iron clothes, sets up her ironing board facing the television set in the living room. She wants to get a look at this Oswald character live as he's being transferred from one police building to another—for security. I watch, too, wanting to see the Schaeffer look-alike, but they're late bringing Oswald out, so eventually I wander off to another part of the house.

Suddenly, Mom's screaming. Oh my God, my God. They shot him! I come running in, just in time to catch the pandemonium.

The newsman says Oswald's been shot! Oswald has been shot! Now Dad is running into the room, too, and he and Mom watch in astonishment and disbelief. Dad is shaking his head angrily again. This kind of thing isn't supposed to happen in America. Eventually, Dad becomes aware of my presence. Sees me staring.

Jimmy, go sit on the steps outside, he says. Dad doesn't want me to watch anymore. I know why—it's like Dad always tells Mom . . . little pitchers have big ears. Be careful of what you say in front of the children.

But what's happening this weekend is too big to hide. Way too big. Like Dad says, this kind of thing isn't supposed to happen in America.

Later Sunday afternoon I go for a walk. The streets are empty. It gets cloudy, starts to rain. Dismal, depressing. But I don't pay the rain much attention—I'm too busy trying to make sense of the shootings. The whole wide world gone crazy. Grown-ups killing grown-ups.

But the longer I walk, the less sense it makes. And I walk for a very long time.

Next day is Monday, but school is cancelled. They bury the President, horse-drawn casket through the streets of our nation's capital, sidewalks lined with people crying. Mrs. Kennedy all in black, little John-John saluting and breaking the people's hearts.

Then it's back to school on Tuesday, resume a normal life . . . whatever that is. Nothing's ever going to be quite the same as it was before November 22nd. Mom says a prayer for the Kennedys, and for our new President. Grandmom lights her customary candle under the statue of the Blessed Mother. The new President is obviously going to need all the help he can get . . . and then some.

They put JFK to rest under the eternal flame. But with Lee Harvey Oswald gone like John Wilkes Booth, the truth remains in the shadows, and the country stumbles forward, afraid to look too closely. Our teachers give us our lessons, act reassuring, and say nothing about November 22nd.

Little pitchers have big ears.

Reading Is Fundamental

Mrs. O'Shaughnessy has the "smart" fourth-grade class, even though they don't exactly tell us kids this, we all know. The School District has just tested everyone's reading skills, and the Longstreet administration is eagerly awaiting news of the results. When the test scores come in, Mrs. O'Shaughnessy announces that five children from our class are reading at least two grade levels above the fourth-grade standard, and are therefore eligible to attend a specially funded reading class once per week. That's the good news. The bad news is Mrs. Dietrich, the enormous, red-faced lady who teaches the slow sixth-grade class, will get to conduct the special session with the eggheads. Probably something of a plum for her since she's got to deal with those blockheads all day.

Problem is, Mrs. Dietrich has a great booming voice, shouts a lot, and has the reputation of being something of an ogre. Still, this is quite an honor, sort of an advanced placement, so we look around the room, try to figure out who made the cut. Everybody likes extra attention, whether they admit it or not, and would no doubt welcome the recognition that goes with being in this prized new group of reading geniuses.

Despite the spitballs, the practical jokes, and all the tussles on the playground with my hair-trigger temper, I'm not that bad a student. And reading is my favorite subject. Especially when it comes to reading stories. Faraway people, faraway places, the realm of imagination. I like the movies even better, but reading comes in a close second. Every year, without fail, Mom and Dad buy me at least one book for Christmas.

This year I got *All about Dinosaurs* by Roy Chapman Andrews. It's the best book I've ever read, about an adventurer who goes to a desert in Mongolia in search of ancient human bones, but finds fossilized dinosaur eggs instead. The first dinosaur eggs ever found anywhere, and they said it wasn't possible. The book is really very cool.

Still, there's a lot of smart kids in this classroom, getting much better grades and studying harder than me. Plus, most of them don't get suspended at least once per year, the way I seem to do, for brawling in the schoolyard or pulling a gag. I don't see how it's possible for me to be on the list.

There's only room for five. . . .

Mrs. O'Shaughnessy stands at the head of our class, clears her throat, reads from the list.

She announces, The five students who will be joining the Special Advanced Reading Program are—

Ruth Cohen. . . .

Ruthie is all smiles, and her friends congratulate her.

Sarah Webber. . . .

Sarah blushes. She's the shy girl who loves everybody, even Coleman. Sarah smiles, her little face turning redder, and looks embarrassed by the nomination.

Rachel Moskowitz. . . .

Rachel is a big, dark-haired girl with freckles who's kind of quiet and keeps to herself. She's not that bad really . . . for a girl.

Phillip Buckley. . . .

A skinny bubblehead whose mother thinks he's going to be a rocket scientist or some other big deal . . . sends him to school with his own little briefcase, if you can believe that. Kids are always knocking the dumb thing out of his hand, and Physical Phil gets terrorized at recess by all the boys, everyone can beat him up. Last month somebody broke his glasses . . . I'd almost feel sorry for the kid if he wasn't such a clueless moron. A hi-IQ moron, but a hopeless case just the same.

Only one name to go. So far, no surprises.

And finally, James Morris. . . .

For a split second I start to turn, look around, search out James Morris. Then I realize he is me. The class is stunned, I am stunned. Mrs. O'Shaughnessy tries to act normal, smiling appropriately, just one more name on the list, no big deal.

But it is a big deal. What's wrong with this picture? A fourth-grade goober with a briefcase and a sign that says KICK ME, three nice Jewish girls, and me—bad boy James "Dizzy" Morris. And I'm not the only one looking around as if there's been a miscarriage of justice. Ruthie and Phillip both look puzzled, even offended, as if I can't possibly be lumped in with their snobby little clique.

James Morris . . . in the Advanced Reading Program, two grade levels above the standard? Must be some kind of clerical error, a snafu with the paperwork. I'm the one with the suspensions, remember? The regular visits to the guidance office, they've got a seat down there with my name. And parent-teacher conferences to solve, once-and-for-all, the problem of what the devil is wrong with James Morris. They're not supposed to put "bad" kids in with the teachers' pets, that's not part of the program.

Even my partner in crime, bull-necked Sherman Sykes, is perplexed.

Sherm says, Nice goin', egghead. What did you do, blackmail Mrs. O'Shaughnessy or somethin'? Steal the answers to the test? What?

Nothing, Sherm. I just like to read, that's all.

Yeah, right.

Best of all is how Claire Miller is taking it. Man, is old Horse Face really sore. She's glaring at me like I ate her lunch . . . which, in a way, I did. I'm in the special reading program—and Claire isn't.

Way cool.

The first couple of weeks with Mrs. Dietrich go real swell. Just me, bubblehead Phillip, and three nice Jewish girls reading some harder stories for older kids. Part of each story we read in

111

class, and the rest we're supposed to read at home. Later, when we come back for our next session, Mrs. Dietrich goes around the little circle and asks us questions.

Then one week it comes time for special reading class—the past week's story is about a group of kids who live in a little town in Brazil. Only problem is, I forgot to finish the assignment. Got distracted by my transistor radio instead.

Now Mrs. Dietrich is going to ask me questions about how the Brazil story ends, and I'm not going to have the answers. Then she's going to holler at me in front of the others with that great booming voice of hers. The more I think about it, the more nervous I become.

But I know a solution—I'll cut reading class. That's it. Head off to Mrs. Dietrich's room with Bubblehead Buckley and the three nice Jewish girls, then make like I'm going to the lavatory. Maybe Mrs. Dietrich will never miss me.

So I duck into the lavatory for a few minutes, wait until the coast is clear, and scout the hall looking for a hiding spot. In our cloakroom I see long yellow rain slickers hanging down and several pairs of galoshes parked below them. This gives me an idea. I stand under the longest slicker, which droops backwards to the floor, and slip into some waterproof overshoes. Suddenly I'm invisible, hiding in plain sight. Better yet, I can hear all the talk from Mrs. O'Shaughnessy's classroom.

All goes well—for about five minutes. Then a messenger comes down from Mrs. Dietrich's room. Where's James Morris? He isn't here, isn't he in reading class? The messenger is sent down to the office. Within ten minutes the whole school administration is combing the halls looking for me, from the principal, Mrs. Glass, on down to Sherm's pal, the janitor. They're worried I got lost, or worse yet, snatched. Mrs. O'Shaughnessy is the most upset of all. She comes through the cloakroom, Mrs. Glass comes through the cloakroom, they all come through the cloakroom. But nobody sees me shaking under the hanging, oversized yellow slicker standing in the big, ugly galoshes. I'm the Invisible Boy.

Near the end of the reading hour, while Mrs. O'Shaughnessy is in the hallway leading the search party, I quietly slip from the cloakroom into the classroom and take my seat. Kids' eyes light up, James where've you been?

Now Mrs. O'Shaughnessy is in the room and Mrs. Glass is there, too. And here comes fat, old Mrs. Dietrich. I'm telling them I was sick, I was in the lavatory but no one's buying my story. Finally, I fess up. Tell them how I hid in the cloakroom, how I forgot to read my assignment about the kids from the town in Brazil, and how I was afraid Mrs. Dietrich would holler.

The grown-ups are all shaking their heads, and the kids are all laughing and pointing, isn't James so silly? No wonder they call him Dizzy.

Cutting reading class and hiding in the cloakroom wasn't such a hot idea.

Well, they decide to let me stay in Mrs. Dietrich's special reading class, but the girls are told to watch me on each trip upstairs so I don't duck out and cause another commotion. They don't tell Bubblehead "Physical Phil" to keep tabs on me, because if he did and then turned me in they know I'd smack Phillip silly first chance at recess or after school. Probably trample his sorry briefcase, too.

So it's a very embarrassing situation, being the bad kid in the Advanced Reading class. It's supposed to be an honor for teachers' pets, but everybody at Longstreet knows keep your eye on James Morris—he can't be trusted.

Maybe the other kids are right, I don't belong in Advanced Reading. Not Sherm's little sidekick, the one who's always in a scrape on the playground or sitting in the principal's office for misbehaving—again.

Sherm has himself a good laugh when he finds I was hiding in the cloakroom the whole time under the rain slicker wearing a pair of galoshes, the old Invisible Boy trick.

Sherm says, Nice move, retard . . .way to go.

Maybe Gram has a saying that explains the whole sorry mess. . . . *You can't make a silk purse out of a sow's ear.*

And you ain't gonna make no boy genius outta some foul ball like Dizzy Morris.

Dream Bike

I come downstairs Christmas morning and there it is, beside the tree, too big to wrap—my very own bicycle. For months I've prayed and waited and hoped, and now my biggest wish has come true. It's a Schwinn, and a real thing of beauty. Fire-engine red and shiny silver that sparkles under the blinking, multicolored Christmas lights. I thank Mom, thank Dad, thank my lucky stars, this is the best Christmas present I've ever had. Wow.

My bike's got training wheels, but I'm not going to need them. Learned on Jackie "Bugs" O'Hanlon's bike last summer and now I'm itching to go. Only problem is it's winter outside and I'm going to have to be patient waiting for the warmer weather. Down to the cellar goes the Schwinn, spring can't come fast enough, and now I'm marking off the days on the calendar, pedaling in my dreams. I envision a summer with rides up and down the Parkway, out to suburban Hayden with all the Victorian mansions, over to Gram's house on 61st. With this new set of wheels, my world has suddenly expanded.

The first few rides in March are cold and windy, but exhilarating. The wind in my hair, sneakers pumping the pedals, the reassuring whir of the spokes. Master of my own destiny.

On the first warm Saturday morning in spring, I cruise north to Digby Avenue, then west over to the Parkway. Head south to the 65th Street bridge and back, then a quick romp over to leafy, lawn-covered Hayden. Double back into Philly, swing around the cemetery, and over to Gram's house on 61st. This is a blast. I can go anywhere, do anything. I'm free, summer is coming, and the whole world has been laid at my feet. Life has never been so good.

I stop by Littlefield at noon. All that riding has made me thirsty. And hungry. I lay my bike against our shared stoop, run inside, I'm only going to be a few minutes. Gulp some iced tea, grab a quick PBJ on Wonder bread, and, what the heck, a cookie, too. And a second one for the road. Clean up in a flash, run back outside.

The bike is gone.

I freeze. Blink. Nope, still gone. Look up Littlefield, down Littlefield. My bike is nowhere to be found. I run back inside, start screaming.

Mom gets very upset. Why did you leave the bike outside, Jimmy? Why?

It was only for a minute, Mom. Not even a minute. I swear.

She calls the cops, gives them the make, the model, the serial number. It's all on record. Maybe somebody will turn it in. I canvas the neighborhood, tell the neighbors, tell my friends. Be on the lookout, one brand-new, fire-engine-red Schwinn with all that shiny, silver chrome. Belongs to Jimmy Morris, got it for Christmas.

No one has seen my bike. I cry, throw a fit, threaten to punch the thief's lights out, no matter how big or how mean he might be. But none of this is any use. The Schwinn is gone for good. Sayonara.

So what am I supposed to do now with this stinking set of training wheels?

Catholic school lets out for the summer, then public school. Jackie is riding his bike, Frankie the Fruit is riding his bike, pretty near every kid my age is riding a bike, and here I am hoofing it. Same as usual, same as it ever was.

Forget Santa, my folks saved for months to buy me that Schwinn. Can't just run out and buy another. Bikes cost— especially Schwinns. Man, did I really blow it. Big time.

Later, Mom finds out that the police have a garage in North Philly where they collect bicycles that were lost or stolen, then eventually recovered. Problem is they're not open on Sundays. Dad can't skip work to take me, and Mom doesn't drive.

That leaves Grandmom Kane.

One sweltering July day, she loads me and Howie in her early '50s clunker, and we make the long drive up north. The streets up here are run down, dilapidated. Lots of abandoned factories, boarded-up houses, trash on the sidewalks. We park most of the way down the street from the police storage facility.

A couple of big, beefy cops are inside lounging in the shade, wearing police T-shirts and baseball caps, sipping soft drinks. Grandmom has the serial number and the receipt, and I wonder if Howie has figured out this means Santa Claus didn't come down our chimney last December. Of course our little sister Laura is still clueless, but then she's just a baby.

My jaw drops when I see the numbers of bicycles that have wound up here. Hundreds of them, all shapes, sizes, colors, and models. My heart soars . . . surely, with all these recovered bikes, mine must be amongst them. Just has to be.

But an hour later, after an exhausting search in the hot, stifling confines of the police warehouse, examining row after row of mostly dented and damaged merchandise, I must accept defeat. My fire-engine red Schwinn with the shiny, silver chrome is not here. Who knows when I'll ever own another bike again.

More people are starting to arrive. Is this the place? Is this where they're auctioning off the bicycles??

Yes, ma'am. Fifteen minutes till auction time, answers one beefy policeman.

After a certain length of time during which a recovered bike hasn't been claimed, the city can sell the bike at auction and keep the money. Guess it makes the best of a bad situation for both the cops and the citizens, especially the thrifty customers.

They start with the nicest bikes, the newest, the most expensive models.

Fifteen dollars, who will give me sixteen dollars? Sixteen dollars right here to the man in the red checkered shirt. Do I hear seventeen dollars? Seventeen? Sixteen going once, going twice . . . sold to the man in the red-checkered shirt!

Howie and I see some bikes that we like, but Grandmom tells us just be patient. They're still not in Grandmom's price range. When I was Howie's age, I used to think Grandmom was one of the richest people around. She always carried a purse full of nickels, dimes, and quarters—her tips from working as a waitress at the automat. But now I know better. The really good-paying jobs get you the green money, not coins.

Eventually the crowd begins to thin. Most people have bought what they came for, paid their money, loaded their bounty onto their cars, and are now headed home. Away from this grungy garage in the middle of an even grungier, decrepit neighborhood.

$5, $4, $3, $2 . . . the bids go lower and lower, the bikes get older and more tattered. Finally, only a handful of bidders remain. The auction is nearing its conclusion.

They wheel out a small, stubby bicycle that looks as if it might have been formerly green, can't be sure. Most of the paint has either faded, peeled, or fallen off. The chrome has rust spots. The basket is lopsided, looks like it was smushed in a bad fall. I can see many patches on the balding tires. Well, at least the bell works. I know, because the helper man is ringing it, smiling all the while as if this were the best bicycle in the entire joint.

All right, do I hear three dollars for this bicycle? Three dollars??

Howie and I look around. No takers.

Grandmom?

Not yet, Grandmom whispers. Not yet.

All right, folks—two dollars. Who'll give me two dollars?

Howie and I look left, look right. Still no hands.

The auctioneer barks, One dollar! One dollar for this solid, dependable little bicycle, ladies and gentlemen. A steal at this price, if I may say so. Who'll give me one dollar?

After a long, uncomfortable pause, Grandmom calmly raises her hand.

The auctioneer smiles, points at my grandmother. One dollar to the lady on my right with the two young boys. One dollar going once, going twice . . . SOLD to the lady in the green blouse. Please pay the cashier and good luck with your bicycle.

Grandmom pays the man the dollar as Howie and I merrily begin the task of wheeling our prize toward the exit. Never expected this little bonus.

Wait, says Grandmom. Stay with me.

The three of us walk together, heading toward Grandmom's early '50s old-timers' relic at the far end of the dilapidated street. There are a lot more people outside on the street than when we came earlier this morning. Black people. Some sitting on stoops. Others sitting sideways in second-story windows, one leg dangling out and one leg in. A few pay us no mind, but several stare as we pass. I can feel their eyes latching on, following us, watching our every step.

Coleman James at school doesn't do that. Why are they eyeballing us like that? I look up, spot a teenage girl lounging in an upstairs window frame. Her eyes meet mine, hard and decidedly unfriendly. I see her wrinkle her nose, give me a contemptuous sneer.

Grandmom, I whisper, why are these people staring at us?

It's all right, Grandmom whispers back. Don't worry about it, honey. Don't look back. Let's just get to our car.

Grandmom tries to act nonchalant, but I can sense her fear. And still feel all those pairs of disapproving eyes on our backs. Howie senses something is up, starts glancing around trying to figure out what it is.

We reach Grandmom's car without incident, squeezing the bike as best we can into the trunk. Grandmom takes some string, hastily ties down the trunk hood, we climb aboard, and we're off. Back to Southwest Philly and Kings Cross.

Back to home sweet home.

Later that week the "new" bike's front tire goes flat. I take two dollars from my savings, buy a bicycle repair kit. New patches, new inner tubes, some special glue. Fix the old tires up the best I can, pump them up at the old filling station on 57th. Not good as new, but as good as it's gonna get.

The following month I scrounge up another three dollars. Mom gives me a few quarters, one of my uncles gives me some more, the rest I have stashed away in a sock drawer. Buy this super-dooper deluxe bicycle chain and lock at a shop down on Lester Avenue. Use this to anchor my stubby two-wheeler to the wooden balustrade on our front porch.

So now I've got my $1 bike with $2 in patches and a $3 bike lock.

It's not the fire-engine-red Schwinn with the shiny, silver chrome, but it's got two wheels, pedals, brakes, handlebars with one grip missing, a crumpled basket, and a bell that rings. So it'll do—because I don't have any other choice. It's all I've got.

Oh, well—maybe next Christmas. At least this time I'll have a good lock.

Rock and Roll Will Never Die

I'm over at the house on 61st Street because Gram's new calico cat, just a kitten herself last Halloween, now has her very own litter of four. She went into the bedroom closet by herself the other night, and now all of a sudden we have five cats. Presto! One kitten is midnight black, another grey, a third is faded calico, and a fourth grey & white with six toes on each foot. None are as pretty as mom, who's snow white, midnight black, and fiery orange with marble-green eyes. But mom's a wild one, almost as mean as she is pretty. We call her Top Cat because she's the boss lady, in charge of all the felines.

The television is on in Gram's living room. While I'm watching the kittens in their cardboard box, tiny eyes just starting to open, Uncle Joe is waiting for the *Ed Sullivan Show*. This is the big night, the American television debut of The Beatles, a group of mop-topped rock and rollers from Liverpool.

Dad says they're a fad, nothing but a gimmick that won't last—no talent. Destined for oblivion. Not like Tommy Dorsey, Glenn Miller, or the Mills Brothers. It'll all blow over in a month or so, you'll see. Next year no one will even remember their names, let alone their so-called music.

Ah, yes . . . the Big Band sound, Dad reminisces. Now *that's* what I call music. Not this idiotic teenybopper crud they pass off as entertainment today.

Uncle Joe argues differently. Says no one's ever risen as far and as fast as The Beatles. Proclaims they're the real deal. Could very well change the history of music with their stylish pop sound and youthful new approach. Uncle Joe's sure these long-haired types are something special, something unique.

Me, I'm more interested in watching the kittens, hoping maybe one will turn out to be like my long-lost buddy Herman.

Ed Sullivan is finally on the tube, looking like a dead guy somebody robbed from a graveyard in one of my Saturday afternoon matinee horror flicks. Yes, it's gonna be a really big shooe, a really big shooe. . . .

Now The Beatles are on, with *I Wanna Hold Your Hand* and *She Loves You, Yeah, Yeah, Yeah*. . . . Uncle Joe says this is great, absolutely fantastic. The audience is going wild. Seventy-three million Americans are mesmerized, at home glued to their sets. Teenyboppers everywhere are going tapioca, coming completely out of their young, impressionable skulls. Dad is wrong. Uncle Joe is right. History is being made. Music will be changed forever. A new era has begun.

Uncle Joe asks, So what do you think, Jimmy?

I mouth my father's words . . . Aaaahhhh! . . .Buncha boys who look like girls and sing like weirdos! Uncle Joe just frowns, shrugs, then cracks a smile. Hey, lemme see those kittens again. Top Cat sure is a good mom. . . .

When I get to school all the kids can talk about are The Beatles, The Beatles, The Beatles. Boys like them, girls love them, and the whole world is buying their music. They're number one, no one's even close. Not Elvis, not Sinatra, nor even The Beach Boys from sunny California can touch 'em. Dad may not like it, but The Beatles are in a league all to themselves, for sure. A force to be reckoned with. Got to give The Devil his due. Top of the charts, Beatle movies, Beatle cartoons, Beatle dolls, jam-packed tours, Yankee Stadium. They're more than just a musical group—they're a happening. The television and magazine people call it Beatlemania. Girls screaming, girls crying, young people in hysterics over a bunch of long-haired crooners.

Silly. Totally ridiculous. The entire country is out of its cotton-picking mind.

Me, I have more important things to worry about . . . like the upcoming baseball season. And, praying that one of the kittens will turn out to be just like Herman, even though none of 'em have his striped raccoon look and gigantic head. Yep, maybe the whole world's gone crazy over some rock-and-roll jokers from across the Pond, but not Jimmy Morris . . . junior or senior. We're not swayed by all the hype or the bandwagon mentality.

Now boys want to grow their hair long, too, and parents are hitting the roof.

Insanity. They're like lemmings, every last one of them.

Me, I only have one question . . . who the heck's this Tommy Dorsey guy—and what's his story, anyway?

CHAPTER 6

Cast The First Stone

Throwing stones might be a harmless diversion if one were living out in the country. Southwest Philly, however, will never be confused with Montana. In a row house neighborhood jammed with buildings, cars, garages, street signs, street lights, and people, chucking rocks can only lead to one thing: trouble. With a capital T. Nevertheless, spurred on by my infatuation with baseball, I enjoy the fine art of hurling rocks. Gradually, my stone-throwing habit becomes something of a passion. Then an obsession. And finally—a full-blown compulsion. No harm is ever really intended . . . but as they say, the road to Hell can be paved with good intentions. Clearly, I'm on the wrong road. Now not only does my mind have a mind of its own, but so does my left arm. See the stone, seize the stone, throw the stone. It becomes eerily irresistible, almost automatic. Very low impulse control. Just one more time . . . one more.

Outside of pets and people, almost anything and everything is fair game. It's not about malice, but about challenge. I see common, everyday objects as targets. Can I hit them or can't I? Only one way to find out. A simple pass-or-fail test, often without regard for consequences.

Garage windows hold special appeal. Small, square, shiny. Hidden away in empty driveways, an invitation to disaster. Eventually, I get caught breaking one and am reprimanded. But my compulsion doesn't end there. Again I am spotted, identified, caught, and punished. Soon I have a neighborhoodwide rep as a window-breaker. Doesn't always matter if it's me who's done the throwing . . . if a window gets broken, my parents are called. Reflex response. The situation gets so bad my poor father winds up spending his Sundays installing neighbors' windows. Not much fun when you're already toiling away the other six days of the week in a stuffy, noisy, auto repair shop.

At first my parents try reasoning with me. Then they just yell a lot. Eventually I lose my allowance and get sent to bed with no supper, can't go to the movies, and am grounded for weeks. There are some not-so-subtle references to the Bad Boys Home, where neighborhood incorrigibles are rumored to be sent. But none of this cures me. First good chance I get—POW! There goes another pane of glass.

No choices left, now my father is resorting to the strap. This commands my attention . . . at least for a little while. There's also an ominous warning that gets served up along with the corporal punishment.

My exasperated father promises, Next time, I'm going to take that throwing arm of yours and tie it to a chair. And if you think I'm kidding, boy, just you try me.

It's isn't that I don't take what my father is saying seriously. I do . . . when I stop to think about it. But the temptation, and impulse, finally get the better of me.

Unfortunately, as luck would have it, my timing couldn't be worse. Sure enough, the very next time I chuck a stone, my father sees me. The Old Man blows a proverbial gasket. Drags me up the front steps, throws me into the living room, and yanks some extension cord out of the closet. Then, true to his word, he ties me to a dining room chair.

So there I sit, stunned. Thirty minutes. An hour. My mother looking frightened, certain my father has gone too far. I hang my little head in shame and disbelief. Then my parents are in another room and I can hear them . . . arguing. Later Mom turns to pleading, but Dad doesn't budge.

I made him a promise, Pam, and I'm keeping it. The boy's got to learn. . . .

Then, just when I think things couldn't possibly get any worse, they do. In a hurry. Comes the sound of a car pulling up outside, stopping. Car doors opening and closing, the sound of footsteps . . . up the stoop and across our front porch. A knock, and the living room door swings open.

Gram and Uncle Joe.

Oh, no. Not now. Please any other time but now.

Gram sees me. Big smile on her face. She takes a step toward her favorite grandson, *Mr. Jimmy*, her precious little cookie-maker. Stops. Catches the pained expression I'm wearing. Looks down. Finally notices that I'm tied to a dining room chair with a heavy-duty extension cord.

Gram screams. Uncle Joe rushes over, starts undoing the knots, looks confused. My mother arrives downstairs while my father rushes up from the basement.

World War III is about to commence, and I'm at ground zero. Uncle Joe fumbles a tad more with the cord, then I'm free. Gram puts her arms around me and gives me a quick squeeze. My eyes never leave the floor. At this moment I wish I could disappear from the face of the Earth. Depending on how this all plays out, I may yet find my request granted.

Jim, what's in God's name is going on here? Gram challenges. What's your son doing tied to this chair?

My father gives a fast-forward synopsis of my recent transgressions. He's reached his wit's end with his elder son. With each word, Gram's face gets redder and redder. Her bottom lip quivers. Next to my Uncle Joe, I am surely the apple of my grandmother's eye.

So you tied him to a *chair*? Jim, are you out of your mind? Why, he's just a child. I've never heard of such a thing. It's, it's—medieval!

Pop tries to respond, but Gram won't hear a word of it. She turns, marches toward the door, and motions to my uncle.

Joe, let's go. We're leaving.

And so they leave. Footsteps across the front porch, down the stoop. Car doors opening and closing. Joe's Studebaker starting up, pulling away.

Dead silence.

Seizing the opportunity, Mom whisks me upstairs to the relative safety of my room. The door closes, and I sit alone on the edge of my bed. Sobbing. In shock. One tiny little boy thrust into the eye of a hurricane of his own making. All because I couldn't stop myself from chucking a lousy rock.

After some time passes, the bedroom door pushes open. I glance up, expecting my mother. Instead it's my father who fills the doorway, and I instantly turn away and tremble. Now I'm about to get the strap like never before. Tensing for an imminent explosion, I remain motionless except for the involuntary tremor.

My father sits down beside me, puts an arm around my shoulder. What's this, no strap? I'm perplexed.

He whispers, Jimmy, you're not a little baby any more. Do you understand me? These things you're doing, like the rock-throwing, can get you into a world of trouble. Big grown-up kinds of trouble. Something could happen one day that your mother and I won't be able to fix.

Dad pauses a moment to let the words sink in. My father's face looks sad, not mad. Do I detect a slight quiver in his voice? I still can't believe I'm not getting the belt.

Then it hits me. Hard. The Bad Boys Home. It's not as if I wasn't warned. Now they're going to make me pack all my clothes. Tonight I am going somewhere far, far away. Away from my bother and sister and parents and grandmothers. Off to live with other incorrigibles. Born to be bad, I am now beyond saving. Nobody else to blame but me.

Jimmy, are you listening to what I'm telling you?

I look into my father's eyes, unable to speak. The walls creep closer, and the rooms seems as if it's starting to spin. My whole life spinning . . . wildly out of control.

Suddenly, Dad is scooping me up like when I was a toddler, kissing and hugging and squeezing me. Tighter, tighter. He begins to rock me gently, his rough face pressing mine.

Jimmy, Jimmy, Jimmy. . . .

I hang there, a trembling rag doll, arms dangling at my sides. My mother hugs me. My grandmothers, too. But my father? I don't know what to think, what to do. His shiny black hair pushes against my nose, my eye. My nostrils fill with the scent of Old Spice, sweat, and Brylcreem. A little dab will do ya.

Something splashes on my shoulder. And again. To my horror, I realize my father is crying. I never knew that men cried. Little boys sure, but not men. Least of all not the strongest man in the whole world.

Jimmy, I'm sorry. I love you, Jimmy.

Squeezing me tighter and tighter. Hard to breathe. Afraid to breathe. This is worse than any strap. Far worse.

Finally, my father loosens his grip. Wipes his eyes. I pretend not to notice.

Now, Jimmy, he says softly, though a bit louder. Jimmy, you have to promise me. No more throwing stones.

With my head down I nod, watching my sneakers dangling above the bedroom floor.

Look at me, Jimmy. Do I have your word?

Looking up quickly, again I nod. Harder.

My father stands. All right, Jimmy. I believe you. You're mother's putting supper on the table in a few minutes. Get yourself washed up and hurry downstairs. We'll start fresh as if this all never happened. Okay? How's that sound?

More vigorous nodding, halting glances. My father leaves my room, goes downstairs, and I have my second chance.

As if nothing had ever happened.

For the most part, the stone throwing stops. When I do feel the urge, I look carefully before I begin hurling . . . usually down at Dobbs Creek. No more angry neighbors at the door, no more Sunday glass-replacement for my father.

Then, six months later, comes the familiar hard knock at our front door. My father has just returned from dropping me off at his mother's house over on 61st near Parkland. I'm spending Saturday afternoon with Gram and Uncle Joe.

Dad answers the door. It's Mr. Wisnewski from around the corner on Wennington Street. My buddy Larry Wisnewski's father.

Mr. Morris, your boy just threw a rock at my garage, Mr. Wisnewski snaps. Then, to top it off, he had the nerve to stand there and curse at me, too!

My boy? answers my father, surprised. You mean Howie?

No, not Howie, Mr. Wisnewski corrects him. I'm talking about Jimmy.

Jimmy? Are you sure?

Of course, I'm sure! Mr. Wisnewski shoots back. I know Jimmy when I see him. He's the little mouthy one with the glasses and dark red hair.

Dad takes this all in, says nothing for a moment, then laughs. This startles Mr. Wisnewski, who stands there confused and speechless.

I've got an idea, my father announces. Wait here just a second.

Dad goes into the house, returns shortly with a copy of the Philadelphia Yellow Pages. Opening the book, my father flips the pages, then finds what he's searching for. Here! he motions, points to a spot on the page, hands the book to our neighbor.

Here? Here what? demands Mr. Wisnewski. I don't have a clue what you're talking about.

Well, if you're certain my Jimmy just hit your garage with a rock, explains my father, then I think we should call this number.

What number? Larry's father frowns, totally mystified.

The number for the front office of the Philadelphia Phillies, my father deadpans.

The Phillies? Mr. Wisnewski explodes. What in the world do the Phillies have to do with this?

Dad says, Because I just dropped Jimmy off at my mother's house, and that's over on 61st near Parkland . . . well over a mile away. So any kid with an arm that can hit a garage window from over a mile away, I think he's got a heck of a future in Major League baseball. Don't you agree, Mr. Wisnewski?

A Message for Coach DeLuca

It's summertime again. Baseball season. Time to haul out my Pee Wee Reese infielder's glove and proudly put on the black and gold jersey of the two-time Little League champs, the mighty Knights of Kings Cross. Last year's shiny trophy still sits atop our dresser in the bedroom Howie and I share. Invisible, forgotten—a distant memory.

The trophy's gathering dust, but now I'm rarin' to go. The breeze is warm, and the ballpark is alive.

Now that I'm nine, a whole year older, maybe Coach DeLuca can start substituting me in a few games here and there. You know, just for an inning or two. Like when we're eight runs ahead, which the Knights often are. After all, I was last year's most valuable Twelfth Man. Saved the Knights from forfeiting the championship to our arch rivals the Bisons when Ryan Mullen didn't get back from the shore until the fifth inning. Without Super Scrub Jimmy Morris, we would've lost. End of story.

Coach DeLuca even said so himself.

So this year, maybe things will be a little different.

We have a few preseason scrimmages—against the Hawks, the Owls, and the Kings. Preseason games are at Dobbs Creek, while the regular season meetings are at 49th & Lester. And just as I had hoped, Coach DeLuca remembers to put me in left field for the final two innings of each game. I'd rather play infield, because I can't judge the fly balls when they're way up in the air. Pee Wee Reese was an infielder, and that's the model glove I'm wearing. But Coach DeLuca says it's out of the question . . . lefties don't play the infield, period. And so that's the name of that tune.

I get a walk in my first time at bat. Feels great standing on first base, a real player, looking to score. But then I strike out next time up—and again and again. By the time I can get a fix on the ball with my bad eyes, it's already crossing the plate, plopping into the catcher's glove. No use starting your swing when the ball's already going by.

One game, I'm standing there all alone in the outfield, and nothing is being hit my way. Pretty soon I'm looking at the cars going by on Dobbs Creek Parkway, watching people coming and going in the park. A kid with a kite, a flock of birds, a plane droning along up near the clouds. Daydreaming.

Suddenly, shouting and general pandemonium jolt me back to my senses. Coach DeLuca is shouting, Jimmy—JIMMY! I look up. See a spinning white baseball come flying in my general direction. But I'm too late, the ball smacks the ground to my left and keeps on going. Now I'm in pursuit as fast as my skinny little legs will carry me.

By the time I track down the ball I'm way deep in left field. Reach down, grab it, turn, give a mighty heave. The ball sails back toward the infield. Takes a hop, the third baseman Keith Stillman snags it on one bounce, wheels, fires a strike to our catcher at home plate.

Too late. The batter has already circled the bases, safely touched home plate. Inside-the-park home run. All because Dizzy Jimmy Morris is daydreaming.

People on the sidelines look at me and laugh. Some of my teammates put their hands on their hips and give me the cold stare. The Mighty Knights have a rep, and it doesn't include bonehead miscues by some pint-sized, four-eyed goober who belongs on some other team that doesn't much mind a losing record.

When I come in after the third out, Coach DeLuca says, Nice arm, Morris. But you have to catch the ball first. You can't be standing around sleeping. Get your head in the game, son.

Seems like baseball's no different from school. Teacher calls on me to answer a math problem, and my mind's a thousand miles away. The deserts of Mongolia, green hills of Ireland, rain forests of South America, Sherwood Forest in Merry Old England. Or riding a rocket ship to Mars, Venus, Jupiter, maybe another galaxy altogether. Some movie I saw, some book I read. Before you know it, I'm out there, drifting. Sure, the lights may be on, but little Jimmy Morris definitely isn't home.

Then, suddenly, I'm back on Earth. Back home. Back in familiar, everyday Kings Cross. And everyone is looking at me, laughing. As usual.

Same old, same old. Get your head in the game, son.

The official Little League season begins, and I'm back riding the bench. No one- or two-inning assignments for me when we're pounding the other team. No anticipated cameo appearances. No pinch-running for the catcher on the two-out, speed-up rule. No nothing. Just riding the pine, collecting the splinters, that's all. Game after game after game. Every official contest counts toward the playoffs. And when it counts, Coach DeLuca gets deadly serious, no fooling around.

Winning isn't everything, it's the only thing.

After a few weeks fellow bench-mate Chuckie Long from Beaufort Avenue decides to pack it in. Figures he's got better things to do than to come to games and watch some other kids play.

Now, halfway through the summer, we're undefeated, and Coach wants to keep The Streak alive. The Knights could be the first undefeated Kings Cross Little League team in recent memory. No sense jeopardizing The Streak by sticking Little Jimmy in the lineup. No sense risking an unprecedented third-straight championship. No sense endangering another predestined, preordained Coach of the Year Award. Not where Coach DeLuca is concerned.

Grandmom keeps coming to as many games as her waitress schedule permits. Same spot in the bleachers at the game field on 49th & Lester, down by the commuter tracks. She's always cheering, always clapping when we score a run, always rooting for my Knights. That's my Grandmom. If she's disappointed that her grandson never gets to play, you'd wouldn't know it.

Me, I'm starting to watch the trolleys roll by up on Lester Avenue. Checking out all the people coming and going in the park. The birds, the planes. The deserts of Mongolia, green hills of Ireland, rain forests of South America. Sherwood Forest in merry Old England. Sometimes riding a rocket ship to Mars, Venus, Jupiter, or perhaps another galaxy altogether. Something in some movie I saw, some book I read.

My head's anywhere *but* in the baseball game. Baseball isn't fun any more. I'm bored. Even if we do go undefeated, win a third-straight championship, I'm starting to care less and less. Sorry, Mr. DeLuca, it's just the way I feel.

I finally get up the courage to tell Mom. I don't want to be on the Knights any more. Don't want to ride the bench forever, be a total zero.

Surprisingly, Mom doesn't put up a fuss. She just says, Okay. If that's what you want to do, Jimmy, it's up to you. It's your decision.

They don't come right out and say it, but I figure Mom, Dad, and Grandmom aren't thrilled with the way Coach DeLuca plays some kids and not the others. How he forgets this is the Little Leagues, not the Major Leagues. Maybe it'd be better if I were on the Hawks, with Jackie. Or on the Owls, the Kings, or even the

Bisons. Any team but the Knights. But once you're drafted, that's it, they're your team. Seems I'm destined to be a Knight forever.

Hey, last year's champs always get the very last player in the draft. That's just the way it is, luck of the draw. The way it's always been, always will be.

Maybe I might get to play some by the time I turn eleven. Or twelve. But when you're only nine, two or three years might as well be forever.

So I say goodbye to my dream of being a baseball player. Green-grass diamond, crack of the bat, roar of the crowd. Keep the black and gold jersey, and the shiny, embarrassing, gold-colored trophy collecting dust on top of the dresser. Spend my remaining summer hours in the countless number of informal games of boxball, stepball, wireball, wallball, sock-it-out, and touch football back home on Littlefield Street. Where we hardly ever keep score. And even when we do, no one tallies the wins and losses. Every kid who wants to play plays. And when I drop the ball, nobody gets too bent out of shape. Except maybe me.

After a while, with all the daily practice, even with my bad eyes I start to turn out to be a fairly decent player. Certainly not "Hammerin" Tommy O'Hanlon, or even little brother Jackie. But decent.

I never give Coach DeLuca the word. Instead, I just stop showing up at games. Nobody calls, nobody asks. Coach probably hoped I'd give up all along—never really wanted me on his Mighty Knights in the first place.

So, Coach DeLuca, if you're out there somewhere, I've got a message for you.

I don't care how many games you win, how many champion-ships you bag, how many Coach-of-the-Year awards they heap on you.

You're a lousy coach. I wish some other team had drafted me. The Hawks, the Owls, the Kings, the Bisons, anyone. Any team but your Mighty Knights.

Oh, and one more thing, Coach DeLuca. . . .

P.S.: *I quit.*

Cowboys and Astronauts

I am nine, Howie is seven, and we have decided to become cowboys. Every night the boob tube offers yet another western: *Bonanza, Have Gun Will Travel, The Rifleman, Maverick, Sky King, Wagon Train, The Virginian,* and of course, our very favorite, *Gunsmoke.* Howie wants to be a cowboy comedian like Festus. I want to be 6' 6" with broad shoulders like Sheriff Matt Dillon and make the guys in the black hats back down in fear for their miserable, despicable lives.

In pursuit of our chosen career, I look in the Philadelphia Yellow Pages to see if there might be a local school where we can enroll as apprentice cowboys. However, although I find lots of opportunities for aspiring welders, TV repairmen, electronics technicians, and dental hygienists, no Philadelphia trade schools are offering courses on riding, shooting, calf-roping, nor bounty-hunting. Howie and I fall into a temporary state of despondency. It seems one must be born in Wyoming or Montana and live on a ranch to become a certified, real-life cowpoke.

Then one day, out of nowhere like magic, arrives a possible solution to our dilemma. Dad comes home from the auto repair shop to announce at dinner that his good friend and coworker, Harry, is a budding star on the Pennsylvania rodeo circuit.

Did he say *rodeo?* Rodeo, as in bucking broncos, charging bulls, and lassoes?

For two months our father gets no peace as we bombard him with requests to attend the rodeo. Eventually, Dad relents and schedules a July 4th trip to the York County Fair to see Harry ride his famous mare in a top-flight barrel racing contest. My brother and I can hardly contain ourselves until the big day arrives.

After a long drive from Philadelphia in the backseat of our baby-blue and white 1956 Chevy Bel Air we arrive at the rural outpost of York County, Pennsylvania. The rodeo is held in a corral next to a hill, which serves as natural bleachers. The show is swell. Cowgirls do tricks jumping in and out of lassoes. We watch calf-roping, barrel-racing, and best of all, the rodeo clowns. Harry and his horse are splendid. We stuff our faces with hamburgers, hot dogs, and ice-cold Pepsi-Cola. What more could a couple of kids and aspiring cowboys possibly ask for?

132

Intermission arrives and all the performers take a break. The corral is empty. We look at our father. He's in a good mood. Can we go inside the corral for a few minutes, Dad? Sure, why not. Howie and I slip through the fence and soon we're in hog heaven. In a real, honest-to-goodness, western-style corral and rodeo. I grab a handful or dirt and shove it under Howie's short, pudgy nose.

Know what this is?

No, what?

Real cowboy dirt!

Yeah! Real cowboy dirt!

However, as I get the nerve to go up close to one of the horses along the outside of the fence, I'm struck by the sheer size and power of this colossal animal. Horses don't look nearly so big or dangerous on television. One well-placed kick from this fella's hoof and he could knock my block clean off. Then, as I almost step in a huge pile of pungent horse manure, I realize yet another important detail—you can't smell the horses through the boob tube, either. Yeeecchh!

Suddenly, a big man in blue coveralls blows a whistle. We stop short, thinking he's tooting the whistle so we'll get the heck away from the corral. But it's not me and Howie he's concerned with. Another man in farmer's clothes is holding a pig, and the big man announces, All children wanting to enter the Greased Pig Contest please gather 'round. First prize is five dollars. Howie doesn't have the foggiest idea what a Greased Pig Contest is, but a prize of five dollars is involved so he's in. I'm a little more cautious, so I go over and ask Dad, What in the world's a Greased Pig Contest?

Dad explains that whoever catches the greased pig in the corral wins the five dollars. I go over to get a closer look at the pig in the farmer's arms. It squirms, it squeals. Oink, oink! I go back over to Dad and say, I don't think so, I'll stay out here on the hillside with my hamburger and my Pepsi, thank you.

Suit yourself, says Dad, but it seems only fair since you're the guy who always eats the BLT sandwiches. I ask him what that's got to do with a Greased Pig Contest and he says, Where do you think the bacon comes from? I take another look at the pig, and it says Oink, Oink.

By now twenty farmers' kids in blue overalls are lined up in the corral with Howie, who's wearing a Phillies cap, Eagles sweatshirt, and basketball hightops. Typical Philly street-kid attire. The big man says, Get Ready, Get Set, Go! and blows the whistle. The other country man drops the pig and it starts running for dear life. Oink, oink! The twenty kids take off in a pack headed straight after it.

But not my little brother Howie. Ol' Shoelace, he just stands there looking around the corral, up at the crowd, and down at the cowboy dirt. Real, honest-to-goodness cowboy dirt.

C'mon, Howie! We holler. Go, Shoelace, go!

It's no use. Little Howie just stands there, mouth open, eyes wandering every which way. He hasn't a clue as to what to do in a Greased Pig Contest. To be honest, neither do I.

Meanwhile, the pig is running, running and the farmer kids are chasing, chasing. And in the oval corral, that means pretty soon you're going to wind up right back where you started.

In other words, right smack where befuddled Howie is now standing. Imagine that. . . .

Here he comes! We shout to Howie. Okay, get ready!

Howie crouches over into a three-point stance as if he were Ray Nitschke of the Green Bay Packers waiting for the snap from center.

Twenty yards, fifteen, ten . . .

The pig never sees Howie. The animal is far too busy looking over its shoulder at the twenty pursuing farmer kids in a sea of dark-blue overalls.

Howie is looking to make the five-dollar tackle, but somewhere within ten yards our Shoelace loses his nerve. He turns his back and tries to run, but it's too late for that. There's no time to get up a head of steam. Within two or three strides, the pig catches up and barrels square into the back of Howie's legs. Howie goes down flat on his face as if he'd been shot. The pig scrambles madly across Howie's prone body, leaving dirty hoof prints on his sweatshirt, steps on the back of Howie's head, and jumps off. Howie screams, tries to roll over, get up, and run for cover, but he's out of time again. The mob of blue-clad chasers knock him rudely to the ground. I watch as my little brother disappears in a billowing cloud of brown cowboy dust. As the chase continues and the dust around my brother settles, I see his chubby little body lying motionless under the bright rodeo lights. Dad and I jump into the corral and carry Howie out to the safety of the hillside. Howie tries to cry but there's so much dirt shoved down his throat and up his nostrils that we have to pour a couple of cups of Pepsi into his face before he can spit out all the crud. Howie is not a happy camper, to say the least. He wants us to call 911, the State Police, and the National Guard. He has had enough of rodeos and wants to go back home to Philadelphia. To tell you the truth, I'm with Howie.

On the long ride home from York County in the backseat of the '56 Chevy Bel Air, Little Howie and I come to a thoughtful conclusion. We no longer want to become cowboys. Too much dirt, too much hurt, and too many wild, smelly animals. Instead, we hit on the idea of becoming astronauts. Hey, remember John Glenn? It's positively brilliant. Riding in a space capsule orbiting high above the globe. Talking to Houston on the radio, and with the President on television. You get your name in all the papers, sign a bunch of autographs, and best of all there's no smelly animals. Just kick back in a nice, clean, quiet space capsule with lots of Tang to drink. We'd be the first astronauts in the history of Southwest Philly. Maybe they'd even have a ticker-tape parade for us down 58th Street past Longstreet Elementary School.

Roger, that's a 10-4, Houston. We're gonna get us a little shut-eye up here. Over and out, Daddyo.

Measuring Up

There's an amusement park way out in the country called Lenape Park, named after the local Lennai Lenape Indian Tribe. It boasts the hottest, wildest roller-coaster ride on the East Coast, or so they say. One trip on that baby and you're guaranteed to lose your lunch. The call it The Beast. Up, down, and around, corkscrewing at blinding speed and unbelievable Gs. People are pale, nauseous, and disoriented by the time they finally step off—if they're still able. Half of the kids in the neighborhood have been out there, and I've just gotta go. I'm not scared of any park ride, and I can't wait to boast to Jackie and Bobby that I tamed The Beast.

One hot Saturday, Mom and Dad load us all in the car, stop over at 61st to pick up Uncle Joe, and then we head for the country. Lennai Lenape Park. Land of hot dogs, cotton candy, funnel cake, merry-go-rounds, fun houses, and most of all, The Beast.

So there we are, Mom, Dad, Uncle Joe, Little Howie, Baby Laura, and me, and I'm having a ball. Hamburgers, well done. Lots of root beer. Making faces at the clowns. Laughing at the monsters in the fun houses. Watching them spin those colorful wheels of fortune, numbers going 'round and 'round.

Now I've got my ticket for The Beast. The line stretches for nearly a hundred yards. Uncle Joe keeps me company in line. Inch by inch, I get closer, closer. Two younger kids in front of me are getting scared, but I'm not scared. This promises to be the absolute highlight of my summer. Three breathtaking, head-spinning minutes on the infamous mechanical Beast. We're getting closer now, and I can hear the screams, the roar of the roller coaster as it rockets its way down the tracks. Just a few more minutes, and that'll be me screaming. Boy, am I gonna have a blast.

At last, I'm standing near the entrance to the ride, and people are coming off from the last run. They look pale, they look queasy, and they all look like they've gotten their money's worth . . . every penny of it. The two younger boys in front can hardly contain their excitement. They hand the carnival man their tickets and practically skip up onto the loading area. I turn and see that Mom, Dad, and Howie have arrived to witness the big moment. I wave and they all wave back.

All right, Jimmy, Uncle Joe whispers. You OK? You ready?

Sure!

There you go. Just hold on real tight, understand.

Yep.

I step up. Uncle Joe hands the carnival man my ticket. Ride Man looks down at me suspiciously, squinting in the bright sunlight.

Just a second, young fella, says the carnival man. Step right over there. I do as the man says and find myself standing next to a metal pole with a painted line just above my head. I look at Uncle Joe and can tell he doesn't know what's going on either.

Put your back right up against the pole, son. Stand up real straight.

I do as I'm told, all the while looking up at the man's leathery face. Carnival Man frowns and shakes his head.

Sorry, son. I can't let you on the ride . . . you ain't big enough, he announces. The carnival man then turns and hands my ticket back to Uncle Joe. He can go on all the other rides, the man explains, but not this one.

The finality of what the man is saying takes a moment to sink in. Too little? I can't go on the ride? Huh? What?? It's not *fair*! I turn to Uncle Joe, who sees I'm ready to explode. He quickly gets right up into Carnival Man's sad, tanned face.

Hey, Mister, wait a minute. We've been in line almost an hour. You gotta let this boy on the ride. C'mon, be a pal.

Carnival Man replies, Sorry, friend—but I can't.

Yeah? What about those two little kids in front of us? You let them on, and they're both younger than Jimmy!

Doesn't matter, says the operator. It ain't how old you are, it's how tall you are. And if you don't reach the mark on this pole here, you can't go on. Them's the rules. It's the danged insurance company, you know? They make us do it.

But he's plenty strong, Joe argues. He's not gonna fall out.

I know, but it ain't up to me.

Now my head is whirling around worse than The Beast could ever make it spin. The shame, the embarrassment, the humiliation. I'm ready to cry, but now I see my father striding over, coming to the rescue.

What's the problem? my father asks. Uncle Joe gives my Dad a rundown. Meanwhile, another park employee has stepped in to help take tickets, and I'm watching all the other, larger kids load up for the next ride.

Listen, buddy, come here for a second, my father whispers to the carnie. My Dad whips out his wallet, pulls out a crisp five-dollar bill, and slyly offers it to Carnival Man. The man steps back, shakes his head, and throws up his hands. Sorry, chief—no can do. I could get fired if I let that boy on. Like I told the other guy, it ain't up to me. If it were, I'd let the boy on in a heartbeat. I know this is rotten, but there ain't a damned thing I can do about it. The ticket's still good on all the other rides.

This has become a big scene. We are holding up The Beast. People are staring. People are talking. My father nods, puts the five-spot back in his wallet, and puts his arm around my shoulder.

All right, let's go, Jimmy. We'll try some of the other rides.

We walk slowly away from The Beast. My whole world is collapsing. I try not to cry, but I feel the tears start to fall, my body start to shake.

All right, Jimmy, that's enough. Behave yourself.

Uncle Joe is really mad now. That's not right, he snarls. Not fair. What a rip!

I find my mother and run to her. She gives me a hug, pats my head, but I can see the hurt in her eyes as well. The whole trip to Lenape Park, just to ride The Beast, and now this. I break free from my mother's arms and run back into the little clearing next to the ride.

I don't need your stinkin' ride, Mister! I scream. I don't need your stinkin' park, either! And I'm never comin' back to stinkin' Lennai Lenape Park for as long as I live!!

True to my word, I don't eat another hot dog or hamburger the rest of the day. And I don't go on another ride. If I can't ride The Beast, then I don't want to ride at all. Period, end of sentence.

I haven't felt this humiliated since Coach DeLuca of the Knights kept me on the bench for an entire baseball season.

After a while, Mom and Dad realize the situation is useless, there is no consoling me, and so we call it an early day and head back to the city.

What a rip, says Uncle Joe. Man, that's not fair at all.

Not just about the ride, I think, but about me, too. Why do I have to look this? How come I've gotta be a cock-eyed little shrimp with fiery red hair and Coke bottle glasses? What did I ever do to deserve this sorry fate? It certainly is a rip, a gyp, and a rob job if there ever was one.

Jackie O'Hanlon's coach on the Hawks let him play in all the Little League games. And I bet you they'd let Bugs ride The Beast at Lennai Lenape . . . even though Jackie is nearly two months younger than I am.

I tell you, it's just a *rip* and a super *gyp* is all it is.

Americans for Goldwater

Extremism in the pursuit of liberty is no vice.

Hey, it sounds pretty good to me. Unlike the 1960 Nixon-Kennedy contest, here's something on which my parents can finally agree. They think Barry Goldwater is the greatest thing to happen to the United States since Harry Truman. Maybe even better.

Mom's going to vote for Goldwater even though he's not an Irish-Catholic. Dad's going to vote for Goldwater even though he's not an Anglo-Saxon Protestant. In fact, it's no secret that Barry Goldwater is Jewish. Yet he's the perfect stars-and-stripes candidate.

Goldwater's main man in our Kings Cross neighborhood is Uncle Joe. Yep, he's turned Gram's enclosed porch on 61st Street into Goldwater Central. Posters, leaflets, flyers, stickers, buttons—you name it. Uncle Joe's Studebaker is a rolling Goldwatermobile. We're going to *WIN WITH BARRY!* Hey, forget the *All the Way with LBJ* crud. My favorite gag is the GOLDWATER soda pop can . . . AuH_2O. I think these are a scream . . . really clever.

So it's not long before I'm pressed into service as the country's littlest street campaigner. My final week of summer vacation is spent hoofing it door-to-door, sliding *GOLDWATER!* flyers under doormats and through mail slots. Never realized before just how many doors there are in Southwest Philly. This is a crowded neighborhood. Row houses are like that.

I fill the basket of my $1 police-auction bicycle with flyers. Ride up one side of the block and down the other ringing the handlebar bell. Then I'm on to the next street. A regular Paul Revere. Uncle Joe hits the parallel streets and supervises what I'm doing. Guess that's one of the reasons why they made him Goldwater's district manager. Maybe Uncle Joe is going places—if only AuH2O can pull off the biggest upset since Truman nipped Dewey at the wire.

Uh oh, now some nasty kids near Lester Avenue are chasing me. Hollering, taunting—these Bozos are for Johnson. Later on another group of kids hassles me on Bellaire Avenue. Yep, they're for Johnson, too. Things soon become painfully apparent . . . maybe Uncle Joe and all the Morris clan are for Goldwater . . . but the vast majority of Kings Cross residents are for Johnson. No doubt about it.

Me, I don't get it. Goldwater strikes me as kinda like Superman . . . he's for truth, justice, and the American way. But most of all he's for liberty, individual responsibility, low taxes, and getting lazy people off the welfare rolls. Plus he's a hard-liner on the red menace, even if I'm not totally convinced that one school kid getting a whole row in trouble is necessarily a bad thing. Otherwise, all baseball players might really be Communist, since one player can let the whole team down.

Basically, this Goldwater is a hard-liner on almost every-thing—just like us, the Morris family.

Dad says Lyndon Johnson just wants to throw hard-earned money at every government program coming down the pike . . . sort of like a sailor who pulls into port after a month at sea. And since Dad was in the merchant marine, I figure he knows what he's talking about.

Campaign slogans aside, all you have to do is take one quick look at the two candidates. Goldwater is handsome, charming—

even dashing. A straight shooter with a gift for words. Johnson, on the other hand, looks like a 6' 5" basset hound that just ate the family's Christmas turkey. Besides, with that cornpone Texas accent, he mumbles like a man talking with mouthful of cotton.

I don't get why just about everyone else is for this Johnson character.

Dad, Mom, and Uncle Joe are livid about the latest Johnson commercial: *10, 9, 8, 7. . . .* People are saying Goldwater's gonna drop "the bomb."

Dirty pool, says the Morris clan. That scallywag's just buying votes with promises he can't keep. Never mind the accusations he can't back up. Never could trust those whacky Texans. As the saying goes in the Lone Star State, Johnson is *All hat and no cattle.* Wise up, people.

And so I pass out boxes of Goldwater flyers, do my part to save our country. Uncle Joe and I crisscross our section of Southwest Philly until my feet ache, and I'm actually glad it's time to return to school and hit the books just so I don't have to hit the bricks any longer.

Well, almost glad. . . .

Believe it or not I've got Mrs. O'Shaughnessy again—she's moving up from fourth grade to fifth right along with her last year's class. Since Mrs. O'Shaughnessy's my favorite teacher in all of Longstreet Elementary, this is fine by me. Mom says I'm teacher's special pet and she spoils me. Well, at least she doesn't call me "Dizzy" the way Mrs. Weinstein did way back in second grade.

So nothing much has changed at the old school . . . well, almost nothing.

The blacks are finally here, and I mean not just Coleman. Bused in from somewhere east of here and down from the north. They're calling it "school desegregation." My folks aren't pleased, and neither are the other Longstreet parents. Some have been holding meetings and protesting downtown at the School Administration Building. Many more are writing letters. But all this changes nothing. We don't exactly know who wants all these black kids here, but they're coming anyway . . . along with a daily parade of big, fat yellow buses.

Since the grown-ups are doing all their grown-up business behind the scenes, we kids don't have a clue until we show up in September. Suddenly there are all these black faces, in the halls and in the schoolyard . . . except in my class. Sure, we've still got Coleman in Mrs. O'Shaughnessy's room, but these new black kids are all over with the slower fifth-grade group. So you don't really notice all these colored kids until we go outside for recess. That's when everyone in the fifth grade comes out together. Then you notice.

Oh, and one more thing is different, too. They've got this new rule. Teachers are stopping kids and going through their pockets, checking what's inside. Have you ever heard of anything so crazy in your life? What do they want to look in your pockets for? All I got in mine are baseball cards, sticks of chewing gum, and some spare change for the occasional candy bar. Jeez, maybe I should write to Goldwater about this.

Great news! Maybe I won't have to write to Goldwater— maybe I can just ask him in person. Goldwater is coming to Philadelphia this week. In fact, his campaign motorcade is scheduled to come right down 58th Street past the Longstreet School—during school hours! Can you believe it? Our very next President in flesh and blood, not just on TV. So I have Uncle Joe slap on the biggest GOLDWATER button he's got. Seems we're having a special recess so we can greet the passing Republican dignitaries.

That afternoon, Mom, Uncle Joe, and hundreds of neighbors line 58th Street across from the school to catch a glimpse of the Man from Arizona. In the schoolyard, Mrs. O'Shaughnessy brings our class to the fence, where we peer between the wrought-iron bars in anticipation.

A murmur arises in the crowd. Okay, here he comes, here he comes! Police motorcycles first. Then the lead car. Next the open limousine, Goldwater smiling and waving from on high in his specially constructed observation seat. They begin to pass our ancient, three-story school building, and my mind for a moment flashes back to Dallas. November 22, 1963. The terrible day that changed America forever.

No, lightning never strikes twice . . . does it? Well, at least those Oswald look-alikes, our next-door neighbors the Schaeffers, are safely tucked away over at the Catholic school on 56th at Lester.

Then, just as the Goldwater car approaches the schoolyard, I hear another sudden surge of noise. Pushing, shoving, hollering from behind. . . what's going on? Quickly I turn around . . . it's all the slow classes just released from upstairs. Those new colored kids booing and screaming, yelling bad things as our guest passes. Waving our man on, giving him the thumbs down.

I'm embarrassed for Longstreet School, and mad, too. Hey, so what if you're for Johnson? That's no excuse for being rude. I certainly wouldn't boo the President, even if he does talk funny and look like a man in a giant basset hound costume.

Later I ask my mother why all the black kids were booing Goldwater. Why are they so mad at Goldwater, Mom?

They just are, Mom says . . . and leaves it at that.

Next day Mrs. O'Shaughnessy gives a civics lesson in presidential elections. For fun, she takes a sample poll. Good old democracy in action again.

Show of hands. How many for Goldwater?

One little boy starts to raise his hand, looks around, then thinks better of it. One of the girls looks around uncomfortably, then drops her head, folds her hands together as if embarrassed. Was she also about to raise her hand for Goldwater?

I wave my hand high and proud. AuH2O, the formula for success. *Extremism in the pursuit of liberty is no vice.*

The class begins to laugh. There's goofy James again, joking around. Nobody, but *nobody* is for Goldwater. He's a sure-bet loser.

But I'm for Goldwater. Really, I am. For a second I wonder if maybe Goldwater prefers cats to dogs, root beer to colas. Just a thought.

Hey, and how come if Goldwater is Jewish, none of the Jewish kids are for Goldwater? What gives?

Okay, class, how many hands for President Johnson?

It's unanimous . . . well, almost. I hate to break this to Uncle Joe, but I think Barry Goldwater's goose is cooked.

That weekend us Morrises gather around the tube to watch a final Goldwater rally. Thousands of Goldwater hopefuls carrying placards—cheering, smiling, shaking their fists. This makes me feel better. Maybe we just happen to live in a weird neighborhood, that's all. And maybe our man Barry can come from behind, steal it in the end like good ol' Harry Truman. Just maybe.

Later I see Grandmom Kane, tell her about the rousing Goldwater speech and the mob of people on television for Goldwater. Thousands, Grandmom, thousands. All that work Uncle Joe and I did, street after street. All I want now is for a grown-up to confirm for me that Goldwater's still got a chance.

Grandmom sighs, says . . . It's over, Jimmy. Shakes her head sadly. Adds, He doesn't have a prayer. Even though I know that Grandmom has offered up many a prayer down at the Catholic Church. And lit many a candle.

I just flat out don't get it. *Extremism in the pursuit of liberty is no vice.* This is inspiring stuff. George Washington himself would've been proud.

And what's so hot about President Johnson, droopy-eyed hound dog with that mouthful of cotton? What do folks see in *him*?

Jeez. . . .

Philly Heartache

They're calling it the greatest collapse in professional sports history. The Phillies have only twelve games left in the 1964 season, and they're six and a half games in first place in the National League. It'll be their first time in the World Series since Richie Ashburn and the Whiz Kids lost four straight to the New York Yankees in 1950, long before I was born. Can't lose, right? Sure thing, right? They'll get another chance at the Yanks, right? The Phils' front office is already accepting reservations and printing tickets for the World Series—right here, at our very own Connie Mack Stadium. The entire city waits in anticipation. . . .

And so the Phillies promptly go out and lose something like ten straight. The clincher is when some banana named Chico Ruiz of Cincinnati steals home to beat the Phils 1-0, knocking them from first.

Philly is in a state of shock. So close, yet so far. We're all living in a bad dream. Then it comes down to the last day of the season. The Phils must beat the Reds, and the Cardinals must lose to those Amazin' Mets, the worst team in all of Major League baseball. I watch the Phils–Reds game at Gram's house, cheering every time the Phils score another run in that Cincinnati bandbox they call Crosley Field—the park with the weird terrace in the back of the outfield near the warning track. Our collective fingers crossed, the Fightin' Phils slaughter the Reds 10-0. Now it's up to the Mets to pull off a miracle.

But it isn't to be. Word comes in later that afternoon—the Cardinals beat the Mets to win the National League pennant. The Cardinals, not the Phillies, are going to the World Series. Our Big Pretzel dream has turned into a bizarre, surreal nightmare.

Yo, ten in a row? How'd you like *them* apples? Everyone says, Well, just wait till next year. In Philadelphia, it seems we're always waiting till next year. It's the city's unofficial pastime.

But not Uncle Joe. He just wants to know if the ball game is over yet, because he's got to watch Dick Clark and *American Bandstand.* Couldn't care less about baseball or the Phillies. He'll take those mop-haired Beatles and their rock-and-roll music over sports any day. Don't know why—that's just my Uncle Joe. And with our luck in Philly, maybe this isn't a bad way to be. If it weren't for bad luck, we wouldn't have any luck at all. . . .

Except for, maybe, that Chuck Bednarik and the Philadelphia Eagles. The Eagles' dramatic championship in '60, back when I was too young to understand football. Of course, Concrete Charlie retired last year—last of the two-way players. Guess football will never be the same, much less our upstart Eagles.

So it's wait till next year again. Spring will come around soon enough, and with it a whole new baseball season. . . .

Go, Phillies!

Dethroned

Sherman "Tank" Sykes is the unofficial heavyweight champion of our fifth-grade class. I am the lightweight champ. Sherman lives in the orphanage off Dobbs Creek Parkway, where most of Longstreet School's hard cases reside. Tank may not be the tallest kid in Mrs. O'Shaughnessy's room, but he certainly is the strongest and toughest. Crew cut, no neck, big shoulders . . . doesn't says much—the quiet, sulky type.

One surprise is that while Sherman lives at the orphanage, he's not really an orphan. His dad's still alive, but can't take care of Sherman since his mom is gone. So Mr. Sykes visits Sherman on the weekends, teaches him jujitsu. I know because Sherman wants to try out the latest move on me first thing every Monday morning.

One day I come to school, go to hang up my coat in the cloakroom. Next thing I know, the ceiling is spinning and I'm sailing through the air. Bang! I hit a wall, slide to the floor, can't breathe. Look up, see a fat face smiling down on me. Crew cut, no neck, flat features. Sherman the Tank.

Hey, James . . . how'd you like that one? My dad taught me that just yesterday.

Yeah. . . . That's . . . gr-great, S-Sherm.

Here, lemme help you up.

Oowwwwww.

With friends like Sherman, who needs enemies?

Then a new kid transfers to our school, into Mrs. O'Shaughnessy's class. Big kid. Tall, lanky, kind of bashful. Hardly says hi or goodbye. His name is George Williamson. Sure enough, first week, Sherman decides to lean on the new kid in the schoolyard. Bumping him, calling him names.

Leave me alone, says George. For George, this is something of a speech.

But Sherman doesn't leave George alone. Instead he persists. Keeps bumping the new kid, calling him a sissy, picking a fight. Finally, George has had enough taunting. Kids gather round to watch George get hammered. It's been a long time since anyone's messed with The Tank . . . and for good reason.

Sherm and George square off. Sherm rushes George, tanklike. But like a matador, George steps aside. Sherm comes again, but George uses his height and long arms to keep the Tank at bay. Now Sherm bull rushes, comes in swinging. George ducks, then swings back. Pop . . . right in Sherman's kisser. Red-faced, Sherman sets himself and charges once more, but George is waiting. Bang, bang . . . a left and a right stop Tank in his tracks. Sherm knows only one way to fight, face first. He makes one final attempt, runs straight in, and BANG! Another shot to the head.

Sherman turns away, stunned. Waves his hand to signal defeat. We have a new class champion, Big George Williamson.

Back in the hallways, and up in Mrs. O'Shaughnessy's room, everybody is whispering. Did you see Sherman get beat up? Can you believe it? Wow!

My buddy sulks in his chair, and I try to console him. Not your day, Tank. Kid got in some lucky punches.

To his credit, Sherm shakes his head, stares straight ahead. No, the guy's just tough, that's all. Beat me fair and square.

Covering all bases, I later congratulate the winner. Nice fight, George. Way to go, big guy.

George just shrugs, gives me a modest smile. Thanks, he says.

Well, at least I'm still the lightweight champ. And unlike Sherman, I don't try to outmuscle guys, or run them over like a tank. I punch and move, punch and move. Back in second grade I saw a small kid beat a bigger kid with one punch. Realized right then that punching was the ticket, not wrestling. Whenever I wrestled, I usually wound up with some kid sitting on my chest, pinning my arms against the ground. Not good. But if I kept my hands free and punched, most times one or two good shots would do the trick. Even with kids a lot taller and bigger. So I practiced my punching and my ducking, got better and better. Most people give up once they get socked in the eye, the nose, or the mouth. So that's what I go for . . . because it works.

Badabing, badaboom.

Then, about a month after George whips Sherman, another kid transfers in. This time from Catholic school into the slower fifth-grade class. Some Our Lady of Perpetual Peace kids do that once they've made their Confirmation, Holy Communion, or some other Catholic milestone. Don't know much about him, but I see him around on the playground. Just a runt of a kid, no bigger than me. Name's Petey Ianelli. Dark hair, dark eyes, olive skin. But I pay him no mind—until one day Petey picks a fight with me. Hey, doesn't this joker know who I am? The name of my game is pain.

I carefully remove my spectacles, roll up my sleeves. Now the boys gather around in a circle, smiling. Should be fun watching this little Italian boy get hammered. The way James can punch, this shouldn't last long.

And they're right—it doesn't.

I throw a left, and Petey ducks. Come back with the right, but it bounces harmlessly off Petey's shoulder. Catch my balance, start to reload, and BLAM! Then BLAM, BLAM! again. Next thing I know I'm sitting on the seat of my pants, stars in my eyes and sharp pains in my head. Bawling like a little baby. I hear Petey's friends congratulating him, patting him on the back. Toughest little kid in *all* the fifth grade, now lightweight champion of all the classes.

I get up, run into the school, covering my face. Don't know what's worse, the pain or the humiliation. After a few minutes, the pain starts to go away but not the shame. Now I'm smarting on the inside . . . big time.

One of my friends sees me. James, what happened to you?

I tell him I fell during recess. But it's no use lying. By the end of the day everyone knows . . . Petey Ianelli beat James Morris. TKO in round 1. No contest, not even close. Boy that Ianelli kid is really tough! Beat James to a pulp in no time flat.

Now I know why Floyd Patterson wore sunglasses and hid from everybody for an entire year after what big, bad Sonny Liston did to him. Robbed him of his pride, the way Petey did me.

Never thought anyone my size could beat me the way Petey cleaned my clock. How'd he do that? One second I'm the reigning champ, getting set to throw my knockout punch, and the next second I'm sprawled on the ground, the down-and-out chump.

Even worse than getting beat was crying about it like a baby. At least Sherm took his whipping like a man, which is more than I can say about yours truly. Me, I cried my eyes out.

Now me and ol' Tank are nothing but a couple of washed-up has-beens.

Live by the sword, die by the sword.

S.O.S.

Mom and some of the other parents at Longstreet Elementary have formed a group to protest the new busing policy. They're calling it S.O.S., short for "Save Our Schools." Problem is Mom and the other ladies don't think our schools are really *our* schools any more. Instead they say people who live elsewhere, who don't send their kids to school here, are calling the shots. Pushing this crazy desegregation idea on us, using our hard-earned tax money to flood our schools with outsiders, experimenting with the lives of little children for some harebrained, pie-in-the-sky social scheme. And for what? Certainly nobody in Kings Cross is in favor of it. Probably not even the people whose kids are being bused in are in favor of it. It's a mystery to all of us down here in Southwest. None of this makes much sense.

But now they've got this new cockamamie law, seems some court somewhere made a ruling. Handed down on stone tablets. Presto—just like that, as if by magic. So the yellow buses keep on rolling, delivering all those black faces to our schools every morning, and carrying them back to their own neighborhoods every afternoon. . . .

. . . . Like clockwork.

So what kind of lamebrains do they appoint to these courts anyway? What gives?

Dad says it's all the fault of these rich, so-called do-gooders like the Kennedys. Always sticking their busybody noses in everyone else's business, exactly where they don't belong. Think they've got the right to tell everyone else how to live, they're so smart. But half of them need a servant just to wipe their own bottoms and help them put their pants on straight. Can't even run their own lives let alone somebody else's. Live in mansions and walled compounds in places like Hyannisport, where you practically have to be a Kennedy to live. Or out on Philly's ritzy Main Line where the houses are all so fine, no row homes there. Don't have to worry about *their* kids' safety—sending all their kids to fancy prep schools and hiring private tutors. Certainly no yellow buses filled with black faces are descending on these respected neighborhoods.

Oh, well. Since these folks get to make the rules, they send all the buses to Kings Cross instead.

What hypocrites, Dad says. It could do some of these meddling, blue-nosed politicians and like-minded professors at these ivory tower schools some good to spend a few weeks in a place like Southwest. Just for a little change of scenery, you understand. Maybe smell some spaghetti cooking for the first time, or even the dreaded boiled ham and cabbage us kids know and hate so well. Give these out-of-touch snobs a whole new perspective, let them see things from a different angle altogether.

But that's never gonna happen. Seems these high-born people who couldn't find Kings Cross on a map know more about what's best for our community then the working stiffs who were born and raised here. Local people who have a stake, a vested interest, after all it's *their* home.

But what's that got to do with anything, right? How dare we hold up progress.

Sure is a fruits-and-nuts kind of world we live in these days, as if maybe the whole country is turning into one giant California. Might be for the best that the whole thing should just slide right into the sea, New York to LA. *Splash!*

Mom says, if the colored schools are that bad, maybe they should take the money they're spending on all these new buses and fix up those other schools instead. Just let us be in Kings Cross and keep our kids out of it, thank you very much.

Sure, people have a right to be concerned about the welfare of these colored kids. But what about *our* welfare? And the welfare of *our* children? Where do we fit in their lopsided equation . . . or don't *we* count any more??

So the Longstreet moms make the phone calls, distribute the flyers, pass around the petitions. Even march on the School Administration Building downtown with their homemade placards: S.O.S., Save Our Schools. Very catchy, very controversial. Most folks wish them the best of luck. First and foremost, everyone's concerned for the children. We should do what's best for the children. The children should come first.

But every weekday morning the yellow buses continue to roll. Back and forth, back and forth. There's no stopping them. In Kings Cross we don't have the clout.

Privately, off the record, many of the Jewish mothers agree with S.O.S. They're concerned for the safety of their children, too. But few of the Jewish mothers want to get involved. They never show up, don't make phone calls, won't distribute the flyers, decline to pass around the petitions. And they certainly aren't joining up with any big march on the School Administration Building. That wouldn't be kosher. Seems protesting and carrying signs isn't something nice Jewish women tend to do.

Then quietly, one-by-one, the **FOR SALE** signs start popping up on the postage-stamp lawns of Kings Cross. Many of these **FOR SALE** signs are posted in front of Jewish homes. This development catches the eye of many Kings Cross residents, including several members of the S.O.S. Committee.

The whispers soon begin. *The Jews are running.* Lots of head-shaking, finger-pointing, and nail-biting. *The Jews are running, those slimy cowards.*

Exasperated, my Catholic mother turns to her own kind for help. Invites several of the Catholic moms from Littlefield and Wennington over to our house for coffee. Mrs. O'Hanlon, Mrs. Schaeffer, Mrs. Pellegrino, Mrs. Deemer. Mom's usual bingo crowd from Our Lady of Perpetual Peace. Mom reminds the women that this is their neighborhood, and their schools, too. You're paying taxes, you should have a say. If the public schools go to Hell in a handbasket, next thing the whole neighborhood goes down, and then we're all going down along with it. Trust me, we're all in this boat together. This is your fight same as everyone else's, it's time to make a stand. Are you with us? Can we count on your support?

The Catholic moms hem and haw. Yes, everyone's concerned for the children. We should do what's best for the children. The children should come first.

Sure, Mom agrees. But that's not the point. The point is, *can we count on your support*? We need you to get involved, immediately.

The women shrug, look away, look down at the floor. This whole busing business is very awkward. No psyched volunteers in this crew, they're not jumping at the chance to make a commitment.

We really, *really* need you on this, Mom emphasizes. I can't tell you how important this is. It's for your sake, too. We're all in this together.

It's Mrs. O'Hanlon who clears her throat, finds the words to speak first.

Pam, says Jackie's mom, it's not that we don't agree with you. We don't much like this busing nonsense either. But all our kids are in Catholic school. I really don't see where this affects us. I'll sign your petition, sure. But that's all, I'm sorry. It's not our problem.

Mom is stunned by her friends and their strangely apathetic attitudes. Okay, so maybe the Jews don't have any backbone. But the *Catholics*? Spineless as well? From them, Mom expected better.

Mrs. Pellegrino tells my mother perhaps she should consider putting all us Morris kids in Catholic school. Says we'd get a much better education, and Catholic schools teach discipline. Mrs. Schaeffer and Mrs. Deemer second the motion.

But it's not about whether parochial or public schools provide the best education, Mom argues. You're not getting the big picture. It's about our neighborhood—our future!

Mrs. O'Hanlon disagrees, and my mother explodes. She's getting her "Irish up" again, and Mrs. O'Hanlon can pretty much match her in that department, as her name would suggest.

Sandy, Mom tells Mrs. O'Hanlon, if this busing problem starts getting out of hand, you'll be the first to run. Count on it!

Me? Run? That's ridiculous! We're not going anywhere, Pam. This is my home. They'll bury me from this neighborhood, I promise you!

Sandy, I hope you're right, Mom replies. I sure hope you're right.

It's time to go, and the Catholic ladies all thank my mom for the coffee and the Danish. It's been a very educational evening.

Good luck with everything, Pam. See you at Bingo on Tuesday night . . . the usual time?

CHAPTER SEVEN

Morris for Dogcatcher

Okay, so Johnson clobbered Goldwater. Biggest presidential landslide in history. A blowout. I think maybe I've had enough of this democracy stuff for a while. What good is one man, one vote, if the majority of citizens are out to lunch? Tell me how it's possible for the far better candidate to lose by millions and millions of votes?

Add in the Phillies blowing the National League pennant, and I am major league depressed.

But Longstreet's teachers, fresh off the Johnson success, are now on something of a democracy kick. All fifth- and sixth-grade classes are to hold classroom elections. Each room is to elect a class president to be a representative on the school's student committee.

Big yawn.

Soon it's apparent that in Mrs. O'Shaughnessy's class the presidential race will boil down to the two logical candidates: smart Ruth Cohen for the girls and popular Ken Richardson for the boys. And as class clown, my philosophy is—if you can't beat 'em, at least make fun of them and have some kicks.

Ruthie and Ken are so serious about this it's hysterical. The election is a sham, and won't make one bit of difference. The principal and all the teachers run the school one hundred percent. We're just the kids. We don't really have any say.

But then I get an idea. . . .

MORRIS FOR DOGCATCHER!

In some local election, I heard a man on the nightly news say that both candidates were so bad they couldn't get elected as dogcatcher. So I decide to let Ruthie and Ken prepare their mundane speeches while I get set for some serious goofiness.

MORRIS FOR DOGCATCHER!

Mrs. O'Shaughnessy doesn't see the humor, but decides to let my idiocy run its course. She ignores me. Maybe if Dizzy James gets no attention, he'll stop. But as Goldwater's littlest campaign manager, I've learned a political trick or two. I start shaking hands at recess and stumping in the hallway.

Hi, I'm James Morris, running for dogcatcher. Really hope I can count on your support. It's time Longstreet had a dogcatcher that everyone can trust, and not just some crook. That's M-O-R-R-I-S. Remember me on election day.

All the kids get a big hoot out of it. Crazy James is up to his old tricks again. Haven't had this much excitement in class since the school district's doctor went up and down the aisles checking each kid's head for cooties.

Using construction paper, I put a few flyers together, pass them out. Before class I sneak into Mrs. O'Shaughnessy's room, write on her blackboard. *DON'T FORGET. MORRIS FOR DOGCATCHER. WRITE-IN CANDIDATE!*

Soon I'm running harder than either Ken or Ruthie, and attracting more attention. Not to mention getting under Mrs. O'Shaughnessy's skin—big time. My little stunt is starting to become a major distraction.

Election day comes to Longstreet. We write our votes on notebook paper, then drop them in a cardboard box. Secret ballot. Our teacher tallies them and announces the results.

The final vote total, says Mrs. O'Shaughnessy, for fifth-grade class president of Room 305 is as follows: fourteen votes for Ruth Cohen, and thirteen votes for Kenneth Richardson. Congratulations, Ruth.

A big hand for President-elect Ruthie; condolences for runner-up Ken.

Someone asks, What about dogcatcher? How many votes for dogcatcher?

Mrs. O'Shaughnessy frowns, looks directly at me. She says firmly, There was no race for dogcatcher.

I shrug, apologetically. Make a goofy face.

James, teacher says, if you'd put half as much effort into being serious as you do into acting silly, you might be surprised at what you could accomplish.

Giggles from around the room.

Speech! someone calls out.

Stand up, James, says Mrs. O'Shaughnessy, folding her arms.

I stand.

Now, asks Mrs. O'Shaughnessy, Might you have something constructive to add to our election, Mr. Morris? Something *worthwhile*?

More giggles, then silence. Teacher is waiting, arms still folded.

Um, um . . . maybe one thing, Mrs. O'Shaughnessy.

Very well. Go ahead, James.

Big gulp.

Umm . . . didn't they elect a Vice-president to help President Johnson run the country?

Yes, James. Our new Vice-president is going to be Hubert Humphrey.

And President Johnson used to be Vice-president for President Kennedy, right?

Yes, James. That is correct.

Well, then, maybe it wouldn't hurt if we had a Vice-president too. Two heads are better than one, right? And Ken got almost as many votes as Ruth. So if we made Ken our class Vice-president, then everyone's vote will have counted, and the boys and the girls will both have a say.

Stunned silence from the class. A big smile crosses Mrs. O'Shaughnessy's face.

Well! I must say, grins Mrs. O'Shaughnessy. That may be about the best idea anyone's had around here in a long while. In fact, I think it's just splendid. Class, what do you think?

All heads nod in agreement.

156

Class, how about a round of applause for James? I think he deserves it.

The entire class gives me a hearty round of applause. Ever the showman, I stand, bow politely, then take my seat.

James, Mrs. O'Shaughnessy adds, sometimes you do surprise me. I believe I do detect a brain buried somewhere in that thick skull of yours.

Yep, I know I have a brain. Problem is, I just don't know what my brain's going to be doing from one moment to the next. My zany mind's always had a mind of its very own.

Maybe I should write to President Johnson. Tell him to scrap this Hubert Humphrey fellow and bring in Goldwater. Then, at least Uncle Joe and the rest of my family might feel a little better about the pounding our man took. Maybe give us *some* say in how this crazy country of ours is being run nowadays.

Well, at least, that's my theory. . . .

Spartacus

I come down the stairs on Christmas morning and there it is, under the tree, big as life . . . my very own Radio Flyer wagon. Sleek, new, fire-engine red steel with shiny black tires and sparkling white hubcaps. I've been praying for (and hinting about) this gift for weeks. Now Santa has not forgotten me, even though I did get Cs in Math and Citizenship, and was just as often naughty as nice.

Along with the Radio Flyer wagon, I get a cool paleontology book called *Search for a Living Fossil* by Eleanor Clymer. It's about the 1938 discovery of the amazing coelacanth off the coast of South Africa. This coelacanth is a kind of dinosaur fish that the experts thought became extinct about eighty million years ago. But when a local fisherman catches a live coelacanth in his net, Dr. J. L. B. Smith and a woman named Marjorie Courtenay Latimer, who runs a museum near Cape Town, must set out to prove that the coelacanth is more than just another fossil. It's a rare but living, breathing fish that's remained undetected by frequenting underwater caves hundreds of feet below the ocean's surface. This is probably the best book I've ever read, except for

157

maybe *All About Dinosaurs*, when Roy Chapman Andrews went exploring the Gobi Desert in Mongolia and found the world's first specimens of fossilized dinosaur eggs.

But the Radio Flyer red wagon is really in a class by itself, because it's a way to earn some spending money, a steady stream of quarters and dimes. Translated this means a never-ending parade of Saturday afternoons at the Parkland Theater's double-feature matinees. Just about all the women in our neighborhood shop at either the local A&P on Lester Avenue or the Acme by my elementary school on 57th Street. Many don't have a car available, so they pay enterprising young boys like me to cart their orders home in their Radio Flyer red wagons. Problem was, I didn't have a wagon. Now I've got one. Brand new, top-of-the line, deluxe model. The Cadillac of grocery haulers.

The first reasonably clear Saturday morning I'm on my way to the 57th Street Acme bright and early. Kicking a can ahead of me, pulling that wagon through oil slicks and the remnants of gasoline rainbows. The local Hatfield and Partridge Street boys haven't arrived yet, and I'm one of the first wagons on the scene.

Take your order, Ma'am? Take your order?

With my spiffy new cart, I get a customer almost immediately. I load the lady's grocery bags into the wagon and walk behind her to her home on Meadows Avenue. I help her carry the bags up to the door. She gives me a dime and a nickel. I thank her kindly and hustle back to the supermarket entrance, pulling my prized wagon close behind. Fifteen cents in less than fifteen minutes. Next run is north on 57th up near Digby. This time I earn a quarter. Wow. Forty cents in little over half an hour. But when I get back to the market more kids have shown up with their wagons, and it takes almost a half-hour to land my next client.

Take your order, Ma'am? Take your order?

This time I've got a lady who lives over on 57th and Beaufort, just around the corner from my house. Twenty cents for my trouble. Not bad, not bad. Ten cents is considered skimpy, fifteen cents is the going rate, twenty cents is bonus territory, and a quarter is gravy-train payment. I've now taken three runs for sixty cents in less than an hour and a half. I'm on a roll . . . until I return to home base at the 57th Street Acme.

It's now pushing 10 o'clock, and the Hatfield and Partridge boys have arrived. This is their territory and they don't take kindly to strangers moving in on their lucrative turf. I line up near the market entrance with my wagon and try to look as nonchalant as possible. That lasts until freckled-faced Tommy Kearns starts giving me the stare. Tommy is hardly any bigger than me, same age, but he's feisty and pushy, and thinks taking orders at the 57th Street Acme is a proprietary local business. He's backed up by his sidekick goon, some gargantuan blonde-haired bozo named Stevie, who's at least a year younger but a full head taller.

Hey, Four Eyes, who invited you? Tommy taunts me. I shrug, look away from Tommy, but hold my ground.

Yo, Four Eyes. I'm talkin' to you! Why don't you get lost before maybe somebody gets hurt?

It's a free country, Tommy, I reply. I'm still not budging.

Now Tommy and Stevie start crowding me. They're making faces and trying to intimidate. Doing a pretty good job of it, too. But still I stand fast next to my Radio Flyer wagon, sixty cents jingling in my pants pocket and hungry for more.

When the stares and the remarks don't work, Tommy gives me a little shove.

Knock it off, Tommy. I ain't botherin' you.

Yeah, you are. Scram, Four Eyes. Tommy punctuates his suggestion with another push, only this time harder. I immediately shove him back. Lay off, Kearns, I warn, trying to sound as threatening as possible.

Oooohhhhhhhh! chime in all the Hatfield and Partridge boys, egging the two of us on for a fight. Tommy isn't scared. He smiles at all his buddies, then turns his full attention back to me.

Hey, did you just push me, Four Eyes . . . or am I imagining things?

You push me, I'm gonna push you back, Tommy. So lay off!

Oh yeah? Tommy punches me in the arm. C'mon, *fair one*, he says. Right here, right now.

Ooooooooohhhhhhhhhh!! adds the boys' chorus for effect.

Tommy and I face off. I don't put my hands up or make a move. I just return his stare. Tommy struts back and forth in front of me, playing to his hometown crowd. Then puts a single finger on my shoulder and pushes. C'mon, Four Eyes. Like I said. . . . *Fair one.*

He's scared, Tommy! laughs one of Kearns' cronies. He's not gonna do anything.

Tommy pushes me again . . . and then again.

Don't push me any more, Kearns.

Oh yeah? Or *what*, Four Eyes? Huh? What are you gonna do about it?

More chuckles from the gang. Tommy laughs, enjoying the moment. He relaxes, looks over to his pals, then BAM! Tommy has spun around and given me a quick, powerful shove, knocking me back an entire step.

That does it. I coil my arms, spring forward, and give Tommy an equally unfriendly knock. Thummppp!

All right, Four Eyes. You asked for it! With this Tommy runs into me, knocking me backwards. But something goes terribly wrong, my legs give out, and suddenly I find myself falling head over heels through space. . . . Smack! Slam the side of my head and shoulder against the hard concrete sidewalk. Instantly feel the searing, dizzying, sickening flash of exploding pain. Hold my head as I roll over, look back, try to focus, and see that fair-haired weasel Stevie. Baby Huey is getting up from a crouch where he had slipped in behind and under me. That punk Kearns set me up, and I was dumb enough to fall for it.

The whole gang laughs and points. Stevie and Tommy laugh the hardest. I try not to cry, but can't help myself. The tears come fast and furious. The laughs and taunts continue unmercifully, salt rubbed into an open wound.

Hey, Four Eyes, someone barks, Take this piece of junk outta here. The boy puts his foot on my Radio Flyer wagon and kicks it toward me. Yeah, adds another kid, We don't need no crybabies around here. It's bad for business. Go on home—beat it.

Defeated and humiliated, that's just what I do. Lug my Radio Flyer wagon all the way back to Littlefield Street. My own little corner of Kings Cross. My mother knows something is wrong the minute I walk through the door.

What's wrong, Jimmy? What happened to you?

Tommy Kearns and this real big kid named Stevie beat me up and kicked me out of the Acme. They don't want me taking orders there any more.

Well, you'll just have to tell 'em you will be taking orders at the Acme. Same as them. That's why you got the wagon for Christmas. They don't own the 57th Street Acme.

Yeah, I agree. I tried to tell 'em that, Mom, but they just laughed and bounced me off the sidewalk on my head.

My mother gets some ice, wraps it in a towel, and presses this hard freezing lump against my head. I tell Mom I don't think I want to go back to the Acme any more.

Your father doesn't like everyone he has to work with either, Mom explains. But still he goes to work every day.

Yeah, Mom, but at least they don't sock him in the face while he's trying to fix somebody's car.

My mother shrugs. I promise I'll go back next Saturday. If I go back to the supermarket now, I won't make it on time for the matinee. Besides, today's double feature at The Parkland is *Godzilla vs. Mothra* and *Spartacus*. I've been wanting to see *Godzilla* all week, and Howie can't wait for *Spartacus*. I smile and show my mother the 60 cents I made.

Later, Howie, Jackie, Bobby, and I all make the long walk to 63rd & Parkland Avenue for the 1:15 show. I pay my 35-cent admission and have enough money left over for a soft drink and a box of French burnt peanuts. The theater darkens, some Looney Tune cartoons in brilliant technicolors are shown, then it's time to get down to business: *Godzilla vs. Mothra*. I really love the science fiction movies, especially any with dinosaurs. And Godzilla is a radioactive mutant T-Rex with the protective, spiky armor of a stegosaurus. But by the end of the story, I find myself rooting for Mothra, the football-field-sized insect from a tropical Pacific island who's only trying protecting her giant egg. Mothra gets killed anyway, although not before she manages to save Tokyo and half of Japan from certain annihilation.

At intermission they show a preview for an upcoming film, *The Man with the X-Ray Eyes* with Ray Milland. Everyone wants to go because it looks as if Ray Milland's experimental glasses will allow him (and the audience) to see under women's clothing. They'll let you watch dozens of violent acts in a single matinee scene without giving it a second thought, even have a fire-breathing monster trample to death half the citizens of beleaguered Tokyo. But no nudity is allowed. So we all want to come back next Saturday to sneak a clandestine peek. Parents have obviously not seen the risqué preview.

Then *Spartacus* starts, as do the numerous homicides. When the gladiators rise up and start slaying their evil masters, the audience loves it. I may like sci-fi the best, but it's the gladiator muscle flicks that really pack the neighborhood house. So when Spartacus dunks one of the hated, sadistic guards in a giant cauldron of boiling soup, snuffing him out, I find myself cheering along with everyone else. But in the end, Spartacus gets himself killed, same as Mothra, although he does manage to go out in style as everyone's righteous hero. Boy, those Romans sure were a real bunch of stinkers, if you ask me. They probably all deserved to go for a swim in the hot soup.

I find the late afternoon sun, though weak, a bit disorienting after sitting in a darkened theater for two feature-length films. Howie, Jackie, Bobby, and I trudge back toward 56th Street and Our Lady of Perpetual Peace Parish, reenacting some of the better scenes and dialogue in the epic *Spartacus*. Near 60th we take a shortcut through a driveway that empties onto Kings Cross Avenue. In a moment of inspiration, Jackie spots a discarded mop handle and scoops it up. Then he swipes a not-so-discarded trash can lid and instantly transforms himself into a Roman-era gladiator with mighty broad sword and shield. Bugs next advances on Bobby, challenging him with a duel to the death, sending Bobby scurrying quickly in search of armor. Soon Bobby has found a pointy tree branch that doubles as a lance. Meanwhile I've scrounged up a broken car antenna, while Little Howie withdraws a dented, plastic whiffle-ball bat from somebody's ash can. Bobby, Howie, and I take a hint from Jackie, each co-opts a resident's trash can lid, and now the games are ready to commence. All that's missing is the sound of trumpets heralding the prelude to our confrontation.

Hail Caesar! We that are about to die, salute you. . . .

The Kings Cross warriors advance, weapons at the ready. Within seconds the sounds of pitched battle are bouncing off the backs of two opposing rows of squat brick houses. Not exactly the Coliseum, but close enough for government work. Jackie squares off against Bobby, and I against Brother Howie, a.k.a. Shoelace, with his forehead full of scars.

Clang, clang sing our echoes. Cling, clang.

Jackie sets himself, coils, and unleashes a mighty roundhouse swing with his trusty mop-handled sword. And again . . . *crack*! Poor Bobby's pointy branch shatters upon impact, splinters flying in every direction, and he is left instantly unarmed. Another thrust from Jackie's sword and *CLANG!* vibrates Bobby's improvised shield. Bobby beats a hasty retreat, and Jackie goes in for the kill, stalking him behind a parked car, where Bobby desperately grabs a length of garden hose. Bobby tries swinging the hose like a cowboy's lasso, but water comes dribbling out the business end, and so he drops the hose and turns to run. Jackie pursues Bobby behind a trash can, then kicks over the can. Chops his mop-handle sword in the direction of Bobby's noggin. Clang! sings out Bobby's shield. Bobby leaps over the fallen trash receptacle and, at close quarters, returns the favor, bashing Jackie's metal shield with his own. *CLANG!*

Meanwhile, Brother Howie's whiffle bat is no match for the speed and power of my rapierlike car antenna. Soon I grow bored, and disarm Little Howie with a single swipe of my silver sword . . . whooosh! Howie then retreats behind a row of smelly garbage cans and begs for peaceful surrender. I approach as if bent on delivering the coup de grace.

I command my little brother to . . . Kneel, slave!

Howie just blinks.

Kneel or die! I repeat my order, raising my sword as if to strike. Howie's mom didn't raise a fool, so he kneels . . . right beside the filthy garbage can. By now Jackie and Bobby have ceased their personal duel to come and watch. I yank the lid from the garbage pail and swivel my nose away. It's plenty ripe even though the winter air is cold—but at least the maggots have all packed it in for the season. Not exactly a pot of boiling soup, but it'll have to do. Okay—put your head right in there, slave!

Little Howie sneaks a disgusted peek and wrinkles his nose. He looks as if he's about to lose all the Juicy Fruits he wolfed down during the lengthy double feature.

Put you head in or die, slave! Howie, on the verge of barfing, involuntarily recoils from the stench. Jackie then draws his mop handle and advances.

On your feet, slave, Jackie announces. I release you from your cruel master! Jackie then turns his sword on me. Clang! rings out my metal shield. I return the favor. Clang! rings out Jackie's battered, rounded lid.

Just then a back door swings open, and this fat old lady in pink hair curlers comes out brandishing a rolling pin. She shakes the implement at us menacingly and scowls.

She scolds, I've had just about all I can stand from you kids! Drop those trash can lids this second and scram, else I'm callin' the cops!

Clang, clang, clang, clang! comes the sound of four trash can lids bouncing off the concrete passageway. This is closely followed by the sounds of four pairs of Converse high-tops and PF Flyers pounding the pavement in a rush for the driveway exit. We laugh and screech and run all the way up to Lester Avenue.

Man, what a Battle Ax! says Bobby. Wouldn't want to be the gladiator that tangles with that lady, adds Jackie. Howie just giggles and shakes his head. Meanwhile, I can't get the image out of my head of Spartacus dunking that guy in the industrial-sized pot of boiling soup. I picture myself sticking Hatfield Stevie in that soup. Then freckle-faced Tommy Kearns. Over and over and over again. Thumbs down, no mercy.

Next Saturday it drizzles. I grit my teeth and tote my Radio Flyer wagon all the way down to the 57 th Street Acme. Hardly any kids are there because of the weather, and I clean up early. Twenty cents on my first order. Then another twenty cents. Then twenty-five. A few of the Hatfield boys show up, but say little and do nothing. There's plenty of business for everyone right now, and we're all too busy taking orders. I take a lady's groceries out to Loomis Street and pocket another fifteen cents, plus some cookies she throws in as a bonus. But when I get back to the supermarket, I see Stevie. No Tommy, just his dumb, overgrown second fiddle. I keep my distance but the big blonde-haired boy sees me and starts right up.

Hey Four Eyes, how's your head? Maybe we'll bust your face today instead.

Yeah, you and who else? Aren't you gonna wait for Tommy so you can gang up on me again?

Tommy's staying over at his cousin's house this weekend. I don't need Tommy to help me beat your face, Four Eyes. I'll do it all by myself.

Get lost, Stevie. You're not going to do nothin' to nobody.

Oh yeah? Stevie walks over to me and looks down. Straight down. He may be younger, he may be goofy, but he's really, really big. I gulp involuntarily. Stevie reaches out and gives me a shove. Here we go again.

Unlike last week, I don't waste any time trying to avoid this fight. Instead, out of fear and built-up rage, I just reach straight back and throw my hardest Sunday punch. Stevie is so tall he's hard to hit in his ugly face, so instead I aim lower. The punch lands dead center where the chest meets the stomach. Pow! The well known solar plexus shot. Stevie's face grimaces in pain. He doubles over, clutches his body, and gasps for breath.

His beady eyes start to bulge out of his blotchy face, a look that says he can't believe this is happening. Sensing the kill, I take a step forward and cock my fist, ready to unload again.

You'd better take a hike, Stevie. That is, if you know what's good for you.

Stevie blurts out that I'll be sorry, then takes off across 57th Street, grimacing and holding his gut. The small group of onlookers, the same boys who jeered me so heartily the previous last Saturday, are stunned.

Wow, did you see that? One punch . . . he took Stevie with just one punch!

A somewhat lucky punch to be sure. But that's for me to know and these goobers to find out.

I take my place in line for the next order as if nothing has happened. The others give me plenty of room, say little, and glance in my direction as if they're still trying to comprehend what they've just witnessed. But just when I'm just starting to feel proud and all full of myself, I look up to see Stevie coming back down 57th Street . . . this time with what is obviously his older brother.

Stevie's *GIGANTIC* older brother.

That's him, says Stevie, pointing straight at me. That's the one who hit me . . . the one with the glasses.

Stevie is big, but his brother is a Goliath. Already over six feet and on his way toward seven feet. He comes closer, closer, towering over me like the Frankenstein monster, and I'm looking for the neck bolts. . . .

Gort! Klaatu barrada nikkto?

No, won't work. I'm dead meat.

Wait a minute, I think. This kid is familiar. I've seen him somewhere before . . . can it be? Of course! He was one of my teammates from the Kings Cross Knights, my old Little League baseball team. Keith Stillman, the colossal third-baseman and uppercutting homerun king.

Hey, Keith, I wave, nonchalantly acknowledging the behemoth. I try being a good actor, but my knees are starting to wobble.

The monster looks down on me and squints in recognition. . . . Hey, I know you. Your name's Jimmy, right? Used to play for Mr. DeLuca on the Knights.

Yep.

Can't remember your last name. Something like Morgan? Or Moran?

Uh-huh. It's Morris. Jimmy Morris.

Then his face gets harder looking again. This is business, not some social call. So, Jimmy, why'd you hit my little brother?

I explain to Keith how Tommy and Stevie suckered me and bounced me off the sidewalk last week, and how Stevie picked a fight this morning by shoving me.

Is that right, Stevie? Is that what happened??

Yeah, Keith. Be he's older than me by a year, maybe two years. He shouldn't have punched me like that.

Keith, I explain, what else could I do? Your brother's like a foot taller than me. If he doesn't want to get punched, he shouldn't go around shoving people. Besides, I didn't know he was your brother, or that he was a lot younger than me.

Keith thinks this over for a second, then gives Stevie a funny look. Turns back to me and says, Listen kid, if he ever gives you any more trouble, you just tell me. I'll take care of it.

Sure thing, Keith. No problem. Whatever you say.

Stevie stammers, But, but, Keith . . . he punched me! He punched me real hard!

Yeah, replies Keith, and I'm gonna punch you real hard too if I hear you're gangin' up on somebody with that punk friend of yours Tommy Kearns. You hear me?

But—*but, Keith*!

But nothing, moron. Get on home now or I'll smack you silly right here in front of your pals.

Overgrown Stevie just stands there, pie hole hanging open like the clueless dimwit he is.

Now! Keith points menacingly, taking a step forward. For the second time in less than an hour, Stevie's big, fat, dumb, ugly face turns beet red, and he stomps off sullenly in the direction of his Hatfield Street home.

And that goes for the rest of you low lifes, too! Keith warns. I hear any more about you guys jumpin' kids down here I'll be comin' around and kicking some butt. Everybody got that?

Valuing their miserable lives, no one offers a word in protest, and Keith turns and follows in Stevie's footsteps up 57 th toward Hatfield.

Wow, I should've guessed Stevie was a Stillman. The Stillmans have about six brothers, each one bigger than the next. The oldest was a star football lineman at Western Catholic and went about 6' 7" and 280. I think they called him "Tiny" Stillman. Used to rule Kings Cross before Sal Cusumano's time. I've got no idea how they fit all these huge brothers into one tiny row house on Hatfield Street. Maybe they all have to inhale, use a giant shoehorn, or sleep in shifts. Supper must look like feeding time up at The Zoo. My guess is they must bring the food in by forklift.

Anyway, seems my problem with Stevie Stillman and most of the Hatfield Street gang is now solved. Except, of course, for one little detail . . . Tommy Kearns. I still have a personal score to settle with our little freckle-faced predator. And, as fate has it, I don't even have to wait until next Saturday to exact my revenge.

One day after school, I'm sitting on my front stoop, minding my own business, when guess who comes cutting through the driveway behind 56 th Street? You guessed it, none other than Tommy Kearns, bobbing along like Howdy Doody himself. Somewhere a light flashes on in my brain. The Acme supermarket may be in Tommy's neighborhood, but Tommy has to come through my territory on his way home from Catholic school.

Solid!

I jump up from the stoop and intercept my number-one tormentor before Tommy can continue down the driveway. He's wearing the standard Catholic school outfit: white dress shirt, loosened tie, dark trousers, and shiny dark shoes. Tommy does a little double take, startled to see me, and comes to a momentary stop at the driveway's entrance.

Hey, Tommy, old pal . . . so, how's it goin'?!

Tommy smiles awkwardly, mumbles something, starts moving again, he's trying to get around me. But I slide over and block his path. Get right in his face.

What's the matter? In some kind of hurry, Kearns?

Y-yeah. C'mon, I gotta get home.

Oh, you do, huh? Well, not so fast, buddy boy. Stick around for a while. Relax! I want you to feel just as welcome in my neighborhood as I do in yours.

Listen, I'm real sorry about the other day. I didn't mean to bother you at all, Jimmy. I swear.

Really? Now that's funny, Tommy. Cause I wasn't tryin' to bother anyone either. But then you and Stevie show up, and the next thing I know all of a sudden I'm falling on my head. Isn't that a strange coincidence?

C'mon, Jimmy. I was only kidding—honest. I didn't mean nuthin' by it. It was Stevie's idea.

Oh, it was *Stevie the Retard's* idea, huh? Yeah, I'll bet. Like you'd really let Jumbo the Dumbo call the shots. Well, guess what, Freckle Face? Here's another idea—every day when you come home from school, you gotta go through *my* neighborhood. And you know what that means?

W-w-what?

This! I reply, giving Tommy a shove.

Quit it! Tommy complains. Look, I promise not to bother you any more over at the Acme.

Tommy is trying to sound more annoyed than afraid, but I catch the quiver in his voice.

Oh yeah? Well that's real swell of you Tommy—except for one little thing. My head's still sore from when you and Stevie dropped me on the sidewalk. How about that?

I see Tommy squirm, shifting his book bag, looking for an opportunity to make a quick getaway. So I smack the book bag out of his hands.

Hey!

Tommy pushes me back, but the shove lacks real conviction. He's strictly on defense here, not a Hatfield boy in sight to back him up. I grab Tommy and we start tussling. He's trying to break loose, not to get me down, and soon I have the advantage. I push him against our hangout ledge for wallball just across the street, where we go toppling onto Mrs. Stern's postage-stamp lawn. Tommy tries to get up but I wrestle him back down.

Let me go! Tommy yells.

Tommy is strong, but he's really no bigger than me. And I'm mad. *Very mad.* My answer to Tommy is to push him into the grass, pinning him. Now he's getting all kinds of dirt and grass from rolling on the back of his nice shirt—you know his mom's gonna be especially pleased.

I said, let me go!

I get Tommy in a headlock and his freckled face gets redder and redder. Aaaarrrrggghhhh! A muffled scream, he's choking. Suddenly, that scene from *Spartacus* comes jumping into my mind again, the one where Kirk Douglas breaks the guard's jaw and dunks him in the cauldron of bubbling tomato soup. I slide one hand around Tommy's face and push down. . . hard. Lower, lower. Now Tommy's face is in the dirt and he's screaming. It crosses my mind to let Tommy up, then I get another flash of me bouncing off the supermarket sidewalk on my head. I remember the pain, the tears, the humiliation.

With all my strength I give one last great shove and mash Tommy's freckled mug into the turf. Then, finally, I let go. Tommy comes up, slowly. He's balling his eyes out, totally beaten. There's a big patch of dirt on one cheek. Blood and snot are coming out his snub nose, which looks even flatter than usual. I briefly admire my handiwork; poor Tommy Kearns sure looks a mess.

Go on, beat it! I command. With crooked tie and tousled hair, Tommy picks up his book bag and departs, tail between his legs. I'm tempted to feel sorry for him, and I even feel a twinge of guilt. But I smile, too. I did what had to be done, and Tommy had asked for it. With that last shove I was sending a message. I won't have to worry about Saturday mornings and the Hatfield boys. And that's all that really matters. Tommy and his cronies will just have to find someone else to bully, that's all. That's life in Southwest Philly. Someone is always getting beaten up somewhere . . . just make sure it ain't you.

Saturday, as expected, goes like a breeze. I clean up early, and the Hatfield boys give me some room and a little respect once they start showing up. By the time I head off to the theater, I've got about $1.20 in my pocket. Soon I'm settling in with an extra box of French burnt peanuts to enjoy *Zotz!* . . . . Not to mention *The Man with the X-Ray Eyes*. *Zotz!* I like a lot—it's all about a professor who discovers this coin with magical powers and then loses it down a sewer grate. But I'm not happy with the *X-Ray Eyes* flick, it's a bit of a con job if you ask me. The movie doesn't live up to the teaser preview, and it's both lame and tame, no scandalously naked people as advertised. By the second half of the film, kids are booing, throwing popcorn, and wanting their money back. The ushers are really earning their pay this afternoon. Oh well, maybe *In Search of the Castaways* with Hayley Mills will be better next week. I really like Hayley Mills.

And so it's steady as she goes on Saturdays for a few months down at the Acme. The pay is good, and the resulting movies are a blast. *Robinson Crusoe on Mars. The Nutty Professor. I Married a Monster from Outer Space. Gorgo. The Blob. Day of the Triffids. The Brain That Would Not Die. Hercules versus the Moon Men.* Real matinee classics.

Then, one Saturday just as the weather is starting to get warmer, it all comes to an sudden end. The runty Conigliaro brothers pull a stunt that gets us all kicked out of the supermarket . . . indefinitely. Could be for just a week, could be for months. Easy come, easy go.

Talk about having all the wheels come off your wagon. Here I am with this shiny red Radio Flyer deluxe model and no place to take grocery orders.

What a rip. How are the ladies supposed to get their groceries home now? If I were Spartacus, maybe I'd start some kind of revolt at the supermarket. Overthrow the goofy red-faced store manager and feed him to the lions. Or at least have the local populace pelt him with his own rotten tomatoes and bowling-ball-sized-heads of cabbage. Run that man out of town, for sure.

Hail Caesar! We that are about to die salute you. . . .

171

New Kid

A new family has moved into our neighborhood. Mother, father, and a boy about the same age as me. They're in the house between the DeLuca clan from Little League and Mrs. Rosenberg, who throws nickels around like they were manhole covers. Over on 56th Street, right across the driveway from our house, their garage faces our little patch of backyard.

Around the corner and down our block, we kids are talking, whispering. Grown-ups are gossiping, too. We haven't had neighbors like these people before. For us this is a first.

Have you seen 'em?

Who?

You know—*them*! That new family with the new kid.

Uh-huh.

Is it true? Are they really . . . you know . . . *colored*?

Yep—black as the Ace of Spades.

The arrival of the Barnett family in our little corner of Kings Cross is cause for much speculation. Sure, they've been busing black kids into our public schools for the better part of a year now. Longstreet, Sanders, Burnham . . . they've all got their mostly colored classes these days. And we know that some black folks have been moving down south of Maryland Avenue, and east from 49th. Nibbling around the edges of this far-flung streetcar suburb, our little oasis far removed from Philadelphia's more embattled areas.

My mind flashes back to Coleman James, a lone black face in a sea of whiteness, the only colored kid in my class at Longstreet. Quiet, unassuming . . . lives all the way up by Maryland Avenue. Not all the way down here, almost to Lester Avenue. Right *here* is different.

So now this thorny issue has finally arrived, planting itself squarely on our row house doorsteps, no place to hide. So what are people to think, to do, to say? What's going to happen next?

Neighbors quickly align themselves into two opposing camps on the controversial Barnett question. There's the "live and let live" crowd, which is willing to take a "wait and see" attitude and give the Barnett Family an even break. Then there's the "not in my backyard" crew, which is certain that black people moving into Kings Cross can only mean one thing: trouble. From these folks, the Barnetts are getting the cold shoulder.

Standing outside on the sidewalk in front of our house, Dad and Mr. Pelligrino get into an argument concerning our new high-profile neighbors. Tutti Frutti's father says, if we let even a few colored move in, next thing you know, they'll be flooding the neighborhood, house prices will fall, and decent people will have to move out. Same as in North Philadelphia, West Philadelphia above Merchant, now West Philly below Merchant, and lots of other places, he's seen it before. Mr. Pellegrino says this is one camel you can't let get its nose under the tent, else it'll be the end of us all and everything we've worked for. Just kiss Kings Cross goodbye, because down the tubes it'll go, sure as the sun rises in the east and sets in the west. Done deal.

Dad tells Mr. Pellegrino that maybe he's jumping the gun, coming to some mighty fast conclusions. Granted this plan to bus school kids in from God knows where is a bad idea, and that's why Pam's been active with the protest group. But you gotta be fair. What if these people who move in have steady jobs, work hard, and keep their homes neat and clean? Surely a handful of well-meaning colored is no cause for alarm. Besides, Dad points out, I can't hold anything against people who never did anything to me. No reason for me to carry a grudge.

Mr. Pellegrino gets red in the face, gets all excited and starts waving his arms the way the Italians do, tells Dad he'll be sorry. Why do some people always gotta learn the hard way? Jim, just remember I told you so. . . . Okay? Cause when the time comes you can't walk the streets of your own neighborhood in safety, then you'll understand. Believe me, you'll realize what I'm sayin' the day you'll be forced to sell, for pennies on the dollar—and be glad you get even that. But by that time it'll be too late. Way too late. Just remember I told you so, Jim. Mark my words on it.

Soon it becomes clear Dad and Mr. Pellegrino are far from the only ones who don't see eye-to-eye in this matter. Some of us are allowed to play with the new kid, and others aren't, and it gets sort of awkward for the first weeks. But after a while, the stony resistance wears down, and the novelty of the Barnetts soon begins to wear off. The new kid's just another kid, same as the rest of us, except he's colored. Hangs out with the neighborhood crowd on the steps by Nolan's Grocery Store. Mountain Dew is his beverage of choice. Joins us in boxball, stickball, and sock-it-out. He's just one of the guys. Likes James Brown instead of *The Loving Spoonful* or *The Beatles*, but, hey, it's a free country.

All I want to know is why's this man Brown singing a song about Papa's brand new bag? Anybody can get a new bag, they give sacks away free down at the supermarket. Take as many as you want. It's a stupid song, if you ask me, and the guy does more shouting than singing. Makes all these screeching sounds like maybe he's stepped on something sharp.

By the way, the new boy's name is Dré. Leroy André Barnett to be precise. His mother and father refer to him as simply Dré, and so that's what we call him, too. Mr. Barnett works for the city, and Mrs. Barnett works as a nurse's assistant. They're real nice, soft-spoken, and very respectful. And whenever Dre´ goes to school or church, he's always dressed up like a little prince. White shirt, dress pants with cuffs and sharp creases, shiny shoes. Very spiffy.

Some of us guys like baseball, others basketball, and a few even favor football. But not Dré. Dré's passion is professional wrestling. Muscular villains, heroes, and buffoons in gaudy costumes. Wrestling by the script, playing to the crowd, it's an obvious fake. But don't tell Dré, he thinks it's for real, on the up-and-up. Wants to be a wrestler himself one day, even though he's just a tall beanpole with feet three sizes too big. Looks like the Scarecrow from Oz, only with a better tan.

Since the Barnetts don't have a car and their garage is empty, Dré puts down some mats and turns the Barnett carport into the Kings Cross School of Professional Wrestling. Kids come most weekends to practice their flips, choke holds, body slams, and pins. Plus Dré's got the ultimate collection of wrestling magazines you can thumb through. Lady wrestlers, tag-team wrestlers, midget wrestlers—Dré's got it all in glossy Technicolor. Even the blood running down their faces, which is fake, comes from these little capsules they hid in their trunks. . . . Only don't tell Dré.

Dré's favorite wrestler is Bobo Brazil, this huge, glistening, black guy with muscles coming out his ears. Most of the other kids like Bruno Sammartino, who's the champ and has been for like five years or more. Then there's me, who has to go and favor somebody altogether different. My main man is Baron Mikel Scicluna from the Isle of Malta. Six feet, three inches, built like Steve Reeves in *Hercules*, jet-black hair combed straight back in a slick pompadour. Cool sideburns, too.

I wonder if Malta is where they invented malted milkshakes?

If pro wrestling wasn't so fake, this Scicluna character would win every time, I know it. Betcha he could take both Brazil and Sammartino together, single-handed. But Scicluna is a villain, and the villains don't ever get to beat the top good guys. They whip up on the second-string good guys, then get to wrestle Brazil or Sammartino in some super match, all the marbles on the table. And always, just when it looks like Brazil and Sammartino are going to lose, get pinned, get killed, or worse, they turn the tables on the bad guys at the last second and come out with the victory. Like magic. Happens every time.

Sometimes I don't know if I root for Baron Mikel Scicluna because he's the biggest and baddest and best, or because, in the end, I know he's always going to lose. Usually the only question is how.

All I know is they never let the villain be the champ, it's not in the dumb script. Lex Luther never beats Superman. The Joker never wins against Batman. Spiderman always comes out on top against the Green Goblin. Good always conquers evil. That's just the way the story goes. Got to have a moral, and a satisfactory ending.

Well, at least in comic books, and in pro wrestling. Which are pretty much the same thing. Only don't tell Dré, he's a true believer. Asked Dad once to be sure, and he said any decent pro-footballer would wipe the street up with these fat clowns in tights.

I wonder if one day they'll let Bobo Brazil beat Sammartino. That would sure make Dré a happy camper. But for now, Brazil isn't allowed to beat Sammartino. He can whip everyone else, but not the champ. It just ain't in the script. Bobo's job is to play second fiddle to Bruno, no matter how many muscles he's got coming out his ears.

Lots of mornings Dré, Howie, and I walk to Longstreet Elementary together. Talk about Sammartino, Brazil, the Baron, all the other big-time wrestling stars. We imagine a great battle royal with all our favorite ring gladiators. Gorilla Monsoon. The Sheik. Abdullah the Butcher. Killer Kowalski. The Beast. The Mongol. George the Animal. Chief Jay Strongbow. The Crusher. Smasher Sloan. Haystacks Calhoun. Plus Sammartino, Brazil, and The Baron. Who would come out on top in the free-for-all of the century? Don't know, but no doubt it would be a world of fun to watch. Super boss if you ask my opinion.

Like me, Dré's in fifth grade. But he's in a different class— the one with the loads of colored kids. Coleman James is still with us in Mrs. O'Shaughnessy's class, but that's it. Guess any more colored kids in our class just ain't in the script. So they've officially integrated our school, but not quite. It's not until you go to recess that you realize just how many black kids they've bused in. Plus the ones like Coleman and Dre′ who are starting to move here.

It's a lot now. Maybe one day they'll be as many of them as there are of us. At this rate, maybe one day soon, who knows?

Meanwhile, Dré continues to be the only colored boy in our section of the neighborhood. White shirt, dress pants with cuffs and creases, shiny shoes. Real nice, soft-spoken, and very respectful.

Living in a fishbowl, all eyes on the "colored" kid.

Sometimes I feel sorry for the Barnetts. It sure is easier blending in with the crowd, wearing dungarees and PF Flyers and looking like everyone else. Okay, so maybe I'm a little shorter, have a carrot top and four eyes, but that's not what I mean.

But then, again, it was the Barnetts who chose to move down here. They could've stayed in their colored neighborhood up near Merchant Street. Then Dré would look like everyone else and not have to live in the Kings Cross fishbowl, walking on eggshells and standing out everywhere like a sore thumb.

So who knows, don't ask me to explain it. I just live here, don't make the rules.

One day us boys are all horsing around in the driveway, nothing better to do, and we start practicing our body boxing. It's like regular boxing, no hitting below the belt, only you can't hit in the face, either. Dré body boxes with a few kids, and it's obvious he's very good. Then it's my turn. I'm the informal body-boxing champ of the Wennington/Littlefield youngheads, so my rep is clearly on the line. What starts out as a friendly sparring session quickly develops into a heated contest. We're both ripping shots and grunting, sweat pouring down our faces. Forget the slapping and the sparring.

Dré gets the better of me early, I can't figure out his novel defense. He's got long, bony arms like a spider and uses this weird cover-up, cross-over technique to protect his body. Dré keeps making me lean to get inside, shuffles his oversized feet, then slams me with shots before I can move and cover up. One punch to my rib cage brings tears to my eyes, and I've got to suck it up and pretend everything's fine. But any more punches like the last one and I'm going to lose my precious title. Finally, I find a way to get inside. Lean over, tap Dré on his side with a hook. Lean the other way, tap Dré's other side. Slide, crouch, punch. Slide, crouch, punch. Dré's getting tired now, we both are. Then I fake to one side, and Dré moves his elbow out to block the hook that never comes. In a split second I come up the middle straight as an arrow. Bam! Inside with the old solar plexus punch to the pit of the stomach. Works every time if you can land it cleanly.

I see the pain in Dré's face as he pulls away and bends over. He can't defend himself anymore, no wind, and I finish the job with another crisp one-two. Dré raises his hand to signal the end of the fight.

Chalk another one up for the Dizzy Jimmy. Little four-eyed boy with the very fast hands. Don't be fooled by the baby face.

I know colored people are supposed to be super-tough and super-strong, like Cassius Clay and Sonny Liston. Or Dré's big hero Bobo Brazil. But I saw the pain on Dré's face when I landed the solar plexus special. The pain was real.

Dré' may be plenty tough, but Dré is human, same as the rest of us.

Spare Change

Dad works Monday through Friday at the downtown Brimstone Auto Service Center, plus a half-day on Saturday. After a week of wrestling with mufflers, brake jobs, and front-end alignments, he's generally beat. At the shop, the Old Man showers and changes into a dress shirt and slacks. Then, upon arriving home, he again switches—into jeans and a sweatshirt. Pop usually just leaves the shirt and slacks hanging from the knob on my parents' bedroom door. The pants pockets are so heavy they droop down, nearly scrapping the hardwood floor.

You can often hear my father coming—the man jingles when he walks. Quarters here, dimes there. Spare change everywhere. My mother complains he's ruining perfectly good trousers, wasting his hard-earned money. But the Old Man pays Mom little mind. Dad figures he's not properly dressed unless he's got that jingle-jangle going. One day I ask Pop why he lugs around all those coins like he's some kind of walking vending machine.

You grow up during the Depression, Jim senior explains, ninth out of ten kids, you never have any money. I used to sit on the corner, down by the drugstore, just watching the adults pass by. Listen to all those coins clinking in people's pockets. So one day I swore to myself that when I grew up, I'd always have a pocketful of money no matter where I was going, no matter what I was doing. Money for a cold drink, a sandwich, a seat at the movies . . . money for whatever I wanted. Sometimes I still think back, remembering myself sitting on that corner, not a nickel to my name, dreaming. Dreaming about how someday I'd always have myself a pocketful of money. . . .

Dad's wallet is generally crammed with paper money, too. Pays for everything in cash. No checks, no credit, just cold hard cash. My mother can only shake her head. It's foolish, she says, your father's just asking for somebody to come along, brain him, take everything he's carrying. But you're not going to tell your father any different . . . he's the most bullheaded man you're ever going to meet. Don't waste your breath.

So I ask Pop why he doesn't just put his money in the bank like everyone else. You know, maybe take it out little by little whenever he needs it.

Wouldn't be the same, Dad smiles. I like my money in my pocket. Where I can see it, touch it, feel it . . . that's just the way I am. No big deal—it's nobody's business but mine.

Dad tells me most folks didn't have telephones at home back when he was a boy. When they needed a phone, they just used the one down at the drugstore. Which is a big reason why Dad and his pals hung out at that particular location. For incoming calls, the druggist would pop out the door, pick out one of the Highland Street boys. Hopefully, my father.

Hey, Jimmy . . . got a call here for Mrs. Brown over on Slocum Street. You know where the Browns live?

Sure, I know where! I'll take it, Dad would volunteer.

Then he'd run as fast as possible to the Brown's porch, let Mrs. Brown know she had an important call waiting at the drugstore. If he was lucky, maybe there'd be a five-cent tip in the deal. Going rate.

But, instead, maybe the beat cop would drop by and chase all the kids off the drug-store corner. Too many kids hanging around with too little to do often meant trouble—if not sooner, then usually later.

First time around the cop would almost always tell the boys politely. But if he stopped by a second time and you still hadn't moved, you were liable to get the business end of his nightstick across your shin. Just a tap, mind you, but enough to get your feet moving in a big hurry.

And that certainly might be enough to put a different kind of jingle in your walk—forget the five-cent tip.

"Urban Cowboy"

My father and pony pose on Upland Street during the mid-1930s.

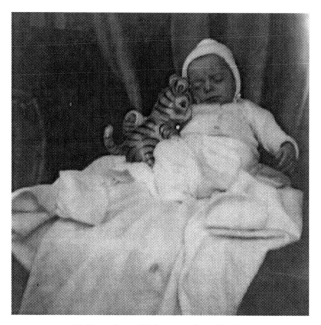

Me and my little grrr tiger (top)
and with Grandmom at Gram's house on S. 61st St. (bottom).

Brothers informal (top)

And formal (bottom)

The old Nixon Theater in West Philadelphia, where my father in his duties as usher once ejected basketball star Wilt Chamberlain and friends.

(photo courtesy of Don Stott)

"Bertie the Bunyip" of Philadelphia children's television fame
(photo courtesy of Billy Ingram at TVParty.com)

The Route 46 trolley stops at 58th & Warrington in the summer of 1957. This was the last year of service for the 46 (a classic Brill double-ender model manufactured in Southwest Philadelphia). By the time of my family's 1960 arrival on nearby Litchfield Street the 46 had been replaced by a PTC bus line.

(photo courtesy of Ed Havens)

Chuck Bednarik "knocks out" Frank Gifford in 1960 championship.

(photo purchased from sports memorabilia dealer)

The Route 13 trolley approaching Kingsessing during the 1960s.

(photo courtesy of Jerry Appleman)

South 55th Street just below Baltimore Ave., the "Angorra" section where we rented an apartment before moving to Litchfield Street. The area was named after a 19th-century cotton mill that pre-dated the neighborhood. (photos courtesy of Bill Myers)

On 55th Street, posing for the camera on my first day of school.
This was the highlight of my career at Longstreth Elementary as things
basically went downhill from here.

"Uncle Joe" striking a pose with a signed photo of Roland,
Philadelphia's resident vampire and late-night television host.

Summertime in the city. We cool off during the early '60s in the
driveway between Litchfield Street and Warrington Avenue.

Me, "Jackie O'Hanlon," and "Frankie Pellegrino" with baseball trophies.

Aerial photo of Connie Mack Stadium in North Philadelphia
(old publicity photo purchased from Sports Collectibles of Houston)

Ticket for the illusory 1964 World Series at
Connie Mack Stadium

(photo courtesy of Joe O'Brien)

Two Southwest Philly movie theaters long-since closed:
the Benn (top), and Benson (bottom).

(photos courtesy of Don Stott)

191

The '56 Chevy Bel Air, an automotive classic and the family car during most of our Philadelphia "row house" days era.

An early 50s Studebaker Champion with the distinctive bullet nose, very similar to what my uncle used to drive during the '60s.

My maternal grandmother, waitress at Linton's Restaurant
for 49 years. She retired only when the chain closed its doors.

Grandmom and one of her ancient clunkers out in front of our house.

My maternal grandfather, who amassed a stock market
fortune by age 29 but died broke at age 39.

Gram and "The Rat"—my paternal grandparents in happier times.

Mount Moriah Cemetery, where the much-maligned caretaker
"Crazy George" carried a bird gun loaded with rock salt.

Shown above are the imposing nineteenth-century gatehouse at
the front entrance on Kingsessing Avenue (top),
and the desolate rear entrance by Cobbs Creek (bottom).

(photos courtesy of John Ellingsworth at mountmoriahcemetery.org)

Artist's rendition (okay, mine) of a "pimple" ball
sliced in half for "halfball."

The Ohio company that manufactured this legendary product
closed its doors decades ago.

Litchfield Street in the summer of 2004.
Our house, which once stood at the top of the block on the left, was
destroyed in a fire several decades ago.

(photo courtesy of Bill Myers)

All smiles upon my graduation from William C. Longstreth,
the local public grade school.

The remnants of our immediate neighborhood's "Mom & Pop" store
at 56th and Warrington, circa 1990.
Small businesses like this once thrived throughout the area.

(photo courtesy of Glenn Myers and Bill Myers)

Most Blessed Sacrament (MBS), the Roman Catholic church that still towers over our former Kingsessing neighborhood. During the 1960s, MBS boasted the largest Catholic elementary school in the world. Today the school is closed and the former MBS convent is now a home for "chemically dependent" women.

(photo courtesy of Bill Myers)

CHAPTER 8

Spidermen

Don't ask me how it all started, I'm not really sure. Legend has it that some kid way back in the early 1950s came visiting his cousin who lived on our block. The out-of-town kid was working on a school project about insects and arachnids, and he had chosen spiders as his specialty. So the kid went out collecting spiders, and his cousin from Littlefield tagged along as his dutiful helper. Pretty soon the cousin was hooked, too—fascinated by the wonderful, mysterious, and creepy world of this silent predator.

And so one thing led to the next . . . when another Littlefield kid discovered something else about spiders—they fight. Boys love to watch a good tussle.

I love to watch anything fight, says Salvatore "Cuz" Cusumano. People, dogs, cats, spiders . . . anything. Fighting's just the way of the world. It's a natural.

And being the toughest "oldhead" in our entire neighborhood, Cuz also likes to participate in fights. Problem is, Cuz is so tough, has such a rep, hardly anyone ever takes him on. The few who were dumb enough to try got knocked out—early on. Very early.

Like last year, when Cuz and some of his boys were walking in Dobbs Creek Park. Along comes a group of colored boys from up north somewhere, definitely out of their neighborhood. One word leads to another, and pretty soon the leaders of the two gangs are squaring off in a clearing.

Cuz is maybe 5' 8" or 5' 9", with biceps like softballs from pumping all that iron. The colored boy is skinny, but goes like 6' 5" or 6' 6", with long arms, long legs. He smiles at Cuz, enjoying himself, thinks this is a terrible mismatch. Next thing he knows Cuz is leaping forward and WHAM! Nails the tall kid cleanly with one mighty hook. Fells him like a tree. Fight over, end of story. Cuz and the boys move on, and the colored boy's buddies are still trying to revive him. Hey, could sure use some smelling salts over there.

Yep, the guy with a rep in our section of Kings Cross is definitely Sal Cusumano, known far and wide as Cuz. I hear he rules Western Catholic this year, toughest kid in the whole school, even though he's not yet a senior.

So Cuz keeps the official spider collection in a dark corner of his front porch, inside an industrial-sized pickle jar. And the boys from the 5600 blocks of Littlefield and Wennington scour the neighborhood with flashlights looking for achaearanea tepidariorum, the common house spider. Beneath stairs, in garages, down in basements, inside hollow trees, in sewer pipes, under culverts . . . wherever it's cool, dark, out-of-the way, and there's plenty of fat, juicy bugs available to snare in a web.

House spiders are blind, don't bite people, and are totally helpless out of their web. But that doesn't stop people from freaking when they see us handling them. Especially the girls. Girls have a thing about spiders.

Usually if you find a good catch you can just scoop it right out of its web. Other times, if it's hiding in a hole or a hard-to-get-at spot, you've got to coax it out. This means tossing a live ant or fly as bait into the center of the web. Or, if you're really good like me, you can put your finger in the web and give a little wiggle— tricking it into thinking there's a juicy meal in the bargain.

I can pick up spiders by the single strand of web they trail behind their bodies. Then make them walk up and down that dragline just like your regular Duncan yo-yo. No sweat, if you know how.

The general idea is to catch the biggest, baddest spider in the whole neighborhood. Quantity doesn't mean a thing—it's quality. You're looking for that one tough, nasty monster that's going to eat everyone else's spiders. That's when you've got yourself a champ.

Spiders grow by molting. Seven times, according to the book on spiders I took out of the Dobbs Creek Library up on Maryland Avenue. Every now and then you'll find a spider that's far bigger than normal. Cuz's theory is that such goliaths happen when nature goes astray and causes them to molt an extra time. Whatever the reason, it happens only in perhaps one in fifty specimens, maybe less.

These "overgrown" spiders with the extra growth molt are usually the champions. Not always, but usually. Sometimes it takes a whole month to find one. Even then, some other kid's entry may eat your challenger for lunch. When it's yours, it's painful to watch.

Like Cuz says, fighting's the way of the world. Spiders are born a hundred or more to an egg sack. They come spilling out all at once, far too tiny to catch any food. So the way they survive is by eating their brothers and sisters. Only the biggest and baddest spiderlings get to become grown-ups. Even then they still fight over turf. So spiders are born fighting, grow up fighting, and die fighting.

Funny thing about spiders, the females are the warriors, and the males are the wimps. The females are twice as big as the males and come in all different shades and patterns . . . grey, black, tan, striped, swirled, spotted. The males are licorice red, frail, and skinny, and usually don't last very long. If the female is hungry or just plain in a bad mood, she'll bite the male, inject him with venom, wrap him up like a fly, and suck out all the juices till there's nothing left but the shell. That's because spider skeletons are on the outside.

Cuz is the official referee when we hold the spider fights. He'll take the challenger, drop it gently into the big glass jar on the other side of the web from the champion. Usually it doesn't take long. The champion senses something new in her web and shakes the web angrily, making a statement. If the challenger is game, she'll shake the web right back and move forward. Blind, suspended in mid-air on spider silk, they meet in the middle of the jar. There's a short feeling out process, legs touching legs, then a violent collision as they grapple. Some like to fight up close, biting and grabbing. Others like to rear back and shoot sticky webs, aiming with the back legs. The first method leaves the head and major organs exposed, while the second exposes the backside and soft underbelly. The winner is usually the spider who can do the most damage the quickest.

Not all fights are to the death. Often the loser will turn tail and run, the winner in hot pursuit, kicking the vanquished spider from the web. But if you're bitten in a vulnerable area, or get your legs tangled by a shooting strand of silk, you're a goner. Not only do you lose, but you get to be today's lunch.

Kids name their champions, and sometimes a ferocious spider will rule the jar for an entire summer, defeating all comers. We've had Blackie, Spud, Flash, Godzilla, Fang, Jersey Jerry, Spot, Killer, Kong, Maniac, and Gadzooks, to name just the standouts in our Spider Hall of Fame.

Cuz and I are the best spider hunters in the neighborhood and boast the most champions. But we have different theories about what makes a champion and where to hunt for 'em. Cuz likes looking in Dobbs Creek Park, especially in hollow trees and under culverts. Cuz says the "country" spiders are tougher, living outside in the elements and hunting for some of the nasty creepy-crawlers that live by the creek. Me, I favor the damp, unlocked garages with lots of old junk and dusty corners in which a spider can make the perfect home. The way I see it, the more they eat, the bigger they get. Garages are the perfect spider incubators.

Last year I caught the biggest spider I've ever seen, what a mutant. Bet it molted an extra two times, not just one. Caught it in my Uncle Patrick and Aunt Marilyn's basement in Derby while we were visiting. I was so excited I named it right away. . . .Wilt, because it was so humongous. Put Wilt in a bottle, kept it by the cellar steps to take home. But Uncle Patrick got a little tipsy at the family barbecue, came downstairs for something, and accidentally kicked over the bottle, breaking it into a hundred pieces. I came in and there was my prized Wilt, giant legs all broken and gushing spider blood.

I cried, Uncle Pat, Uncle Pat—look what you did to my spider!

Uncle Patrick rubbed his eyes, steadied himself. Sorry, Jimmy, he apologized.

But I was inconsolable and gave Uncle Pat a dirty look. I'd never find another spider like Wilt . . . this specimen was truly one in a million.

Perturbed, Uncle Pat then made a face of his own. All right, Jimmy, if it makes you feel any better, we'll put him in the car and rush him over to Fitzpatrick Mercy Hospital.

Very funny, Uncle Pat. I didn't have a champion all last year, either. But this year I've got Concrete Charlie, named after the great Chuck Bednarik of Philadelphia Eagles fame. Charlie's a beige-colored beauty with thick, blood-red legs and a real fighting machine. Goes for the quick kill every time, and usually gets it. Nothing fancy, just pure power and aggression. I think Charlie's got a chance to rule the jar for the rest of the summer.

I like owning the champ.

As a little sideline, I've found I can make some money with my knowledge of spiders. It's an easy trick. Just put a house spider in one jar, and a Daddy-long-legs spider in another jar. Then bring the jars where younger kids can watch. Once they get interested, tell 'em you're going to put the two spiders together and have them fight. Hey, wanna bet?

Nah, say the kids. That's not fair. One spider's way bigger than the other.

Of course, they're right. The daddy long-legs is three, maybe four times longer. Makes the house spider look like a pudgy little shrimp.

I say, Tell ya what I'm gonna do. Just to be fair, I'll let you pick the one you want.

Really?

Sure, why not?

Okay, I pick that one. The big one.

How much you wanna bet?

A quarter?

Nah, too much. I don't have that much to lose. How bout a nickel?

A dime. I'll bet a dime.

Okay, whatever—you're on. . . .

Greed will getcha every time. Only these little crumb-grabbers don't know that yet. But they're about to learn. The hard way.

Oh, one more thing. Before we start, let's see the money.

203

The mark pulls out a dime. So do I.

Ready?

Uh-huh! He's all smiles, already counting his winnings.

I gently open the bottle for the house spider, coax it out, dump it into the jar with the daddy long-legs. The long-legs shakes the web menacingly, and the stubby little house spider moves forward. We're on.

It doesn't last very long. The long-legs is very big, very long, but also very fragile. The house spider can't reach the long-legs' body, but it doesn't have to. Instead, it just seizes one of the beanpole legs in its jaws and pulls. Pop, off comes Daddy-O's eighth leg. Now there are seven.

Pop, pop, pop.

Now the daddy long-legs is trying to run, but it only has four legs.

My pigeon says, What's happening? What's wrong with the big spider?

Looks like he's in a little bit a trouble, I explain. Having a rough time of it in there. Happens to the best of 'em.

Pop, pop, pop . . . POP.

Now all eight legs are off the daddy long-legs spider, and my champ goes in for the leisurely kill. Bites the legless, quivering thorax, injects the deadly venom. Soon the insides of the loser will turn to liquid goo. Spiders don't eat actually eat their prey, they drink 'em.

I say, Tough break, kid. Reach my hand out, pocket both dimes.

The pigeon puts up a protest. Hey, that's wasn't fair!

No? Why not? I let you have your pick, didn't I?

The kid rubs his head, confused.

I tell him, Hey—listen. Don't worry about the dime, maybe I can make it up to you. Do you collect football cards?

Yeah . . . so?

Well, do I have a deal for you! Just so happens I've got last year's Pete Retzlaff of the Philadelphia Eagles right here in my back pocket.

Really? You got Pete Retzlaff??

Oh, absolutely. . . . I wouldn't lie to you, buddy.

In the words of the immortal W.C. Fields, another Southwest Philly product, *Never give a sucker an even break.*

Barry Craig

Okay, so the Phillies blew the National League pennant race last year. No problem. *This* year's going to be the year. Callison, Gonzales, Bunning, Short, Taylor, Wine, Dalrymple . . . the boys can't miss. The season's baseball cards are out, and someone gets hold of the new card for Cookie Rojas, the Phillies second baseman from Cuba. Little guy, moon face, glasses . . . looks familiar. Yep, sure looks something like a Latin version of me, Jimmy Morris. And I'm not the only person to notice. It becomes official in the neighborhood once Sal "Cuz" Cusumano christens me "Cookie" Morris. The nickname catches on almost immediately. And, I have to admit, it sure beats the heck out of "Four Eyes" and even "Lefty."

Hey Cookie, Cookie, lend me your comb. . . .

Once school lets out, stickball, boxball, sock-it-out, and baseball-card collecting get into full swing. I decide to add to the fever by starting my very own unofficial Cookie Rojas Fan Club. The first three members are me, Howie, and Howie's best friend Barry Craig.

Barry is a tow-headed kid from down the street, tall for his age and a budding athletic talent. He's a Tommy O'Hanlon in miniature. When the kids my age need another ballplayer, Barry is always the first of the younger "youngheads" selected. Lanky and fast, his long legs eat up the ground when chasing fly balls or running the bases. Only seven, Barry looks like eight or nine and plays like ten. Everyone should be so lucky.

No surprise, Barry's a chip off the old block. His old man played in the city championship game for Burnham against Wilt

Chamberlain and the boys from the Brook. Had more success against The Big Dipper than some of those trees have in the NBA today. At least Wilt didn't do his Hershey 100-point number on Barry Sr. and his Burnham teammates.

One hot July day my mother decides to surprise the members of the Cookie Rojas Fan Club. Buys us three white T-shirts, takes a red magic marker, and starts drawing up some homemade jerseys. Prints "**Phillies**" on the fronts of the shirts, and "**Rojas**" "**16**" on the backs. We proudly display our new digs for the whole neighborhood, vowing to wear them for the entire summer, or until they fall apart, whichever comes first.

Later that afternoon, some of the Littlefield/Wennington boys decide on an excursion down to Dobbs Creek Park. The sun climbs high into the sky, along with the temperature . . . 88°, 89°, 90°, 91°. . . . Howie and I get permission from Mom. Mrs. O'Hanlon gives Jackie the OK. Donnie Fahey is good to go, as is Tutti-Frutti.

Barry Craig gets the green light, but his mother wants him back by four o'clock. Mr. Craig works the early shift at UPS, and the Craigs always eat supper before everyone else. So we all gather round and head down to the park.

Mickey Farrell sees us, decides to tag along. Mickey, free as a bird, *never* has to check in with his parents. What a life.

We take a detour through Mt. Lebanon Cemetery, skirting headstones, keeping an eye out for legendary Crazy Sam, the cantankerous caretaker. But it's too hot for even Crazy Sam, who's probably taking a siesta in his office. After a while, we move on to shadier pastures—Dobbs Creek. Explore the murky water line, hunt for spiders, climb up and down the steep bank.

The older boys, Jackie, Donnie, Tutti Frutti, and myself vote to explore the upper section of the park to the north. We have our gloves and a baseball with us, there are a couple of ball fields up at that end, and maybe we'll have ourselves a little hardball practice . . . something we can't do back in the neighborhood. Too many broken windows, too many angry adults.

Two of the younger boys, Barry and Mickey, want to hang back and stay at the creek. Besides, Barry's gotta be back by four

206

anyway. Torn between his friends and mine, Howie finally decides to tag along with us older boys. So, we wave goodbye to Barry and Mickey and hit the dirt trail going north.

More exploring, more hunting for spiders, and a half-hearted attempt at hardball practice in the suffocating heat. We take a long break under an ancient tree, listen to the bugs buzzing by, the babbling creek, the distant sounds of traffic from up on Dobbs Creek Parkway. Just another lazy, endless summer day like so many others—too much time and not enough to do. Hazy, hot, and humid, not a care in the world, school almost two months away . . . an eternity.

Meanwhile, back in the lower park, Barry and Mickey still want to stay, but it's almost four o'clock. They decide to head home so Barry can ask his folks for an extra hour. But when Mr. Craig says no, Barry and Mickey sneak back anyway. They find an old, homemade raft someone has abandoned, and soon Barry and Mickey are having a grand old time on the gently flowing creek. Just like Huck Finn and Tom Sawyer on the great Mississippi.

It's been a long day, and by five-thirty we older kids plus tagalong Howie are all starting to feel tired, hungry, and thirsty. So we make the long trek out of Dobbs Creek Park, down the Parkway, and up Venice on our way back to the neighborhood. As we approach the corner of 57th and Venice, we see a familiar figure peering down the street toward Dobbs Creek Parkway. It's Mrs. Craig, Barry's mother, and she looks plenty worried. Arms folded, shifting her weight impatiently, tapping her foot.

Have you boys seen Barry?

Not since earlier this afternoon, Mrs. Craig. He was with Mickey, down by the creek.

We continue on, turning up 57th toward Littlefield and Wennington. Mrs. Craig stays anchored to her post, arms folded, shifting her weight, tapping her foot—all the while continuing to stare in the direction of Dobbs Creek.

Man, we say, Barry's sure gonna catch it tonight. He's in big, big trouble—probably be grounded for a month.

Howie and I arrive home, wash up, get ready for supper. Dad's running late, so Mom has us kids eat right around our tiny kitchen table. Soup and sandwiches, lots of fun when it's just us kids—me, Howie, and little Laura. I crack a joke, and Howie laughs so hard, milk comes running out his nose.

Halfway through dinner we hear a disturbance outside. Voices, people milling about out front on the street. Mom goes to see what's the matter. Curious, I soon follow.

From our porch I see that Littlefield is filling up with people, like an impromptu block party. Groups of neighbors in haphazard clusters. Shocked looks on all their faces. Whispering, murmuring. Something bad is going down.

Did you hear the news?

What news?

Barry Craig just drowned in Dobbs Creek.

The awful, incomprehensible words cut me like a knife. My little mind freezes, unable to fully comprehend or accept the horror of what has happened. Barry? Dobbs Creek?? Drowned??? No, no it can't be. He was playing with us just a few short hours ago. In his handmade Cookie Rojas jersey, the one Mom had custom made for our fan club. Laughing, smiling, seven year-old blonde-haired boy full of life. He can't be dead.

Can't be.

From up the street we watch as the police climb the stairs to the Craig's front door. Next come the stunned grandparents from just a few blocks away, faces flushed with anguish.

Finally, the ruddy-faced priest, dressed all in black and looking very stern, the weight of the world pressing down on his weary, burdened shoulders.

It's official now. Barry is gone—gone forever.

Mom whisks me inside, tries to have me finish my soup and sandwich. But I have no appetite. Dad comes home, and Mom takes him aside, I can hear them whispering. Dad doesn't eat, so I guess he's lost his appetite as well.

Poor brother Howie is inconsolable. Barry was his very best friend.

Later, I find sleeping to be even harder than eating. I want all of this to be just a bad dream, a nightmare from which I can awake. But next morning, when the sun comes shining through my bedroom window, Barry is still gone, and I begin to come to grips with the hard reality.

My mother and all the other women spend the day baking food for the Craigs. Ham, turkey, lasagna, potato salad, soup, bread— enough food for a half-dozen families. Somehow I doubt the Craigs are going to be hungry. I know we still aren't.

Numb, unable to help, my father and all the other men go off to work as usual, robotlike, silent, with the thermos bottles and dangling lunch pails their only companions.

The rumors begin to spread like wildfire. Mickey got angry at Barry, pushed him into the water. Mickey waited most of an hour to go get help. Barry's foot got stuck in an underwater pipe, holding him just below the surface. The Craigs got a hundred thousand dollars in insurance money, but Mr. Craig was so grief-stricken he took a book of matches and burned it all up. Crazy talk mostly.

So many stories, it's hard to separate fact from fiction. And no one's about to ask the Craigs. Not now, not later, not ever.

They bury little Barry from Our Lady of Perpetual Peace. Dress him up in his First Communion suit. Handsome, sleeping blonde-haired boy in all white, everyone's picture of the forever angel. His final resting place a giant, rolling, Catholic cemetery well beyond the city limits in the far-reaching western suburbs of Philadelphia.

Gone, but not forgotten. In our minds and hearts but rarely on our tongues, except for the occasional whisper. Here one moment, gone the next in a savagely cruel twist of fate. And the harsh lesson is not lost on any of us. Least of all the boys who spent that last afternoon with poor Barry. It could have just as easily been Jackie or Donnie, Howie or Mickey, Tutti Frutti or even myself. There's no rhyme or reason to it. It's not supposed to make sense. It just happened.

Now I know the awful truth, what Grandmom was trying to tell us the time we watched those boys hitch a ride on the bumper of that delivery truck in the snowstorm.

They make those coffins in all sizes, boys. In *all* sizes. . . .

The reality is death isn't just something for old people and the olden days of polio, small pox, scarlet fever, diphtheria, and The Great Flu Epidemic. Death is for the here and now, for all people, and for all times. Always lurking, unseen, waiting to jump at the right opportunity.

We'll miss you, Barry Craig. Forever and a day.

Evil Eye

It's another regular Saturday morning down at the 57th Street supermarket. Kids are back with their red Radio Flyer wagons lined up to take orders, walk someone's groceries home for a quarter. Another day, another $1.00. Maybe a $1.25 if tips are good.

Take your order, ma'am? Take your order?

The store manager pretends not to see us so long as we behave ourselves. Unwritten rule. He doesn't bother us if we don't bother him—simple. We provide a useful, though entirely unofficial service. But if there's just a hint of trouble, he's gonna come outside and yell that we've gotta hit the bricks. Scram, you kids. Get lost—beat it!

One more run and maybe I'll have enough for this afternoon's double feature at The Parkland, with a cup of fountain root beer and box of French burnt peanuts thrown in.

The first movie is a Jerry Lewis comedy about joining the Army, and the second film stars the British heavy Christopher Lee as super villain Fu Manchu, who's cooking up yet another devilish scheme for world domination.

Hey, Jerry Lewis isn't bad. I really liked *The Family Jewels*, where he plays something like eight different parts. And *The Nutty Professor*, where Jerry's a nerdy college teacher who drinks the potion and does the Jekyll and Hyde thing, is an all-time classic. But the Fu Manchu flick is the one I really want to see.

210

The Face of Fu Manchu sounds really boss, I saw the preview last week.

Just one more order, then I'm outta here.

On this day business is brisk early, but by eleven or so it slows way down. Too many kids, too many wagons, not enough customers. Two of the junior entrepreneurs are twins named Lenny and Leo Conigliaro. Neither runty brat has gotten an order for almost an hour, and now they're getting antsy. I hope they don't pull their usual stunt, get us all kicked out. The twins are a couple of real flip-tops, about nine cents short of a dime, if you ask me.

Sure enough, here comes an old lady with her personal two-wheeled cart, no profit opportunity there. But as she passes, Lenny gives Leo the sign and they go into action. Big fight breaks out, Leo shoving Lenny, Lenny shoving Leo. Then Lenny chases his brother past the lady with her personal cart crammed full of eggs, milk, bread, and coffee.

Lenny reaches out his brother, who turns, ducks, then . . .

WHAM!

Leo runs smack into a hollow metal support pole.

BOONNGGGGG!

The pole vibrates loudly upon impact. Everyone outside the market turns to see. Leo flops to the ground, writhing in pain, holding his head. He really looks as if he's badly hurt.

Aaaaaaaahhhhhhhhh! My eye, my eye!

Lady with her own grocery cart stops, leans over to help.

Are you all right, little boy?

Leo cries, It's my eye. I hit my eye!

I'm sure it's not too bad, the lady comforts Leo. Here, let me take a look.

Leo whimpers, It hurts, it hurts real bad. Meanwhile, his eye remains tightly shut.

Now, now . . . let me see, coaxes the lady. I'll be gentle.

211

Okay, Leo agrees softly. How does it look?

Leo *s l o w l y* opens his eye. There's nothing but an empty socket staring back at Cart Lady. The entire eyeball is missing. Gone.

Now it's the nice lady's turn to start screaming. Only this part of the show is no act.

Aaaaahhhhhhhhhhhhhhhh!!

She bowls over her cart, destroying the eggs, breaking the milk bottle, tearing open the sack of ground coffee, and smushing her fresh loaf of Wonder bread. We last glimpse her scrambling back into the market in a state of uncontrollable hysteria, knocking startled patrons aside.

No, this poor lady hasn't forgotten her green stamps.

Leo and Lenny quick grab their wagons, rush off around the corner, laughing as they go.

Leo had cancer as a baby, and the doctors had to remove the damaged eye. He's got this glass one in its place, looks almost real. Easy to take out, easy to pop back in.

Only shocked, grossed-out Cart Lady doesn't know this.

Me and another boy start to pick up Cart Lady's ruined groceries and return them to the toppled container. Do our good deed for the day. But we're too late. Here comes our not-so-friendly store manager. Red-faced, smoke pouring from his ears, clearly pushed beyond his breaking point.

OUT! All of you! NOW!!

But it wasn't us, mister. It was Leo. . . .

Yeah, and Lenny, too.

I don't care! Leave NOW. Get away from my store. And don't ever come back, EVER! Else I'm calling the cops!! Do you hear me?

Aw, jeez. . . .

Ever is a long time. We'll probably be back next Saturday. Definitely before the end of the month. Chase goofy Leo and Lenny away if they show their grimy little faces.

I make it to Parkland in time to catch the double feature. Buy my French burnt peanuts and slip into the darkness, they're already showing the warm-up cartoons. No root beer though, thanks to the Leo and Lenny Show. I really could've used another grocery run, another quarter.

Their little thing with Leo's eye is getting old. I'm surprised Cart Lady fell for it, especially since I think she's a regular shopper at the 57th Street store. Anyway, the Conigliaro Brothers should definitely cool it, cut the stuff. Somebody may have a heart attack, then they'll be sorry. Why do Italians seem to have this thing about the eyes? They believe you can put the whammy on someone by giving them the old Evil Eye, bringing on the bad luck. Maybe, maybe not. But I doubt it could be as bad as the shock Leo and Lenny can spring on people. I know, because I got a good look at Cart Lady's face as she ran screaming into the market, groceries spilling onto the sidewalk.

Well, the Lewis film is a scream, he and Dean doing the buck-private routine. But when the *Fu Manchu* movie starts, I'm in for my own little nasty shock. The flick starts with Christopher Lee hiding out in an underground command post somewhere in London, ready to launch another brilliantly conceived scheme for world conquest. But a secret agent has infiltrated the Fu Manchu organization, gotten the goods on the entire diabolic plot, and is now ready to spill the beans. Only problem, the spy is discovered before she can get the word out. The price for such treachery is death, and Fu Manchu witnesses her execution personally. His henchmen put the poor woman in a glass chamber, pleading for her life, no way out. The signal is given, some big valves are turned, and suddenly muddy river water comes gushing into the chamber from the mighty Thames. Faster, faster . . . higher, higher. The young victim fights and claws and scratches at the glass, no use. The chamber fills to the top, no more air, and finally the bubbles come pouring out of the girl's nose and mouth. She's drowning, so horrible, no one there to save her.

I can't watch any more, shut my eyes, turn my head in revulsion. My mind flashes back to Dobbs Creek, Barry Craig, and the Cookie Rojas T-shirt, #16. The day Barry fell in the muddy water, no one there to save him except for little Mickey Farrell who was too small. The day none of us can change, it always ends the same way, over and over, Barry gone forever.

I gulp, force myself to look up at the big screen again. The agent's limp, lifeless body hangs suspended in the murky chamber. Her face floats by the glass, frozen in terror, eyes wide open but not seeing. No more bubbles.

Close-up of Fu Manchu . . . wicked, satisfied smile beneath the infamous, drooping mustache. That merciless, cold, steely Evil Eye. He likes what he sees, bigger monster than Godzilla, King Kong, and Ghiddra combined.

My stomach is doing flip flops, and now I think I'm glad I didn't have the money for that cup of root beer. French burnt peanuts, soda pop, and an upset stomach are a potentially explosive combination, especially in a darkened, crowded movie theater. No need to add to the audience's horror, they've already got more than enough trauma up on the big screen.

I shut my eyes again, sit very still, and think of Cart Lady. Hope she's doing better than me, 'cause right now I don't really feel all that great.

Guess I'm not cracked up to be a Fu Manchu fan after all. Next time I oughtta stick with Disney. Maybe catch that upcoming *Flipper* movie. Keep my stomach nice and calm, let the cute dolphin with the weird smile do all the flip-flops and somersaults.

Under Wraps

To Trick-or-Treat, or not to Trick-or-Treat . . . that is the question. On one hand, I am now in the sixth grade, definitely getting too old and too cool for going door-to-door in some cheesy Halloween costume like a lowly third-grader. On the other hand, why miss out on an easy score of Mallo Cups, Hershey Bars, Chunkys, Raisinettes, Clark Bars, Zagnuts, M & Ms, and dozens of other goodies just ripe for the picking in our densely populated row house neighborhood?

However, much like Shakespeare's Hamlet, I procrastinate and let my decision slide right up until October 31st. Too late to order one of those boss, real-life masks from the back of *Famous Monsters Magazine*. They've got Cyclops, Werewolf, The Mummy, Screaming Skull, Gorilla, a wickedly green Frankenstein, and even an authentic astronaut's space suit that costs probably half of Dad's take-home pay at Brimstone. Not to mention my flat-out favorite, the Melting Man mask looking like something right out of Vincent Price's *House of Wax*. I'd like to sneak up and toss that next to some burning building and watch the firemen's faces when they see the Melting Man face in the rubble.

But a mail-order mask is academic now, and the only thing left for me is to hoof it down to Woolworth's on Lester Avenue and buy one of those flimsy plastic masks with the cheesy rubber band in the back that are, say, 59 cents and a rip-off even at that price. I hate the thought of stooping so low, maybe I'll just have to wait until next year. What to do, what to do?

Brother Howie is going out in his San Francisco Giants baseball uniform, a present from my Mom's Aunt Emma who lives up in New York City. Aunt Emma and her husband Uncle Richard are still big Giants fans, even though the Giants left New York for the West Coast years ago, Say hey, Willie Mays. And I don't care for the Giants much because they're always giving the Phillies a serious whipping, especially when that Juan Marichal guy is pitching, big windup and leg-kick high up in the sky.

Our next-door neighbor Bobby Schaeffer is going out as a pirate, black patch over one eye, handkerchief on his head, fake gold tooth made out of foil, and black mustache penciled in. Doesn't matter, he still looks like the assassin Lee Harvey Oswald at twenty paces, shiver me timbers.

And then there's Jackie "Bugs" O'Hanlon from just down the street. Jackie is going for costume of the year, maybe costume of the century. He's Robbie the Robot from the movie *Forbidden Planet* and television show *Lost in Space*. Mr. O'Hanlon is helping Bugs to make his costume, which has been kept a big secret until tonight. It's really very cool, a small cardboard box fastened on top of a larger box. Jackie climbs inside, and it's got a plastic bubble dome on top, filled with old vacuum tubes and wires from a junk radio, and disguised peepholes out the front for Jackie to see. Not to mention a mess of fake dials and electronics pasted all over the boxes in the form of shirt buttons, colorful plastic spray can tops, bottle caps, electrical switches, flashlight bulbs, and various odds and ends from Mr. O'Hanlon's basement workshop. The high-tech effect is completed with what looks like a discarded utility meter protruding from the front and center of the lower, bigger box. Even Jackie's arms, which stick out through holes on the sides of the main box, are encased in corrugated, neoprene, lightweight industrial tubing to give Jackie an authentic, Robbie the Robot machine-type look.

Bobby, Howie, and I can only say one word . . . Wow!

Best costume in the whole neighborhood, replies the robot's voice, sounding very much like Jackie "Bugs" O'Hanlon. The O'Hanlons always have the very best.

The sun is going down, supper is over, and I have less than an hour before Trick-or-Treating goes into full swing. Frantically I search boxes in our basement, closets in the bedrooms. Finally, I look in the closet in the bathroom.

There I see it—an ace bandage. Hold it up, let it unfold. Perfect! With enough of these, I can wrap myself up, become murderous Kharis, The Mummy. Boris Karloff would be proud. Quickly I scoop up the meager savings from my dresser drawer, borrow some more change from Mom, then dash around the corner to Sperling's Drug Store on Venice Avenue to stock up on ace bandages.

Back home I unroll the new bandages, learn to hook them together using the handy silver clasps they come with, and make one long bandage that Mom wraps around and around my shirt. Then, with the final bandage, I rub in a touch of yellow mustard to simulate the rotting that a proper 3,000-year-old mummy must have. This last bandage Mom wraps around my head and face, leaving a small slit over my eyeglasses.

I do a fast rehearsal learning how to drag one leg behind and hook my fingers into a frozen claw, then I'm good to go. Meet Kharis, killer mummy on the loose in Kings Cross. Now I can't wait to go door-to-door, score a bunch of sweets.

So me, Howie, Bobby, and Jackie get started on our side of Littlefield. Hopping the banisters, crossing the porches, making a beeline for the doors with our little brown grocery sacks for the loot. Only problem is, Robbie the Robot in his square boxes and plastic bubble top can't climb the railings. Jackie's got to shuffle off the porches, onto the steps, then back onto the porches. Slowly.

C'mon, guys . . . wait up!

But soon we leave our buddy Bugs O'Hanlon behind. Sure, he's our friend. But free candy is free candy—and you get your chance only once per year.

Hey, Trick or Treat . . . smell my feet. Give me something good to eat!

Our little street is crawling with kids, like the giant armored water bugs that surface from below on hot summer evenings whenever we've experienced an extended drought. Bums, beatniks, werewolves, Draculas, princesses, football players, witches, skeletons, Bozo the Clown, the Devil himself toting a mean red pitchfork. Suddenly an apple goes hopping and skipping down the street, pieces breaking off. Some kids' heads turn, voices laughing under the costumes.

Mrs. Thorne must be giving out apples again, snickers Bobby Schaeffer.

Yeah, but still—kids shouldn't be chucking them down street, says Howie. That's not right.

Wouldn't happen if she gave out candy bars same as everyone else, shrugs Bobby, his one-eyed Lee Harvey Oswald pirate face pouting at the thought of Mrs. Thorne's grievous breach of Halloween etiquette.

Through wrapped bandages, I chip in my two cents, say I heard somebody somewhere in Philly put razor blades inside apples last year.

Great, laughs Bobby. Goes to show you not all the world's monsters are just at the movies. Giving razor blades to kids— what a sicko!

Hey, asks Howie, did anybody bite 'em or swallow one?

Nah, I answer. But almost—word is it was a pretty close shave. Hardy har har.

Bobby, Howie, and I finish one side of the street, then start on the other side, our sacks growing heavy with chocolaty, sugary loot. Our approach is for the pirate and the ballplayer to ring the bell, get their candies first. I hang back, wait on one side of the shadowy porch, then do the slow Kharis mummy walk to the door, dragging my injured leg behind, clawing the air with a talon-like gloved hand.

Trrrrriiickkkkk . . . . O-o-o-r . . . . *Trrreeeaaaatttt*!

Grown-ups smile and laugh. Sometimes they even throw an extra goodie in my bag. Unlike at Longstreet Elementary, it pays to be a ham on Halloween.

We hop the next railing. Bobby and Howie knock on the door, say their Trick-or-Treats, collect their bounty. A big guy with a beer belly holds a tray of Tootsie Rolls, one for you kids and maybe a couple for me, watching my Kharis shuffle entrance.

Yo, Mr. Mummy, he points. Looks like you're losin' a little somethin' there.

I look down. Oh, no! Unfortunately Mr. Beer Belly is quite correct. There go my prized bandages I've been dropping like so many breadcrumbs in the forest. They lie, each bandage tied to the next, draped over the porch banister, trailing behind into the shadows across the previous porch. Mr. Mummy is coming unwound, now practically naked. Not exactly what I had in mind for the legendary Mummy's Curse.

Quickly I reel in what's left of my unraveled bandages. Some of the silver clasps are missing, and it's too dark to attempt a proper rewind. So I ball up the bandages, grab my bag of sweets, and hurriedly head for home.

Mom tries to hastily fix the damage with the help of some safety pins, but I'm missing too many wraps, Kharis the Killer Mummy is history. Just when I was really vacuuming in the munchies, too.

Mom empties my bag, says to continue on with just the bandage on my head.

Ridiculous! What kind of sad excuse for a mummy is that?

Oh, just tell them you're a mental patient and you bumped your head in an accident, Mom explains.

Mental patient? Accident? What accident?

Who knows, says Mom, exasperated. Just tell 'em you've got amnesia and can't remember.

Amnesia? What's *that*?

See? You re forgetting already. Just tell them you can't remember. They'll give you the candy.

This is stupid. But Mom's right, they'll probably just give me the candy, anyway.

Mom says wait a minute, goes into the kitchen, gets the ketchup bottle from the refrigerator. Smears a dab of the red stuff on the bandage above my eye. Ketchup on top of the original mustard, I'm now a walking condiment. Well, who cares, so I grab the empty sack and hurry out the door to catch Bobby and Howie. Hey guys, wait up!

Bobby and Howie laugh when they see me in my new getup. What's *that* supposed to be?

I'm a mental patient, I tell them.

No kiddin', Bobby the Buccaneer snickers. I woulda never guessed.

Just knock on the door, Bobby.

Bobby knocks. A woman answers, looks us over. Says, And what do we have here, tonight? What are you boys supposed to be?

I'm an outfielder, answers Howie.

I'm Blackbeard the Pirate, says Bobby.

I'm a mental patient, I explain, without much enthusiasm.

A mental patient, huh? Escaped from the state hospital, I presume?

I don't know, Miss. I was in an accident or something like that.

An accident? What kind of accident?

I don't know, Miss. I can't remember. I've got um, um . . . I've got amnesia.

The woman bursts into an immediate fit of uncontrolled laughter. Runs inside to get her husband. Hey, Bill . . . you gotta see this. We got this kid who's an escaped mental patient—with amnesia to boot. He's so cute.

This whole mental patient thing is dumb if you ask me. But the dumber I play it, the more laughs I get, and the more junk they toss in my sack. At this rate of chocolate-bar acquisition perhaps I should bump it up a notch, play the raving lunatic. But I stay with what's working, because if it ain't broke, don't fix it. Not when precious sacks of goodies are involved.

When our bags get full we make a quick detour home to make a delivery. Along the way we spot a familiar, forlorn figure on the sidewalk. Boy besides pair of crumpled, grass-stained cardboard boxes, dented plastic bubble, wires and pieces of metal hanging off. The sad remains of Robbie the Robot.

Hey, Jackie! What's up? What happened to you??

My lousy costume, whines Jackie. That's what happened to me! First I couldn't climb the railings. Then it got too hot inside the boxes, and way too heavy—especially carrying around that dumb bag. And then I couldn't see, missed a step, and fell right over onto this lady's lawn. Splat! Dropped my candy all over the place, smashed up my lousy costume and everything!

Man, are you all right? Bobby asks.

Yeah, mutters Jackie. Stupid costume. Now all I have is one measly half of a bag of candy. This really stinks.

We're all nodding our heads in sympathy with Bugs, but inside I'm really laughing. Jackie had the best costume, hands down as usual, nobody can beat Robbie the Robot, but he's barely got half of a sack of the sweet stuff. And me? I'm forced to drop my half-baked, last-minute attempt at Kharis the Killer Mummy and switch to something lame like being an escaped mental patient wearing a single ace bandage and a dab of ketchup. Yet I'm coming home with my fourth bag, every one overflowing, quite a haul if I say so myself.

Mom's eyes grow big as Howie and I return home for good toting with our final catch of the night. Wow, says Mom. I've never seen so much candy! Where did you boys all go?

Instantly I go into my confused mental patient routine. Scratch my head, gawk around as if I'm in some kind of fog.

Sorry, but I don't know, Miss. I can't remember. Amnesia, I explain, tapping my bandage alongside the splotch of ketchup mixing with the underlying mustard.

Mom says, Don't get smart with me, mister . . . else I'll give you some *real* amnesia to worry about.

But Howie and I just laugh, watching Mom as she sorts through the mountain of treats on the dining room table. Can't eat anything until Mom checks it out . . . you know, with stuff like razor blades in apples going around. Mom slips us each a Hersheys Milk Chocolate & Almonds, tells us to eat them quickly and get ready for bed.

Next morning, as Howie and I prepare for school, Mom leaves a single treat for each of us. Hey, Mom—what gives? Only one measly chocolate bar after bringing home a mountain of the good stuff piled so high?

Mom says one candy bar a day is plenty. Any more is un-healthy, it'll rot your teeth and spoil your appetite.

But Mom . . . what did you do with all our candy? Where'd you put it?

Mom folds her arms, smiles her devilish little know-it-all smile. Says she can't remember—must be a case of the amnesia coming on. Guess this disease is contagious.

Aw, Mom. . . .

Never you mind, Mom adds. Now hurry along or you'll be late for school.

Fish Story

Sometimes when you walk home from school, same route day after day, you are bored. And when you are bored, looking for a little fun and excitement, you can get into trouble. Quickly.

As third- and sixth-graders in a K-to-6 school, Howie and me are cocks of the walk. This could definitely change come junior high school. But for now, nobody gives us much trouble . . . especially not those safety patrol nerds in their little space cadet belts at the corner of 57th Street and Venice Avenue. Pulling the safeties' chains no longer holds much challenge, so naturally we look for bigger and better targets on which to act out our devilish tendencies.

Eventually, our attention is attracted to the sleepy little kosher fish market that faces onto 57th Street just south of Venice. Maybe this is for no better reason than it's just there – unavoidable, directly on our daily path back to Littlefield Street. But, mainly, I think it has to do with those two big plate-glass windows that invite your eyes to go exploring inside. Sort of a people-sized version of a sidewalk-facing goldfish bowl.

The grumpy-looking man who runs the store is middle-aged, balding, and slowly turning to Jell-O. Every day we walk past, and every day Grumpy stands behind the counter in his stained apron, slicing fish and waiting on the occasional customer. Waiting and slicing, talking and wrapping. Slice, slice, slice. Beady eyed and rumple faced, never even a little smile. Scaly silver fish, red insides coming out, heads chopped off.

So we begin to make Mr. Grumpy's day a little more interesting. We make smiley faces at the Fish Man. Smile and wave, wave and smile . . . with a few jumping jacks thrown in for good measure. Howie blows kisses, puckers his lips, and presses his chubby nose against the glass, wide-eyed. At first, Grumpy just frowns and waves us away. Then, as the afternoons go by and his stares and gestures only serve to encourage us, Mr. Grumpy decides to change tactics and give us the cold-shoulder treatment. He'll simply act uninterested, drop his eyes when he spots us, and continue on with his grisly work. Slice, slice, slice. Pull the bone and peel the skin. Chop off the head.

Yum.

Naturally, it's brother Howie's bright idea to step up our psychological warfare on Grumpy the Fish Man. Some paper, a little planning, a big red crayon, and VOILA!! Protest signs are firmly pressed against the plate glass window for Grumpy to read:

FREE THE FISH!

YOU'VE GOT FISH BREATH!

GONE FISHING!

I SMELL SOMETHING FISHY!

SMILE, YOU'RE ON CANDID CAMERA!

THROW IT BACK!

HEY, SQUID FACE!!

This gets Fish Man's attention. Once again he's back to trying to wave us away, gesturing emphatically. And again we hold our ground, press our faces against the glass, and hold up the sign de jour:

SHARK BAIT, $0.19 LB.

FISH MAN, YOU'RE OUR HERO!

HEY, HOW 'BOUT A FISH   HEAD FOR MY CAT?

SORRY, CHARLIE!!

Whenever dumpy Grumpy makes a move for the front door, we're up the street before he can scoot around the counter and reach the sidewalk. In time, poor Fish Man becomes sullen. Humiliated, he avoids looking at us. But we can always tell he's angry by the way he slices those fish. Slice, slice, slice. Faster, *faster*, *FASTER*. Silver scales flying and red Technicolor insides coming out. Once, His Grumpiness tries racing around the counter and lunging for the front door, but we're up to Beaufort Avenue and out of harm's way by the time he's reached 57th Street, waving his ever-present knife. It seems the tormented Fish Man can't win. He is simply destined to put up with our shenanigans until I graduate from Longstreet and mosey along to junior high school, where we'll more than likely begin terrorizing someone else. But in the meantime, my graduation day remains months and months in the distant future.

Then, one cold and sunny day, wiseguy Howie makes one of his nastiest signs to date:

I'D RATHER BE THE GARBAGE MAN. . .

IT STINKS LESS!!

Fish Man glares. If looks could kill, we'd be fish food. Grumpy shakes his fillet knife at us in anger, then goes back to work. Sullen, moody. Slice, slice, slice . . . silver strips of skin flopping everywhere, gross-looking red insides coming out. I give Fish Man a wave. Howie presses his lips against the glass and rakes his fingernails across the window with great effect. Enraged, Grumpy retreats to the storeroom in the rear, seemingly to fetch a new batch of dead fish to gut and slice.

We figure the show for today is over. Slowly we back away from the big window and begin to shuffle on up toward Beaufort Avenue. Not a care in the world, just a pair of happy-go-lucky brothers, school all done for the day.

But just before we reach the alleyway, there comes a blood-curdling scream. We freeze in our tracks, stunned.

Now I've got you, you little devils! booms a maniacal voice. Slowly, a familiar fillet knife appears from the shadows of the alleyway. Next a hand, and then a face. A familiar, fat, fleshy, balding head with a fiendishly unfamiliar smile. Grumpy has faked us out by pretending to go into the storeroom. What he was really doing was hustling out the back door and sneaking up the alley lickety-split. Now we feel like a couple of flounder on Fish Man's well-used cutting board. The man's beady eyes twinkle crazily. Fish Man is more than ready to explode with simmering, pent-up rage.

Fish Man looks a terrible sight, his white apron all soaked with blood and splattered fish guts. The big fillet knife gleams in the afternoon sun. Instinctively I step back, looking to flee. But Howie remains statue-like, transfixed by the blood, the glint of stainless steel, and those twinkling, revenge-minded eyes. My little brother's mouth hangs open like so many of the fish we have seen Grumpy cut and mutilate.

Suddenly, Fish Man lunges forward and grabs Howie by the scruff of the neck. Holds the bloody blade before my brother's freckled little nose. Old Shoelace the Scarface looks cross-eyed at the red-drenched steel just inches away from his tender gullet. Howie's face suddenly goes white like a bowl of vanilla ice cream, his eyes rolling up into his head, and his body falling limp.

I hear someone scream. It is me. I'm shouting, Let him go! Let him go!! We're talking pure 100% panic.

Fish Man's wild eyes flash, and he screeches this crazy, high-pitched laugh. The world stands eerily still for what seems like an

224

eternity. Then, Fish Man pulls the gore-encrusted fillet knife away from Little Brother's Throat and gives Howie a shove toward the street.

See you tomorrow, fellas, he taunts, waving the blade. Stop by any time!

My heart feels as if it's going to beat right out of my chest. Howie is dazed, in shock, and mumbling incoherently. Somehow, I manage to drag Howie halfway up the block. I looked back to see the Fish Man, wiping the bloody blade on one of his apron's few remaining white patches. He seems to be rather enjoying the warm afternoon sun, smiling his first real, honest-to-goodness smile in months.

Needless to say, we never bother Fish Man again. Not ever. Coming home from school we no longer tarry at Fish Man's now infamous corner. And we always stay on the opposite side of the street, keeping our eyes peeled for a fleshy, balding man wielding a gore-covered knife and a seriously dazed expression.

For months after Fish Man's revenge, whenever our family has fish sticks and stewed tomatoes on Fridays, I can't help but think of Fish Man and how he has gotten the last laugh. And he who laughs last, laughs best as they say. So obviously, Grumpy is now in stitches. No doubt he sees us some days, far across the street, slinking by his storefront. Now it's poor Howie and I who have been humiliated, and who are dreading further contact.

Howie and I had escaped with our lives. My mother, seeing the untouched plates of fish sticks and stewed tomatoes, figures we are silently striking for pepperoni pizza. Some kind of coordinated protest against her Catholic no-meat-on-Fridays taboo. Little does she know, for even less do we tell her.

Slice, slice, slice. I wonder if that's how Jack the Ripper got his start way back when? Whatever. All I know is we eat all the macaroni and cheese, but leave the stewed tomatoes and fish sticks. We have tasted our fill of the Fish Man, and may he cut and gut his little fishes in perpetual peace.

Just leave little brother Howie and me out of the equation.

Sorry, Charlie.

CHAPTER 9

College Material

One cold winter evening Mom's in the kitchen with Howie and Laura, while Dad's busy upstairs. I'm alone in the living room watching *Combat!* There's Lieutenant Hanley with his carbine, bayonet, and Colt .45 mixing it up with the Jerries somewhere in France during WWII. Right in the middle of a breathtaking action scene my father comes downstairs, heading for the kitchen. He stops at the TV, turns off the sound. No more *Combat!* for the moment.

Do your homework yet, Jimmy?

Some of it, Dad. Mom said I could watch *Combat!* and then finish the rest.

Jimmy, I want to ask you something important. If you could wish for *one* thing in the whole wide world—what would it be?

This is a weird question, especially coming from Dad. I'm not sure what to pick, because it's something I've never given any thought. You don't get stuff just like magic simply because you want it. If there's some fairy godmother out there somewhere waving around a wand and granting wishes, she's never made a side trip to old Kings Cross near as I can tell.

So I say, Um . . . a vacation to Hawaii, I guess. Sure hope this is the answer Dad's looking for. Saw an advertisement the other day for vacations in Hawaii, and I really liked the idea of spending a week in Honolulu paradise. Especially during a frigid Philadelphia winter. Lying on a hot tropical beach in January, sipping a cold fruity drink. The only time I like winter is when I'm earning money shoveling snow from other people's sidewalks. Otherwise, I'll take summertime in a heartbeat. They say Hawaii has summer twelve months a year. Lucky stiffs.

Dad says, Let me tell you something that's even better than a whole week's vacation to Hawaii.

Yeah, Dad? What's that?

A college degree.

Really?

Yep. And do you know why?

No, Dad . . . why?

Because, Jimmy, if you've got a college degree, then you've got your vacation to Hawaii. Do you understand what I'm saying?

I shrug. No, I don't really understand.

You see, Jimmy, Dad explains, once you've got that college degree, then you can *buy* your trip to Hawaii. Year after year after year. Or a new car, or nice house, or a brand new pair of shiny shoes—or anything else if that's what you really want. That degree's your ticket, Jimmy. Never ever forget that.

Dad doesn't have a college degree.

Now do you understand what I'm saying?

I think so, Dad, I reply. But being a sixth-grader I'm still mostly in the dark.

Don't worry, Dad says. You'll understand better when you're older. Right now, all you've gotta do is one thing . . . keep after your studies. Keep hittin' those books. Keep doing well in school. We'll find a way to get you into college. I promise. Somehow, some way. Okay?

Okay, Dad.

Dad turns the TV sound back up, heads for the kitchen, and I finish watching my thrilling, action-packed episode of the boys from Kings Company. Now that Lieutenant Hanley is done killing his quota of Jerries for the week, I go upstairs and get out the dreaded homework. But I can't concentrate, can't stop thinking about what Dad said.

Something here doesn't add up, doesn't make any sense. The downtown Brimstone service station where Dad works sits right across the street from two universities. Dad sees the college people every day . . . some are even his regular customers. Professors, students, office people—Dad works on all their cars. And the Old Man swears these are some of the dumbest people God ever put on the face of this Earth. Says most don't know their you-know-whats from a hole-in-the ground. Totally hopeless.

The professors are arrogant, nerdy, nincompoop know-it-alls who, for all their great theories and ideas and studies, can hardly tell you the time of day nor which end is up. The office people shuffle paper, push pencils, avoid hard work like the plague, move at glacial speed, and are the laziest group of slugs this side of the employees down at Philadelphia's City Hall. And the students? Well, they're the worst of all. Generally, the college kids all have rotten manners, exhibit no more common sense than a head of cabbage, and probably need assistance with wiping their own bottoms. How anything of real importance or value is ever taught much less learned at these universities is a complete mystery to my father.

Dad's prevailing theory is that colleges serve as a sort of dumping ground for society's misfits. Allergic to hard labor? Sign on at the university. Can't cut it in the real world, solve real problems, get real results? There's a spot for you on the faculty. Listen to weird music, wear strange clothes, sport an outlandish hairdo, talk bizarre politics? You'll fit right in on campus.

And so far as all their great experiments, studies, analysis, and research is concerned, Dad says the college crowd needn't bother. They'd get it right by a far higher percentage by just flipping a coin, and it would save them a great deal of time and trouble. These academic types are like a bunch of house cats chasing their own tails . . . a flurry of activity and great fun to watch, but when all is said and done, nothing much gets accomplished, and they predictably wind up right back in the very place they started.

The Old Man says that no matter what the subject, the college folks who drop in from across the street are sure to take the wrong end of any argument. Guaranteed. So take away their books and classes and laboratories, and let 'em flip a coin when it comes right down to making a decision. At least this would ensure they'd probably get it right close to half the time . . . although with the college types you never know, because they'd find a way to botch this completely—even something as simple as a coin toss. It's like watching the *Wizard of Oz*, where the scarecrow's got straw stuffed between his ears, but someone hands him a piece of paper that says DIPLOMA, so now everyone assumes the dimwit must have a brain . . . after all, he's college educated.

One of Dad's favorite customers, this big-shot professor with a wall full of diplomas, couldn't get his car started on one of the coldest nights of the year. So, instead of looking under the hood and discovering the loose battery terminal that could've been tightened by hand in a jiffy, Professor Genius lights his pipe, curls up inside the car on the middle of the campus parking lot, falls asleep, and nearly freezes to death. Later, when my father asks the good professor why he didn't think to check under the hood, Mr. I.Q. has a most profound answer. He says, That's what I pay other people to do. Dad thinks a wind chill of fifteen below zero would motivate any relatively sane person to at least have a look-see. But, says Pop, what do I know? Hey, I'm just a mechanic, that's all.

Basically as far as the Old Man is concerned, they're doing the country a great service by identifying and segregating all the oddballs, goldbrickers, incompetents, and chronic malcontents. Better just to stick them off by themselves in this place called "college" so they won't be getting in the way of normal, productive people doing all the necessary work that makes the world go 'round. Otherwise, if you let these looney-tunes have the general run of the everyday world, there's no telling what kinds of destruction they may cause if left unchecked. And, Lord knows, working people already have enough problems to contend with, thank you very much. So, by all means, keep these goobers on campus and off the road, and let working people be.

Dad says, if a person really wants to get an education, have a look at the way the real world works, there are far better options than college. For instance, such a person could join the Army— the way Uncle Hank did in the Korean War. Or maybe even see the world from an oil tanker, the way Pop did just out of high school by signing up with the merchant marine. Of course, that's not an option these days, with Our Majesty John Kennedy having put his John Hancock on treaties that sunk our once-proud merchant navy forever. Sheer lunacy. And who do you suppose is going to be delivering the baked beans and toilet paper for the next war, let alone the precious oil? It borders on treason, it does.

Yes sir, it's a safe bet that anyone planning on college is looking for an easy life, something for nothing, and the chance to skate through adulthood without doing a single, solitary day of honest work. Not a lick.

Which all makes me start to wonder why Dad has now pegged me for a college boy. Sure, fractions and long division have sometimes stumped me. And Dad's biggest complaint about James Morris Jr. is my laziness. Every single teacher I've ever had says I don't concentrate, don't work up to potential. But have things gotten to the point that maybe Dad's decided I won't be able to cut it in a real job? That I'll never be able to do an honest day's work as long as I live? Never drive a nail, fix a flat, or shine my own shoes? Have I become such a hopeless case that I'll need to be separated from normal working folks for my very own good . . . not to mention for the good of society at large?

I'm curious, so I decide to run this college thing past Mom, who's now finishing up in the kitchen.

Mom, I was wondering, do you think I should go to college?

Of course, Jimmy.

But what if I want to do something else?

Nonsense. You've got the brains for college. Why not go?

Well, what if I just don't want to?

Then I'll break both your legs, Mom warns. You're going to college, and that's final. Did you finish your homework?

I guess this means my parents are serious—about me going to college that is, not about breaking both my legs.

Still, I don't know much about this college stuff . . . I've never even seen one except to drive past. But I guess what all this means is I'll be going, whatever that involves.

You know something funny? I always did wonder what it'd be like to smoke a pipe. Pipes look sharp, and they smell pretty good, too. Way better than cigarettes.

Professor Jimmy Morris. Hate to admit it, but I think I like the way that rolls off the tip of my tongue. Now all I have to do is find some important-sounding subject I can study to go with the impressive title. Nothing, of course, that'll get my hands dirty, you understand. . . .

Alphabet Soup

His name is Gregory Zyglowicz, but everyone in the sixth grade calls him Greg, or simply Alphabet. Alphabet is a big, husky kid . . . not so large or strong as Sherman Sykes, but sizeable enough. I don't know how it starts, but somewhere, somehow the bad blood between Alphabet and me begins. A misinterpreted glance here, an accidental bump there. Out on the playground, I can sense that Alphabet is looking for a fight. Why with me, I don't know. But I've got my rep, despite the Petey Ianelli disaster in fifth grade, and I can't let Alphabet push me around, regardless of his size.

One day I'm at recess, minding my own business, when I happen to stroll by Alphabet and a few of his friends. They're in line playing hopscotch or something dumb, and I'm heading for the kickball contest at the far side of the yard. As I go by I catch Alphabet giving me the stare. So I slow down, stare right back. Alphabet replies by making a face and crossing his peepers . . . he's obviously making fun of my lazy eye. The eye doctors say this strabismus thing will one day require yet another operation.

I make a face at pudgy Gregory in return, puff up my cheeks. Referring to Alphabet's not-so-svelte physique, I call him Mr. Pork and Beans, to which he takes exception.

Buzz off, Four Eyes.

Drop dead, Alphabet.

Wanna make somethin' of it?

Hey, it's your funeral, Pork and Beans.

With that we're in each other's face, first bumping, then pushing. But this is a losing bet for skinny little me. No way can I match Mr. Pork and Beans in a shoving contest . . . pretty soon I'm going to find myself sprawled across the concrete, with Gregory sitting on my chest, then Longstreet's entire sixth grade will be laughing at me. So I escalate matters—by hauling off and socking Alphabet in his fat kisser. Next thing you know we're grappling and tussling, and I can hear the entire schoolyard full of kids come running in our direction.

Holding on for dear life, I try to break free so I can sock Alphabet some more. But Zyglowicz is very strong and won't let go. He gets me off balance, tries to swing me around and toss me like a rag doll. I bang my knee hard on the cement but refuse to go down, hanging on like a terrier. We stumble into the brick wall by the entrance to the fire escape. Kids are crowding around, cheering and screaming and jostling for a better view. Cheap entertainment until a teacher comes along and breaks us up.

Alphabet tries to slam me against the wall, but I brace myself and don't get hurt. Frantically, I try pushing Pork and Beans away, but can't. But while I'm shoving and tugging, I see an opening. Zyglowicz is leaning forward, arms extended, pushing, his jacket loose and bunched around his shoulders. Quickly I grab a handful of material and yank for all I'm worth, pulling the jacket's collar up over Alphabet's thick noggin.

Hey, who turned out the lights?

Instinctively, Alphabet lets go of me and tries to pull down his garment. Wrong move, Mr. Pork and Beans.

Wham, wham, wham. Now I'm popping my defenseless adversary square on his covered-up but still ugly head. Sightless, Zyglowicz tries to duck and turn away, but instead falls into the wall.

A few well-placed shots to the skull and old Mr. Pork and Beans will never dare cross his eyes at me again. I take a half-step back, wind up with my Sunday punch, then step forward for the kill.

But before I can throw the coup de grace, someone from behind grabs my arm. Alphabet's friends coming to his rescue in a fair one?

Enraged, adrenaline already pumping to the max, I spin and lash out. Again and again. Roundhouse right, roundhouse left. I feel the meddler's grasp loosen . . . step back to admire my handiwork—poised to strike again.

Longstreet's new fourth-grade teacher, Miss Townsend, is standing there all disheveled, long brown hair messily out of place. Her head is down, and she's holding the side of her pretty face where I just bopped her a good one.

I mutter, Miss . . . Miss . . . Miss T-Townsend. I'm, I'm sorry!

Teacher steadies herself, collects her composure. *To the office*! she barks.

I hear the sound of a hundred children, in unison, say . . . Ooooooooooooooh!

James Morris is in *t r o u b l e* now.

He's going to be suspended! He's going to get expelled! They're going to send him to Kardo!!

Mrs. Glass, our principal, arrives, along with several other teachers and various members of the Longstreet constabulary. Someone seizes me roughly by the shoulder, and I'm quickly whisked inside the building toward the now-familiar principal's office. To the place that has a chair with my name on it—and another for my buddy from the Dobbs Creek Orphanage, Sherman "Tank" Sykes.

Friends, enemies, boys, girls, teachers, secretaries, big kids, little kids . . . they all look at me with the same pitiful expression. A strange look of morbid curiosity mixed with shock and revulsion. They stare, then look away, shaking their heads in disgust.

Can you believe it? Hitting a *teacher*?? How awful. . . .

It's the unpardonable sin, the most basic of taboos. Even worse than Catholics eating meat on Fridays.

Mrs. Glass tells her secretary, Call his mother . . . you have the number. Then brings me into her office where I'm told to sit. Soon we're joined by the school psychologist, both women now looking at me as if I'm some kind of caveman just captured and brought in from the jungle.

Why did you hit the teacher, James?

My scratchy voice cracking, But I didn't know it was a teacher . . . honest!

But you hit her more than once . . . how could you not know?

I was turned around. She grabbed me. I thought it was the other boy's friends, and I was scared.

Why were you fighting, James?

It was Gregory Zyglowicz's fault. He started it.

The other boy hit you first?

Well no, not exactly.

You hit him first?

Yes.

Why, James?

Because he looked at me!

He looked at you?

Uh-huh. He looked at me funny!

Alphabet isn't the only one looking at me funny today. The principal and then psychologist are both looking at me like I'm some kind of Martian just off the spaceship. They'll never understand. Never.

And now I'm definitely going to be suspended. Maybe expelled. Perhaps even sent to that lunatic asylum they call Kardo. It's where they dump all the school district's hard cases, the worst of the worst. Named after Caesar Kardo, a black man from Philadelphia during the Revolutionary War days. When the British attacked Germantown in what is now Philadelphia's northwest corner, the illustrious Caesar Kardo picked up his trusty slingshot and fired some rocks at the advancing Redcoats. He got a musket ball right between the eyes for his troubles. And so now they've got this school for bad kids named after him.

Some consolation prize that is.

Maybe this time the Longstreet School's had enough of James Morris, and now I'm about to get it right between the eyes. POW, to the moon.

I probably won't be the first student ever from Longstreet sent to Kardo—the teachers are always threatening me, Sherm, and some of the others with it. But I imagine I'll be the first ever to go to Kardo straight out of the advanced reading group, the one with all the nice Jewish girls and Bubblehead Phillip Buckley.

Mrs. O'Shaughnessy's going to be really disappointed when she hears about this. Teacher's pet really let her down big time today. So much for her special fourth- and fifth-grade project. Looks like I'm going to be history before the sixth grade graduates, earning that one-way ticket to the Bad Boys School.

This hole I've dug's so deep I'm never going to climb out.

Sure enough, I'm suspended for three days. And grounded at home for a month—no TV, no movies, no out, no nothing. Luckily they're not expelling me, but a big parent-teacher conference is scheduled before I'm allowed to return. I've had parent-teacher conferences since the first grade, Mom is a regular visitor here for both me and little brother Howie. But this time I know they're serious. . . .

They even make Dad attend the conference. Guess there's a first time for everything.

So Mom is there looking concerned, Dad is looking glum in his Brimstone mechanic's overalls, and the Longstreet constabulary is acting as if they've had to put up with six straight years of John Dillinger Jr. It's all there in the file . . . teachers' reports, the biting incident in first grade, the playground scrapes, the practical jokes, the pea-shooters, the spitballs in class, the clowning around, the daydreaming and not paying attention, the prior suspensions, my illustrious campaign for dogcatcher in our class elections, the typical James Morris escapades, the everything.

Dad's face burns red, and I see him wince.

But Longstreet is going to give me one more, and they stress *one* more, final chance.

Outside in the hallway, Dad pulls me aside. Shakes a finger in my face, and I'm glad we're standing in the school, or else I could be catching worse.

Things are going to change, Dad says firmly, eyeballs just inches from mine. You got that, Jimmy? This nonsense stops here.

No more mention of college. But I guess that's where I'm still headed. They'll never let me have a real job, like fixing trolleys, painting buildings, or driving a delivery truck. Not with my record, anyway.

It's off to college with me, where they'll make me into a professor and lock me away in some dusty office where I can shuffle papers, smoke a pipe, and contemplate great theories at which normal people will laugh hysterically because they're so absurd and utterly useless. This must be my fate, because if I were allowed to do any real work, I'd only make a mess of things, and then somebody would have to get paid to come along and clean everything up.

But if I'm only allowed to shuffle papers, smoke a pipe, and think great thoughts, surely no harm can come to anyone from that. Then, maybe the trolleys will continue to run, the buildings will get painted properly, and all the stores will get their deliveries.

Then one cold night I'll go out to start my car at the university, but it won't run, and I'll have to spend the night freezing inside it because I don't have the common sense to fix anything.

And the next morning all the mechanics, firemen, carpenters, electricians, plumbers, steamfitters, and deliverymen will be laughing themselves silly, because the great professor James Morris Jr. was too dumb to tighten the battery cable or some-such part and nearly froze his sorry toucas sitting there like a clueless nincompoop.

A sad, sad case indeed.

Falling for Rachel

Rachel Moskowitz, one of the girls from last year's advanced reading group, sits next to me in Miss Silverman's sixth-grade class. She's not like the other sixth-grade girls, all stuck up and bossy, looking down their very grown-up noses at any sixth-grade boy. You can talk to Rachel almost as if she's a normal person. Sometimes that's just what I do while Rachel and I are waiting for the teacher to begin the lesson.

Rachel's a large girl for sixth grade and very smart. She has big brown eyes, long dark hair, freckles, and smiles a lot. Everybody in our class seems to like Rachel because she is easygoing, acts very mature, and is usually very nice. Unfortunately, I cannot say the same thing for Claire Miller, old Horse Face herself. I can only wish that Claire someday transfers out to another school. Then I will organize a party with cake and ice cream for our entire class.

Rachel's favorite thing in the whole world is The Beatles, and she collects all of their records. I pretend to like The Beatles more than I really do, so that Rachel and I will always have something in common to talk about. To tell you the truth, I like The Beach Boys and Herman's Hermits way better. Making friends with a girl seems to have different rules, and I'm just trying my best not to mess up.

Way back in second or third grade, when I was just a little kid, I had sort of a crush on tiny Janet Bennett. Best guess would be this was because of Janet's pretty blonde hair, because she wore glasses same as me, and because she was one of the very few girls in my grade who wasn't taller than me. Janet never figured out I had a crush, mostly because I never told her. Chucked a snowball at her once, but that probably doesn't count. Anyway, the more I got to know Janet, the less I liked her. She whined a lot and usually acted real dopey and immature. Then, after a while, I realized I didn't have a crush on Janet Bennett any more. This girl's still around, in Miss Silverman's class with Rachel and me, but I no longer pay her any mind. Janet, in my book, is history.

But Rachel with her big, brown eyes and warm smile is different. I think maybe now I have a crush on Rachel instead.

One day I'm stopping to buy a chocolate bar for myself on the way to school, and it crosses my mind that maybe Rachel might like some chocolate, too. So I spend my last dime and buy her a Hershey's bar. I wrap it up in a note that says I HAD AN EXTRA CHOCOLATE BAR TODAY AND THOUGHT YOU WOULD LIKE IT. . . . JAMES.

Next day when I come to school there's a Mallo Cup on my desk with a letter. THANK YOU, JAMES, FOR THE CHOCOLATE BAR. THAT WAS VERY NICE. . . . RACHEL. Mallo Cup is about my very favorite candy, next to Chunky. Creamy marshmallow inside, milk chocolate outside, gourmet delicious. How did Rachel know this? I think I am in love.

Rachel lives up on 56th and Meadows Avenue, two blocks east of Longstreet Elementary. I live south of the school. But now I'm noticing that once in a while Rachel walks south after school, same direction as me. So one day I see her up ahead and hurry to catch up. I ask Rachel, Where are you going? Rachel tells me she's going to the Jewish school on 57th and Beaufort, practically on the next block from me. She goes to special Hebrew classes one day a week, and shows me her Hebrew books. They're full of all these squiggles, dots, and funny little lines, and I can't make heads nor tails out of any of it. Looks more like a book full of musical notes than pages of words and lessons.

Rachel explains how Hebrew is the ancient language of the Jewish people, very old and very sacred. That sounds fine by me, but what I don't understand is why they just don't translate the entire mess into English, like they do with The Bible. Certainly putting it in English would make things a whole bunch easier on Jewish kids such as Rachel, who then wouldn't have to learn all this Secret Agent Man code with the funny lines and squiggles going in every which way that regular people can't read.

The Jewish people have some other funny deals going on, too, like the strange foods only they can eat. Lox and bagels, gefilte fish, and matzo bread for starters. I even heard that somebody's grandmother up in New York City keeps live carp swimming around in her bathtub—I mean, what's the story with that? Mr. Lerner, the man next door to Grandmom, once gave me a piece of matzo bread at Passover, which is the same week as Easter, only the Jewish people don't celebrate Easter. So it's all kind of confusing and mixed up. . . .

Mr. Lerner's matzo bread wasn't too bad, but it was very dry and stuck to the roof of my mouth. Maybe I prefer good old Bond bread just the same. Especially when you put on some good ol' bologna, liverwurst, or tuna fish.

Of course I like Jewish pickles, the kind the Nolans keep in the big, dark, wooden barrel in their corner store. But everyone in our neighborhood puts the Jewish pickles on their sandwiches, so I guess that's different. Don't ask me why, it just is.

Meanwhile, every week Rachel and I sort of have a date. I walk her to the Jewish school on Beaufort where she spends the afternoon studying the sacred text of Israel. Then I continue home

238

to play boxball with Donnie, Jackie, Howie, Frankie, Larry, and all the rest of our Littlefield gang. I figure it must be extra hard being a Jewish kid, going to school twice in the same day and having to learn things in both English and Hebrew. And when the Jewish kids aren't going to Hebrew school, they're off somewhere taking lessons on the clarinet, violin, tuba, cello, or some other such musical instrument. Always something to study and learn.

Makes me very glad to be a Gentile. We Gentiles just say a few short prayers and then go about our merry way. And I'll take playing stickball over playing the cello any day. Never played the cello, but I'm sure I'd prefer stickball just the same.

Soon I'm carrying Rachel's Hebrew books and we talk and laugh all the way to 57th and Beaufort. Did I mention she has really big, brown eyes? Something tells me that Rachel is beginning to like me, despite my reputation for being a scrapper.

Then, it happens. I'm walking Rachel to the Hebrew school, same as usual. We've got less than a block further to go, and I decide to take a chance. For some time now I've been thinking about holding her hand, same as in The Beatles song she likes so much. Only I haven't been able to work up the courage—until today.

It's sunny afternoon. Rachel is smiling. The whole world seems to be smiling. We're just walking, talking . . . same as always. And so I just do it. Reach over, hold her hand . . . like it's no big deal. My heart is pounding and I've got the goose bumps, but I try to act real cool and nonchalant. Like I do this all the time.

Rachel pulls her hand away and comes to a dead stop in the middle of the sidewalk, sudden mad look and big, brown eyes squinting.

What do you think you're doing, James?

Flustered, I pull away too, feeling my face and ears starting to burn red. The absolute height of embarrassment. Not the foggiest as to what to say next. But Rachael does.

My mother warned me about boys like you!

Standing there like a complete dummy, I don't have the faint-est clue as to her mother's warning. All I did was try to hold Rachel's hand. Didn't know this might be a bad thing.

What happens next confuses me even further. Imitating a place kicker in a football game, Rachel steps back, runs up, and POW! Boots me squarely in the shinbone.

Oooowww!

I immediately drop her Hebrew book and papers all over the pavement, grab my aching shinbone, and proceed to hop around on one foot like a funny man in a bad comedy.

Hey, Rachel, what did you do that for?

Rachel's immediate reply is to back up again, run forward, and give me another swift kick . . . this time to my one remaining good leg. Left without a leg to stand on, I collapse to the sidewalk in a jumbled heap of pain.

Yes, I have clearly fallen for Rachel . . . although not quite in the manner I had expected. In a matter of seconds Rachel is scooping up her Hebrew text and papers with all their squiggly bars, dots, and lines of ancient, sacred code. I now realize that Rachel may be even harder to read than her incomprehensible books.

Rachel gives me a curt, Hmmpphh! Then, turning away, throws her curly dark hair over her shoulder and marches smartly off toward the entrance of the mysterious Hebrew school.

I sit there, totally dumbfounded, rubbing my sore shins, watching Rachel as she disappears into the flat brick building for an afternoon of learning some five-thousand-year-old language.

And mazeltov to you, too, Rachel Moskowitz!

After a few moments I get up—gingerly—and limp the short distance to my house. There's some question as to whether I'll be able to participate in our street's daily game of boxball, but after a short while I recover, go outside, and take my customary position in the game.

Next day, my legs are feeling much, much better, but I'm still smarting on the inside. No telling what the repercussions will be at school, if any. It doesn't take me long to find out. Every sixth-grade girl I see points and giggles until she's laughed herself silly. Rachel has blabbed, and now everyone knows—if not firsthand, then at least through the tangled Longstreet grapevine. Talk about your supreme humiliation. I might as well be wearing a sign that says KICK ME.

Horse-faced Claire Miller is by far the worst with all her taunts and snickers. I can forget about walking any other girl home. I'll never, ever, live this one down. Where did I go wrong? What did I do to deserve this?

Rachel sees me as I slide into my seat next to her in Miss Silverman's class. She simply turns away, tosses her dark hair, and puts her freckled nose in the air.

Another "Hmmpphh!!" is all I get. Take that, James Morris.

Strange. I wonder if all this hype about girls is really all that it's cracked up to be. Seems like maybe they're far more trouble than they're worth. At least that's my theory, anyway.

Very weird. Like dealing with aliens from another planet. All I did was hold her hand. And what kind of boy was Rachel's mother warning her about? I wonder why other kids don't have these kinds of problems. Certainly, when it comes to girls, I must be a real dummy.

Jeez. . . .

And I still say The Beach Boys are better than those dumb Beatles. Way better.

A Standup Guy

We're at recess out on the schoolyard, just another sixth-grade day. The girls are busy at their hopscotch and jump rope. A group of colored boys are on the court shooting baskets. The rest of us are divided between wallball, sock-it-out, hanging out under the open-air pavilion, or just aimlessly wandering our sloping expanse of fenced-in concrete.

Suddenly a pimple ball squirts by one of the wallball participants. The boy turns to give chase, his eyes focused dead ahead on his rolling quarry. A split second later one of the hoopsters fires an errant pass, which sails past the outstretched fingertips of the intended recipient. This second boy also wheels around, intent on tracking down the basketball.

Tunnel vision. Neither kid sees the other until it's too late. BANG! A minor collision occurs, nothing serious. The black boy spins, stumbles, regains his balance. Now he's glaring at the back of the white boy who's continuing on to retrieve the still-rolling tennis-sized pimple ball before it squirts under the wrought iron fence and out into Partridge Street. New pimple balls cost 15 cents, a hefty investment, and unlike the basketball they don't belong to the school. Gotta bring your own.

Nobody's allowed off the playground for any reason, it's Longstreet's number one recess rule.

One of the other black kids calls to a passerby near the pavilion. Yo—little help? Somebody scoops up the wayward basketball, bounces it back toward the court.

Meanwhile, the black boy who got bumped continues his hostile stare . . . shouts, Hey! Why don't you watch where you're goin', man?

Sorry, apologizes the white boy as he returns toward the basketball court, 15-cent pimple ball in hand. His name is Larry Lawrence, just a regular guy in Miss Silverman's sixth-grade class. Someone I once beat up on the schoolyard in fifth grade, but we're on good terms again. Not best buddies, but friendly.

I'm a player in the wallball game, too, standing idly around with the others waiting for Larry to bring back the ball. Leaning against the brick wall at the back of the supermarket down the far end of our playground. Watching as Larry passes the semicircle at the top of the key, right near where all the colored boys are standing.

Then it happens. The black boy who's still miffed scoots over and shoves Larry in the back—hard. Sends Larry hurtling, he almost falls flat on his face.

Larry catches himself, turns, and tries to protest, red-faced. Hey, kid! I said I was sorry!

Shut your mouth, snaps the black boy. Else I'll shut it for you.

Larry just stands there, mouth open. Not a clue as to what to say next. Doesn't want to retreat but doesn't want to fight. He's trapped in no man's land. Heads are beginning to turn, eyes watching.

The black boy takes offense at Larry standing there, mouth hanging open.

What, you got a problem, man? The kid strides up, gets in Larry's face, next gives him a shove from the front.

Larry yells, Quit it! He's standing his ground, but not fighting back.

Yeah? Who gonna make me, chump?

My feet are now moving under me. I come up besides Larry, show of force. Next time the black boy is going to have to push both of us.

The circle of black boys are staring back: all smiles and one mean face ready for a scrap.

I say, Leave him alone. It was just an accident—he said he was sorry.

The one with the angry face snarls. So who asked you, Four Eyes?

I answer, Nobody asked me. . . . Nobody had to. Feel my ears doing the sudden burn.

Then bug off, Four Eyes!

By now I'm wondering when some backup is coming. Sherm, Petey Ianelli, the other kids in the wallball game. Somebody around here with a pale face besides me and Larry. Anybody.

The angry black boy steps forward, chin out. I step closer, remaining defiant.

One of the basketballers shouts his encouragement. You ain't gotta take nothin' from him, Troy. Go ahead, beat his butt!

As if on command, Troy steps closer and gives me a push. I immediately respond in kind.

Get him, Troy!

Troy hauls off and throws a big sweeping roundhouse right. I see it coming and duck. Pop back up and throw my own counterpunch haymaker with Troy off balance.

Smack! Troy goes down on one knee holding his fat mouth, face distorted in pain.

Kids are running over to watch. Close, but not too close. I look up, look down. Troy is doing his best not to cry, all the while threatening to get me, hurt me, kill me.

I look up again, see these black faces gathering around. Closing in. White faces way out on the edge looking confused and nervous. Why isn't anyone helping me or Larry? There's far more of us, fewer of them.

But we're standing there all alone, just the two of us—encircled and outnumbered.

All the smiles are gone. The group's biggest black boy gets right in my face. Looks down on me sneering, glaring, jaw tightly clenched.

Why you do that, man? Why you hit my boy?

He pushed me first, then swung on me. What was I supposed to do?

Someone out of view says, Get him, Darnell! Smack his face!!

I can't understand—*Why isn't anyone coming to help??*

Darnell and I lock eyes. He's got a mean, cold, hardened look. Nothing like Coleman James or Dré Barnett. And he's so, *so* much bigger than me . . . wonder how many grades this boy's been left back. Maybe if we were closer in size, I'd have a chance in a punchout. Try to land a lucky shot. But this time I'm in over my head. Way over.

Darnell is bumping against me now, chest out, I can feel his hot breath. Our eyes still locked, I'm waiting for him to make the move. Maybe I can get in a quick shot or two before a teacher comes and breaks us up. It's my only chance. Nobody else is stepping up.

C'mon, Darnell! Mess him up!!

One second in eternity. Two seconds. . . .

I *really* hate myself for being so small.

BBBBRRRRIIIINNNGGGGG!!!

School bell—recess is over. Time to head inside. The white kids on the outside of the circle move first. Then some of the black boys on the inside shuffle away. Troy is up now, dabbing at his mouth. Larry Lawrence has since slinked off to only God knows where.

Slowly, reluctantly the crowd breaks up. As if by a magnet, kids are being drawn toward the school entrance. Looking back, over their shoulders, not wanting to miss any action. You can't help but look when somebody's getting pounded, it's like rubbernecking at a car wreck.

Thirty kids, twenty, ten, five, three, two. . . .

Finally it's just Darnell and me, staring and staring. Nobody moving. *High Noon* at Longstreet Elementary.

Someone calls out, C'mon Darnell. Three of his buddies are still hanging back, halfway in school and halfway out, waiting.

Eventually, Darnell turns and starts to trudge back toward the doors. Swivels, throws me one long, last dirty look over his shoulder. Then he and all the black boys disappear inside.

I stand there silently in the now empty schoolyard. Heart pounding, chest heaving. Watching the now ominous school entrance. After two or three minutes, I sneak over, slide as quietly as possible through my usual door, eyes darting around. Expecting an ambush in the stairwell, loads of colored boys jumping up and swinging.

Nothing. The stairwell is empty. Everyone's already in their classrooms, colored boys included. Now I'm going to catch it from Miss Silverman. Climbing the stairway I quickly make up a story about finding a glove and returning it to the Lost and Found. Nothing original, but it's the best I can do on such short notice.

After school we're in the cloakroom collecting coats and kids are coming up to me with smiles, patting me on the back.

Attaboy, James. Way to go. That was really brave the way you stood up.

I'm smiling too. It feels good to regain some of the rep I lost back in fifth grade when Petey Ianelli knocked me flat with just three punches. Now I'm Bad Man on the Playground again, you'd better give Crazy James some room.

Then one of the wallball players starts patting me on the back as well, and I'm getting testy again. Hey, how come you didn't help me? Where were you when I needed you?

The boy drops his eyes, all flustered and apologetic. Sorry, James. You were doing OK, and I didn't want to start any trouble.

Yeah, agrees a second boy. You gotta be careful with those colored kids. You never know what they're gonna do.

That weekend, back on Littlefield Street, I recount for Jackie O'Hanlon and Diet Donnie Fahey the details of my brush with the gang of boys from the mostly colored class.

Figures, snorts Diet Donnie. Them Jewish kids won't fight—they'll punk out every time. All the wieners go to public school. You should get your mom and dad to transfer you to Catholic school with us.

Donnie's right, adds Bugs O'Hanlon. We don't have many rugheads in our school. And the ones we've got aren't any problem. Besides, the minute they started something down at OLPP, we'd finish it. They'd be crazy to even try.

Guess that's one point in favor of Catholic school. I sure don't like the thought of having to face down Darnell and his goons all by my lonesome. But from all I've heard, Catholic school is no picnic either. Nuns in penguin suits smacking kids with rulers, making them write 500 times *I will not lose my copybook ever again*. A hundred kids or more to a classroom, including just about all of our neighborhood's hardest cases. All the real JDs go there. The girls all have to dress in scarlet uniforms with white collars, and the boys are all duded up in dress shirts and ties. Copy this, copy that, memorize this, memorize that, never any time for art or reading stories. It goes beyond strict—I even hear they take homeroom attendance at Mass on Sunday. Can you believe it?

Wow, what kind of school is *that*? Yet Jackie and Diet Donnie say they wouldn't think about going anywhere else. Same with Bobby Schaeffer, Tutti Frutti Pellegrino, and lots of other kids in Kings Cross.

Well, I guess it doesn't matter anyhow. I'm never setting foot in Catholic school, period. Not with the kinds of things my father says about The Pope, Wednesday night Bingo, all the money collecting they do at Mass, the 50-50 chances they sell, Confession, the situation in Northern Ireland, no meat on Fridays, and a dozen other papal conspiracies they're always cooking up in Rome at this secret command post they call The Vatican.

Anyway, as it turns out, Darnell, Troy, and the other colored kids don't give me any more problems except for the occasional funny look. In fact, one day at recess I happen to overhear two of the black boys talking. One says, Is that him? The one with the green shirt? And the other boy replies, No, not *him*—*that* one, the little white boy wearing the glasses. Don't mess with him . . . he don't look like much but the boy's got some heavy hands.

I like it. Maybe I could paste some kind of sign above my hook on the cloakroom wall:

JAMES MORRIS

Little white boy with the heavy hands.

Has a certain sort of ring to it, don't you think?

If there's any more trouble, maybe I can borrow some of the Catholic schoolers as a loaner.

Surely Diet Donnie would know who to ask. Bugs, too.

A Day in the Park

I've got my flashlight with new batteries and a handy mayonnaise jar, I'm ready for a spider hunt. Over to Dobbs Creek Park, spring in the air, summer not far behind. Checking the culverts, the hollowed-out trees, the holes in the massive bridge wall beside the stream. Gonna find me a monster spider, this summer's champion, one that'll eat all the other guys' spiders for lunch. The Godzilla of arachnids.

Don't have too much luck under the bridge, so on a hunch I decide to try the campgrounds in the upper section of the park. Up north just below the suburban train line and Maryland Avenue.

They've got some old stone buildings used by the summer day camps that don't open until after school lets out for the year.

Just as I approach the main stone building, a boy comes into view. He's crossing the playing field, heading in my direction, tossing a football one hand to the other, back and forth, back and forth.

He's a black boy, and that could spell trouble. But I don't see anyone with him, or anyone else around, so I go about my business as I case the stone headquarters wall for shiny new cobwebs. Pretend not to notice the kid coming, but keep a wary eye on him just to be safe. Closer, closer . . . something familiar in the way he walks, where have I seen him before?

Another couple of steps, then . . . *recognition*. Of course! Sigh of relief, it's my longtime classmate Coleman James from Longstreet Elementary. The quiet, shy kid who's got his first name last and last name first.

I sing out, Hey, Coleman! Over here!!

Soon Coleman is tagging along on my spider expedition. I show him where the spiders like to hide, how they spin their webs, what they like to eat. All the basics.

Underneath a window sill I nab a newly molted adult with long slender legs. This one's a keeper, but is definitely going to need fattening up with juicy flies. The remains of the discarded old skin still cling against the hiding spot, you can count the eight legs. Looks like a rumpled pair of tan-colored spider pajamas.

Carefully I handle my prize catch in cupped hands as Coleman wrinkles his face in disgust.

You sure that thing's not gonna bite? It might be poisonous—you know, like maybe a black widow.

I explain to Coleman that Philadelphia is too cold for black widows, and how I've never seen one in all my years of spider hunting. And how black widows have big red hourglasses on the undersides of their bellies, you can't miss 'em. These ones I'm catching are just plain, old, everyday, garden-variety house spiders. They aren't poisonous, can't even see you, and aren't even capable of biting through a person's skin.

If you never saw a black widow before, Coleman prods, how can you be so sure what they look like?

Books, I tell Coleman. I've studied lots of pictures.

I find a second spider, cradle my hand, scoop it out of the web. Put it down on the ground, watch it crawl. Like magic I pick this one up by the invisible strand of silk all house spiders trail behind. Play out the dragline, make it go up and down like a Duncan yo-yo on its string. Haven't figured out yet how to do the sleeper or a walk-the-dog maneuver with a spider on the end of the thread, but I keep trying.

After some time, Coleman tires of the spider show, guess it's an acquired hobby people don't take to right away. So I put aside my flashlight and mayonnaise jar for a chance to toss around Coleman's football.

After a few minutes of lobbing the pigskin, two things are obvious. First, Coleman has better hands for catching the ball. And second, I've got a better arm for throwing it. Soon I've got Coleman running pass patterns, with me impersonating an NFL quarterback, dropping back and firing.

Next, I'm playing the punter, booting the ball to Coleman who's the return man. With the whole grassy field to ourselves there's no way I'm catching Coleman—he's got slippery moves and speed to burn. Sometimes he slows down and lets me get close, then steps on the gas before I can zero in for the two-handed tag. He's good and makes it look so easy.

Winded, Coleman and I take a break seated under the park's jungle gym, iron bars overhead. We talk, laugh, stretch out, watch the white puffs of clouds drift by. Coleman has been in my class since the second grade, but this is the first I've ever spent any real time with him. Before today he was always just the quiet black kid on the other side of the room. Now, after all these years at Longstreet, Coleman has become my friend in one short afternoon. All by accident. Funny how some things work out.

Eventually I grow restless sitting under the jungle gym. Jump up, grasp the horizontal bar overhead, do some chin-ups. Now I'm showing off, still embarrassed by Coleman's speed to burn. Coleman smiles his big pearly white smile, decides to join me. Swings on the bar, tries to match me chin-up for chin-up. But it's no use—Coleman may have the flashy quickness, but I've got the edge in strength. Maybe it's because I'm always practicing on the low-hanging tree limb in Gram's yard over on 61st by the B&O railroad tracks.

Coleman drops from the bar, exhausted, shaking fatigue from his arms. With a surge of adrenaline, my arms and shoulders burning, I manage to do three more chins before releasing and falling to Earth. Plop!

Listen, James, says Coleman, I've gotta be going. I promised my mother I'd be home by four-thirty.

Guess I'll see you in school on Monday.

Okay, James.

Hey, Coleman. . . .

Yeah?

We're not in school, you know. You can call me Jimmy. All my friends call me Jimmy.

Okay, James.

This makes me laugh. Coleman isn't trying to be funny, which makes what he's just said all the more laughable.

Coleman, don't you have a nickname? How about Cole, or maybe CJ?

No, my new buddy says. Just Coleman.

Well then, see you Monday.

Okay, James. . . . I mean, Jimmy.

It occurs to me later that some of the other colored kids I've known don't have nicknames, either. Dré is sort of the exception. One boy I know is Thomas. Not Tom, or Tommy—just Thomas. Another is Robert. Not Rob, Bob, or Bobby. On Littlefield Street, we have Bobby, Jackie, Johnny, Frankie, Donnie, Howie, Mickey, and even Cuz. Everyone has a nickname. No one calls me James, except in school. So it makes me wonder what the deal is with colored people and nicknames.

Later, when I drop by Grandmom Kane's house for a glass of Kool-Aid, I ask her why the colored kids all go by their real names. What's the story?

Well, that goes back to slavery, Grandmom explains. Back then the masters gave nicknames to each and every slave. Willie, Billy, Charlie, Richie, Freddie, Lonnie . . . you know, little boys' names. The master would be called Mr. Jones or Mr. Johnson, but no matter how old the slave got, whether he was eighty, ninety, or even a hundred years old, he'd still be a Willie or a Freddie. So ever since Lincoln freed the slaves, black people prefer to be called by their given names, not by nickname. Same deal with the hats. You always see colored men wearing hats. During slavery, only men were allowed to wear hats. And slaves could never be men, only boys—no matter how old they were. So now you know why colored men always use their proper name and wear a hat. Understand, Jimmy?

I think so. Thanks, Grandmom.

You know, Jimmy, it wasn't right what they did to the colored. Took them from their homes in Africa to a strange new place way across the ocean, broke up their families, forced them into being servants. It wasn't right at all.

I know, Grandmom.

They've been through a lot, Jimmy. For a whole lot of years, too. And it's going to take a lot more time for them to catch up. Something like that just don't happen overnight. And people can't expect it to, either. Not after all that's happened.

What Grandmom is trying to tell me makes sense in a weird sort of way. I can understand that colored people have had a rough time of it and now have some serious catching up to do. And that folks have to learn to adjust to the colored being equal to white.

But what I can't understand is how slavery ever happened at all. I mean, it's so dumb.

Besides, I can't imagine myself running around, barking orders to a Coleman or a Dré. Much less to the likes of Troy or Darnell from the schoolyard at Longstreet. Do this, do that . . . they'd never pay me no mind anyway. You can forget about these

251

kids being slaves. From what I can tell, they seem to do pretty much what they please. Especially the ones like Troy and Darnell who walk around all cocky and flip with a big chip on their shoulder always looking for trouble. People like that could use some heavy-duty attitude adjustment if you ask me.

All I can say is, it must've been a totally different world way back over a hundred years ago before Lincoln freed the slaves. That yes master, no master stuff is out the window, you can kiss those days goodbye forever.

So nowadays they're putting all these colored kids in our schools and sending their families here to live right next to us white folks, like it or not.

Don't ask me how this is all going to play out—nobody knows, it's a brand new idea. And an entirely brand new world. As Grandmom says, it's going to take some time for things to get sorted out.

CHAPTER 10

Penny Candy

The Nolans are the first adults I've ever been taller than, and I still don't stand five feet. They run the local corner convenience store—an older couple from Eastern Europe whose real name is Nolansky or something like that. Northwest corner of 56th and Wennington . . . you've got to walk down the steps and duck under the overhang to enter their basement business. His name is Irv, hers is Pearl. They've got milk, canned goods, candy bars, Tastykakes, cigarettes, cold sodas, lunchmeats, produce, breakfast cereal, a barrel of Jewish pickles and, of course, penny candy. Six and a half days a week the Nolans are open, sunup to sundown, booking profits on as little as a fraction of a penny per transaction. Although their store seems to be their actual home, the Nolan's official residence is close by on Beaufort Street—you can see their house just across and down the alley from our bedroom window.

One of the Nolans' trademark marketing schemes is their colorful outdoor bubblegum machine. It sits by the store's entrance, beckoning children at a penny a pop. The special allure is the yellow gumball "winners" that Mr. Nolan stocks like trout in an upstate stream. The yellow winners are encircled with two special green stripes, and they constitute perhaps only one in fifty gumballs. But you can see them through the clear glass gumball holder, and every winner is instantly redeemable for a full-sized chocolate bar at the Nolan's counter. Hershey's, Chunky, Reese's Peanut Butter Cup, Clark Bar, Baby Ruth, Mallo Cup . . . just take your pick.

During one month-long stretch my brother Howie rides on a hot streak. Day after day after day, brother Howie is the lucky kid who gets the winner. Monday, Tuesday, Wednesday, Thursday . . . brother Howie can't miss. The Nolans are amazed. News spreads, and the neighbors are perplexed. Howie's buddies are jealous. They rub Howie's crew cut for good luck, feed their pennies into the machine, but don't get any golden winners with the prized green stripes. Howie smiles, pulls out another winner, and marches in for his umpteenth chocolate bar.

Finally, as the Nolans are about to declare bankruptcy, my mother discovers Howie's amazing little secret. No, it's neither psychic ability, good karma, his Black & Decker type haircut, nor astounding luck. It's plain old food coloring. Howie has been using Mom's green food coloring to paint his winners using all the plain yellow gumballs the Nolan's machine spits out. Howie, a born maestro when it comes to arts and crafts, does the winners up better than Mr. Nolan himself.

Now Howie's been had, and must go to bed without any supper.

But Howie isn't the Nolan's only headache, not by a long shot. The steps by Nolan's store are where me and all of my buddies "hang." Diet Donnie, Bobby Schaeffer, Jackie O'Hanlon, Scotty Morgan, Frankie Pellegrino, Dré Barnett, Larry Wisnewski, and the rest of the neighborhood crowd. And with both of the Nolans being under five feet tall, they're the natural target for boyish pranks. Nothing personal—they're just handy, that's all.

Sometimes we stage a fake fight outside their 56th Street door. Two kids, rolling around on the sidewalk, grappling and screaming. We imitate our TV wrestling heroes, use a few packets of ketchup for fake blood. Scotty Morgan, a double-jointed contortionist, pretends to have a broken limb. Irv—Mr. Nolan— eventually comes outside, wearing his ever-present storekeeper's apron, his tiny, wrinkled face contorted in worry and upsetment.

Boys, boys! . . . That is enough! No fighting in front of the store. Do you want I call the police?

Then, he'll hit us with our very favorite Nolanism . . . What has gotten into you kids? Have you all gone *haywire* or something? Why so crazy all of a sudden?

The way the Nolans see it, us corner kids are real live wires, never more than two seconds from going completely "haywire." A constant threat to their orderly world of stocked merchandise— neat rows, shelves, boxes, and display cases of everyday merchandise for their paying neighborhood customers. Six and a half days a week, sunup to sundown. Transaction by transaction, little by little, penny by penny. Problem is, the paying customers are mostly the parents of all us "haywire" kids. So the Nolans will put up with a certain level of nonsense, and we know it. Our job is to come as close to the imaginary line as possible without crossing it.

One day Jackie and Larry come really, really close. Instead of a fake fight, they stage a fake accident. Unconscious twelve-year-old in the gutter outside the store, seemingly struck by a hit-and-run driver. We scream inside to the Nolans for help . . . Call an ambulance, call 911! Mr. Nolan emerges from the store, wringing his weathered hands on that ever-present apron, looking ready to throw a coronary. He approaches the lifeless young figure on the ground, bends over, reaches out—when suddenly the "victim" springs to his feet and races around the corner, all the while howling and laughing with delight.

Mr. Nolan shouts angrily, All you kids away from the store! I've had it . . . have you all gone haywire or something? Are you all crazy?

We try to explain to Mr. Nolan that the boy wasn't hurt as badly as we thought—and has apparently made a miraculous recovery. But Mr. Nolan's nerves are shot. He'll call our parents if we don't leave for the rest of the day. We take off, knowing we've already got one foot over that imaginary line.

One summer afternoon we're lined up buying Tastykakes and sodas when Tutti Frutti bumps into Jackie's arm, causing Jackie to loose his quarter. By chance the coin plops straight into the open wooden barrel containing the Nolans' ever-popular supply of Jewish pickles. Jackie immediately complains to the Nolans, and Irv comes out from behind the counter, rolling up his sleeve, all the while muttering Yiddish under his breath. Mr. Nolan reaches way down, pickle brine up over his elbow, and retrieves Jackie's quarter. Over the proceeding week we don't miss a day without some smart-aleck kid "accidentally" fumbling a coin into the pickle barrel . . . until Mr. Nolan gets wise and announces that he's not retrieving any more money from the barrel for haywire kids so you'd better hold onto your change or you're out of luck.

About a month later, Jackie and Howie hatch a plan to get even with "mean" Mr. Nolan for refusing to return the "accidentally" lost quarters and dimes. Jackie comes across one of those industrial-type road flares, the kind truckers use on the highway for alerting motorists to a disabled vehicle. These babies are meant to fire up in all kinds of weather, even the wettest of downpours. So, while Howie asks for a can of something off the shelf right behind where the Nolans are standing, Bugs fires up the flare and tosses it into the pickle barrel.

Jackie complains loudly, Mr. Nolan, Mr. Nolan, I dropped both my quarters in the pickle barrel!

At first Mr. Nolan refuses to come help, but Jackie contains to whine and fuss about his quarters. Reluctantly, Mr. Nolan comes out from behind the counter, muttering incomprehensibly in Yiddish. Rolls up his sleeve, begins to reach toward the barrel—stops dead in his tracks.

An angry red glow emanates from somewhere deep under the brine, like the opening scene in Disney's *20,000 Leagues Under the Sea*, where Captain Nemo's *Nautilus* appears in the depths as an angry sea monster with hot red coals for eyes. Bubbles are breaking furiously to the surface, and all those Jewish pickles are doing a lively jig. Mr. Nolan steps back, points angrily toward the door.

What is this? What is this? All you kids out of the store. Look at my pickles! Are you kids crazy? Have you all gone haywire or something?

We all run from the store, exhilarated. We'll give the Nolans a couple of days to calm down—but then we'll be back. After all, it's our corner. And our parents are the customers. Mr. Nolan would never call the police, and only resorts to calling our folks once we cross that point-of-no-return line.

One of the Nolans' neighborhood services is to let their better customers buy on the tick—on credit. Their prices may be higher than supermarket prices, but the Acme, Food Fair, and Philly Fruit don't let you pay at the end of the month. The Nolans do. The accounts are meticulously kept in Mr. Nolan's well-worn copybook. Almost all the families use the system, and Mr. Nolan will send a kid home with a gentle reminder for the mother when they've bumped up against the limit and a payment must be made. Everyone buys on the "tick"—that is except for the older people. People who were adults during the Great Depression of the '30s, when families couldn't pay their bills and suffered through the shame of losing everything.

But these are different times, and the younger families see no disgrace in purchasing convenience store groceries "on the tick."

My mother's mother is one of those old-fashioned types who never buys on credit. Remembers the days when folks stood in bread lines, soup lines, and sold apples on street corners for pennies. One weekend my grandmother buys a 99-cent box of laundry detergent at Nolan's, puts a dollar bill on the counter.

That's a dollar-five, Mrs. Kane, Irv explains. Six cents state tax on soap.

Grandmom fishes for the nickel, doesn't have it. No problem, says Mr. Nolan. Don't worry, Mrs. Kane.

Grandmom smiles, thanks Mr. Nolan—she thinks the shop-keeper is letting her off the hook for the tax. Not so. Irv reaches for the handy copybook, starts outlining a whole new page. Mrs. Kane, owes 5¢.

Horrified, Grandmom races home, finds a nickel, then races back to the corner store. But it's too late. Grandmom has already bought on credit, on the tick. She now has her very own page in the Nolans' book.

Grandmom comes over to our house for supper, tells the story. She's still very much perturbed at Mr. Nolan, the temporary five-cent debt, and the Nolan's shameful ledger. We don't know which is funnier—Mr. Nolan creating an entire page in his copybook for a five-cent debt, or Depression-era Grandmom hurrying home in search of a nickel, bothered by the thought of owing anybody anything for even twenty minutes.

Some of the neighbors think the Nolans are a bit stingy and swear there's a little thumb action on the scale when they're slicing and weighing the salami and the liverwurst and the provolone. A few even believe that the Nolans show preference to their Jewish customers, despite the fact that the Jews buy by the ounce and the Catholics, with their big families, buy by the pound. They chuckle and imitate the thick Yiddish accent of some of the older Jews. . . .

I'd like a quarter of a quarter pound from the *chuicy* end!

One day it starts to snow as Howie, Laura, and I are leaving for school. We come home for lunch, the snow piling higher and deeper, and Mom gives me a $5 bill and tells me quick rush over to Nolans, get a pound of bologna and some American cheese. The line is long, it's the lunch hour, people are panic buying before the storm. I finally get the bologna and cheese, run home, and Mom starts making the sandwiches to get us fed and back to school on time. But as she unwraps the bologna and starts putting the slices on the bread, one slice after another is spotted with green. The bologna is moldy. Seriously moldy. Quick, Mom says, rewrapping the lunchmeat, take this back to Nolan's. I hurry back, tell Mr. Nolan the problem, but he says, Sorry, you can't return lunchmeat once it's been opened. I go home, tell Mom, and now she's furious, with hungry kids, green rancid bologna, and the lunch hour almost over. She grabs me, the suspiciously green bologna, and stomps off to Nolans.

The line at Nolans is still long, but Mom barges right up to the counter, demands a refund. Mr. Nolan restates store policy—no refunds on opened lunchmeat, no exceptions.

Mom yells, Then you feed it to your family!

Why, what's wrong with it, Mrs. Morris?

Mom shouts, It's *GREEN*, that's what's wrong with it! Flings the bologna up in the air, rancid slices falling this way and that way, customers scurrying to take cover.

It is one of Mom's finest moments, a story she delights in retelling. Every year her bologna grows a shade greener, the snow an inch or two deeper.

Me, I think the Nolans should reconsider their marketing strategy. If they want to sell green bologna to neighborhood Irish-Catholic families, they might do better to unload it in mid-March around St. Patrick's Day.

Little brother Howie could give the Nolan's some tips on applying the green food coloring. Then they might really have some winners. Bon appetite.

Kiss Me—I'm Half Irish

Us kids are eating cereal and hustling to get off to school when Mom comes in with these buttons. The say "*Kiss Me I'm*

Irish" and Mom is sticking them onto our school clothes. Then, of course, I remember today is St. Patrick's Day. Next Dad comes into the dining room, hurrying so he won't be late for Brimstone, where he's got a long day ahead sweating through tedious brake jobs and front-end alignments.

Pam, what is this? Take these things off the kids. I don't want our kids wearing this nonsense. Mom takes the buttons off but she is not happy. Dad is orange and Mom is green, and they've been at it for as long as I can remember. Seems Dad's people and Mom's people have been fighting for 800 years, and from what I can tell, they're just getting started.

It makes you wonder how they ever got married. Maybe if you marry someone from the other side, it's easier to spy on what the enemy's doing. Or if you're married to the other side and live together it's easier to get your shots in from up close.

I'm not sure yet whether I'm supposed to take sides, be orange or green, English or Irish. Only one thing is for sure . . . I know I am confused.

At the end of St. Patty's Day, my father comes home tired and wants a beer. Mom opens him a bottle, pours it in a glass, and mixes in some green food coloring. When she hands the beer to Dad all foamy green and weird-looking he is not amused. Down the sink it goes.

C'mon, Jim, says Mom. Lighten up.

Dad grumbles that a working man can't even enjoy a decent glass of beer without harassment, and pours himself another glass minus the green food coloring. And yes, he'll gladly celebrate St. Patrick's Day when the rest of the country starts celebrating Orangeman's Day . . . which is in July, thank you. But everyone ignores Orangeman's Day in America—except for my Dad and his brother Hank.

You're trying to turn the kids into Irishers, Dad complains. But Mom denies it. Then Dad starts in on the Pope, The Vatican, and the Catholic Church in general. Next he moves on to the Irish, who drink too much, like to complain, and talk tough without backing it up. Maybe they should all go back to Dublin, Limerick, Donegal, and wherever else they came from, and let decent people be.

Can't go back to Derry or Belfast, Mom observes, they're British occupied.

Don't start with that, Dad says. Northern Ireland is for the Protestants, the rest of Ireland is for the Catholics. It's been that way for a long time, and it's not about to change. Get over it, Pam.

England should be for English, and Ireland for the Irish says Mom.

Well, says Dad, if the Irishers were only half as tough as they all talk, they'd have no trouble taking Ulster in a month. But when it came time for serious action in the Big War, when the world had to stand up to those Germans, no, the old Fightin' Irish had no stomach for it. Declared themselves neutral and left the British and Churchill to face the Nazis all by their lonesome. Now the Irish are content with planting bombs in pubs and blowing up statues of dead English heroes whom they wouldn't have had the guts to mess with way back when they were alive.

Mom just shakes her head and goes into the kitchen to prepare supper. No one can compete with the Old Man when it comes to what the politicians call a filibuster. He's the champ . . . that is, except for maybe his brother Hank.

Soon dinner is being served, and Dad has quieted down. Ham and cabbage, our traditional St. Patrick's Day meal. Dad may dislike the Catholics and the Irish, but he's a ham and cabbage man. Mom digs in, too, and now both are eating with gusto. At least this is one thing on which they can agree. Problem is, nobody asked us kids. We all hate ham and cabbage, big time.

Okay, so the ham isn't half bad, but it gets badly polluted by the cabbage juice running all over our plates. I force myself to eat the ham but leave the cabbage, which has been boiled to death, then boiled again. The cabbage sits there, soft and greyish white, looking like the brain that got dropped on the laboratory floor in that Frankenstein movie. It smells bad, tastes worse, and turns my stomach. Mom makes me eat a few mouthfuls, but soon it's all mushy, shapeless, and cold, and I refuse to take another bite.

Since I didn't finish my supper, I can't have any dessert. Morris house rule.

Mom, I ask, why can't we have cole slaw instead of cabbage? It's made from the same stuff but tastes a whole lot better. Mom says that's not traditional for St Patty's Day, not the way it's done in Ireland. If this is traditional Irish food I can begin to understand how they had the famine, and why the people had to flee that country on ancient slave ships, with people dying and being thrown overboard to the sharks until the rest arrived safely in New York, where perhaps they were able to get their first decent meal in recent memory. If I had to survive on ham and cabbage every night, I know it wouldn't be long before I too was a starving skeleton all bony and grinning like the Jolly Roger.

I figure maybe next year I can wiggle a St Patrick's Day invitation to Frankie "Tutti Frutti" Pellegrino's house for dinner. Mom says the Pellegrinos eat spaghetti three times a week, and spaghetti is my favorite, next to hamburgers. On the other nights the Pellegrinos eat lasagna, pasta pizule, pizza, antipasto, and all sorts of good stuff. Then they have cannolis, biscotti, and perhaps some pizzelles for dessert. Maybe I wouldn't mind being called a wop, guinea, greaseball, dago, spaghetti-bender, if I could eat Italian food every night. Italian is the king of food, and I hate to admit it, but our soggy Irish food comes in last. Behind Chinese, Greek, Mexican, German, Polish, and even Jewish in my book. Yep, Irish is dead last. At least that's the opinion of this starving, sorry, half-limey, half-mick for what it's worth.

I wonder if Frankie's Italian family has this north vs. south deal going like the Irish. Even our United States got into a similar mess back when we had the Union and the Confederacy facing off. Or could maybe the Italians be lined up East vs. West? And if Frankie's mother and father are on different sides, I wonder how that plays out. From what I've seen of Italians, they'd probably holler a lot, gesture, and cuss up a storm. They're a feisty bunch. And if the going got really tough, they might even resort to throwing rotten tomatoes and old wine bottles, and then it'd be time for everyone to duck for cover and start running.

At least that's my theory, anyway.

Oh, well. At least my situation's not half as bad as this boy Diet Donnie knows from Catholic school. Carl Fosco is the kid's name, and according to Donnie this Carl's father is Italian but his mother is Polish. I asked Donnie how Carl handles this, and

Donnie shrugged and said it gets kind of weird when you're a wop and a Polack all rolled into one. It's as if poor Carl walks around mad all the time, but doesn't quite know who to hit . . . he's in a permanent state of confusion.

Fair One

It's a sunny Saturday afternoon, not a care in the world. Dad is over at Uncle Hank's house in suburban Alton, Mom is in the kitchen baking cookies with sister Laura, and brother Howie is who knows where—same as he always is. I've got the living room and, more important, the TV all to myself. Bottle of root beer and a pack of Tastykakes all saved up and ready. All I've gotta do is warm up the set, adjust the rabbit ears. . . . It's game time, our Phillies vs. the cross-state rival Pittsburgh Pirates, and I settle into Dad's easy chair all comfy as they play the national anthem.

Not six pitches into the first inning comes a knock at our front door. Aw, jeez.

Mom steps out from the kitchen, hands all covered in cookie dough, Jimmy, would you get that please?

I oblige grudgingly, pull myself away from the ball game, and swing open the screen door. It's a young boy about my age, maybe a little older, certainly somewhat bigger. Arms tightly folded across his chest, a determined look on his cocky face. Never seen him before, don't have the foggiest.

The boy asks, Are you Jimmy Morris?

Yeah, I answer, wiping away chocolate cupcake frosting from the corners of my mouth. What do you want?

The boy replies, Mind stepping outside? This comes as more of a demand than a request.

I comply and step onto our porch. Somehow I'm getting a bad feeling about the situation. The only person I know going door-to-door in this neighborhood is the Fuller Brush Man. But that guy's old, bald, and carries a thick case crammed with dozens of cleaning samples. Besides, he was just at our door last week, and wouldn't know me by name if his life depended on it.

The only thing this kid's carrying are dirty looks and bad intentions.

My suspicions are confirmed when the mystery boy gets right in my face and growls, So you're the one who's supposed to be so tough, huh? Gonna wipe the street up with me, huh? Well here I am, punk. I'm not afraid of you. In fact, I'm bettin' you're the one who's chicken!

I ask, Hey, what's goin' on, kid? What's your problem?

Mystery Boy just sneers, bumps me in the chest, and announces, Fair one! Just you and me, Four Eyes. Right here, right now!

Our neighbor, Mrs. Schaeffer, spots trouble brewing and comes onto her front porch. Jimmy, she asks, is anything the matter?

Umm, nothing I can't handle, Mrs. Schaeffer.

Why are you two arguing? You're not going to have a fight, are you?

I look at Mrs. Schaeffer and shrug, since I'm entirely clueless. Give Mystery Boy the blank stare, since he's the only one who really knows the score here. Or even what game we're supposed to be playing.

Mystery Boy says, C'mon, kid. You just gonna stand there all day or what? Your little punk brother with the big mouth says you can take me. Well, here I am . . . I'm callin' you out.

Little punk brother with the big mouth. That, of course, would be Howie . . . I should've guessed, should've known.

Now my mother comes to the door, apron tied around her waist. She's quickly wiping the cookie dough and flour from her hands.

Jimmy, is there a problem?

This kid wants to fight me, I explain.

Why? What for?

Nothing. I don't know, Mom. Honest.

Mom frowns, swings open the screen door, steps onto our porch. Now Mystery Boy retreats down the steps and onto the sidewalk. Points back up at me and glares.

I'll catch you later, punk. Some other time when there won't be nobody around to save you. Then you'll be mine, Four Eyes. *All* mine. Just you and me. . . .

With that, Mystery Boy saunters up Littlefield to 56th Street, turns the corner, and disappears. I never see him again, never find out who he is, where he hangs, he's just Mystery Boy forever and ever.

Later, little brother Howie, the troublemaker, comes wandering home, not a care in the world. I take him aside, give him a shot in the chops. Okay, maybe two or three shots. Explain to now blubbering Brother Howie that, in the future, when he shoots off his big mouth and tees someone off, he's going to have to learn to fend for himself. It's not my job to straighten out his every mess, especially since he seems to like playing the wise guy and smarting off every chance he gets.

Hey, its not like I don't usually stick up for my little brother— I do. But somewhere there's a limit. And just because Howie wants to give someone lip doesn't mean I have to be the chump to end up with the fat lip. There's a certain code involved here, and Howie is violating that code.

Besides, I never had the luxury of having a big brother to back *me* up. And maybe that's why I'm not so quick to start trouble and give people a lot of guff. Especially feisty, ornery-looking people I don't know.

Button Nose

A bunch of the guys head down to The Parkland to catch a matinee. Turns out to be one of the worst movies ever made, this stinker called *I'll Take Sweden*. Stars that insipid old fogy Bob Hope and some new blonde actress named Tuesday Weld. Afterwards, along the walk home, we all compare notes and figure the movie owner ripped us off. Wasted our precious Saturday afternoon with this garbage. For the princely sum of 35¢, we deserve much, much better. Give us The Three Stooges. Jerry

Lewis. Steve Reeves as Hercules. Christopher Lee as Fu Manchu. Any of the outer space aliens or mutant terrestrial creatures covered in *Famous Monsters Magazine*, my absolute favorite publication.

Just don't give us that geezer Bob Hope and his insufferable cornball routine.

Seems only one of our gang sat riveted to his seat. *No*, not because of Bob Hope's dreadful one-liners. . . .

Because of rising starlet Tuesday Weld.

Jackie O'Hanlon says Tuesday Weld is the most fantastic-looking movie actress there ever was, or there ever will be. Drop-dead gorgeous, a regular goddess from heaven. Immediately this kicks off a raging debate as to who is the most beautiful woman on the planet as kids begin announcing their first-round draft picks.

Ann-Margret, says Diet Donnie. Did you guys see *Viva Las Vegas*? Ann-Margret is absolutely boss. Totally awesome.

Larry Wisnewski says he'll go with Raquel Welch. *One Million Years B.C.* did it for him. Welch in that cave girl bikini getup. Va-va-voom!

Frankie the Fruit declares he's a Sophia Loren man. Does the wavy thing with his hands to show she's got the super shapely curves.

Donnie smirks, Shoulda known you'd go for the Italian, Fruit.

Bobby Schaeffer votes for everyone's sentimental favorite, the legendary Marilyn Monroe. Can't go wrong with that selection, right?

Diet Donnie laughs, shakes his head. Marilyn Monroe? You can't pick her, Bobby. She's dead!

Bobby gives us that Lee Oswald sneer and snaps back, Even dead Monroe looks better than some of the dogs you guys picked!

Touché, Bobby Schaeffer. We all get a good laugh out of that classic zinger. But then when the laughing dies down, Donnie realizes someone hasn't yet cast his vote. *Me*.

Yo, Cookie—so who do you like, huh?

265

Don't have to think about it, my mind was made up a long time ago. But the guys will never believe it. This is way too embarrassing.

Who, Cookie? C'mon, Jimmy . . . tell us!

I gulp, swallow hard. Guess it's time to fess up, get this one off my chest.

Hayley Mills, I say softly. She's my favorite. But my buddies, as expected, seem somewhat stunned.

Hayley Mills? Donnie gasps. She's just a kid, for Chrissake!

And flat-chested, too, Bobby observes matter-of-factly.

She's a goody two-shoes, adds Frankie the Fruit. They only put her in that silly, goody two-shoes Disney stuff.

Yeah, chuckles Jackie in disbelief, I think she turns into a *nun* at the end of her last movie.

I haven't gone to Catholic school like the others, so I don't know yet how you're supposed to run the other way whenever a nun starts coming in your general direction.

But none of this matters much, it's not going to change my mind. I've seen Hayley Mills in *The Parent Trap*, *In Search of the Castaways*, *That Darn Cat*, and her latest and greatest, *The Trouble with Angels*. And yes, Jackie is correct, as Catholic school student Mary Clancy, she *does* become a nun at the end of *The Trouble with Angels*. But not before she spends the entire movie terrorizing the sisters of the all-girls' school faculty with her smoking, lying, scheming, and general all-around teenage rebellion.

Scathingly *brilliant*, as the spunky Mary Clancy would say.

Therefore, I don't care if Donnie, Larry, Frankie, Jackie, and Bobby pick life-sized Barbie dolls such as Ann-Margret, Raquel Welch, Sophia Loren, Tuesday Weld, and Marilyn Monroe. I'm sticking with Hayley Mills all the way, there you have it. Flaxen hair the color of morning sunlight, the way she wrinkles her girlish button nose when she giggles, the mischievously warm smile that fills the big screen at The Parkland Theatre. . . .

Cookie, you sure got a lot to learn about women, Donnie sniffs.

I just shrug, water off a duck's back.

And besides, says the Diet Man, you better get rid of that pompadour of yours. No girl is ever going to go out with you looking like that. The Wet Head is dead, get with the times.

Oh, yeah? Then what's your Ann-Margret doing with Elvis Presley, Mr. Slick himself?

That's just Hollywood stuff, Donnie smirks. I'm tellin' ya, all the girls today they go for the dry look. Brylcreem's for real old guys—like in their twenties.

Donnie and Larry are already wearing their hair dry, combed forward and down. It's the new, popular, Beatles look. Kids love it, parents don't. Even Frankie and Bobby are starting to go a little shaggy on the sides. This is the *in* thing.

Jackie O'Hanlon, on the other hand, still looks like goofy Dennis the Menace with short sandy-brown hair, rabbit ears, and buck teeth thrown in. I'm glad somebody looks almost as hopeless as I do—misery sure does loves company.

Ah, yes—little old me . . . still sporting the fast-fading '50s look. Same as Cuz, Dad, Elvis, and all the oldheads in Kings Cross. Hey, a little dab *used* to do ya, now maybe it won't. I hate to admit it, but maybe Donnie is on to something here. It's weird how the slowest kids in school like Diet Donnie and Bobby Schaeffer seem to know so much more about life's other stuff— girls, Marlboro cigarettes, booze, fast cars. Even my bull-necked buddy Sherm was that way back at Longstreet Elementary. Seems like the more Jackie and I pull ahead in our studies, the slower we are around the neighborhood. Not everything you learn in life is in books.

Meanwhile, Donnie and Bobby couldn't care less about their studies. They're too busy earning their diplomas on the streets, enjoying every minute.

No way will I ever dare tell these guys about my second-round draft choice . . . Carolyn Jones, the raven-haired actress who plays spooky Morticia in *The Addams Family* television show, dressed entirely in black. Lives at 1313 Mockingbird Lane with Thing,

Gomez, Lerch, Uncle Fester, Cousin It, and the rest of the loveable oddballs. *Tish, you spoke French—that drives me wild*!

Squeaky clean Hayley Mils is bad enough. But if these guys find my second favorite looks like a vampire, they'll never let me live it down. Maybe they'll figure the Kings Cross Boogeyman got hold of me one day, pulled me down into the sewers, bit me on the neck. Now I'm suffering under his terrible spell and somebody needs to drive a wooden stake through my heart.

This makes me wonder—do you suppose the Boogeyman still wears Brylcreem? Or is he doin' the Beatles thing too?

I just wish the incomparable Hayley Mills had her own television show. That way I could watch her every single week. Dad would probably approve of Hayley, since she's English. But Mom? Mom's got this funny thing about blondes. Once when Mrs. Deemer was over for coffee, I heard my mom and Johnny's mom talking about another neighborhood woman who teases her hair into curls and bleaches it very blonde. Mom, who has red hair, and Mrs. Deemer, who's a brunette, were not impressed.

Mom said, These blondes, they get away with *murder*! Then she and Mrs. Deemer just laughed and laughed until their sides ached. Don't ask me to explain this, because I can't.

I just know I'm a definite Hayley Mills man, and I'll drink to that. Well, maybe a root beer at least.

One day I hope to have a girlfriend just like Hayley Mills, all sunny-haired and button-nosed. That would be great, the absolute best.

Betcha Hayley Mills wouldn't kick a boy in the shins the way Rachel Moskowitz did the day I walked her to Hebrew class earlier this year.

I still don't know what the story was with *that*.

Keeping Up with The Joneses

My longtime friend and best snow-removal customer, Mr. Lerner, is dead. Mrs. Lerner, who is getting too old to take care of herself, moves in with her daughter, and the family sells the house.

Enter the Joneses, the second black family on our block after Mr. and Mrs. Pratt, the schoolteachers.

The Joneses are the model of propriety. Mrs. Esther Jones, single mother of John and Mary, is a religious, no-nonsense lady who works as a secretary down at City Hall. She is mother, father, and drill sergeant all rolled into one. With Mrs. Jones any back talk is simply out of the question, and her kids don't dare think of straying from the straight and narrow. The Bible teaches us to honor thy mother and father, and by God if the Jones children don't honor Mrs. Jones, there'll be Hell to pay.

The Jones children work hard at school, spend most of Sundays praying in church, and have little time for foolishness. Neither seems to own any play clothes. The Jones boy, who is twelve, a year older but in the same grade as me, is always seen in shiny shoes, sharply creased dress pants, and crisp white shirts. He is tall, light-skinned, handsome, as outgoing as his mother, and makes friends easily. When speaking to adults, he calls them sir and ma'am, and this is quick to bring the smiles and nods of approval.

Big sister Mary, fourteen, has her mother's dark chocolate complexion, but is reserved and keeps mostly to herself. Her skirts and dresses are old-fashioned and modest, and there's an air of seriousness you don't expect from someone still in junior high school.

The Jones' house is kept spotless, the sidewalk swept, the postage-stamp yard well tended, and all the white folks breathe a little bit easier. People point to the Joneses with pride. See, they say, these are decent colored people. They're not the kind we're worried about. The Joneses are welcome in *our* neighborhood. It's not as if we're against *all* colored people.

Soon my grandmother and Mrs. Jones grow friendly, sitting in their porch chairs and talking across the banister. Jew and Catholic have been replaced by Baptist and Catholic, black and white. Two single working women in a man's world, having sacrificed so their children may have it better. Religious, purposeful women. With so much common ground, Mrs. Kane and Mrs. Jones discover they are far more alike than different. Far more.

As for me, I still miss my friend, the kind and generous Mr. Lerner. Plus, with the Jones kids always doing the chores, I don't have a prayer of shoveling *their* sidewalk. In fact, I half expect John to be out there first snowfall knocking on doors, shovel in hand, and giving me some added competition. It worries me, this new kid who says sir and ma'am and gets the nods of approval.

Yep, because that's the way that Cookie's business crumbles.

Rumble City

Mostly we get along with the kids from Beaufort Street, pronounced "Bewfort" in Kings Cross parlance. They go their way and we go ours. Beaufort is Littlefield's sister street—we share a common, narrow alleyway. But us Littlefielders hang with the kids from Wennington Avenue, and the Beaufort Streeters hang with the guys from Venice Avenue. It's always been this way and probably always will be. My friend Chuckie Long is from Beaufort. Chuckie and I were pals in class at the Longstreet School and commiserated together on the bench of the mighty Little League Knights. But when we're back home in our neighborhood, Chuckie's got his boys and I've got mine. Littlefielders and Beaufort Streeters don't normally mix. Sorry.

It seems sharing a common driveway brings neighbors closer together, while an alleyway serves as more of a dividing line. We share a driveway with Wennington, while the Beaufort Streeters share a driveway with Venice. That's just the way it is—we didn't build Kings Cross or make the rules.

One day a Littlefielder takes a shortcut up the driveway the runs behind 56th Street, southeast from Venice to Wennington. As he crosses Beaufort Street, a few kids hanging on the corner property give him some guff, and our boy gives it right back. Kids at our end of the driveway pick up on the commotion, halt the boxball game, and head down toward Beaufort to lend our buddy some support.

The tussle between the youngheads, which starts as a mere exchange of unpleasantries, quickly escalates into a nasty barrage of taunts and threats. Before you know it, someone picks up a stone and flings it. Now the battle is on. Rocks, stones, and chunks of debris go flying up and down the sloped, partially shaded, concrete-paved driveway. These missiles are bouncing off the pavement, the 56th Street garages, my house's brick wall and stone foundation.

This is crazy, someone is going to get hurt.

I see Chuckie Long with the Beaufort Streeters, along with another semireasonable kid named Andy. So I yell down to them . . . *Chuckie, Andy—tell your guys to quit it, will ya?*

Then I turn to some of our guys . . . Diet Donnie, Bobby Schaeffer, Bugs O'Hanlon, Frankie the Fruit, Dré Barnett, Larry Wisnewski, little brother Howie, and some others.

Donnie, Bobby, Jackie, Frankie . . . *cut it out, will ya?*

Diet Donnie, who's preparing to pick up an egg-sized piece of loose cement and hurl it, gives me a look of utter disbelief. The Round One follows this with a sneer that says, If you ain't gonna help us, Jimmy, then get outta the way!

Not five seconds later, out of the corner of my eye, I see this silver object come hurtling up the driveway in our direction, spinning end-over-end. *SMACK*, it hits something solid.

Frankie the Fruit screams, grabs his head, collapses onto the hard pavement. Crying, moaning, writhing in pain. The twelve-year-old now curls up in a fetal position. Meanwhile, the pitched battle temporarily pauses, nervous kids at both ends of the driveway standing around watching, waiting.

Jackie goes to Fruit's side, kneels down.

Jackie says, Frankie, let me see. Coaxes the Fruit to remove his hands from the front portion of his scalp.

A section of Frankie's dark hair grows wet and matted. Blood flows freely down to the hairline, spilling onto the forehead, then falls to the ground. Drip, red. Drip, red.

Bugs recoils in horror, exclaims, *Oh God!*

His worst fears confirmed, Frankie buries his head in his hands once again and resumes his bawling.

I look down, spot something lying at my feet. Silver, metallic, shiny. Bend over, pick it up. A stout, meaty Eveready flashlight battery, size C. Not the kind of thing you want bouncing off your unprotected coconut.

Someone has already run down Littlefield Street and knocked on the Pellegrinos' door. Now we see Mr. Pellegrino coming off the porch and down their front steps in a pair of ancient brown slippers. He hustles over to where Frankie lies stricken, sees the blood, the ugly scalp wound, and cries out, *Oh Jesus! What happened, Frankie? Who did this?*

Immediately a half-dozen adolescents and pre-adolescents point down the driveway toward the Beaufort Street culprits. The Beaufort boys have retreated, eyeing the unfolding events from a safe distance, ready to bolt if Frankie's dad starts coming their way, well-worn slippers or not.

Mr. Tutti Frutti's got no time to play detective, first things first. He scoops up Frankie in his arms, hurries back down Littlefield to the family station wagon. Eases Frankie onto the passenger seat, then runs around, hops in, and takes off for Fitzpatrick Mercy Hospital to get his son's noggin sewn back together.

Once Mr. Pellegrino's wagon is around the corner and out of sight, Diet Donnie turns his attention angrily toward Beaufort Street. Hollers down the driveway, You guys are gonna get it now. Youse in BIG TROUBLE!

Oh yeah, Fatso? comes the reply. Like what are *you* gonna do about it?

Red-faced, Diet Donnie turns to Jackie and whispers, Go get Cuz.

Bugs takes off down Littlefield to get The Man. The most feared and respected oldhead in all Kings Cross. Muscle shirt, softball biceps, sunglasses, greased hair slicked back into a shiny black DA. The one, the only, the undefeated Salvatore J. Cusumano, a.k.a. "The Cuz." A legend in our own time.

Cuz will straighten this little problem out no time flat. He eats Beaufort Streeters for breakfast. No contest.

Two minutes later, Jackie is coming back up the street. Motions for Donnie to meet him halfway, where the two converse.

When Jackie and Donnie rejoin us, I ask, Where's Cuz?

Shhh, Donnie orders. He'll be here any minute, the Diet Man lies. When Donnie shows his face again at our end of the driveway, the Beaufort taunts continue.

So what about it, Fat Boy? What's it gonna be? We're waiting!

Donnie looks down Littlefield Street. Pretends to see someone coming. From where the Beaufort kids are, blocked by a row of houses, they can't see what we *don't* see.

They're right down here, Cuz! Donnie points down the driveway. Said you punk out . . . said you wouldn't show your face.

Donnie starts laughing. I glance down the driveway, and even from a distance can see the looks of concern spreading across the Beaufort Streeters' faces.

Donnie, who's giving an Academy Award Performance, waves to the imaginary Sal Cusumano. Beckoning him on.

Donnie shouts down the driveway toward our Beaufort Street adversaries, You wanna see what we're gonna do, you fags? Tell it to Cuz, 'cause youse morons got like maybe ten second to live, all of youse.

Donnie puffs his chest out, starts walking down the driveway, straight at the Beaufort Boys. Whispers to us behind him, C'mon, youse guys, follow me.

We all take the cue, puffing our chests up and striding confidently into what seems a sure beating.

But the sight of us advancing, and the thought of Cuz coming along right behind, is too much for the nerves of the Beaufort Streeters. They begin to break ranks and flee. First one, then two, then the entire motley crew.

By the time we reach the end of the driveway, Beaufort Street is deserted, with the Beaufort and Venice kids all beating a hasty retreat to the comfort and safety of their homes and high front porches.

We laugh happily and slap each other on the back, returning to Littlefield in the best of spirits. Diet Donnie, the hero of the day, grins from ear to ear. All this fuss has made Donnie thirsty for a Diet Pepsi, so we decide to head to Nolan's Grocery for soft drinks and a celebration.

Sitting on our corner ledge outside Nolan's, root beer in hand, I dream about the day I'll be one tough oldhead like Cuz. Muscle shirt, softball biceps, sunglasses, head full of greased hair slicked back like Elvis. That'll be the day.

Yep, tough enough to clear a driveway full of punks just by the very mention of my name. No need to throw a punch. I can hardly wait.

Maybe I should ask Cuz to get me started on lifting weights. Cuz hasn't developed his softball biceps by accident, you know.

Better say your prayers, morons, 'cause here comes Jimmy Morris. Baddest man in all Kings Cross. I could have you Beaufort Streeters for breakfast.

Subterranean

Brother Howie and his buddy Johnny Deemer are climbers. They go way up in the trees, over fences, up on roofs—you name it, whatever is available, because it's there. They even climb the hard, craggy faces of imposing rock formations that dot the far bank of winding Dobbs Creek. Lose your footing or handhold in one of those crevices and you can easily twist an ankle, break an arm, or worse. But don't try warning the Daredevil Twins, they're busy having too many thrills, getting high on going high.

Howie and Johnny especially like the roof atop the flat, one-story Hebrew school on the 5700 block of Beaufort. Not because it's particularly challenging—the chain link fence that runs behind the building is the hardest part. Instead, Howie and Johnny love the excitement of being chased by the school's slow-footed caretaker. Their favorite trick is to stamp on one side of the roof, get the caretaker's attention, then escape down the other side before this long-suffering man can draw a fix on them. So far they've lucked out, but one day they're just asking to be caught. It's only a matter of time—and bad karma.

Me, I don't do climbing. Don't care for heights, don't like the sense of being exposed. I have these recurring nightmares about twisting ribbons of metal in the sky—sort of like steel girders except they curve and lead off into nothingness. Find myself out there walking on one. Slowly, carefully, trying my hardest not to slip. But the walkway grows narrower and narrower. Soon I lose my balance, tip over, begin to fall, and let out a horrible scream. Then I wake up in bed in a cold sweat, with my heart pounding like mad. No matter how many times I dream this big fall, I never do make it all the way to the ground. They say a coward dies a thousand deaths. Well, it seems as if I've dreamed this dream a thousand times. Always scary.

One summer day me, Howie, Jackie, and Johnny go on a spider-hunting expedition down to Dobbs Creek Park. Howie has seen cobwebs under the lower ledges of the rock formations he climbs and thinks we might be able to catch ourselves this summer's eight-legged fighting champ. But upon closer inspection, we discover the rock ledges offer the slimmest of pickings in the spider department. So far, our expedition is turning into something of a bust.

So the four of us head farther downstream, scouting for new places to hunt. Hurry up past the spot where Howie's good friend Barry drowned last summer. Little is said, but we all have a sense of foreboding and have no desire to linger. Follow the muddy bank, around one bend in the waterway, then another. We can hear but can't see the passing cars up on The Parkway above us and to our left. On our right across the water we catch glimpses— through breaks in the tangled vegetation—of the Hayden section of Mt. Lebanon Cemetery, headstones on hillsides baking in the midday sun.

Then we see it. Hidden on our Philly side of the creek in a tangle of dense thicket and overgrown brush. A big square block of concrete set against the hillside, dark oval opening perched above the sleepy green water's edge. A big corrugated metal storm drain, invisible from the sidewalk up along The Parkway. Definite spider potential. We decide to move in for a closer look.

A few feet inside the drain's opening, just out of the rays of sunlight, we bag two spiders in gleaming webs, eight-legged sentries on either side of the tunnel entrance. Once we drop our catch into the mayonnaise jar, Jackie aims his flashlight further back into the shadowy gloom. The culvert runs straight back into the hillside, no end in sight.

Wonder where it goes, I remark.

Don't know, says Jackie, but *I'm* not going in there.

Me neither, adds Howie, with Johnny nodding in agreement.

I borrow the flashlight, hoist myself up, and begin to duck walk down the ribbed metal tube into the buried unknown.

Be careful, Cookie, Jackie warns. There could be rats.

Yeah, or maybe roaches, observes Johnny.

And alligators, too, Howie giggles. Maybe even the Boogeyman!

You'd think, with Howie being my brother, he'd be the one most concerned for my safety. . . . But no. With Howie everything's a gag.

During my first subterranean excursion I follow the storm drain all the way up the hill and under the Parkway, cars rumbling overhead. From here the tunnel branches off in different directions, with connection lines under the roadway. Whenever a vehicle runs over a manhole in the road there's a tremendous BAM—BAM! The sound reverberates throughout the tunnel—bounce, bounce, bounce. Down here all sounds are magnified. Listen closely enough and you can even hear your own heartbeat.

When I reemerge fifteen minutes later my buddies are duly impressed, and I do my best to describe what lies hidden under the hillside and The Parkway. Next time I'd like for someone to join me, but to my dismay I get no takers. Too creepy, they say.

Soon I find myself making more subterranean excursions. Alone. Exploring, branching out from culvert to connecting culvert, building a mental map of this Dobbs Creek underground highway. Quickly I learn to wear old dungarees, long-sleeved sweatshirt, and a ball cap—the latter for keeping the dirt and cobwebs out of my hair. The storm-drain maze is surprisingly clean except in places where a branch gets hung up, and over time this catches cans, bottles, the occasional discarded sneaker, and other debris in a mini-logjam. At the very bottom of the tubes settles this sort of sandy grit that's forever damp. But when I duck walk the wetter parts and crawl along the dryer stretches I can make steady progress. After a while my nose gets accustomed to the dank, musty, stale smells and I realize this isn't such a bad little world. Not overly scary if I keep my head and plan my moves. No rats that I can see, although I'm sure they're down here somewhere. Quiet too, except for the hollow echoes and eerie splish-splashing of water. A weird but not unpleasant form of sensory deprivation. Refreshingly cool and dark even while topside it's oppressively hot and bright.

A very different kind of place. But then I'm a very different kind of kid.

Here and there I come across junction rooms that act like roadway intersections, pipes running off in different directions, lots of smallish side tunnels, some made of concrete instead of ribbed metal, some dead-ending, others leading to who knows where, circular empty tubes stretching endlessly into the blackness. Learn to trust my memory and study the landmarks— because down here I discover how easily one's sense of direction can be led astray. Only thing for sure is these tunnels all wind up draining down into Dobbs Creek—a big help so long as I figure out to move in the right direction.

Just hope my trusty flashlight never goes out, I could really use a spare. Even so, it's not entirely dark down here in most places. Especially up along the shoulder of The Parkway, where light filters through the slits in the regularly spaced grates and little golden beams shoot down the holes drilled though the bulky iron manhole covers.

One time I stick a can of soda in my pocket and take a leisurely break next to a square sewer grate up along the Parkway's sidewalk. My very favorite resting spot. While relaxing undetected by all, sipping and stretching and listening to afternoon traffic, I hear these two voices approaching from somewhere above. Girls' voices. As they pass over me, I cup my hands in the darkness and poke my face up near the bars at the surface.

Hey, Miss! Hey, Excuse me, Miss! Can you help me, please?

. . . .Oh my *God*! There's somebody down there!!

Down where?

Down *there*! In the sewer!

Miss, you wouldn't happen to have an extra ham and cheese sandwich on you, would you? Or maybe a PBJ? I could sure use something to eat down here. Haven't had a bite in weeks.

N-n-n-no!

How about a cigarette? Oh, and a light, too . . . if you don't mind.

N-no. W-who are you, and what are you doing down there?

Who, me? Oh, I live down here. You see, I'm your friendly, neighborhood . . . BOOGEYMAN!

Screams, then the frantic slapping sounds of racing feet fading away. Ah, yes—along came a spider and sat down beside her. The exhilarating feeling of omnipotence and complete power. Seeing and not being seen; knowing and not being known. Big smile crosses my lips down in my safe little hideaway lookout. So close to the real world just above and yet so far. A fellow sure could get used to this.

Perhaps one day when I grow up, I'll be lucky enough to join Ed Norton from *The Honeymooners* in his brotherhood of the sewers. Sure beats driving a bus like his buddy, Ralph Kramden. Some guys just get all the breaks. They really have it made.

Just don't ever ask me to be a tree surgeon or telephone lineman. I'll leave those jobs to the likes of Howie and Johnny. The thought alone is enough to give me some serious vertigo. Trust me, I'll stick with the underworld.

Speaking of Howie and Johnny, they're waiting for me at a manhole cover just a hundred yards or so down the road. There I'll find the exit, climb the rungs, knock on the underside of the metal plate, wait for my seconds to slide the circular barrier away, and then do my Jack-in-the-Box thing. Pop goes Jimmy into the blinding, dazzling sunlight. Back into the overworld of sun, sky, trees, fresh air, and acres upon acres of green park grass.

Sometimes Howie and Johnny bring friends and acquaintances along as spectators. Boys watch as the amazing Jimmy disappears into the mysterious storm drain in one section of the park, only to reemerge forty minutes later at some entirely separate location. Voila! Hey, how'd he do that?

Kids look at me with an odd mixture of curiosity and respect. This I enjoy. As with Howie and Johnny up in the trees, I've conquered the fear, mastered the danger, done the unthinkable. I've gone where none of the other kids have gone before. I can do something special . . . even if it is maybe a tad on the weird side. Okay, so I'm he Boy Who Crawls Through the Sewers, that's my thing, and I'm mighty proud of it. Just give me a flashlight and some batteries, and I'm good to go. See you at the next culvert. Later, alligator.

Maybe one day I'll start venturing out of the Parkway to explore the sewers underneath the rest of our neighborhood. There's got to be an easy access—I just haven't found it yet. But I know now there's another world down there under the surface streets of old Kings Cross. A quiet world of dark, unexplored passageways just waiting to be conquered. Same as Christopher Columbus. Or Admiral Perry. And Sir Edmund Hillary. Even my astronaut hero John Glenn, he of the right stuff. They all accomplished important firsts in their fields of expertise. Why not Jimmy Morris?

Sometimes when I walk the sidewalks of Littlefield, Wennington, and Venice, I find myself gazing over at the inviting sewer grates. Imagine myself crawling, duck walking, and generally hanging out down below. My very own underground kingdom—who knows what secret, hidden treasures I'd find? Just ripe for the picking.

But our local neighborhood streets are a long way from the big drains that empty into Dobbs Creek. And there's another factor that causes me some squeamishness . . . the ancient dried creek bed that runs under Littlefield, Venice, and Wennington. Don't know where exactly, but it's under there for sure, according to the grown-ups. It's where all the giant armored water bugs live. Thousands of 'em, maybe millions. You rarely see the water bugs except for the odd summer night following a long, hot dry spell. Then they surface, en masse, as if out of some Grade-B horror movie over at The Parkland. Swarms of creepy, crawling, thirsty, black bugs scurrying for water under the midnight moonlight. Shells so thick they crunch when you step on 'em. You can hear people yelping after the buggers begin to surface. Chasing people off the sidewalks, off the stoops, into their houses, don't dare be caught outdoors in your bare feet.

Eww, eww, eww, eww! Bugs! Big ones! They're all over the place!!

By next morning's sunrise they're all gone. Underground again. Burrowed down into the dried creek bed that lies buried just beneath the homes and the streets and the sidewalks. Out of sight and out of mind. Lurking, waiting.

I never want to be down inside a tunnel when the water bugs come swarming. Gives me the willies just thinking about it. Bad enough just walking on the street during their invasion, let alone crawling underground where I'd be outnumbered a gazillion-to-one.

So for now I stay down in The Parkway, in and around the big storm culverts that empty into the creek. Never far from an easy escape route. And away from the rats and the menacing water bugs.

But then it happens. Something totally unforeseen. I'm crawling into my familiar storm drain, same as usual, with Howie, Johnny, and a gang of curious spectators agreeing to meet me at some designated manhole at a familiar prearranged park location.

All is ho-hum routine until I reach for the metal rungs beneath the agreed-upon exit and tap on the bottom of the heavy iron cover.

No answer.

I tap harder, give a little shout.

Nothing except the muffled sounds of passing Parkway traffic.

Odd. I know I'm not lost. Climbed out of this particular manhole at least a half-dozen times before. So I grunt and groan, manage to slide the cumbersome metal plate sideways. Carefully, so the cover's lethal edge doesn't drop back into the hole and conk me on my skull.

Poke my head above ground, nobody there. Start to do a 360° like the gun turret on one of those new-fangled Army tanks when . . .

WHOOAAA!

Giant, black, flaring nostrils in my face, great bulging white and brown eyeballs. It's horrible. Monster, he's going to eat me! I scream and drop back down the hole, heart pounding, I'm dead meat for sure, perhaps only seconds to live.

Pause. . . . Waiting for the gruesome end.

Comes a voice from on high. . . . *Come on up out of there, son!*

I remain frozen, hunkered down, shivering with fright. What the devil is happening? What kind of monster talks?

Again, the booming voice. Let's go, young man. Come up here on the double!

I grasp the rungs and slowly raise myself up to ground level. This time I glimpse a looming horse head just inches from my escape hole, bare teeth nibbling on blades of grass. Look up, see a man about twenty feet way up in the air wearing a Smokey the Bear hat.

Uh oh, Park Guard. Well, at least I'm not about to be eaten alive. Not yet, anyway.

OUT, I said! Now the mounted cop is growing testy, losing his patience.

I comply with his command—but only halfway. My nerve ends are jangling. The horse's head keeps chewing, chomping, then starts moving my way again. It's bulging eyes dart in my direction. Watching me. I definitely don't like the looks of those big teeth. Don't want to be eaten alive by the likes of Horse-Face Claire Miller's twin, four-legged brother.

He won't bother you, promises the guard. Pulls on the reins, turns his horse sideways so that the animal's head is pointed off in another direction. Now I'm climbing out of the hole and the man in the saddle only looks to be ten feet in the air. But I'm still straining my neck to look so high.

All right, what's the big idea? What do you think you're doing down there?

Who, me?

Yeah, you! See anybody else around here I'm talkin' to?

No, sir.

What's your name, kid?

Umm, Jimmy Morris.

And what were you doing down in the storm drains, Jimmy Morris?

Umm, looking for this ball I lost. It kind of rolled down in there.

Don't lie to me, boy. You didn't lose your ball. You were crawling around in the storm drains on purpose, having a little adventure—weren't you?

I lower my head, nod yes. No doubt Dudley Do-Right here saw my buddies messing with the manhole cover, and one of my guys 'fessed up.

Too late, no use making a run for it—the Mounties always get their man.

Listen up, kid. This is for your own good. I don't want to be the one who has to fish you out of the sewer after you've been down there rotting for a week. What do you think would happen if you ever got lost? Or couldn't get out fast enough if it started to rain? Ever see a body after all the roaches and the rats and the worms have gotten to it?

I gulp. . . . No, sir.

Well, it's not pretty a pretty sight, Jimmy Morris. And the smell . . . you never forget that smell—not for as long as you live. Sometimes, of course, we never do find the body at all. Stays down there forever until even all the bones are gone. Or maybe a storm washes what's left of you into the creek, then you float down to the Delaware River and out into the bay. Is that what you want, son? You want to wind up being snack food for all the fishes?

No, sir. Now Dudley's inside my head, he's got my attention, and I'm trembling something terrible. My mind's thinking about Howie's little buddy Barry Craig drowning in Dobbs Creek last year. I'm flashing on my lifeless body lying there caught in the back of some unknown culvert. Or having to ride up high on the dreaded horse to the Park Guard station. Getting arrested. Having the Mounties calling Mom and Dad. Mom and Dad coming to get me and take me home.

Lots of bad things I hadn't stopped to consider. Heck, I was too busy having so much fun.

Go on home now, son. This time I'll let you off with just a warning. But I never forget a face, and if I ever catch you messing with these storm drains again, I'm going to come down on you like a ton of bricks. You got that?

I nod.

Suddenly the big horse rears its ugly head, whinnies, and lets out this terrible snort. Before I know it without thinking my sneakers are flying and I'm running down The Parkway headed straight for home.

And so ends my shortened career as the mighty explorer of the fabled River Styx and the untamed subterranean world of old Kings Cross. I never return to the sewers again. I leave their uncharted depths to someone else's fertile imagination, and move on to other pursuits.

I really don't like horses, especially the smell. Makes me wondered how I ever wanted to be a cowboy.

Guess I was just born to be a city boy, and that's the name of that tune.

CHAPTER ELEVEN

Monkey Wrench

What we need in this neighborhood is a pool. Low dive, high dive, thousands of gallons of fresh, chlorinated city water in an aqua-blue rectangle of paradise. Come June, July, and August, when school is out, the temperature in the cool, green suburbs can climb to 90°, 93°, 95°, and above. But here in the dense cityscape you can easily add another five degrees to whatever the thermometer reads in the burbs—and that's probably in the shade under your front porch's awning for starters.

♫   ♫   ♫   ♫

Hot town, summer in the city. . . .

Back of my neck gettin' dirty and gritty.

Our urban, Kings Cross world is filled with tar, blacktop, steel, cement, brick, wrought iron, and asphalt. The sun beats down mercilessly. Electric fans, perched in many of the old window frames, shake, rattle, and hum. Other windows just get left open, the occupants hoping against hope for that occasional breeze.

The O'Hanlons have air-conditioning. It's a Fedders, the very best that money can buy. We know, because Mrs. O'Hanlon always tells everyone so.

Out on the forsaken concrete stoops you can probably add another five degrees to whatever it is up on the shady porches. . . . Which, of course, are still five degrees hotter than the green, leafy suburbs.

Then we come to the city sidewalks, which seem to bake at yet another five degrees hotter than the abandoned stoops. As for the asphalt and macadam streets? Well, let's just say that if you wanted to fry an egg. . . .

Harrigan's, the closest city pool, is blocks south of Parkland way down off 68th. That's a long mile, maybe two—in each direction—and through Little Italy to boot. Most of our mothers don't drive. Besides, the pool's already crowded with kids from that area, the rough-and-tumble Haskell section of Southwest Philadelphia. And the locals don't especially appreciate us making it any more crowded. After all, it's *their* pool, you Kings Cross numbskull. Beat it, take a hike.

Meanwhile, we all sit around and melt like butter over here in good, old steamy Kings Cross.

Well, at least we still have nearby winding, wooded, spacious Dobbs Creek Park. But you can't *live* in the park. You've got to come home, giant armored water bugs or not.

And don't you dare think about going wading in Dobbs Creek. Not after what happened to poor Barry Craig last year. Your mother would break both your legs, then tell you, Just wait till your father gets home. Not a pretty thought.

The neighborhood ladies still light their candles for Barry down at Our Lady of Perpetual Peace. A summer later, the memories remain so agonizingly fresh. The day we all rarely talk about. The day we'll never forget.

Today there's Jackie, Donnie, Frankie the Fruit, Bobby, Howie, Larry Wisnewski, and myself all huddled under the shade tree across from the Morris house, next to the brick garage wall that serves as our informal wallball court. But it's far too steamy to play wallball, boxball, stickball, halfball, or anything else. We're already too busy sweating.

We talk, sip Kool-Aid somebody's mom whipped up, and dream of a neighborhood pool that will never be. A passing mirage in the oasis of our urban desert. Then suddenly, out of the monotonous, sultry stillness, comes this great *WHOOSHING* sound. Like a nearby river of water, rushing and gushing.

No, it can't be. We must be hallucinating, our minds playing tricks. Perhaps a really bad batch of Kool-Aid.

But to our added surprise the *WHOOSHing* sound increases. Doesn't go away, instead it's getting louder and stronger. Jackie jumps to his feet, points a finger north. Past my house, down the driveway that parallels 56th, the one that empties onto neighboring Beaufort Street.

Fire hydrant?

Bugs shouts, Look, guys!

Now we see the water. Lots of water, no mirage. A white, foamy wall of water surging along Beaufort, racing downhill toward 57th Street. Energized, we brave the sun and the concrete, head on down the short driveway toward Beaufort—our sister street.

Sure enough, we reach Beaufort and find the fire hydrant on 56th going full blast. Too good to be true. This isn't some wimpy sprinkler the city uses once per month, but the real full-pressure deal. Water blasts across the street as if shot from a cannon, slamming with great force against the retaining wall for the stoop of the corner house facing 56th.

No adults in sight. Somebody must've gotten hold of a monkey wrench.

Solid!

More and more kids are appearing by the minute, arriving from all directions. Beaufort kids, Littlefield kids, Venice kids, Wennington kids, kids from all over. Hey, it's party time!

Some of the older boys have gotten hold of a football and are hiking it by dropping it into the thunderous stream of water that rockets from the hydrant's opening. The pigskin momentarily disappears, then shoots out like a stunt man fired from a circus cannon.

Other youngsters romp through the man-made river that rushes downhill, or simply remove their shoes and go wading in the coolness. One boy does wet, sloppy wheelies on his bicycle, while another tries surfing on his skateboard.

The Feeney girls from Beaufort—all seven of them—break out their jump ropes and begin a spirited a round of double Dutch near water's edge. Some of the neighbor girls join them, taking turns laughing and twirling, followed by giggling and hopping on first one foot then the other to the rhythm of the turning twine.

Splish, splash . . . splish, splash . . . splish, splash. . . .

Farther downstream, a toddler reemerges in his bathing suite complete with tiny toy shovel and bucket, as if this were his day at the beach. In no time he's scooping up sandy dirt from a postage-stamp lawn, dumping on the water, making mud pies.

A little blonde girl takes the opportunity to practice with her hula hoop. Wiggle, wiggle, wiggle, splash. . . . Wiggle, wiggle, wiggle, splash.

The crowd grows bigger, more festive. . . . The hydrant is like a magnet, except it draws people rather than iron filings. Closer and closer, cooler and cooler, sillier and sillier.

The temperature on Beaufort feels as if it's dropped a fast twenty degrees.

Even the normally stodgy adults are getting into the act. Removing shoes and sandals, dipping in a toe here, a toe there. So what if the hydrant's on for a bit, what's it gonna hurt? Let somebody else dial the station house if they want.

Old Man Mitchell, a well-known Beaufort Street character, comes out and plops down on his stoop with a bottle of Ballantine beer and a hefty cheese sandwich. Soon the mischievous eccentric is pitching pennies into the passing water. Then nickels . . . followed by dimes. The local munchkins squeal in delight, thrashing through the swirling current in a free-for-all over spilled treasure.

Us older kids watch from a distance, laughing. But if Old Man Mitchell should decide to start tossing in some quarters, I think we'll be diving right in and crowding out the little crumb-grabbers. You can buy stuff with quarters.

Then, just when we're thinking it can't get any better than this, it does. The Rosati's Italian Water Ice truck pulls up, near the corner of 56th. Drops anchor just yards from the gushing hydrant. Now *there's* a businessman who knows how to seize an opportunity. Capitalism at its finest.

Water Ice Man's got no shortage of customers. Dripping kids come wandering over to his window, fishing out the coins. Lemon, grape, cherry, cherry-vanilla, orange, chocolate, tutti-frutti, and even bubblegum flavored Italian ice. He's got everyone's favorite flavor . . . except mine.

What, mister—no root beer? Again?

What the heck . . . I make do with a cherry-vanilla. We all splurge, buy soft pretzels with yellow mustard to complement the flavored ice. No use holding back today. What would you be waiting for? These are those lazy, hazy, crazy days of summer just like in the song. What you dream about on frigid winter mornings all bundled up for the walk to school.

Beaufort Street tingles like a mouthful of peppermint Lifesavers. Summer can't get any better than this. For the briefest of moments, we're living the high life in Southwest.

Uh oh, I hear someone warn. Look up, feel a wave of apprehension ripple through our little impromptu block party. A solitary figure comes into view halfway down the street. Approaching the action, walking hurriedly. It's Beaufort's resident cop, Officer DellaVecchia, striding forcefully toward our illegally flowing fire hydrant.

And also right at us, and our little clandestine celebration.

All around me kids stop doing bicycle wheelies, stop surfing on homemade skateboards, stop jumping rope, stop doing the hula hoop, stop launching footballs into the roaring blast of city water. Stop everything.

All because of Officer Michael DellaVecchia. All eyes are on The Man. Gorilla in a blue uniform. Barrel chest, thick hair-covered arms, mouth bent into a perpetual scowl. Sees every Kings Cross child as potential juvenile delinquent, or a perp with something to hide.

All Beaufort Street is hushed, save for the steady *WHOOSH-ing* of thousands of gallons of refreshing H_2O.

It occurs to me that I've never seen Officer DellaVecchia out of uniform. No matter what time of day, which day of the week, which month of the year. He's always either coming or going. Police cruisers stopping by his house. Lots and lots of overtime. Rotating shifts. Double shifts. A veritable one-man street patrol against neighborhood crime. Sometimes I wonder if Officer DellaVecchia ever changes out of that uniform. Probably just crashes on the living room couch, catches forty winks, maybe an hour or two at best. Then another cruiser stops out front, honks, and within minutes Officer DellaVecchia is back out on patrol, gun and nightstick in hand, ever vigilant.

Now The Man is bearing right down on us. He looks even grumpier than usual, his customary catnap interrupted by some punk kids turning on the city's hydrant. *Officer DellaVecchia's* hydrant—he's The Law. At the end of one apelike arm dangles an ugly-looking, heavy-duty monkey wrench. The serious kind that could bust your skull as easily as cracking open a walnut, maybe easier.

Officer DellaVecchia shakes the tiredness from his weary bones, plants his lumpy black patrolman's shoes on the sidewalk. Expertly grasps the control valve on top of the *his* hydrant with the business end of the monster wrench.

One squeaky turn, and the water cannon softens to a mere torrent.

Scattered boos erupt from those safely at the rear of the crowd.

Another turn causes the torrent to slow to a stream.

Aw, jeez! someone protests.

A third turn, and the stream eases to a harmless trickle.

What a rip, someone mutters. Just when we was havin' a little fun around here for a change. . . .

One final, decisive turn of the wrench, a few feeble drops—then nothing.

Show over. Minus the surging foam of water, an eerie silence returns to Beaufort Street. The sun suddenly feels brighter, hotter, and you can feel the temperature slowly heading back up. Rising, climbing.

Officer DellaVecchia hefts the big wrench, scans the immediate crowd. All eyes remain on the man in blue, on his heavy-duty walnut crusher.

DellaVecchia booms, Okay—who's the wise guy turned on this water? Huh?

Shrugs all around, vacant looks. Kids scratching their mops and crew cuts. Water? What water, Officer?

The old heads, the boys with the football, have wisely slunk off into the shadows. DellaVecchia sees me, Donnie, Jackie,

Howie, Frankie, Larry, and Bobby standing there looking guilty of something.

Hey, youse guys, the patrolman points in our direction. Whaddaya know about this here . . . huh?

Nuthin', Officer. We, um, just happened to be walking by. . . .

Oh, youse were, huh? And where are all youse kids from, anyway?

Littlefield Street, Jackie and I reply.

Wennington Avenue, Donnie and Larry add.

Howie, Frankie, and Bobby stay quiet and let us do the explaining.

Littlefield and Wennington, huh? DellaVecchia grumbles. So whatchu guys doin' down here on Beaufort if youse don't mind my askin'?

Umm . . . nuthin' officer. Like we said, we were just passin' through.

Oh yeah? barks DellaVecchia. Then go ahead—beat it. Shakes the wrench in our direction, adds an exclamation point. . . . *Scram!*

We turn, start heading back for the driveway that connects to Littlefield.

And for the rest of youse people—the cop's voice rises, like a councilman on the stump—this here is *city* water. We get a fire, and we ain't got no pressure, then someone's house is gonna burn. Maybe your house. Maybe your whole block. Youse Einsteins all got that? I catch any one of youse turnin' on this water, I ain't bringin' youse home to Mommy and Daddy. . . . You're goin' down to the station house with me. This is serious business, so don't mess with me here. . . .

Under his breath, Diet Donnie mutters, *Up your nose with a rubber hose, DellaVecchia.*

We retreat up the driveway, leave Beaufort to Officer DellaVecchia and his amazing feats of oratory skill. Back to Littlefield, back to our private oven, back to our few square feet of refuge under the shade tree across from the garage wall that doubles as a wallball court. But in this heat wave we don't expect to be playing wallball any time soon. Not unless we want to do a fast meltdown like the Wicked Witch of the West. Looks as if the most we can hope for the rest of this sweltering day is maybe an impromptu water-balloon fight.

Wrong again.

That evening, news comes of another fire hydrant going into action just off 55th Street. Next night, same thing up on Partridge. Then Windermere. Later, down on 57th Street. Day after day, night after night, the Robin Hood with the monkey wrench strikes, always one step ahead of the men in blue—led by none other than Officer Mike DellaVecchia. Chances are, if you ride your bike around for a couple of hours and listen for that *WHOOSHing* sound, you'll find it. Sure enough, a hydrant somewhere is roaring at full blast. People coming out of their homes, kids dancing in the street, a spontaneous block party breaking out.

Neighborhood speculation grows as to the identity of our Kings Cross version of Robin Hood. He's a growing hero in the eyes of many, especially among us young boys. Visions of Sherwood Forest dance in our heads. But the mystery man's nothing more than an infuriating, smart-aleck street punk to the weary cops. Just some twisted delinquent with an overactive ego and more than his share of good luck. But they'll catch this goober eventually. It's just a question of time. Not to mention who, how, why, and where in the world did he ever get that king-sized wrench??

We ride our bikes at dusk, cruising from one corner to the next. Bingo, there it is, another open hydrant. Once again the police don't arrive until after-the-fact. The sun goes down, and the targeted street glistens under the electric streetlight. Steam rises from the cooling macadam, disappearing into the darkness. Perfect end to a perfect day.

But no way can this last the rest of summer, and it doesn't. The cops finally nab our hero. In the act—*red-handed*, as they say. Confiscate the legendary monkey wrench. Haul this well-known neighborhood troublemaker to the station and book him. Throw the teenaged miscreant into a holding cell, keep him there for several days. Not to protect the neighborhood, mind you—but to protect the kid. Because the police, you see, are trying their darndest to prevent a probable assault and battery. Perhaps even involuntary manslaughter, who knows. Not good for the Kings Cross crime stats. Word on the street is this punk's father is liable to kill him. Tear this slippery, greaser of a teen apart from limb to limb, leather jacket and all.

This glorified punk, our celebrated Kings Cross hero who brought a temporary breath of fresh air to these sweltering streets, is none other than Michael DellaVecchia Jr., a.k.a. Crazy Mike, son of Officer DellaVecchia.

Crazy Mike had been using his old man's city-issued wrench, sneaking out of their Beaufort Street home's cellar door, and then back in again undetected.

All while Officer DellaVecchia was trying to catch his precious forty winks. . . .

Requiem for a Hot Dog

Going to a Phillies game up at Connie Mack Stadium in North Philadelphia is an annual neighborhood ritual. A sacred pilgrimage of sorts. Entire families, Mom, Pop, the kids, dutifully make the trek. Load up the station wagon with the munchkins in their Phillies uniforms wearing baseball gloves to catch foul balls. Once at 21st and Lehigh, you pay some of the local kids to watch your car for a dollar. Translated, this means you give them a dollar and maybe they won't slash your tires. The practice seems to be philosophically written off as part of the price of general admission. Besides, it sure beats being stranded in unfriendly North Philadelphia with four flat tires and the sun going down over the rooftops.

This particular year we get an unexpected bonus. Frankie's dad, Mr. Pellegrino, decides to take some of the neighborhood boys who play in the local Little League to a Sunday game. Myself, Jackie O'Hanlon, Scotty Morgan, Donnie Fahey, Johnny Deemer, Bobby Schaeffer, and, of course, Frankie "Tutti Frutti" Pellegrino. We all pile into the Pellegrinos' ancient station wagon and head north to Shibe Park, now known as Connie Mack Stadium after the famous A's manager, Cornelius Alexander Mack.

We arrive at the stadium early to watch batting practice and maybe snag a few souvenir foul balls. To be on the safe side, Mr. Pellegrino pays the local kids two dollars. You especially don't want to be stranded in North Philadelphia, nighttime quickly approaching, and a station wagon filled with seven little white faces whose safety depends entirely on you. So the two dollars is insurance money.

None of us kids catch any foul balls, and soon the stands are filling quickly. The hated Cincinnati Reds are in town, along with their budding star, Pistol Pete Rose. Philly fans have a rep for booing everybody, Phillies players included. But Pete Rose and his showboating antics are singled out for special attention. Little do these fans know that one day in the distant future Pete Rose will be traded to Philly. He'll help us win the National League pennant and World Series, and become a revered figure in Philadelphia sports history. But in 1966, the name of Pete Rose is mud in the City of Brotherly Love.

About five minutes before the umpire shouts Play ball! and the game gets underway, a woman, man, and little boy take the seats directly below and in front of us just behind the first-base dugout. We are approaching the end of the good old days with fans dressing in their Sunday finest for sporting events, and these folks are most definitely old school in this respect. The man, who isn't young, wears a brown double-breasted suit, paisley tie, and a wide-brimmed fedora just like the film noir detectives from the 1940s. The woman's fashionable dress seems more suited for church than an afternoon at Connie Mack Stadium. But it's the little boy who quickly grabs our attention. Our *immediate* attention. He's five years old, maybe six, which makes him several years younger than our Little League gang. And he sports a complete, brand spanking new baseball uniform with a mini-outfielder's glove as a matching accessory. More precisely, it's a Cincinnati Reds uniform, and includes the letters **ROSE** stitched boldly across the back.

Bad mistake. In Philly, this may be enough to incite a small-scale riot.

Jackie starts in first. Then Donnie. Soon I'm swinging for the fences with my buddies.

Hey, kid! Nice uniform!! What, ya think you're in—*Cincinnati* or somethin'?

The little boy turns and makes a mad face. Now he's compounding his mistake.

I'd like to see that Pete Rose bum strike out! Bugs shouts for our whole reserved-seat section to hear. What a LOSER!

Yeah, I add devilishly. I'll bet he goes oh for four. He's an automatic out.

You got that right, agrees Donnie Fahey. The only reason they got Rose leading off is so he can't hit into more double plays.

This is all too much for our proud, pint-sized Cincinnati Reds fan to take. He jerks around in his seat, dislodging his Cincinnati Reds cap in the process, and defiantly sticks out his dimpled little chin.

Pete Rose is the best player in baseball, and I bet he can beat your stinky old Phillies any old time!

The seven of us reply in unison . . . Oooooohhhhhhh! Like we're *really* impressed, kid. Take a hike, Mergatroid.

You'll see, promises the Cincinnati Kid. Just watch.

Switch-hitting Pete Rose, as usual, leads off for the visiting Reds. He faces the Phils' fireballing right-hander Art Mahaffey. Mahaffey smokes the first pitch past Rose for a swing and a miss. Rose then takes another darting fastball for a called strike, and now Pistol Pete is in the hole, 0-2.

Jackie yells, C'mon, one more! Sit this bum down!

The Cincinnati Kid turns and sticks his tongue out at Bugs. Mahaffey winds, delivers the pitch. A wicked slider on the outside corner. Rose is expecting another heater, and the breaking ball dips under his bat as Rose goes down swinging for out number one.

Jackie starts immediately with the booing and jeering. Go back to Cincinnati, you bum!

Yeah, back to the bush leagues! adds Johnny D.

The Cincinnati Kid is nearly in tears. Not a good sign, since we're still only in the top of the first inning. At this rate we'll have the little squirt practically catatonic by about inning three. Maybe that'll teach him not to dare wear the Reds uniform in *our* house.

The mighty Reds go down in order, and now it's the Phils turn at bat. Immediately they get a rally going, and a hard single up the middle scores an early pair of runs. We're up 2-0, and the joint is really rocking and rolling. Not a great place to be if you're a Cincy fan.

The nicely dressed man and woman try to make small talk with us Little Leaguers, maybe smooth things over a bit. But we have our sights trained on the Cincinnati Kid, looking to move in for the kill. Mercy is not an option for pint-sized Reds fans—especially not with one who's got the annoying habit of sticking his dirty little tongue out at us.

Sensing trouble in his seat down at the far end of our row, Mr. Pellegrino calls for an early snack-break. So we all get up and march single file back to the food concession area underneath the stands in the catacombs of the aging Connie Mack Stadium.

Donnie Fahey leads the way, a smile spreading across his ample features. Donnie may not be the most passionate baseball fan like Jackie or me, but he knows a thing or two about ballpark food. Hot dogs, hamburgers, peanuts, Cracker Jack. Donnie doesn't care who's playing—he wants to know what's on the menu. Lately we've taken to calling him Diet Donnie because of his new-found love of diet soft drinks. In Donnie's convoluted mind, these low-cal and no-cal drinks neutralize all the calories in his high-energy foods. Having some fried chicken? No problem, just guzzle down a Diet Coke. Shazaam, the greasy calories are eliminated. Consuming some chocolate cake? Don't worry, just suck on this Diet Pepsi and fizz away all the fat. Got a craving for some pepperoni pizza? No sweat . . . just pop the top on a can of Tab and nuke all that bad stuff into oblivion. Presto.

Only problem is, Diet Donnie's dungarees are getting tighter and tighter by the month. Obviously something must be amiss with his seemingly magical equation.

We stand in line, mouths watering, and inch our way forward until Donnie reaches the counter. He quickly pushes four quarters at the man in the funny hat and white apron.

Gimme two hot dogs . . . with mustard and relish.

The man looks at the coins. Says, That'll be a dollar twenty, kid.

Donnie's face turns crimson. What? A dollar twenty? But they was fifty cents each when I was here before.

Sorry, kid. They changed the prices last month. Not my idea. Hot dogs are now sixty cents.

But I only have a dollar, Donnie protests.

Sorry, kid. Buy somethin' or step aside. You're holdin' up the line.

Okay, Donnie replies angrily, I'll take one hot dog with *everything* on it!

The man smiles, figures he'll fix the annoying wiseacre Donnie. Puts on extra mustard, extra ketchup, extra kraut, extra onions, extra relish, extra everything. For the love of Pete, you can't see the hot dog, it's buried under a mound of condiments.

Donnie collects his change, stands there holding the super dog with two hands like a bowling ball. Probably weighs nearly as much.

The rest of us get our munchies, then we make the long, arduous trek back to our seats way behind the first-base visitors' dugout. Donnie carries his creation as if it were nitroglycerin. Still, he leaves an unmistakable trail of diced onions and assorted toppings in his slow and steady wake.

Once back in our seats, the game begins to take an unexpected turn. Mahaffey loses the radar on his booming fastball. He's walking guys one after the other, and now the bases are jammed with Reds, no place left to put 'em.

Up steps Pistol Pete Rose in the batter's box, digging in his cleats.

The Cincinnati Kid is up clapping and cheering now. C'mon, Pete. Eye on the ball, Pete. Wait for your pitch, Pete.

Jackie yells, Okay, Mahaffey! Here's an automatic out. One-two-three just like you did before. Sit this bum down!

Cincinnati Kid turns, sticks his tongue out. Reminds us that Pete Rose was Rookie of the Year. He's got the best batting average in the majors. He's a superstar. He's going to knock that Mahaffey and our Phillies into next Tuesday.

Yeah, yeah, yeah. For your information, ya little turkey, Pete Rose is a *bum*. That's all he ever was, that's all he'll ever be. A jug-eared, flat-top, no-good loser.

Oh yeah? Well, we'll see about that!

Rose fouls off a couple of pitches. Works Mahaffey to a count of 2-2. Mahaffey winds, and here it comes . . . you guessed it, the slider. Only this time he hangs it out fat, and Pistol Pete is waiting to jump on this mistake.

Crack!

Rose slaps the ball to the opposite field, down the left-field line. It's slicing toward the foul line but falls fair by inches, bouncing down into the Phils' bullpen in foul territory. Reds runners are tearing up the base paths, the crowd is roaring. We all stand to get a better look. One run scores, two runs score, three runs score. The ball is careening around the corner like a pinball where leftfielder Wes Covington finally tracks it down.

Rose rounds second, fakes like he's applying the brakes—then steps on the gas. He's gambling on a triple despite Covington's bazooka arm. Here comes the throw, right on the money. Here comes Pistol Pete, patented head-first "Charlie Hustle" slide. The ball and Rose arrive simultaneously at third base in a spectacular cloud of dust.

The dust settles. Rose is holding the bag, the third baseman is holding the ball, and the stadium is holding its collective breath. All eyes are on the man in blue.

The umpire flattens his palms, gives the signal. SAFE!

A torrent of boos rains down upon the sparkling green field. Fans can't believe their own peepers. Safe? Come again?

C'mon, he was out by a mile, ump!

Get your eyes checked, buddy!

Where'd they get this moron, anyway—the Cincinnati School for the Blind?

Rose calls time-out. Wipes considerable dirt from the front of his shirt and pants.

Cincinnati Kid can scarcely contain his glee. He turns and points a finger right in Jackie's face. See? What did I tell you? Pete Rose is the best! I told you he'd get a hit!

He's a *bum*, Bugs insists. No, he's worse than a bum. He's a *hot dog*. That's what Rose is—a hot dog!!

Jackie is referring to Rose's fancy catches, his head-first slides into bases, and his habit of racing down to first whenever he draws a walk. In Jackie's book, Pete Rose is a showboat, a pretender, a player with lots of style but little substance. In a word, Pistol Pete's a *hot dog*.

Jackie turns away from the Cincinnati Kid and flails his arms in frustration. However, at this precise moment, Diet Donnie happens to be bending over, holding his condiment-covered hot dog creation in one hand, and flattening his wooden seat with the other.

THWACK! Jackie's demonstrative little outburst causes his arm to strike Donnie's exposed wrist with the blunt force of a karate chop. Bits of onion, ketchup, mustard, relish, and sauerkraut spray in all directions. The previously buried hot dog squirts from it's soggy bun like a daredevil shot from a circus cannon. Up, up, and up. End over end in s-l-o-o-w motion. Then down, down, and THUNK.

The wayward frankfurter lands unceremoniously on the well-dressed man's snazzy brown fedora. Dangles precariously on the edge of the hat's crown, wobbles, succumbs to gravity, then slides snuggly into the center crease of the gentleman's hat.

We sit stunned, not believing our own eyes. Me, Jackie, Donnie, and Johnny. Waiting for the man to jump to his feet and call for stadium security. Or, even worse, for him to lose his temper and beat us to within an inch of our lives in front of thousands of screaming, cheering Philadelphia fans. Yo, mister— hit 'em again!

But none of this happens. To our sheer amazement, the man seems not to notice the meaty ball-park frank lodged firmly in the middle of his Humphrey Bogart–style headware. And even if the guy remains miraculously clueless, we fully expect another adult to lean over at any moment and say, Pardon me, fella, but did you know you have someone's hot dog stuck in your hat?

After Jackie's crack about Pete Rose being a hot dog, surely no one is going to believe this thoroughly unbelievable coincidence. Our story about the incredibly wayward frank, no matter how true, is just one dog that ain't gonna hunt. So collectively we cringe, knowing that any minute now the unpleasant discovery will be made and the entire bunch of us Southwest types will be dead meat. Dead dogs, so to speak. Done in by a carelessly wayward wiener. Definitely not a thought to relish.

Seconds pass, then minutes. Slowly, we dare to breathe again. Tentatively glance around, fully expecting the worst. The razor-sharp Sword of Damocles hangs over our sorry Kings Cross heads. But everyone's watching the game, and no one seems to notice Donnie's ridiculously misplaced lunch, a culinary misadventure if there ever was one.

Out on the field, the Reds are giving the Phils a first-class whupping. Mahaffey is already taking a shower, and the relief pitcher isn't faring any better. Meanwhile, Diet Donnie looks at his lost lunch with sad, longing eyes. Low rumbling sounds begin to emanate from his ample midsection. It's going to be a very long time until supper—assuming we remain alive that long.

By the fourth inning, the Reds are up by four runs when Charlie Hustle slams another frozen rope, this time into the gap in right center. The Cincinnati Kid is doing a war dance in front of his chair while the well-dressed man and woman smile and clap approvingly. With each successive Reds' run and accompanying round of applause, the offending hot dog gets jiggled and bumped. Rolls left a quarter-turn, then rolls right a quarter turn. What ketchup, mustard, and relish remain are slowly being transferred onto the brown fabric of the fedora, giving it a somewhat tie-dyed effect. Now I understand why you never see anyone sporting a tie-dyed fedora . . . take it from me, it's not a pretty sight.

By inning number-six Pistol Pete collects his third hit of the day, as the Reds' rout of the Phils continues. Cincinnati Kid laughs and giggles, turns to us and says, See! I told you so. Pete Rose is the best player in the National League!

We glumly nod in agreement. Sneak another peek at the precariously positioned hot dog. Yeah, kid, Pete Rose is the best in the league, the best player in the world, the best player in the universe. He's Honus Wagner, Ty Cobb, and Stan Musial all rolled into one. Whatever you say, Sweet Pea—we don't care.

We just want to go home. Back to Kings Cross. Away from North Philly, away from Connie Mack, away from the Cincinnati Kid, and definitely away from Diet Donnie's not-so-lost frankfurter.

Our miraculous hot dog survives the seventh-inning stretch intact, but now here comes the sun. Baking, broiling, and shriveling the mystery meat until it begins to turn black . . . as they do when the department store vendors leave them too long under the lamps in those big, glass, see-through machines.

By inning number-eight the local flies have made a discovery and start zeroing in. The well-dressed man is shooing and swatting, still oblivious, but the little green guys keep dive bombing, like so many WWII Zeros, Spitfires, Corsairs, and Messerschmitts.

The game is hopeless, the Phils are down by ten, and we've had enough of the national pastime to last us well into next season.

Mercifully, after what seems like an eternity, the game sputters to its inevitable conclusion. Fans stand up, begin to march antlike toward the exits. The Cincinnati Family strolls just up ahead. If you know what you're looking for, you can still see the tail end of the Donnie's hot dog poking up from the rear of the fedora.

We reach the stadium lot, pass by the stadium's clubhouse door, and Mr. Pellegrino graciously asks if we'd like to wait around for the well-known ritual of scrambling for players' autographs. But when we see the Cincinnati Kid and company lining up for a chance at Pistol Pete's John Hancock, so we politely decline the offer. It's time to make a quick exit, stage left.

No, just take us home, Mr. P. But thanks, anyway.

So we all pile into the Pellegrino family wagon. With no small relief we watch as the Cincinnati folks and other autograph hounds fade into the distance, followed by the arched walls and finally the commanding light towers of our beloved Connie Mack Stadium.

We half expect a Philadelphia blue car which the old-timers call a red car to pull along-side of us at any moment, and for the police to take us in. But eventually we disappear into Sunday traffic and make our way toward Southwest Philly and the familiar surroundings of our old Kings Cross neighborhood. You can tell poor Diet Donnie's never gone this long before without goodies. His stomach rumbles mightily, and our hefty buddy looks as if he could lunch on the Pellegrino wagon's back-seat upholstery if we don't point him in the direction of a well-stocked refrigerator lickety-split.

All Wet

The moms up and down Littlefield have put their heads together and decided to send their sons to the downtown Big Brothers swim classes. Sometimes we go individually, and Mom takes Howie and me on the trolley to Center City—land of skyscrapers, crowded streets, and glitzy, upscale department stores. Other times we car pool, often with Tutti Frutti and his father, Mr. Pellegrino. The regulars are me, Howie, Jackie O'Hanlon, Frankie, Frankie's little brother Carl, and sometimes Scotty Morgan.

♫　　♫　　♫　　♫

When you're alone and life is making you lonely

You can always go . . . Downtown.

♫　　♫　　♫　　♫

When you've got worries, all the noise and the hurry

Seems to help, I know . . . Downtown.

It was just last summer that our Kings Cross neighborhood lost little Barry Craig to the temptation of Dobbs Creek. The

301

moms are doing everything in their power to prevent a repeat occurrence—they can threaten us with grounding but know full well that boys will be boys and that sooner or later one hot summer day we're going to forget about poor Barry and wind up back in the infamous creek. Then what will happen?

In the minds of the moms the danger of the nearby murky water has surpassed the horror of boys doing the soapbox derby thing in busy traffic. The very least they can do is give us a fighting chance and see that we learn to swim. So here we all are at Big Brothers, ages eight through twelve, being taught to float not sink. This isn't about making the next Olympic swim team, this is about keeping us all alive and breathing.

Classes start in the low end of the pool where the water's not over your head and you can stand up and walk around. Safety instructions about what you can do around the pool and what you can't. Just getting us comfortable with the water and the Big Brothers' facility in general. Oh, and no snapping towels in the showers at kids' bare bottoms. Soon they're teaching us how to paddle, how to kick. So far, so good.

Our instructor is a tiny Japanese man, maybe 5' 2" tops, not much bigger than us kids. Bigger than tiny Mr. and Mrs. Nolan who run the corner store at 56th and Wennington, but not by much. The Japanese man is calm, reassuring, and patient. He says, Don't be afraid of the water—I won't let anything happen. Trust me, I will teach you.

Soon the day comes when it's time to go into the deep end of the pool. Mr. Tanaka gives us flotation devices, sees that they're fastened securely, helps us down the ladder.

Jackie is already getting the hang of things, splashing about and laughing. Tutti-Frutti and little brother Carl are close behind. But Howie and I are still terrified, clinging to the safety of the pool's ledge. Barry was Howie's best friend. And me? I'm just plain scared of the deep water, always have been.

Mr. Tanaka goes easy on us the first day in deep water. Lets us practice our kicking, holding onto the side of the pool in our bright, orange flotation devices. Easy does it, not too fast.

Back in the changing room, some kid named Doug from Northeast Philly starts to make fun of Howie for wearing a crew cut and for being scared of the water. Calls him Chicken Little. I step in, tell him buzz off.

Yeah? Who's gonna make me, Four Eyes?

I am, Pigeon Toes!

Four Eyes!

Pigeon Toes!

Someone on Big Brothers' staff comes in, breaks it up. Makes us get dressed and sends us all on our way. Pigeon Toes and his boys to Northeast Philly, me and my gang to Southwest.

Next week Mr. Tanaka has us paddle through the deep end in our life vests. Now comes the moment of truth, the moment I've been dreading. Tanaka helps us take off the preservers, leaves us clinging to the pool's wall. Then he glides to the center, treading effortlessly in the deep water.

Come with me, Tanaka urges in his thick Oriental accent. Come into the deep water, boys!

Jackie laughs and plunges ahead, paddling, paddling . . . ends up by Mr. Tanaka's side. Followed by Tutti Frutti, followed by Carl . . . with some gentle coaxing.

Now it's just me and Howie hanging on for dear life. Howie looks at me for support, then at Mr. Tanaka. Gathers some courage, takes a deep breath, and pushes away from the wall. Halfway out he slows down, splashes wildly, calls for help. Mr. Tanaka propels himself dolphinlike to Howie in seconds, guiding my little brother to where the others are paddling.

Now I'm alone. Mr. Tanaka reaches his hand out. Come, Jimmy, he says. Come into the deep water.

Part of me wants to come, to trust. But fear grips the bigger part, and its hold is more powerful, overwhelming. I can't move, can't run, can't do anything except shiver and grasp the ledge ever tighter. Eight feet of water, no vest. It's even over Wilt the Stilt's head. Feel the panic.

Come, Jimmy, come into the deep water.

Ashamed, I shake my head, turn away, close my eyes, bury my face against the wall . . . holding on for dear life with both hands now. In my mind I can see Barry floating in Dobbs Creek, blonde hair bobbing. Barry in his angel-white First Communion suit, ghostly pale.

I hate this place, hate Big Brothers, hate Pigeon Toes, hate Mr. Tanaka with his funny accent, hate the smell of chlorine. Most of all I hate the fear—and especially myself for letting fear get the best of me. Scared silly, just like pigeon-toed Doug from Northeast said. A coward and a yellow-belly. Like some puny little sissy of a girl. No, worse than a girl . . . even most of the girls aren't afraid of the water.

You can trust me, Jimmy. Come into the deep water now. . . .

Dirty, stinking Japs. I know all about Pearl Harbor—I've seen all the war movies at the The Parkland Theater. Sneaky and treacherous these noodle-eaters are. What if I start to drown? What if Mr. Tanaka doesn't save me? What will happen then? Kids can die in seconds, you know—just like Barry Craig.

They can keep all of their Godzilla movies for all I care, lousy rotten Japs.

I'm so afraid. Afraid of the deep water.

♫　♫　♫　♫

Just listen to the music of the traffic in the city,

Linger on the sidewalk where the neon lights are pretty.

How can you lose? The lights are much brighter there.

You can forget all your troubles, forget all your cares.

So go . . . Downtown.

Things will be great when you're Downtown. . . .

Next week our swimming classes come to a close. I go home to Kings Cross, never to return to the Downtown Big Brothers.

♫　♫　♫　♫

You're gonna be all right now . . .

Downtown . . . Downtown.

304

I'm twelve, it's high summer, we're just a short walk from Dobbs Creek, and I still don't know how to swim.

Nightmare on Beaufort Street

Her name is Rosemary Hughes and she lives four blocks away from us Morrises on the 5200 block of Beaufort Street. I've never been on this block before—rarely do I have a reason to venture east of 54th Street. We don't know Rosemary Hughes, nobody on Littlefield Street seems to either. But on this horrible day everyone in Kings Cross and across Philadelphia will know *of* her.

Rosemary is a young stay-at-home mom like so many in our neighborhood. Blonde and blue-eyed, a petite 5' 2", not yet twenty-seven. She makes breakfast, sees her husband Jay off to work at eight, then cleans house and chases after her two toddlers, Bryan and Kevin. After lunch the boys take their nap and maybe mom can squeeze in a soap or two . . . *Guiding Light*, *As the World Turns*, *The Edge of Night*, *General Hospital*.

Rosemary is an Elvis Presley fan, collects all the memorabilia. Disney characters, too . . . Mickey, Donald, Daffy. And when it comes time for the annual 5200 Beaufort block party each summer, Rosemary is one of the primary organizers.

Everyone, it seems, likes Rosemary Hughes.

On this day, while the boys are sleeping and Rosemary is engrossed in the daily installment of *As the World Turns*, she hears a noise on her row house porch. Again, a bump. Someone at the door? The mailman's already been, and Rosemary isn't expecting visitors. Approaching the window, she sees a man. A strange black man tugging at her front door. Pulling harder and harder, trying to force his way in.

Rosemary goes to the door, opens it a crack, confronts him. Shouting, arguing, trying to keep the man outside. Away from Rosemary, away from her little Bryan and Kevin.

The man is hostile, incoherent. He pulls a knife. Rosemary screams. The man reaches in, grabs Rosemary, pulls her close, and begins to stab. Savagely. Again and again. A brief, desperate struggle spills across the front porch as the life quickly flows out of Rosemary Hughes.

305

The butcher knife is so very large, and Rosemary is so very small.

Neighbor housewives hear Rosemary's screams, race to their porches. The nightmarish sight that confronts them will remain imprinted in their minds for the rest of their lives.

Police arrive in minutes, arrest the crazed, bloodied perpetrator. But there is precious little they can do for poor Rosemary Hughes. This is a job for the parish priest, the coroner, and, finally, the Philadelphia Fire Department.

A river of blood runs off the porch and covers the Hughes' front stoop. Horrified neighbors watch as Father McNulty from Our Lady of Perpetual Peace administers last rites. The inspectors take their grisly pictures. The lifeless, mutilated body is then carted off to the morgue, and the fireman begin to hose everything down. Porch, steps, sidewalk. . . .

Later detectives interview the suspect. He doesn't know Rosemary Hughes. Doesn't know why he was on her porch. Doesn't know why he knifed her. Doesn't remember a thing—it's all a blank. He was drunk, didn't know what he was doing. Now he's sober and he's sorry. Terribly sorry.

But sorry isn't going to bring Rosemary Hughes back to Jay, Bryan, and Kevin. Sorry isn't going to erase this terrible tragedy, this terrible stain from the psyche of our Kings Cross neighborhood.

All of Southwest is in an uproar. Stunned neighbors converse across stoops, over porch banisters, and out on the sidewalks. Rumors race up one street and down the next. Speculation is rife—and so is the building anger.

Why are these people moving into *our* neighborhood?

What do they want?

Why don't they just go back where they came from?

Why do they have to live like animals?

What did we ever do to them?

What's going to happen next?

So many questions, and so few answers. More than anything, there's the fear. You can feel it, sense it, almost smell it. Other parts of our city have "changed." When they built Connie Mack Stadium decades ago in North Philly, the area was all white. Now it's all colored, and people are afraid to go there . . . even during the daytime for the baseball games. Kids ask for a dollar just to "watch" your car . . . meaning maybe they won't trash it if you pay.

So what does the future hold for Kings Cross?

I think about our first black neighbor, Dré Barnett. Quick smile, shiny shoes, sharp creases in his pants. I can't imagine Dré stabbing anyone with a butcher knife. Or shy Coleman James, my quiet classmate from Longstreet Elementary. Or Bible-toting Mrs. Jones, Grandmom Kane's stalwart, Bible-reading, next-door neighbor.

But then again I can't imagine somebody stabbed so bad, over and over again, that the firemen have to come with the truck and hose the porch and steps and sidewalk and everything down because there's so much blood. So, so much blood.

It makes me sick to my stomach just thinking about it.

Grandmom lights a candle at church for Rosemary Hughes, and later next day she talks with me about what's happened. Grandmom works with a lot of colored people at Lyman's Automat, and gets along with just about everybody. She realizes my apprehension.

Jimmy, Grandmom says, You can't judge a book by its cover. There are good black people and bad black people, good white people and bad white people. Always remember that. Let me tell you a story about something that happened years ago in the neighborhood up north where I used to live. . . .

A white lady is riding the trolley one night, coming home from work. It's after dark. She goes to get off at her stop, but this colored man gets up, too, and heads for the doors. Afraid of getting off the trolley alone with him, she decides to sit down and wait until the next corner. She does, and a young white fellow gets off, too.

The man smiles at her, and she smiles back. This isn't my regular stop—the one before is, she tells the stranger. But I was afraid because no one else was getting off except for that colored man.

Well, agrees the white man, you did the right thing, Miss. Now I'll take that pocketbook from you, and don't try anything dumb. . . .

I laugh at the story, and understand what Grandmom is saying. She makes a good point. But later I get to thinking. Last year Grandmom drove me through her old neighborhood, it's way above Merchant Street . . . almost up by The Zoo. Upper part of West Philly, the area is black—and has been for years and years.

And all the white people such as Grandmom's family are long, long gone. . . . Never ever to return.

Tournament

Today is the big day, and us fighters slip quietly down the back steps at the rear of Sal "Cuz" Cusumano's house into Cuz's legendary basement gymnasium. Youngheads congregate outside in Sal's backyard to glimpse the action through dingy casement windows and dusty door panes. Inside Cuz and his oldhead cronies lounge on metal folding chairs, wooden crates, and the cellar steps. I see Bruce Cutler, Davey's older brother. Lanky Tommy O'Hanlon, Jackie's big brother and the star athlete of Kings Cross, is there, too. Ditto for Billy "Con" Connelly, Skinny Sammy Shapiro, and Slippery Bert Snyder. The afternoon's entertainment is about to begin.

Eight fighters in an elimination box-off—a series of seven clandestine fights that will determine the lightweight "younghead" champion of 5600 or "five-six" Littlefield and Wennington. The Cusumano basement has been neatly partitioned by a Maginot Line of makeshift boxes, paint cans, and used end tables. In the front half of the cellar rest Cuz's weighty iron barbells and dumbbells. The grey walls are covered with taped pinup after pinup of famous bodybuilders and strongmen. They stare back stiffly, frozen in various workout positions and bulging-muscle poses. Symmetrical Steve Reeves of Hollywood Hercules fame, grinning Mr. America, grimacing Mr. Europe, muscle-bound Mr. Olympia, humongous Mr. Universe. . . .

That guy makes Steve Reeves look like a skinny man, Cuz explains.

The rear half of the Cusumano cellar, an almost perfect square, remains empty save for the washer, dryer, and slop sink off in the corner. This is the temporary ring, our homegrown field of battle.

Cuz pops his head out the cellar door, cautions the crowd of peeping youngheads to keep the noise down. Don't be attracting any attention from adults, Cuz warns. Else there will be hell to pay. Not necessarily from the grown-ups, but from Cuz.

The youngheads obey and grow momentarily quiet. It is now time for the games to begin. Everyone loves a good fight, especially the spectators watching from a safe distance. But now it's my turn at being the spider in the jar, everyone else watching.

Hail Caesar! We that are about to die salute you. . . .

Back in the cellar, Cuz gives us warriors our final instructions. Each fight is three rounds long, with rounds being the length of whatever rock-and-roll song happens to be playing on the oldheads' official transistor radio. A fighter is considered knocked out when he turns and waves his glove to surrender, falls down and can't get up at the count of ten, or starts crying. After three rounds, Cuz will poll the oldhead judges by asking them to clap for each fighter, with the boxer receiving the most enthusiastic hand being declared the winner.

Good luck, guys, and may the best kid win.

There's a momentary delay as Cuz adjusts the radio, then pours a cup of Pepsi for each smiling, relaxed oldhead. Those of us younghead gladiators who are about to die salute them.

Round one of the opening fight begins with Mick Jagger and The Rolling Stones belting out their colossal hit *Satisfaction*. The wine-red Everlast gloves start flying, the oldheads are shouting encouragement, and the youngheads press their noses against the casement windows in their very cheap backyard seats—standing room only.

♪♪♪♪♪♪♪

Hey, hey, hey. . .That's what I say.

I can't get no . . .Sat-is-fact-shun.

Soon I'm on in the second fight against a tough, little curly-haired fireplug named Greg Mitchell. But while Greg may be very brave and willing, he has little boxing talent, and always leads with his face. I can't miss with my punches as I time his every bull-like rush. By round two, Chubby Checker is doing *The Twist*, and I'm beating a steady tattoo on Greg's pudgy face, which grows redder and redder with every connection. A big overhand right lands flush on Greg's schnozz. He screams, grabs his nose with his boxing glove, and so I immediately slug him one in his unprotected belly. Now Greg is crying, and Cuz steps in to call the match. Raises my glove in victory, and I give a confident showboat wink to the oldhead judges.

♪♪♪♪♪♪♪

Let's do the twist, twistin' time is here. . . .

Somebody helps Greg remove his gloves, pours him a cup of Pepsi as a consolation prize. He'll live. . . . It's just a red nose, Greg's more embarrassed than hurt.

The afternoon wears on with more good fights and scores of hard-driving pop tunes. Len Barry. The Lovin' Spoonful. The Byrds. The Dave Clark Five. Martha & the Vandellas. The Beatles. The Kinks. The Orlons. And, of course, my very own two favorites, Britain's Herman's Hermits and California's smooth-sounding Beach Boys.

The oldheads are really whooping it up, clapping and shouting and spilling cups of soda across the cement slab floor. For my second fight, I draw Terry McBride as my opponent. Terry is tall, awkward, and holds like an octopus, which makes him hard to hit. For three songs, I try my best, but after the last round, *Wipe Out* by The Safaris, Terry is still standing. Still, my volley of windmill punches is more than enough to earn the decision and put me in the championship final against my good buddy Jackie "Bugs" O'Hanlon.

310

Jackie has made quick work of his two opponents, hardly getting his dirty blonde hair mussed. I'm the defending champ, but Bugs smiles cockily after two consecutive early KOs. Besides, last year Jackie and I were the same size, but this year he's inches taller. Which isn't fair, since I'm almost two months older and one grade ahead.

Well, no matter. I'm just going to have to take care of business and defend my title. Bad enough I lost my unofficial fifth-grade crown back at Longstreet School to that Petey Ianelli, so I can't let the same thing happen here.

I stand alone in my corner, and Jackie in his. Cuz positions himself between us, softball muscles bulging, dark Brylcreemed hair glistening, a tiny gold cross dangling from the chain suspended from his thick, brown neck. Cuz doesn't need to win any stinking tournament, he was born the champ of Kings Cross, always was, always will be, some guys have all the luck. Surely the only things that could hurt Cuz are kryptonite or the atomic bomb.

Sam the Sham and The Pharaohs come on the transistor radio belting out *Wooly Bully*, and Cuz signals for us to begin.

♫♫♪♫♪♪♫♪

Uno, dos, one, two, tres, quatro

Matty told Hatty about a thing she saw.

Had two big horns and a wooly jaw. . . .

The room explodes in a flurry of noise and excitement as Jackie and I close the distance and meet in the center of the makeshift cement ring.

Nervous, we both swing and miss. I stalk Jackie, bending at the waist, trying to duck under Jackie's hard right-hand punches. I've got to get inside, go to the body, then up to the head. Keep the pressure on, keep Bugs on the run.

But this year is proving much different from last. Bugs is harder to reach now. His arms are longer, and he's sliding away whenever I try to trap him in a corner.

Snap, snap goes Jackie's left hand in my face. The jab's not hurting me much, but I can't get set to get my punches off. One second Bugs is there, the next second he's gone, and then I've got to load up and try again.

The Pharaohs finish their *Wooly Bully* song, and I know that Jackie has won that first round. Standing apart in my corner I look across the room at Bugs with his freckles, big rabbit ears, and buckteeth smiling back at me. Outside the ring us two are friends, now Jackie's trying to take my title but he can't have it because it's mine, and so I'm gonna knock that silly grin right off his retarded Dennis the Menace face. Maybe remove some buckteeth in the process, practice dentistry without a license.

Time in, the Dovells come on doing their *You Can't Sit Down* number, so Cuz gives the signal, and Jackie and I rush out and start firing punches with bad intentions. A jab bounces off my shoulder, and another glances off the top of my head, so I get mad and start smoking with both hands. Jackie circles, covers up doing the peekaboo, and I keep coming and keep swinging. I'm catching arms, elbows, shoulders, and one roundhouse left sneaks in and catches Bugs on the ear. What's up, doc, is right.

The crowd is screaming, I'm sucking wind, Jackie comes out of his shell and clips me with a right to the forehead, but I shake it off and keep on winging. Then the Dovells do the big finish and the music fades, ending round two. My round, so it's gotta be an even fight. The next and final round is for the championship, the whole bag of cookies. Jackie is good, but I can take him. He's no "Pistol" Petey Ianelli, that's for sure.

I'm standing by myself again in my corner, sucking air. Jackie stands across the way, staring back. The room grows quiet as the oldheads wait for the upcoming song and the final round. Cuz adjusts the volume, holds his free hand out like a traffic cop ordering us to wait.

Waiting, waiting, waiting, and . . . Box!

Jackie and I rush across the floor, nearly bumping skulls.

♫♪♫♪♪♪♫♪

There's a man who leads a life of danger.

To everyone he meets he stays a stranger. . .

♫♫♪♫♪♪♫♪

With every move he makes, another chance he takes.

Odds are he won't live to see tomorrow.

As Johnny Rivers sings about the lonely, dangerous life of the *Secret Agent Man*, Bugs O'Hanlon and I trade blows, going for the gusto. This isn't at all like last year, when I pounded Jackie to the body to take the tournament title. This year Jackie is taller, faster, and stronger. He parries my attempts to get within punching distance. Sticks that jab in my face, roughs me up on the inside when I finally do manage to get there. On the outside, Bugs feints and moves, shades of Cassius Clay. Uses that O'Hanlon family athleticism. But I reload and keep coming, keep swinging. C'mon, Crazy Jimmy.

My roundhouse right sails over Jackie's head. He slides along the back wall, and I keep coming, reaching for the body, trying to dig in a shot. If I can just knock the wind out of him, just for a few seconds, then I can let both hands go and take the round, maybe the fight.

Reaching, reaching, and . . . BAM!

I don't see Jackie's counter right hand until too late. It glances off my unprotected face in a flash of stars and jarring pain. I stumble forward, try to grab, try to buy time to clear my dazed and aching head. Jackie is pulling away, prying me off, shoving and throwing rabbit punches with a killer instinct to follow up on his momentary advantage. Bugs is now doing to me what I've been trying to do to him.

♫♫♪♫♪♪♫♪

Secret Agent Man,

Secret Agent Man,

They've given you a number,

And taken 'way your name. . . .

Out of gas now, I grope, claw, and hold. Throw the occasional feeble punch. Manage not to start crying, and last till the end of the round, when Johnny Rivers finally fades out on

313

Secret Agent Man. Jeez, I never realized this was such a long song.

Now Bugs and I stand in the middle of the room breathing hard as Cuz turns down the radio's volume. It's official now, polite cheers for me, rousing cheers for Jackie O'Hanlon, he's the new neighborhood lightweight champion of the youngheads.

Once again I've lost another title. Now my only remaining unofficial belt is for neighborhood body boxing, which is bare hands and no hitting in the face. I'm great at cracking kids' knuckles by catching them on my sharp, bony elbows. But body boxing is a minor sport, a play-acting version of real boxing, and nobody pays it much mind.

Jackie's the real champ now, hats off to him. Maybe I'll get a little bigger and stronger and then win the title back next year before we become the new oldheads, sipping cups of soda and watching the upcoming crop of youngheads getting it on.

Later, Cuz gets Jackie and me our own cups of Pepsi, I wish he had root beer instead, and then congratulates me on fighting so gutsy and hard-nosed.

Yeah, but I'd rather have won, I tell Cuz. Maybe you can give me some sparring lessons, teach me some new moves.

Gotta shorten your hook, keep your hands up, and learn to slip more punches, Cuz observes.

I nod in agreement, and tell Cuz how this makes two titles I've lost. Got beat by this kid Petey Ianelli over at Longstreet Elementary back in the fifth grade.

Cuz cocks his head at the mention of the name. Ianelli? You mean the runty little kid who lives on 57th and Wennington?

Yep, that's the one.

Cuz laughs. Well, no kidding. His father's Rocco Ianelli, the prizefighter. The boy gets lessons every weekend in the backyard. The old man puts the gloves on Petey and makes him go a coupla rounds. He's practically a baby pro himself by now.

This doesn't make me feel a whole lot better, but it does go a long way in explaining things. That three-punch KO Petey hung on me two years ago was no fluke. I just wish maybe I could get some lessons from a pro like Mr. Ianelli. Or Cuz, who might as well be a pro.

I look again at all the posters adorning the Cusumano basement walls. Symmetrical Steve Reeves of Hollywood Hercules fame, grinning Mr. America, grimacing Mr. Europe, muscle-bound Mr. Olympia, humongous Mr. Universe. . . . I've see all the ads on the back pages of the comic books—the ones with the smiling muscle-bound guy that says, *I was a 98-pound weakling before I started with the Super X Muscle-Building Formula.*

My first problem is I'm not even close to 98 pounds yet. So first I gotta bulk up just to get to 98-pound-weakling status.

It starts me to wondering. Learning to fight, or growing big muscles? Which would be better?

Then I look at Cuz, and I know the answer. In old Kings Cross, it's better to have both precious assets. Definitely.

Hey, I mean, it couldn't possibly hurt—right? Anyway, I for one am game . . . let's bring on the moves, bring on the muscles.

CHAPTER 12

Secret Student

I've graduated from Longstreet Elementary, summer is now over, and my parents are still trying to decide where I'm to go to school. Dad doesn't want me going to Catholic school, and both of them don't want me going to Sanders, the now-infamous, battle-scarred public junior high just a block-and-a-half away—the once-proud school Dad attended decades earlier.

Desperate, Mom and Dad ask a favor of Uncle Hank and his wife Betty. Seems we're going to run a little game on the education system. Enroll me in a nice public school out in the suburbs, register me at Uncle Hank and Aunt Betty's address.

My instructions are clear . . . don't talk to anyone. Not a soul. Take the train at 58th Street below Maryland to the suburban Langford Station, walk the rest of the way to school, keep my mouth shut, take the train home in the afternoon, and nobody will know the difference. Simple.

Sounds good to me, although I'm sure missing all my good friends from Longstreet. I know many of them will be going on to Sanders. Seems like an awful lot of fuss over going to a better school. Langford is miles and miles away.

So every morning I carry my books, wait for the train on a platform full of adults heading for work, and quietly set out for Langford–Alton High School in Delco County, grades seven through twelve. Sure is different from elementary school in the city. They've got real athletic fields, soundproof music rooms, a metal shop, a cooking room for Home Economics, science labs, a great big auditorium with a stage, a padded wrestling room, fancy art rooms with all kinds of painting supplies, mechanical drawing tables, and best of all—a huge lunchroom with every kind of meal, juice, and snack you could possibly want.

All Longstreet Elementary had was a concrete playground, swings, a storage room filled to the ceiling with a mountain of coal, and a makeshift library in the basement. Looked like a medieval fortress. But I liked it anyway—it was our neighborhood school.

Pretty soon I'm settled in at Langford–Alton, and making the adjustment to moving from class to class each period. I've got homeroom with the Home Economics teacher, then metal shop or study hall, English, gym, lunch, Science, Social Studies, Math, and on some days, Music. But the new schoolwork is tough, and the long trip home every day doesn't help. By mid-first quarter my English and Social Studies teachers are sending notices home that I need to bring up my grades.

Unfortunately, my mind still has a mind of its own. And it's so much easier to get into trouble in high school when you're going from class-to-class, teacher-to-teacher. No one person is in charge of watching you, and there are so many distractions when you're so far away from home. . . .

The Long and Short of It

In the morning I get off the train from Philly, same as usual. Hustle through the streets of suburban Langford on the way to Langford–Alton High School. As I'm passing the local Catholic school, grades K to 8, a ball comes flying out of the schoolyard and rolls across the street just up ahead. Must've bounced over the fence. I see a tall black boy in a sea of white shirts and ties waving to get my attention.

He hollers, Yo—little help! and points toward the escaping sphere.

I rush over, grab the ball, fire it back at him. Only my aim is a little off and the ball goes sailing high and to the left, out of his reach.

The black boy looks over his shoulder at the ball zooming all the way across the schoolyard, then turns his attention back toward me.

He yells, Punk! . . . You did that on purpose.

No I didn't!

Yeah you did!

Says who?

Says me.

317

Wanna make somethin' of it?

Fair one, right now!

The black boy struts toward the schoolyard entrance, glaring at me all the way. I cross the street, walk toward the opening to confront him.

The boy is even taller than I realized . . . a head taller than me easily, though young looking. We close the distance and now he stares down at me contemptuously.

The black boy challenges me again. Why you do that, man?

Do what? I didn't do *anything!* Next time get the ball yourself.

He screams, Don't mess with me! . . . Then gives my shoulder a hard shove.

Instinctively I swing back—hard. I aim at his face, but the boy's so tall my punch lands short and slams into his chest. To my surprise the kid steps back, clutches the area of impact, bends over, and starts to cry.

He squeals, I'ma tell my big brother! You wait here!

Like a dummy I do what the boy says—I wait right there. The thought occurs to me that as tall as this boy is, his big brother may look like Wilt Chamberlain. Maybe I should just pick up my books and be on my way.

But as I'm mulling over the situation, the Catholic school's side door opens and the tall black boy reappears . . . along with his "big" brother. The second boy looks a year or two older all right, but he's two shades lighter and also a full head shorter. Perhaps even no taller than runty little me. I blink, not believing my eyes.

The tall one spots me, still rubbing his chest. There he is, Lamont. That's the one who did it!

The two boys stride across the lot, "big" brother in front.

Hey—you the one hit my brother?

Yeah, I did. But he pushed me first.

Sensing a fight, the sea of white shirts and white faces begins to converge around us at the schoolyard entrance. Mutt and Jeff here look to be the only black kids in this entire school.

The tall boys interrupts, He threw the ball over my head, Lamont—on purpose!

Lamont asks me, Why you do that?

I smile, Are you *really* his brother? . . . still not believing what I'm seeing.

Lamont barks, Hey—I axed you a question, Four Eyes. Don't get smart.

I retort, Bug off, pal! . . . You don't tell me what I can say. . . .

Put my hands on my hips for emphasis.

Next thing I know Lamont is tearing into me, fists pumping. Bam, bam, bam! One punch hits me on the cheek, just missing my glasses. I step back, tear my specs off, jam them in my pocket. But before I can get off a punch, here comes Lamont, Bap. . . bap . . . bap. It's like trying to fight an electric typewriter. I've never seen anyone move his hands that fast. Petey Ianelli hit harder, but this Lamont boy is even faster.

I move and duck, wait for Lamont to miss—barely, then grab him in a bear hug, holding on for dear life. We struggle, Lamont tries to break free to throw more punches.

Git 'im, Lamont! cries the "little" brother. Beat his butt!

And "little" brother's not the only one. The crowd of onlookers form a ring, encircling us combatants. They're cheering for Lamont, too.

Lamont starts to wiggle away again, and I go for the headlock. Suddenly, we both topple to the ground. I've got the advantage— no, Lamont's getting the upper hand. I push harder, then pull and flip Lamont over. But no sooner do I get on top than Lamont is hissing and spitting and clawing like a madman, trying to throw me off . . . and doing a good job.

Lamont screams, Let me up! I'ma kill you! Let me up!!

Someone in the crowd says, Uh oh—here comes Sister!

I look up for a split second, see where the crowd has parted for the approaching nun.

The Sister starts issuing orders: Stop that, Lamont! Stop it right now!

But Lamont is foaming at the mouth, tussling for all he's worth. I take a calculated gamble—let go, roll away, jump up, and quick stand beside the rotund nun for protection.

Lamont scrambles to his feet, starts to charge after me, but the nun uses her girth to intercede. She grabs hold of Lamont's shirt. Meanwhile, I'm wisely keeping Sister between me and certain trouble. Just minutes ago I was walking to school, not a care in the world. How did I ever get myself into this mess?

The nun gets a better grip on Lamont, wheels him around and starts pushing him toward the school door.

Get inside, Lamont—now!

Lamont and the nun start for the door, "little" brother in tow. I finally take the hint and start to head in the other direction—for the exit and safety. Go for my books, get ready to split.

Now I hear more shouting, turn around to see what's up. The nun is holding onto Lamont again, tugging him fiercely toward the school building.

Lamont is yelling, I'ma get you . . . you hear me! I'ma whip your butt, Four Eyes! I'ma get you good, boy—when no one else is around!!

I don't doubt Lamont's murderous intentions for a second. But a realization crosses my mind, and I start to smile.

I holler, Oh yeah, Lamont? You will, huh? There's only one problem, you moron!

Lamont has now paused at the school entrance, watching, listening. . . .

Guess what, Lamont—you don't even know who I am, or where I live!

With that parting shot I retrieve my books, put on my Coke-bottle glasses, and continue on to Langford–Alton, where I am already late for homeroom.

The Betrayal

A nice young woman at my Ankorra Mill train stop in Philly has taken notice of me riding to the suburbs every morning with an armful of textbooks.

She says, Hi there—where do you go to school? I see you on the train every day. Do you go to private school?

At first I'm evasive, but then the woman slowly wins my confidence. What could it hurt? It's the other kids at school who Mom and Dad don't want me talking to. So I tell the woman my parents don't like the school in our neighborhood, and are instead sending me to a better one in my uncle's neighborhood out past the city line.

That Friday, no notice, I'm yanked out of study hall, sent immediately to the school office. Get called on the so-called-carpet—by a beefy, red-faced school administrator who chews me out royally. Jumps right up in my face, his thick eyebrows twitching, beady eyes narrowing. Treats me like a criminal.

Don't you know this is illegal? Why aren't you going to school where you belong? It's not fair to the taxpayers of this school district! Blah, blah, blah. . . .

Funny, but Dad says the same thing about Sanders. Says what they've done to the local schools with the forced busing isn't fair to the taxpayers in our Philadelphia neighborhood, the people paying the freight. Damned if *his* kids are going to be somebody's guinea pig, maybe get knifed in the process. You know those ivory-tower college people cooking up these harebrained social schemes aren't going to dare sending *their* kids to a dustbin like Sanders . . . they probably go to some fancy, ivy-covered, lily-white prep school out in the country. Hypocrites, every one of 'em. Playing with peoples' lives, like so many pieces on a chessboard.

Soon I learn about the betrayal. Seems that "nice lady" on the train works in the Langford–Alton School District. Finked on me first chance she got, once she knew the whole story and was wise to our plan. Thanks to me.

Funny, but nobody seems to mind that the "nice lady" lives in Philly with us, but teaches out at Langford–Alton. How come she's not teaching at Longstreet, or Sanders, or Burnham?

No matter. The school administrator keeps asking me questions, but I dummy up. This is grown-up business, and already he knows way too much as it is, courtesy of my big mouth. Dizzy James is already in plenty enough trouble for one day.

I go home on the train. The school calls Uncle Hank and Aunt Betty. All the grown-ups have a conference about me the following Monday, my fate hanging in the balance. But just when I'm sure I'm headed back to Sanders, a compromise is reached. I can remain at Langford-Alton the rest of the school year, but there's just one catch. . . .

I've got to go live with Uncle Hank and Aunt Betty—for real. Stay in the suburbs, ride the school bus each morning. School officials will be checking. If they catch me taking the Philly train during the school week again, it's the Sanders Zoo here I come.

Mom quickly packs all my clothes. She says it's okay for me to come home for the weekends.

I'm told to behave for Uncle Hank and Aunt Betty—I'm their guest, they're doing me a big favor. And one more thing—don't do anything, ANYTHING that would give Langford–Alton a reason to kick me out. . . .

Seems they're just itching for an excuse.

Later that week Aunt Betty takes me to the local mall, to a store that sells school paraphernalia. She has me pick out a scarlet-and-grey gym back with the letters LAHS emblazoned on its side. Not bad—the letters stand for Langford Alton High School.

But the one that really catches my eye is the black-and-gold model with the one-eyed pirate grinning back at me. Jaunty buccaneer cap, great eye patch, I think pirates are the coolest.

That's Triboro High School, Aunt Betty explains, just west of here. They're the Pirates. Not a bad school, but LA is better.

I say, Triboro? What kind of silly name is Triboro, and what joker would ever go to such a dumb-sounding school? Even if they do have such sharp-looking gym bags. . . .

Me and Lonnie McGee

So now I'm living at my aunt and uncle's house and riding the bus to high school, grades seven through twelve. Aunt Betty is a farm girl from the western part of the state and runs a different house from my mother's. Back home, things are more informal. But here in Alton, Aunt Betty is a stickler for cleanliness and rising at the crack of dawn . . . time to "red up" as she says. She's forever on me about showering, "warshing" behind my ears, and brushing my teeth until my gums are sore. But pretty soon I get with the program as if I'd been doing it all my life.

I don't know any of the kids in the neighborhood and just pick any old seat next to anybody so long as it hasn't been taken. Except, of course, if the other person is a girl. Then that's a different story, and I look for a spot elsewhere.

One day on the ride home all the seats are taken except two. One is next to a fat girl named June, and the other is beside the only black boy in the entire town of Alton.

Hard choice. If I sit next to the fat girl, she may think I'm sweet on her. Or, just as bad, somebody else might start the rumor . . . pass it around.

On the other hand, I noticed before that all the other kids avoid sitting next to the black boy—he often sits alone.

I hesitate. The black boy looks my way, and, just for a second—our gazes lock. Then he looks back out the window. But something in the way he looked at me sent me a message. . . . Please, sit next to me.

So I sit next to the colored kid, take out a schoolbook, start reading, mind my own business.

We ride through tree-lined Langford until we reach the Alton borough line. Corner after corner kids get dropped off. The bus starts to empty. I wait for the colored boy to get up, but he says nothing and just keeps looking out the window.

Finally, we're reaching the end of the line, the final three stops for the last streets in Alton. The remaining kids all get off, disappearing in several directions. Except the colored boy, who stays by my side. We reach my new street, and the boy's still with me. I hadn't noticed him before at my stop, or on my street. Now we're all alone, just the two of us. Finally, the other boy speaks.

Hi. My name's Lonnie. Lonnie McGee. What's yours?

Jimmy Morris. I live up this way, on Birch Street.

Lonnie says, I know . . . I saw you the other day—my house is just across the street from yours.

Soon I'm stopping by at Lonnie's house on the way home from school. I'm the new kid and don't know anyone. Most of the other kids ignore Lonnie, and he keeps mainly to himself.

Mrs. McGee gives us milk and cookies. She seems glad that Lonnie's finally made a friend.

Uncle Hank gets a big laugh out of the situation, while Aunt Betty is somewhat annoyed. Here are my mom, dad, aunt, and uncle all conspiring to keep me out of Sanders, which has been overrun with the blacks they're busing in. So now that I'm out in the suburbs in a 99.9% all-white school, what do I do? Buddy up with the only black child on the school bus. Go figure.

Uncle Hank smiles, says since we're just kids, let us be kids. No harm, no foul. Lonnie seems like a nice enough boy.

But Aunt Betty doesn't like it. Doesn't like that the McGees have moved onto Birch Street in the all-white borough of Alton. Her street. I try to tell Aunt Betty that Lonnie's a good kid, good in school . . . always dresses nicely. Aunt Betty agrees but says when you let one in more will surely follow. Like flies, she warns—like a swarm of flies.

We hang out in Lonnie's room, mostly reading comic books. I think Lonnie's got every comic book they ever printed. Superman, Spiderman, The Hulk, The Fantastic Four, Batman—you name it, he's got it. Every edition. He's got 'em piled in closets, under his bed, in chests, on shelves, in cabinets . . . action heroes everywhere. Lonnie's a walking encyclopedia of fantasy. Reads them out loud, acts out the parts.

Bang, zoom, *POW*!

One day I suggest maybe we do something different. Like play basketball, ride a bike, have a catch. Nothing doing. When Lonnie doesn't have his nose in a textbook, he's got it in a comic book. Rarely goes out, except to go to school.

I start to wonder if kids are avoiding Lonnie because he's black, because he's weird, or because he's both. His parents seem normal enough—it's a wonder they don't kick him outta his room from time to time, make Lonnie do something else besides all this make-believe fantasy stuff.

As I slowly begin to make other friends at LAHS, I begin to find excuses for not swinging by Lonnie's house after school. Eventually I stop going altogether. We still say hi to each other in the halls at school, and sometimes Lonnie will slip me a new comic book in study hall. But mostly we've gone our own separate ways, me with my small new circle of friends, and Lonnie by his lonesome in his imaginary world of evildoers and caped crusaders.

Maybe I feel a little sorry for Lonnie, but I don't miss the subtle stares from the other kids . . . the feeling of being an outsider.

And besides, it's made Aunt Betty a whole lot happier about things in general. Me and Lonnie McGee—jeez, what would the neighbors think?

Boys Will Be Boys

I slowly and steadily develop a new circle of friends at Langford–Alton High School. Mostly some regular seventh-grade kids at my table in the lunchroom. My new best pal is Tim Armbruster, who lives just around the corner from Uncle Hank and Aunt Betty. He's in the Boy Scouts, and my aunt remembers him fondly from when she was den mother for the Cub Scouts. Some days after school Tim and I watch television over at his house, work on jigsaw puzzles, or listen to bubble gum records by The Archies or The Monkees. Tim heads up the newspaper drive for his Scout troop, collecting old papers to give to the Junk Man for cash. He and his dad have this derelict car in their backyard which they fill up with newsprint. When the car's full, it's time to unload the stuff and start over again. The boys in those drab-green military shirts and funny neckerchiefs always need more money.

I help Tim go door to door, collect some bundles of papers. Even attend a Scout meeting or two. But I don't think the Boy Scouts are for me . . . all that goody-two-shoes garbage and "I will be square" nonsense.

After all, I've still got a rep to protect back in Kings Cross. Diet Donnie would never let me live it down if he found out I was consorting with known Boy Scouts.

Meanwhile, I've also managed to make a couple of enemies at Langford–Alton. Some of the "cooler" and bigger kids have this thing against wearing white socks to school. Wear white socks and you're sure to get razzed—or worse. It's to the point where some of the boys even wear black socks to gym class . . . sneakers, shorts, and all. I know, it's ridiculous, but it's the unwritten code at my new school.

One day I wear white socks to gym, which is borderline taboo, but then forget to change back into black socks for class. A definite, big-time no-no.

Fred Talbot, our grade's premier bully and a heavyweight wrestler on the junior-high squad, decides to give me grief over, of all things, athletic socks. Not that Fred needs an excuse, but now he has one. He's at the lunchroom table behind us, and I try my best to ignore him.

At first Fred just points to my white socks. Then he's calling me names. Next he comes over and pours milk on my pants— since I like wearing white so much.

Embarrassed in front of my friends, I tell Fred to bug off.

Fred pushes me—hard. Laughs in my face. What did you say, Four Eyes? You tellin' me what to do, shrimp? How about it, Carrot Top?

I try talking my way out of the jam, but Big Fred's having too much fun.

Fred says, I'll see you after school, Loser. By the tree on the far side of the football field. Then we'll see if you're still brave enough to tell me what to do. And don't try to chicken out on me, 'cause I'll come lookin' for ya.

For the rest of the day my friends look at me sadly. Dead man walking, I've only got hours to live, tops.

Big Fred goes about 140 if he's a pound. I'm maybe 85 pounds with rocks in my pockets.

It was nice knowin' ya, Jimmy Morris.

I'm no fool . . . I break my date with Big Fred, hope he doesn't notice. Too bad, he does.

For the rest of the week Fred's looking for me after class, shoving me in the halls, telling everyone I'm chicken, afraid of my own shadow. Worse yet he's told his eighth-grade buddy on the wrestling team, Ernie Imhoff, who's not as tall as Fred but is even stockier. Weighs 150 if he's an ounce. Now they're both torturing me wherever I turn, there's no place to hide.

Friday afternoon our history teacher, mean Mrs. Smedley, catches me peeking at some girl's paper during a quiz, orders me to stay after school. Makes an example of me in front of the entire class. Now I'll have to take the late bus. Fred's in my history class, but I don't take any notice of this—until I leave detention. Sure enough, Fred and Ernie are waiting by the stairwell where they accost me. Two against ½.

Fred laughs, Time's up, chicken. Now you're ours, you little punk.

Fred and Ernie begin to march me through the empty school— toward the rear exit . . . we're headed for that tree at the far side of the athletic field. Nice, quiet, out-of-the way . . . no interruptions.

Only thing is, we pass by the main office on our little march across the building. I see the opportunity, fake like I'm tripping, then break free and dash through the office doors. Quietly take a seat by the Vice-Principal's office, wait for him to come out.

Fred and Ernie peek in, look around. Pssstt . . . Morris. You tellin' on us, ya little pip-squeak?

Don't know yet. Maybe I am, maybe I'm not. Depends.

Ernie makes a slow, silent, slashing gesture across his throat. If I rat, I'm dead meat. They pretend to be threatening out in the hallway, but I can tell my little stunt has these wrestler goobers worried. No telling what I'll say, or what trouble they could be in.

Later the Vice-Principal comes out of his office. I explain I feel sick to my stomach and missed the late bus. He gives me a ride home in his sporty new VW beetle. Nice guy. I think he knows something's up, but doesn't ask. Seems like a pretty cool sort—especially for a vice-principal.

I'm safe . . . for now. But then I lie awake in bed thinking about Fred and Ernie. Friday night, Saturday night, Sunday night . . . until Monday morning rolls inevitably around, with the long bus ride into school.

Pssstt, Fred whispers, first period. Did you tell, chicken? Did ya?

I shake my head. Being a chicken's bad enough without adding "fink" to my lowly resumé. I'd already made enough of a mess of things. Maybe I should've just gone to Sanders after all.

The humiliation only gets worse. Fred and Ernie pass it around . . . James Morris ran into the office and hid from us, he was so scared. Threatened to tell the Vice-Principal, the little weasel. The other kids laugh and point, and my friends don't want to look me in the eye at lunch.

Fred pays our lunch table a visit, pours more milk on my pants.

I thought the city was supposed to be rough, and the suburbs a piece of cake. Boy, did I think wrong.

Eventually, Fred and Ernie catch up with me again after school. This time I don't run or yell for help as they take me out to the tree on the far side of the football stadium. I'm simply out of options—I've got no choice but to fight Fred and get it over with.

I know it's a sin but at this moment I'm thinking that I hate God for making me so small and other kids so big. It's not much to ask to be big. If I were a big kid, I'd mind my own business and not go around torturing 85-pound midgets all around campus. I swear.

But I'm not a big kid, so here I am—about to get pounded. Fred takes off his jacket and I do the same. I hate Fred Talbot and Ernie Imhoff and all the other overgrown dummies in the world with cabbage for brains. But at least these dummies have brains enough to grow big and strong. Me, I'll always be a squirt.

Fred smiles devilishly and puts his hands up to box. I find a measure of comfort in that he's not starting out by tackling me and rubbing my face into the ground as if I were some kind of #2 pencil eraser.

I put my hands up high, begin circling.

Fred throws a punch and misses. Then another—misses again. I can see the blows coming . . . wide, slow, and telegraphed. Most I duck, and a few I block. Fred is clumsy, and probably never fights anybody his own size, except in wrestling. But he's very strong, and if one of Fred's looping shots connects, I'm in big trouble. It'll be down for the count I go.

Ernie yells, C'mon, Fred . . . finish him off. *Hit him*, will ya?

Fred huffs and puffs. I'm tryin', Ernie. But he won't stand still!

I start to counter some of Fred's misses. Just a couple of quick shots here and there that bounce off Fred's arms and chest. No real damage, but it makes Fred angrier. Swing and a miss, swing and a miss. I can feel the breeze.

Fred's face is getting red and he's breathing more heavily. I fake left, fake right, go left, bob and weave.

Fred yells, Stand still and fight, will ya?!

Ernie gets mad at Fred, starts to call him names. Fred starts with the excuses. While this is going on I pick up my jacket, wave to Fred.

Nice fight, Fred. Why don't we shake hands, call it a draw? I gotta catch the bus.

But before I can go, Ernie comes over. Says, Not so fast, Morris. You still gotta fight me, too.

Huh? That wasn't part of the deal. This was between me and Fred.

My turn, Ernie insists. Then we're all done and you can go home.

Disgusted, I take off my jacket . . . again. Not only am I being made to fight the biggest kid in seventh grade, but also the biggest kid in eighth grade—back-to-back.

Within thirty seconds I discover that Fred is Fred and Ernie is Ernie. I make the big eighth-grader miss his first few punches, but he's way better than Fred. Ernie's punches are fairly straight and crisp. He misses with a left, but then follows with the right. Bam, the punch slams into my shoulder with a jolt. Clueless Fred doesn't know what a combination is; Ernie's just thrown the old one-two. This boy knows how to fight a little, and he's twice my size.

Ernie fakes the left. I duck. But when I come up, Ernie's clubs me on the side of the head with his right. I go down on one knee.

Ernie tells me, You gotta say "uncle" when you give. Do you give?

I shake my head no, stand up.

I'm ducking and moving, ducking and moving . . . but it's just a matter of time. Finally, Ernie makes me bite on another feint. A short right hook clips me right in the mouth. I go down again, only this time much harder. I sit up, touch my lip, taste the blood.

Ernie says, Do you give?

I could get up again, but Ernie's only going to hit me harder. And I'm way too small to hurt him back, even with a lucky punch.

I pull myself up on one knee, wave Ernie off. Say the magic words.

I give.

It's all over, I can catch the late bus now. But I'm furious at myself for being weak, for being small, and for being a target. Most of all, I'm disgusted at myself for giving up. No guts. I should've made Ernie knock me out cold. Have them carry me out on my shield—like a true warrior.

Hail Caesar! We that are about to die salute you.

Cuz wouldn't have given up, or Tommy O'Hanlon, or Dad, nor Uncle Hank. A real man wouldn't do that. A lousy little punk would.

But at least it's over. Fred and Ernie will likely move on to their next victim, no use picking on me any more. They've had their little fun.

I catch the last bus to Alton, my lip growing fat and numb. Feels like I've been to see the dentist. In a way I have . . . I can tell Ernie does this a lot, only he operates without a license. Nice work if you can get it. Badabing, badaboom.

When I get home, Aunt Betty sees the fat lip. So, what happened to you?

I tripped in gym class.

Yeah, right.

Hanky-Panky

Seventh-grade science class with Mr. Lugar is right after lunch, down in the basement next to the cafeteria. Which means we usually show up a few minutes before the teacher. One day I'm in my seat early, along with a few others. It's in one of those special lecture rooms where the curved rows elevate toward the back to give everyone a good view. Two boys above and behind me are whispering and giggling, and I lean my chair in their direction so I can pick up on what's so secretly funny.

They're talking about how babies are conceived. The one boy, Charlie, is giving the other boy a graphic description of how it's done. Charlie has just found out and is anxious to share this amazing knowledge—who does what with whom using which parts of whose anatomy. I've heard vague rumors to this effect, but never anything so spectacularly detailed. I try to picture in my mind what Charlie is describing, but it's so preposterously absurd I can't fathom it. Nobody in their right mind would ever even consider doing such a thing with another person, no way José. It's just too gross.

Right about then Mary Alice Resnick enters the room and takes a seat near me, her frizzy hair tied down with a white headband, socks pulled up to her knobby knees, black shiny little girl's shoes with the Pilgrimlike silver buckles. Mary Alice is so skinny she looks downright sickly—can't weight more than 37 pounds tops. If she ever fell down and broke something there'd be no need for X-rays . . . just hold her up to the light.

Now I'm looking at Mary Alice out of the corner of my eye, thinking about the things Charlie is saying, imagining me and Mary Alice Resnick. No, no, no it's just not possible. Charlie needs some serious help, he's one sick pup, and they should throw him some of those ink-blot puzzles straightaway and find out what's up. Must be a screw loose somewhere, maybe a whole box of 'em.

Babies just grow in women's stomachs until they get fat and swollen and have to get rushed to the hospital where the babies can be born, that's all. Charlie is out of his cotton-picking mind, and I look at Mary Alice Resnick one more time just to be certain—and boy am I ever certain.

As I said before, No way, José. Not now, not any time soon, not ever. Gross me out!

But this overheard snippet of illicit conversation bothers me the rest of the school day as I ponder what to do—tell somebody Charlie needs serious help or mind my own business. Somewhere way in the back of my seventh-grade mind there's a fuzzy link between what Charlie's talking about and me getting kicked in the shins back in sixth grade by Rachel Moskowitz. But for the life of me I can't make the connection.

Basically, Charlie is a looney tune and needs his goofy head examined, he's a strange one all right.

Maybe the school nurse can help. It wouldn't be like ratting on Charlie since he's clearly in need of professional guidance. But I can't very well march right into her office and repeat what I heard Charlie say. Perhaps, just perhaps, an anonymous note might be do the trick. . . .

Dear Nurse Strickland,

Charles Murdoch, a seventh-grader, is telling us other students the most disgusting things about how babies are made. I don't want to get Charles in any trouble, but he has a sick mind and needs a lot of advice.

P.S.: I won't tell you what Charles said boys and girls are supposed to do with each other when they get older. You'll have to ask him. But be careful, he might lie and say somebody made the whole thing up.

Sincerely,

X X X

Someone in Charlie's class

But no, I don't write the letter. In the end, I figure Charlie's problems are Charlie's problems and they don't concern me. His parents or teachers are going to have to figure out on their own that Charlie is a serious head case with weird ideas. Besides, isn't that what parents and teachers are for?

I board the bus, watch the world go by my window, forget all about Charlie Murdoch. Start humming that catchy new tune I've been hearing on the radio everywhere, over and over. The funky, wild-sounding one by Tommy James and the Shondels.

♫ *My baby does the hanky panky. . . . ♪ My baby does the hanky panky. . . . ♫*

Burning Issues

Grandmom Kane's old clunker has been on the fritz, so now she takes the early bus. Since before Mom was born she's worked as a waitress in Lyman's "automat" restaurant. South Philly, North Philly, downtown. Serving soup, coffee, tuna sandwiches, lemon meringue pie. Quick food for busy people. Year after year after year. Always on her feet, always on the go.

Years before I used to think Grandmom was the richest woman in the whole world, with her little brown zippered purse that always bulged. Quarters, dimes, nickels, pennies—her bounty of tips for the day. Counting coins at the dining room table, bringing a Snickers or Chunky bar home for each of us kids. Always a smile no matter how hard the day, how tedious her life.

Actually, Grandmom *was* rich once. Long time ago. Well, sort of. Way back when, before the Great Depression. Mother's father was a successful car salesman. An unpredictable, irascible, besotted Irishman blessed by the Blarney Stone. Francis charmed friends, business associates, customers, and Grandmom alike. Never at a loss for a story. Knew how to say the right things at the right times, had that Emerald Isle instinct. Parlayed his salesman's commissions into a sizeable grubstake. Sweet-talked some bank into an otherwise risky loan. Opened his very own used auto lot. Did well. Opened two more dealerships, then secured a bigger line of credit from the bank. Leveraged his growing profits in the stock market. Bought on margin. Made a quick killing. The typical rags to riches, Roaring Twenties tale.

Francis meets Grandmom at—where else?—Lyman's Automat. She's waitressing, serving up the lemon meringue pie, and he's drinking the coffee, serving up his usual blarney.

Soon Francis is sending a car and driver to chauffeur young Elizabeth from the restaurant. Begs her to quit the waitressing job. He's got plenty of mullah, has enough to retire by age twenty-seven. No need her pouring coffee and serving pie for five- and ten-cent tips.

But my grandmother-to-be likes her job. Values her independence. Keeps taking the early bus to the automat. Very stubborn.

Then comes the great stock market crash of '29, followed by The Depression of the '30s. Francis' leveraged house of cards collapses. Loses forty grand in one day—at a time when you can buy a meal for fifty cents and a new car for $800. Sits with his head in his hands on the front porch of the West Philly home of Elizabeth's parents.

I've lost everything, he moans. Everything.

Elizabeth's mother admonishes Francis. You haven't lost everything, you fool. You only lost your money.

Francis vows to get his money back. More fancy schemes, sharper angles. Meanwhile, in the depths of the numbing Depression, my mother Pamela is born. As soon as she's strong enough, Elizabeth resumes taking the early bus. And Francis continues to dream, to plan. A comeback the likes of which the business world has never seen. He'll show 'em . . . show them all.

But for all his jocularity, and the grandiose ideas, Francis has a darker side. Alcohol, the great curse of the Irish. Fueled by premonitions of an early demise.

I won't live a day past forty, Francis confides to Elizabeth in a somber, if not sober, moment.

Elizabeth replies, Don't be ridiculous. How could you possibly know a thing such as that?

I know, answers Francis cryptically. I just do.

Later, when he's feeling a mite better, Elizabeth sends Francis around the corner for some eggs and milk. Three days later he returns—with a loaf of bread and head of cabbage.

It is no use now. Francis continues to worsen, and Elizabeth continues to take the early bus to the automat and care for little Pamela.

Then comes the accident. Francis, too drunk to drive, careens into a telephone pole, his chest crushed by the force of the unforgiving steering wheel. Recovery is slow, painful, uncertain. Then, just as Francis may be about to turn the corner—calamity strikes. Tuberculosis sets in, the dreaded "Consumption." In Francis' already weakened condition the inevitable doesn't take long: his lanky six-foot frame reduced to a skeletal sixty pounds.

Francis, entrepreneur and visionary, alcoholic and incorrigible louse, dies at age thirty-nine, not a penny to his name. Elizabeth becomes a single parent at thirty. Little Pamela is not yet three.

Elizabeth continues to take the early bus to Lyman's Automat. When Pam is old enough, Grandmom Kane sends her away to live with the nuns at the girls' Catholic school near the university. Comes home for Thanksgiving, Christmas, Easter. The "Catholic slammer" is the way Dad describes it when he's needling Mom.

And so on this particular day, as on thousands of days before and on thousands of days to come, Grandmom rises before daybreak to catch her early bus. In the stillness of those wee hours she hears a noise out there in the darkness.

Milkman?

No, there it is again. Out in back, not in front—can't be the milkman. It's someone behind the house, in the common driveway that runs between Littlefield and Wennington. So Grandmom glances out the rear bedroom window. Sees the Fahey roofing truck, parked in front of the Fahey's garage same as usual. And the silhouette of a man standing at the rear of the two-wheeled contraption attached to the roofing truck. It's what the men use to cook the tar they spread across the flat row house rooftops. As Grandmom's eyes focus she can tell he's a young man. Bushy hair, checkered flannel shirt, dark pants probably dungarees, and white sneakers. Probably one of the roofers there to get an early start, maybe fix some faulty piece of equipment. Seems to be holding a metal can of some sort.

Grandmom pulls away from the window, steps back. Remembers she wants to put some coffee on, begins to leave the bedroom. Hears footsteps running, then a tremendous "whoosh-ing" sound from the rear of the house. Turns, sees light flaring up against the curtained windows. Lots of light. Dancing, flickering.

Roofers wear boots on the job, not sneakers. But this doesn't cross Grandmom's mind until later.

The Fahey truck is fully engulfed in fire, a raging inferno. Ditto for the trailing tar cooker on wheels. Flames leap from the burning vehicles onto the family garage. Climb up the wall, lick at the Fahey kitchen windows. Meanwhile, the Faheys lie fast asleep on the second floor.

Grandmom runs for the phone downstairs, dials 911. Hurry, please hurry. There are kids in that house. Hangs up the phone, makes the sign of the cross, says a quick prayer.

The early morning stillness is quickly shattered. Police. Fire engines. Inspectors. Detectives asking questions. Thankfully the Faheys are unharmed. However, both roofing truck and tar cooker are reduced to smoldering, blackened wrecks. The acrid, chemical smell of roasted tar permeates our startled neighborhood. Luckily, the Faheys' sturdily built house of bricks is only singed. Could've been worse. Especially when you're talking row house dominoes, flames leaping from one connected house to the next, an ever-present Kings Cross fear.

It's an all-too-easy assessment for the investigators. Clear case of arson, even without Grandmom's eyewitness statement. Size-nine sneaker print on the truck's rear bumper. That rules out Wilt the Stilt, but leaves in most everyone else. Too dark for Grandmom to see the perpetrator's features. Young white male. Average height, average build. Dark clothing.

Sneakers . . . not for roofing, but for running.

A shaken Buck Fahey announces a reward for information leading to the arrest and conviction of the brazen arsonist. Me, I'm hoping they catch the guy. Send him up the river for a long, long time. The Faheys are my friends. What kind of yo-yo would want to set their truck on fire? Almost burn down the Faheys' house with everyone inside? Crazy, I tell you.

To my complete surprise, neighborhood support for the embattled Faheys is lukewarm at best. Sure, everyone else likes the Faheys, too, they're swell people. But Buck Fahey's little company has decided to defy the mighty roofers' union. The outfit hasn't been doing business by the union playbook. Buck Fahey's been cutting corners, bending rules, creating a lot of animosity.

Soon I begin to pick up on the rumors, neighborhood whispers. . . .

Buck Fahey was warned—but he didn't listen.

And. . . .

Fahey's a nice guy, and what happened was awful. But he was kind of asking for it—he should've known better than to rock *that* boat, you know?

Finally. . . .

Maybe they should've been more careful not to set the house on fire with all those kids. Last thing anybody wants is somebody gettin' hurt. But people gotta do what they gotta do.

This kind of talk really upsets me. Young Donnie Fahey is one of my very best pals. Has been ever since we moved to Littlefield Street. Mr. and Mrs. Fahey have always been really nice to me. Nobody deserves to have their stuff set all on fire. It's against the law, right?

Confused, I bring the subject up with Dad.

Dad listens carefully to my concerns, nods in agreement that the Faheys are good neighbors, wonderful people. His face wears a pained expression. Behind those deep brown eyes, I can almost see the wheels turning, turning. Organizing his thoughts, weighing the words.

Angrily, I continue to press for answers. But why'd they do it, Dad? Why'd they set Mr. Fahey's truck on fire, nearly burn the house down? And how can people think that's okay?

Dad tilts his head in agreement. You're right, Jimmy—that wasn't a good thing, setting the truck on fire. It was stupid, and it was dangerous. But Mr. Fahey's been going down the wrong road. He's at fault in this, too. Maybe you'll understand better when you get a little older. . . .

But I don't want to understand when I get older, Dad. I want to know now.

Dad sighs, bites his lip, rubs his hands together like when he's wiping away the auto grease with Lava soap.

A lot of people have fought many years for the right to belong to a union, Dad explains. People working decent hours for decent pay—that didn't happen automatically. People gave up a lot to get that . . . some even died. Getting treated like a man, like a human being, hasn't always been something you could take for granted. Not when there was money involved. Not when some folks had a chance to make piles and piles of it, usually at someone else's expense. It's called greed, Jimmy.

Confused and frustrated, I interrupt. But Dad, what's all that gotta do with Mr. Fahey and the fire?

Mr. Fahey made a decision to go against the union, Jimmy. Talk is he's been hiring nonunion workers, paying them nonunion wages, working his men on Sundays. I realize he's got a business to run, and he's gotta feed his family, too, but when you start going up against the system that's in place, sometimes there's a price to be paid.

Dejected, I look down at the floor, chew on a fingernail. Well, whatever happens, Dad, Donnie Fahey is still my friend.

Dad smiles, nods his approval. No reason for you to stop being Donnie's friend, Dad reassures. And as far as Mr. Fahey is concerned, well—that's grown-ups' business. It'll all work itself out one way or the other. I wouldn't worry about it too much.

I guess so, I answer half-heartedly.

Jimmy, asks my father, have they ever taught you in school about the Molly Maguires?

The who?

Dad shakes his head. Figures, he says. Well, a long time ago—back in the last century—the mine bosses in upstate Pennsylvania had their men working like slaves. Breaking their backs for pennies a day. Forcing them to buy groceries on credit at the company store. People dying from unsafe conditions . . . cave-ins, explosions, poison air, black lung disease. The owners grew fat and greedy, and squeezed the men down in the mines until there just wasn't anything left to squeeze.

So what happened, Dad?

Well, the men decided to start a union. Everyone sticking together to demand more pay, safer mines, fairer treatment. But the mine bosses wouldn't hear of it, set out to bust the union real quick. They had the local cops on the company payroll, same as the courts and the judges and everyone else, so they sent the policemen in to bust some heads. Tried to scare the men out of organizing. Fired any workers who sided with the union. Brought in scabs to replace those they had beaten, fired, or killed.

So who are these Maguires, Dad?

The union's secret underground organization, my father explains. When the owners got rough, started shooting and beating, the Maguires fought back. Fired at the cops, blew up some of the owners' houses. But they were outlawed, and the owners still held all the power. Eventually, they locked up all the Molly Maguires. Put 'em on trial. Hung a lot of them. Some weren't more than nineteen, maybe twenty years old.

I listen silently, trying to comprehend the horror.

But even though the Molly Maguires lost, a funny thing happened. The mine bosses got the message. Slowly, things began to improve, bit by bit. And the miners' union finally got a foothold. That's how the AFL-CIO got started. So the workers finally got representation . . . better pay, better hours, more benefits. A chance to negotiate on equal terms with the owners, as a block, united instead of all being divided up and powerless. One person can't deal with a big company all alone . . . they just run right over you.

The bottom line here, Jimmy, is that people didn't start getting a fair deal until they fought for it. And more important, they won't *keep* getting a fair deal unless they *keep* fighting for it. . . . You understand what I'm saying?

I nod. It's sort of like the time I stuck up for the kid on the playground at Longstreet . . . but my classmates were too afraid to stand behind me. That's what made me so angry. They all needed to stand up.

Dad says, I know Buck Fahey is only trying to do what he thinks is best for his family. But the man's gotta be careful. He's gotta respect the rules, and not put other peoples' livelihoods in jeopardy. Mr. Fahey is not the only person with a whole lot at stake here—and I think he's got to step back and realize that.

So I take Dad's advice. Decide to ask Mrs. Smedley, my history teacher at Langford–Alton, about what she knows concerning these rebels, the infamous Molly Maguires.

The Molly *Maguires*, sniffs Mrs. Smedley. They were a terrorist outfit, back in the 1800s. Handy with dynamite, if I remember. We don't teach about them—it's not in the approved curriculum. Besides, that sort of thing doesn't happen any more. . . .

It occurs to me that perhaps Mrs. Smedley ought to take a detour through our Kings Cross section. See for herself Buck Fahey's blackened, burnt-out truck with the melted tires. Happened just last week, not way back in the 1800s.

Far from satisfying my curiosity, Mrs. Smedley's response intrigues me even further. Why are the school system and its teachers trying to skip right over this entire episode in Pennsylvania history . . . as if it never even happened? Finally get some stuff that's not boring, but us kids never get to hear about it. What's the deal here?

So I go to the local branch of the free library, do a little research. Read about the appalling conditions, rampant abuses, and blatant exploitation by the mine bosses . . . and the brutal retaliation by the miners. The spectacle of a trial in Mauch Chunk, now the town of Jim Thorpe after the Indian track star, and the condemned young men who were marched off to the gallows.

One of the youngest of the accused, Alexander Campbell, swore his innocence before the hangman slipped on the noose. Put his hand on the stone wall of his cell, left an imprint for all to see. Proclaimed that the mark would remain after his death, a testimonial to his complete lack of guilt and the injustice of a court that had decided his fate long before any testimony was given.

True to Campbell's word, the outline of a ghostly handprint endured. No matter how the prison authorities tried to wipe it off, scrub it out, bleach it away, the mark would ultimately return. Legend has it that the embarrassed warden finally ordered the prophetic wall removed and set aside. To this day, in the coal region of Pennsylvania, the tales of the Molly Maguires are told and retold, and at this point it is all but impossible to tell fact from fiction, history from myth.

But if anything in this world is true, it is surely this . . . truth is often stranger than fiction. And the time of the Molly Maguires wasn't the most enlightened chapter in the annals of our state's history.

Oh, and one more surprising thing. The Maguires were Irishers, the mine bosses mostly English. So for my Orangeman father to take the side of the micks against his brother limeys must mean theirs was a righteous cause.

But later, just when I think this question has been solved to my satisfaction, black vs. white, right vs. wrong, I overhear Mom and Dad discussing the Fahey fire. Now Dad's putting a whole new spin on things. Not black and white, but shades of murky, mystifying grey.

Dad says, I'm a union man, Pam, through and through. You know that. And I've got a right to unionize, it's the law. But a man's got a right to run his own business the way he sees fit— without some thugs tryin' to burn his place down, and his family along with it. Too many of these roofers are just low-life punks, giving decent unions and working people a bad name. Their idea of registering members is you sign up or they throw you off the roof . . . you can forget using the ladder. Now, how apple-pie, Fourth-of-July American is that? No way do I want to get identified with them, Pam, be tarred by that brush. Before you know it, they'll have people pointing their fingers at all unions, calling us all criminals. And that plays right smack into the hands of the company men. It's not good I tell you. Not good at all.

So *now* what am I supposed to think? About the fire, Donnie's father, the Molly Maguires?

Even Dad can't make up his mind. Guess there's two sides to every story. Sometimes even inside the same person's head, duking it out, back and forth, around and around. . . .

Why can't anything ever be easy and simple? No muss, no fuss? Clear as a bell??

Jeez, . . . I'm still all confused.

*

CHAPTER 13

Meatball

Okay, so I can't help it. I've become the designated clown in Mrs. Fox's weekly music class . . . with my new, so-called buddy Fred Talbot egging me right along. Sometimes I try to resist, but my mind with a mind of its own just loves the spotlight—whether the attention I'm receiving is good or bad. The other kids enjoy it, I'm having fun, so what's the big deal? I've never really come close to getting into serious trouble . . . until today.

Our beloved Mrs. Fox is a rather large lady, and she's not getting any younger, that's for sure. Sixth-period music class on Friday afternoon is conducted in a dusty, old, hidden-away music room stashed at the top of a narrow flight of stairs around the far side of the gymnasium. I guess the idea is to keep the noise of musical instruments and group singing well separated from areas of quieter academic pursuits. Problem is, some days it can take Mrs. Fox an extra five minutes to slog all that distance to our culture-enriching hideout. Not always a good thing with antsy seventh-graders who can't sit still for five seconds.

Therefore, opportunity knocks. It's time for the James Morris Variety Show!

Most weeks I warm the stage for Mrs. Fox by doing stand-up imitations of our illustrious teachers. There's the bombastic, animated, arm-waving Mr. Lugar . . . our manic science teacher. Mrs. Smedley, our mean-spirited social studies teacher whom I portray as a real-life double for the Wicked Witch of the West, complete with riding her bicycle to school. Mrs. Stanley, our elderly mathematics lady who's from the Midwest and pronounces anything with the letter "a" funny—not to mention the words roof (like a dog's bark) and room (sounds similar to "rum"). Then there's always Mr. Mayo, our superman of a gym teacher and former state wrestling champion, enthusiastically demonstrating the intricacies of the half nelson or reverse takedown as he crushes his hapless opponent, blood flowing across the mat.

But today I have chosen to imitate none other than the sweet, charming, and hopelessly old-fashioned Mrs. Fox, who takes our musical education and cultural enrichment oh so seriously. I start at her battered grand piano, then move to the podium, gesturing as if I'm leading the entire class in song. I speak in Mrs. Fox's mellifluous, high-pitched, and very proper voice.

Today, class, I will have the pleasure of leading you in song with one of America's old-time favorites, the classic and unforgettable *On Top of Old Smokey*.

Ready class? On three . . . and a one, and a two, and a three . . .

♫ ♫ ♫

On top of spaaa ghet ti. . . .

All covered with cheeeeeese. . . .

I lost my poor meaaaat ball. . . .

When somebody sneezed.

This is a bigger hit than I ever dreamed . . . a master performance. My audience is in hysterics. Kids are rolling out of their seats and onto the floor. Tears are streaming down their appreciative faces. I knew this would be funny, but I never imagined to what extent. I've got 'em eating out of my hand. Watch out, Jerry Lewis. Move over, Soupy Sales. Eat your heart out, Don Knotts.

I sing louder, more forcefully, all the while waving that imaginary conductor's wand in mock seriousness.

Fred Talbot is coming out of his seat, cheering me on.

Then I notice Tim Armbruster, Mr. Boy Scout himself, giving me the high sign. He's catching my eye, pointing over my shoulder. His message is clear. . . .

Turn around, you fool.

I oblige, do an about-face, look up. Mrs. Fox fills the doorway behind me, hands on hips, wearing her best teacher's frown.

Now the class really has something to roar about.

Mrs. Fox says, That's enough. . . . Everyone quiet down. . . . Now! . . .

The class grows quiet except for an escaping, involuntary giggle here and there.

Mrs. Fox continues, That was quite impressive, Mr. Morris. I must say, you are a born entertainer—a natural. And class, you may be laughing hard today, but don't be surprised if sometime in the future you see this young man on stage, performing in front of thousands. What young Mr. Morris here can do is quite a gift . . . put to proper use, of course.

Mrs. Fox turns her very proper gaze back to me, arches one eyebrow . . . waiting.

I drop my head and apologize. . . . Sorry, Mrs. Fox. Then turn to take my seat.

Not so fast, James, Mrs. Fox interrupts. Stay right there.

Mrs. Fox smiles pleasantly to all the boys and girls in my audience. Says, James, I'm now going to sit at the piano. I want you to sing *On Top of Old Smokey* for us. But this time I want you to use the correct words.

In terror I shake my head vigorously, pleading to be excused.

Mrs. Fox asks, What's wrong, James? Don't tell me you have stage fright all of a sudden. . . . Not after the performance you just graced us with a moment ago!

Once again I lower my head, mumble, I'm sorry, Mrs. Fox. But I don't know the words to the real song.

The music teacher nods slowly, understandingly. So I see . . . you know the silly version by heart, but not the original words. How very interesting, James.

Again the class laughs, but Mrs. Fox quells them with another frozen glare.

Very well, James. You may take your seat then.

I make a beeline for my spot on the second bench, relieved and ready to withdraw into my period-long shell.

Oh, and Mr. Morris . . . one more thing.

Yes, Mrs. Fox?

Next time you wish to perform for this class, be prepared to sing the entire *correct* version of *On Top of Old Smokey*. Or else you'll be doing your singing in the office—is that clear, young man?

Yes, Mrs. Fox.

Excellent!

After music class I am the butt of jokes, a regular Bozo the Clown. Tim Armbruster can only shake his head at having such a bonehead for a buddy.

Fred Talbot laughs and punches me in the arm. Hard.

Fred smirks, Way to go, moron.

Sometimes I wish maybe I could be more serious . . . do things the right way. Instead of doing them the weird way, which is the way everything I get involved with seems to come out, like it or not. Don't really know why I'm such a hopeless head case.

Even Steven

It's funny how some things work out. Boy Scout Tim Armbruster is still my best friend at Langford–Alton, and I occasionally pal around with Lonnie McGee when he manages to get his nose out of a comic book. But the weird thing is that one of my best friends is now Fred Talbot. That's right, the biggest kid in seventh grade—the same goober who once made it a point to make my existence 100 percent miserable. Turns out he's not half bad, especially when he's not hanging out with that mug Ernie Imhoff. I think Fred pulls his tough guy act just to impress eighth-grader Ernie . . . although it's getting to be a hard habit to break. Sometimes when Fred starts to pick on a kid when I'm around, I can usually talk him out of it. I'll just give Fred a suggestion like, Why waste your time on this pimple? Or maybe, Hey, give the kid a break, Fred—looks like maybe he ain't had one his entire life.

I can usually get Fred to laugh . . . at which point he generally shows his intended victim a little mercy. Though I have to admit that at times it's feels like I'm walking around school with a leash on my very own pet gorilla. If he doesn't get his banana or wakes

346

up on the wrong side of the cage, then he goes a little ape and ruins some loser's day. Hey, I tried, I really did . . . just glad this time it's not me.

Fred dared me into cutting music class a few weeks ago— even though I promised my parents that I'd never do anything that'd give the LAHS constabulary an excuse to kick me out and send me packing back to Philly. A calculated gamble on my part—a show of good faith to Fred. Luckily, Mrs. Fox didn't note my absence, or never handed my name in to the office. Dodged another bullet, ha ha.

Lately, I've been alternating lunch periods between Tim's table and Fred's table. Tim's group has the normal kids, and I'd rather eat there most of the time. But it doesn't hurt to count the seventh grade's heavyweight wrestler and his cronies amongst your closest buddies . . . even if they can sometimes be wise guys, shameless bullies, and first-class jerks in general.

Aside from impressing Ernie, I think the only reason Fred bullies other kids is because he can. He's just bigger and stronger than the rest of us, and we're handy. Fred's not mad at kids when he picks on 'em . . . it's just a matter of availability and contempt. Sort of the way Gram's cat Herman used to hunt for mice down on the railroad embankment. Spoiled Herman had all the canned cat food and kibble he could possibly eat at Gram's house . . . never had to hunt a day in his life. But the mice were there, and they were catchable . . . so Herman caught 'em. Nothing personal. It's just what cats do—that predatory instinct. End of story.

Maybe the same motivations apply to Fred. I don't know, I'm never going to be the biggest kid in seventh grade. Or any grade, for that matter. So I can't really say.

Another strange thing is, all of Fred's football/wrestler stooges have sort of accepted me—except one. That would be Steve Dwyer, the smallest and meanest kid on the whole wrestling team. Dwyer's only 75 pounds, which is ten pounds lighter than even skinny little me. But Dwyer's sort of a half-mad, half-looney tune flip-top, so people give him a lot of space. Sometimes being a bit crazy can be a big help—especially when you're small. Most folks won't mess with you if they think you're a nut case— because they can't be sure what you're liable to do. Seems like maybe the best defense is a good offense.

347

Next to football, wrestling is by far the biggest sport at Langford–Alton. They even have their very own specially built wrestling room here. Every inch is padded, and it's large enough to hold four matches at once . . . with spectators. And it's also the place where Mr. Mayo, our gym teacher, has been taking us for wrestling instruction every gym period this quarter. Mr. Mayo was state champ in his weight class long ago and is a wrestling fanatic, which is why we're stuck doing wrestling the entire quarter. I can't wait to move on to dodge ball, basketball, softball, or something else more normal. As the saying goes, wrestling just "ain't my bag."

Part of our grade for gym will depend on how we each perform in a series of wrestling bouts staged by Mr. Mayo. He pairs us off by size, with the matches for the bigger kids scheduled first. Today Fred Talbot pins his hapless opponent in about twenty seconds flat, gloating and showing off during the entire pathetic contest. In the middle-sized bouts, Tim Armbruster ekes out a points victory over an evenly matched adversary.

Hail Caesar! We that are about to die salute you.

Now it's time for us lightweights. Surprise, surprise . . . I've gotta go up against none other than feisty Steve Dwyer, the school's 75-pound dynamo with the 50-pound chip on his slender shoulder. Dwyer's got big pointy ears, freckles on a tiny angular face, a long bony nose, and looks like a demented leprechaun with a heavy-duty case of rabies.

Dwyer just sneers at me, laughs in my face, says I'm all his and I'd better say my prayers 'cause I'm dead meat. The feelings of disrespect are mutual, but I don't have Steve's confidence—or his sparkling record in competition. Heck, I don't even *like* wrestling. I'd rather just smack Dwyer a good one, but that's not allowed in wrestling. Besides, Mr. Mayo would probably flunk me, then send me straight to the office. And remember, I'm not supposed to be getting into any trouble, else they could ship me back to Philly in a heartbeat and all that major mess they're having at infamous Sanders Junior High on 54th Street.

Mr. Mayo says, Take your positions. We start with Dwyer on bottom, knees and hands pressed against the mat, and me cradling him on top. Then our gym teacher blows his whistle, and my world explodes into a flurry of action, noise, panic, and extreme do-or-die exertion.

I push Dwyer down, but Steve's like a cross between a gator and a crazed chimp. He twists and leans and fights until suddenly he's got me, but I no longer have him. This kid's got moves like the half nelson, the ankle lock, the hammerlock, the double-arm lock, the grapevine, the leglock, and the scissors thing with his legs. Heck, he's got moves I've never heard of, couldn't even pronounce. I don't believe them even while they're happening; it's as if I'm mainly a spectator . . . someone along for the ride.

All I'm trying to do is hold on for dear life, keep my back off the mat, and avoid the pin. I need every one of these ten extra pounds, wish I had twenty or more. I'm thinking maybe I should've paid closer attention at Dré Barnett's informal garage *wrasslin'* sessions when I had the chance. Oh well, too late now.

Bruno Sammartino I ain't.

Mr. Mayo kneels down, leans in. Dwyer scores one point, then another. Mr. Mayo says, That's a point, Dwyer one-oh. Ho, that's another point, Dwyer two-oh.

Steve rolls me over, goes for the pin. I hear the other kids' screaming, yelling, I'm looking up at the lights now, not a good situation. Somehow I get some leverage, grunt, manage though brute strength alone to throw Steve off. Then I stand up off the mat—and fast. My mom didn't raise herself no dummy.

One point for Morris on the escape! Two-one, Dwyer.

Still, for every move I make, for every way I turn, Dwyer has an answer. But I am bigger than him, and stronger. It's so weird how the usual roles are reversed—I've always been the little feisty one with the slick, nasty surprises up my sleeve. Until now.

I can hear Fred Talbot's voice and some of his stooges, laughing, whooping it up, rooting for Dwyer. Tim Armbruster and some of the others with a little backbone are rooting for me, the relatively sane kid and regular guy. Mostly they're just glad their own matches are all over and done.

Less than a minute remaining. Dwyer fakes like he's going for a headlock, gets me to raise up a little, then submarines underneath before I can react, knocking me off balance. Quickly grabs me in some sort of arm lock, driving my shoulder into the canvass.

Point for Dwyer! Three-one, Dwyer.

Psycho Steve is on a roll. Fred and his band of lesser apes are going nuts.

I'm having trouble getting out of this one. At least I'm glad we're not house spiders, else Dwyer would be applying the deadly venomous bite and in minutes my insides would be turning to a mushy, bloody milkshake. Yum.

I struggle, twist one way, twist another, but Dwyer keeps riding my shoulder into the mat. Mr. Mayo leans in, and I'm sure he's going to award Dwyer the pin, announce that the match is over.

But Mr. Mayo whispers, Use your legs, Jimmy. Arch your back. You can roll him.

I take a quick breath, do what Teach says. Sure enough, I flip Dwyer over.

Point for Morris! Three-two, Dwyer!!

Less than thirty seconds left. Twenty-five, twenty. . . . Time is running out. In fifteen seconds I will have been beaten by a demented leprechaun. I hate losing, especially to ignoramuses like flip-top Steven Dwyer.

To his credit, Dwyer doesn't try to sit on his lead and run out the clock. Instead, he's still going for the pin, probably embarrassed that the match has been so close. Dwyer's a kid who's always got somethin' to prove. Being such a shrimp will do that to you. Believe me, I know.

So I bait Steve with an opening, and he bites. As Dwyer reaches to slap on another hold, I jump him, hang on, get him in the only decent hold I know—the good, old, tried-and-true headlock. Squeeze Dwyer's pointy head like it's in a vise, a pimple I'm going to pop, then pick him up off his feet and give him a mighty shove. Down goes Dwyer onto the soft mat with a THUMP!

Point for Morris. Three-three! . . . TIME!!

Our grudge match is over. Kids are yelling, cheering. I have come from behind to tie rabid Steve Dwyer, vaunted midget wrestler, pint-sized bully, and general nasty all-around pain-in-the-butt.

Dwyer cries, Not fair! He cheated, Mr. Mayo! He used an illegal move!

Save it, Dwyer, retorts the gym teacher. You got cocky, and you almost got yourself beat. Let that be a lesson to you.

But Mr. Mayo!

But nuthin', Dwyer . . . no more of yer bellyachin'—time to hit the shower. And that goes for everyone else, too. Let's get a move on.

We head downstairs to wash up and change. Dwyer gives me some dirty looks, but I'm not worried. Tim Armbruster and some of the others congratulate me, slap me on the back, give me the thumbs-up. Later in the hallway, heading for class, Fred Talbot tells me, Way to go, you wrestled good. Man, you really got Dwyer steamed, too.

Talbot laughs, hauls off, socks me one in the bicep. Hard.

Ouch!

I was really hopin' you might beat him, Fred confides. But a tie is pretty much the same thing to Dwyer. He can't believe you tied him.

Coulda beaten him if I wanted to, I lie. But he's such a nice guy I just didn't have the heart. I mean, you know how it is . . . right, Fred?

Fred laughs, but doesn't buy my line for a second.

So Fred, if you really wanted me to win, how come I heard you rootin' for Steve?

Aw, forget that, Fred shrugs. We're on the wrestling team together, so it'd look bad me cheering for somebody else. You know, team spirit and all that crap.

Yeah, I suppose so, I agree . . . but neither am I buying Fred's cornball line.

351

Later, on the bus ride back to Alton, I get to thinking. I boxed the biggest kid in seventh grade to a standstill, and now I've wrestled the school's toughest munchkin to a tie. So I guess things aren't going all that badly out here in suburban Langford–Alton. That is, except for maybe some of my grades. Seems my report cards here read much like the ones I got back at Longstreet Elementary. Same comments, same criticisms:

James is a very nice boy—if only he could learn to follow directions.

James is a promising student—but he must learn to pay more attention.

James does very good work—when he puts his mind to it.

James will go far—but first he needs to focus his energies.

James is a likable young man—but he must work to control his temper.

James has the ability—but his constant daydreaming presents a problem.

See what I mean? Seems like everyone wants to send me to college now, have me smoke a pipe, shuffle some papers, keep me away from hard-working folks. Man, sometimes these teachers sound like a broken record. James is a nice boy—*but*. Always the same tune, same beat. I wonder if they put this kinda stuff on everyone's report card? Guess if they said everything was going fine, then you'd have nothing to work toward, no gains to look forward to. At least that's my theory, anyway. Let's face it, who *couldn't* stand to "improve their focus" and all that jazz?

It's not that I don't try hard in school, because I do. But sometimes my mind just seems to have a mind of its own. It's not like I *always* do goofy stuff on purpose. Or daydream. Or get bored. Or pop my top. These things just have a way of happening, that's all.

Besides, I'm still only a kid. So gimme a break, huh?

Soldiers

I come home one weekend from Uncle Hank and Aunt Betty's house in Alton to discover that Tommy O'Hanlon has gone though Marine basic training at Parris Island, South Carolina. Now he's come home to Kings Cross before he gets his assignment and the military ships him out to who knows where, most likely Vietnam.

Guess I've been away at my suburban school too long. Didn't even know Tommy had signed up. Now he's parading up and down Littlefield Avenue in his dress blues, younger kids marching behind as if he were the Pied Piper himself. Have to admit Tommy looks really snazzy. That flat, stiff white hat with the bill pulled down low over his ice-blue eyes, and peach-fuzz haircut. Shiny brass buttons on a high-necked, navy blue top, matching dress pants with blood-red stripes down the sides, glossy black shoes that reflect like a pair of black mirrors. The proud Marine insignia, eagle perched on top of the world.

Tommy always did like uniforms—football, baseball, even the Boy Scouts. He's a joiner, a doer, a leader. All for one and one for all. Semper Fi. Once a Marine, always a Marine. Tommy's a natural, he'll be going places.

They should be mopping up this mess in Vietnam any month now, the way the papers are telling it. President Johnson is getting tough with those crazy Communists. More troops, more bombs, more napalm. Vietnam isn't a big country. No way they can take this pounding day in and day out. Maybe it'll all be over before Tommy ever gets there. Heck, we beat the Jerries, then nuked the Japs. So what chance could a bunch of silly, backward people who run around in pajamas possibly have?

Funny, but I remember the Johnson loyalists just a few years ago saying Goldwater was a warmonger. Said our man Barry was looking to get us in a war, drop *The Bomb*. But now it's Johnson who's dropping all the bombs. He's talking tough, escalating, putting the screws to those hated Commies. Some people on TV wonder if the President's doing the right thing. There's some second-guessing that maybe we shouldn't be involved in a war over in Asia. But here in Kings Cross we're sure. We're patriotic people who stand behind the President. Take our hats off at Connie Mack Stadium, stand tall, and sing the *Star-Spangled Banner*, hand over heart. No foul balls around here that I can see.

I always sing the *Star-Spangled Banner* especially hard, since it was Dad's ancestor, Ferdinand Durang, who helped Francis Scott Key put the famous music to the words. He's my great-great-great uncle, or something like that, according to Gram. Still, it's a very hard song to sing, and my voice cracks when I try hitting the high notes.

Diet Donnie comes around with Larry Wisnewski, Johnny Deemer, and some of the Wennington crowd. We all admire Tommy's uniform, shake his hand, wish him well. They should use Tommy on the next recruiting poster. Sharp as a tack, all spit and polish.

Man, somebody whispers. I think those gooks are in trouble now. Somebody ought to tell 'em Tommy's comin'. Gonna kick some yellow tail for sure.

Yeah, Donnie agrees, sipping on a diet Pepsi. And if they give Tommy any stuff, then we'll really get serious . . . send in Cuz. He don't even need no weapon.

We all laugh, imagining Tommy with an M-16, sneaking though the jungle in khaki, camouflage, and greasepaint. Now here comes Cuz with his softball biceps, strutting along in a muscle shirt and leather jacket, tiny gold cross around his neck, cool shades, and DA slicked back with Brylcreem, a little dab will do ya.

Yo, where do all them Cong hang? Like, what corner? I'm callin' those little suckers out right now—fair one!

Larry Wisnewski says the Cong should just pack it in if they know what's good for 'em. But maybe they'll just have to find out the hard way. Their call.

Back in Alton the next week I ask Uncle Hank about Korea. Dad's other brother, Sam, served with the U.S. Cavalry in China during the Second World War. Got a medal for bravery for pulling a drowning GI out of a river just in the nick of time. Gram's got the picture of an officer pinning the medal on Sam's chest, shaking his hand, Uncle Samuel grinning ear-to-ear. And Hank's Army picture is on her dresser, too.

To my surprise, Uncle Hank tries to avoid any talk about Korea. He's quick to change the subject . . . asks about homework, school, that sort of thing. But I persist, keep pushing buttons to see what happens.

I imagine Uncle Hank mixing it up with the North Koreans much the same way Lt. Hanley gets into it each week with the Jerries on the television show *Combat!*

Did you see a lot of action, Uncle Hank? Were you guys fighting all the time?

Uncle Hank frowns, looks away, rubs his chin. No, he replies, not too much. But believe me, a little fighting goes a long, long way.

I know by the way my uncle says this he's seen some pretty bad stuff, more than just the "flesh wounds" they get on *Combat!*, and that he's not going to talk with me about it. So I ask him a different question, try another approach.

Uncle Hank, what's the thing you remember most about Korea?

My uncle gets this faraway look in his eyes, searching the old memory banks. I know he's found the answer when I see him smirk.

The cold, Uncle Hank says. It could get really, *really* cold in Korea.

This answer knocks me back a bit. Korea is in Asia, same as Vietnam. And on the news reports, you can see they have palm trees in Vietnam and tropical jungles. The GIs always look hot and sweaty, some with no shirts. So I mention this to Uncle Hank.

Asia is a big place—an entire continent, he explains. Check your geography book, Jimmy. Vietnam is in the south, and Korea's way up north. Just like Maine and Florida here in the U.S. Believe me, up in those mountains in Korea it gets plenty cold.

One way Korea *is* the same as Vietnam: they're both squared off North vs. South. Just like America once was. And just like Ireland has been for years and years. Always this same deal in so many places, North vs. South, North vs. South. It makes a person wonder.

Don't know. Guess I have a lot to learn about this war stuff, *Combat!* aside.

I'm still not sure what Uncle Hank really thinks about Korea, because he says so little and changes the subject. But I do know one thing he definitely liked about Korea—this stuff called *kimchee*. It's pickled cabbage mixed with lots of hot spices, and Uncle Hank makes it every so often. Gives some to Dad, too. And you're not going to believe how he makes it. Takes the cabbage, chops it up, puts it in a jar with the seasonings, then *buries* it in the back yard for days and days. I kid you not, right down in a hole in the ground, all covered up, waiting for this stuff to ferment. I've heard of some strange food, but this *kimchee* takes the cake. It's probably even weirder than the old Jewish grandmothers with the carp swimming around in their bathtubs. Gross me out!

Me, I'm sticking to my root beer, hamburgers, and PBJs. The usual stuff.

Anyway, I just hope everything goes OK for Tommy O'Hanlon in the Marines. They're in a dangerous business. Grandmom Kane's favorite cousin Martin was a Marine. Got caught on the beach at Iwo Jima along with thousands of others. Some Jap sniper shot Martin in the head, killing him instantly. So many of our guys bought the farm when we invaded that island, they had to bury the bodies right there on the spot, no way to send 'em home. Eight years later the family gets a call from the Government, saying they're finally going to dig Cousin Martin up and ship his remains back to Philadelphia. But Marty's mother said no thanks, just leave my son be. Let my boy rest in peace, haven't we been through enough already?

I wonder after all these years if Grandmom ever lights the odd candle for Cousin Martin under the statue of the Blessed Mother. And I wonder if maybe I should ask her to light one for Tommy. Don't know if it would do any good, but I know it sure couldn't hurt.

The O'Hanlons had already lost one child to lead-paint poisoning before we Morrises ever moved to Littlefield from 55th Street and the little apartment above Lobb's Produce. It was back in the late '50s. A baby girl, curly blonde hair, barely two, Jackie's little sister Jenny.

Surely God wouldn't let anything bad happen to yet another O'Hanlon. . . .

Especially not if Grandmom lights one of those special candles. Tommy will be fine. I just know he will.

Return to Kings Cross

Today is the last day of school before summer vacation and it's bittersweet because I know I'm never coming back to Langford–Alton and this really isn't a bad school after all. They give us our report cards, and we get out early at noon. As I climb aboard the waiting Alton-bound yellow bus and take my usual seat for the last time ever, I see overgrown Fred Talbot, my one-time nemesis, pass by my window.

I wave, Hey Fred! See ya later, Fred. Have a good summer.

Fred comes over to the window, which is cranked open because of the heat.

You comin' back next year, Jimmy?

I say, No, I'm going back to Philadelphia. Can't go to school here any more unless my family moves out to the district and I live here for real.

Too bad, Fred replies apologetically. I betcha we're gonna have ourselves a blast around here in eighth grade. Kinda wish you were comin' back, since you turned out not to be half-bad after all.

You too, I add . . . and Fred and I both start to laugh. Not "half-bad" is about as close to high praise as you're going to get from a seventh-grade bully like Fred Talbot. I just hope maybe he goes a little easier come September when he's breaking in his next sidekick.

Goodbye, Fred Talbot, it was nice knowin' ya.

The bus pulls out, and I make that long, last, hot ride. We cruise under the fully leafed shade trees along Langford's Main Street, lined with late-Victorian houses built around the turn of the century. Over the railroad bridge, more aging mansions, right turn into Alton. Corner stop after corner stop, the bus slowly emptying, excited school kids scurrying off to begin their long-awaited summer vacations. Finally, end-of-the line, last street in Alton, land of the Dutch colonials. I disembark, the bus does the loop around the minipark, and I head off for one last time to Aunt Betty and Uncle Hank's house.

Aunt Betty feeds me some tuna on toasted hot dog rolls, which I wash down with a glass of OJ. She wishes me well as I gather up my few remaining odds and ends in a paper sack. I thank Aunt Betty for letting me stay the school year, then head out the door to catch the dusty, rust-colored, every-half-hour passenger train back to Philly. No one at the station this time of day but me. Sure is a hot one, must be 90° already.

Now I leave behind Fred Talbot, Tim Armbruster, Lonnie McGee, Steve Dwyer, Ernie Imhoff, Mrs. Fox, Mrs. Smedley, Mr. Mayo, Aunt Betty, Uncle Hank, and my school in the suburbs. Alton Station, Langford, Kernwood, the high trestle over Dobbs Creek, and on into Southwest Philly. All the while I'm looking around the train for that rat-fink lady teacher who spilled the beans back when I was a secret student. I'd like to give her some advice on minding her own Ps and Qs. But I don't see our friendly, neighborhood Benedict Arnold on board. I get off at Ankorra Mill Station, climb the creosote-soaked stairs up to 58th Street, and begin the sun-drenched walk south toward home. My real home— Kings Cross, land of the hoagies, cheesesteaks, Jewish pickles, soft pretzels, and Italian water ice. Where kids tie the laces of worn sneakers together and toss 'em up over the phone wires and the power lines—hang 'em high for all to see. A Southwest summer ritual.

Ah yes, the first sweet anticipated hours of summer vacation. Boxball, stepball, wireball, sock-it-out, halfball, buck-buck, Mr. Softee ice cream, summer matinees at The Parkland Theater, hanging on the corner, spider hunting, Phillies baseball, open fire hydrants, a week at the seashore, just plain goofing off. Can't wait to get started, don't know what to do first. Don't have to be anywhere, do anything—my time is *my* time.

Solid.

Block after block, shade tree after shade tree. Huffman Avenue, Ashcroft Avenue, Thompson Avenue . . . sauntering along toward my alma mater, Longstreet Elementary at the corner of Meadows Avenue. And as I walk from corner to corner, past 58th Street porches, storefronts, and side streets, something quickly becomes apparent. There are a whole lot more black faces in the neighborhood than last year. Not just the occasional colored person, such as Dré Barnett or Coleman James, but entire groups and clusters and families of them. They're not just getting bused here for school any longer—they're actually moving in. Right here in our very own Kings Cross.

Like flies, Aunt Betty had said. You let in one, you'll have a hundred, for sure.

Within a half hour I'm home, changed, and out the door for the first game of sock-it-out. They don't play sock-it-out in the suburbs. They don't play any of our street games in the suburbs, except for maybe some touch football. Don't have the row houses, the narrow streets, driveways, and alleyways. It's a whole different world out there, once you get past the city limits, which are just on the other side of The Parkway at Dobbs Creek.

Well, the gang's all here, same as usual. Diet Donnie, Bugs O'Hanlon, Scotty Morgan, Johnny Deemer, Frankie the Fruit Pelligrino, little brother Howie, Larry Wisnewski, Bobby Schaeffer, Dré Barnett, Davey Cutler, you name them. Catholic school has been out since earlier in the week. Dré and Davey got out of Sanders this morning. Now the Cookie Man is back in town from the 'burbs, we're ready to roll. All present and accounted for.

School's out for summer, and it feels great to be home. Home for good. Time to celebrate.

Don't know if I'm going to Sanders or OLPP in eighth grade, my future remains uncertain. I'll see what shakes out in September. But for right now, September is a very long way off.

Donnie sees me and smiles. Hey, Cookie! C'mon, hurry up . . . we need you on our side. Get in the game, Jimmy.

Word comes to us later from Alton that a house has gone up for sale. Right across the street from Uncle Hank and Aunt Betty. The McGee's house. Seems Lonnie's gonna have to pack all his comic books. Dad's sister Marge and her husband decide to take a look, tour the property. It would be great to get their high school kids out of Southwest Philly, out of volatile Burnham High

School. Grab some fresh air in the suburbs, nice schools, little crime—no worries. Have Hank and Betty as their neighbors. But when they show up that weekend for a look-see, they're told they won't be allowed to make an offer. The McGee house is an NAACP house. The NAACP has stipulated that the house is to be sold to colored only, to maintain their foothold in the neighborhood and further the cause of integration.

When news of this gets back to Dad he nearly snaps his cork. The hell you say! Now you're not allowed to buy a house because you're *white*? In a white neighborhood? Come again?? So where are all the Feds now? Or those stuffed shirts up in Harrisburg? How come this isn't illegal? What about our Constitutional rights? Isn't this racism? Just try to tell a black family they can't move into a house in Kings Cross, and you'll find yourself in court up on charges faster than you can say Jackie Robinson.

Maybe, says Dad, Mr. Pellegrino from down the street has a point here.

He of the *Pellegrino Prophecy*.

Light Bulb

It's a hot summer evening right before dark, and since I have my Friday allowance I want to buy a creamsicle stick at Neuman's ice cream joint on 57th. Because my little brother Howie also has his allowance, he wants to come along and buy a creamsicle, too. Next thing I know, Howie's nerdy pal Ray Watts is getting money from his mother and can he come along with us? Already this is turning out to be some kind of ice cream expedition, and I wish maybe Howie and Ray could just wait for the neighborhood ice cream truck instead. Besides, Neuman's is just down the street from the McLaren and Krause houses and who knows, maybe I might see Donna McLaren and Mary Jane Krause there. And who wants to be seen by the lovely Donna and Mary Jane when you've got your little brother and his decidedly odd and defective buddy tagging along?

Ray Watts is a goofy kid with a mop of blonde hair and thick, near-sighted, grey-framed glasses. He's got a case of terminal confusion, and goes around squinting at the world with his mouth hanging open for all the flies to buzz in. Kids call him "Light

Bulb" because Ray is always the last to know what's going on—and when he finally does get it, the expression on his face is priceless. Hence, the moniker "Light Bulb." Seems Ray spends most of his time at Dobbs Creek looking for frogs and trying to catch minnows to bring home in his five-gallon paint bucket. He's the kind of kid who might as well carry a sign that says—Kick Me! At least in our neighborhood, anyway. I was a little like Ray a few years ago but wised up after getting leaned on so much. Now I'm mostly a spectator as I watch other goofy kids getting leaned on. Clueless kids like weird Raymond "Light Bulb" Watts, who's got a hard way to go in unforgiving Kings Cross.

But I figure sure, what the heck, Howie and Light Bulb can come along too. What can it hurt? All I'm really interested in is that orange creamsicle with the delicious white stuff on the inside on such a hot summer night. And if I see Donna and Mary Jane, then I'll just tell Howie and Ray to bug off, run on home, and I'll act like I don't know these two bothersome chuckleheads.

I cross Wennington at 57th, Howie and Ray in tow, and head for the steps below the Breyers Ice Cream sign. There's a kid leaning against the wall of the ice cream parlor named Fat Angelo, who's an Italian from down around 58th Street. Fat Angelo, a.k.a. Jello, is sucking on a cherry popsicle. I don't know what his full name is, just Fat Angelo or Jello, which is already more than I want to know. Jello is a miserable kid about my age, twelve years old, whom absolutely nobody likes. Jello doesn't even like himself, which is one of the reasons he's so miserable, I suppose. His only joy in life seems to be in terrorizing kids a lot younger and smaller than himself. This is how Fat Angelo gets his jollies. He feels better watching someone else having to be even more miserable than he is. Believe me, he's not the only one around who does this. In fact, he's not even the worst. Your only ways of dealing with Jello and his kind are to be either bigger or tougher than they are, or to learn to avoid them altogether. But avoiding Fat Angelo is hard, since he spends so much time on area corners stuffing his fat face with assorted goodies and being his usual intolerable self looking for victims.

I walk by Fat Angelo without a word. My brother Howie walks by Fat Angelo without a word. Then along comes goofy Ray Watts. Jello sees Light Bulb, pops the half-eaten cherry popsicle out of his mouth.

Hey, skuzz ball—just where do ya think you're goin'? says Fat Angelo.

Just to get an ice cream, Light Bulb pleads.

I thought I told you to stay outta my sight, wimp.

I butt in, tell Fat Angelo to give it a rest. Jello says he's got no problem with me or Howie getting an ice cream, but he wants Skuzz Ball here outta his sight. He's tryin' to enjoy his cherry popsicle, and he doesn't want the scenery ruined by no little twerp with the Light Bulb expressions. I tell Fat Angelo it's a free country and he says, Yeah, but not for twerps it ain't. I decide the best thing to do with Jello is ignore him, so I head for the door of the ice cream parlor. Howie follows me, then Ray follows him, strength in numbers. Fat Angelo sticks his chubby arm out and blocks Light Bulb's way.

C'mon, Angelo! whines Raymond.

C'mon, An-gel-o, mimics the Fat One.

Light Bulb tries to go around the roadblock but Jello reaches out and shoves him hard, knocking Ray off balance. Ray catches himself after almost falling, then wheels to face his tormentor.

Hey, knock it off, Fatso!

Fat Angelo gets mad, lashes out, gives Light Bulb a smack across the face. Knocks his thick glasses crooked. Light Bulb grabs his sore face, starts to cry, then runs for home. You're in trouble now, Raymond calls back. He's still holding his scrambled face, a pathetic sight. Fat Angelo says, whatever, he's really trembling in his boots.

I ask Jello what is his problem and he says to mind my own business. I figure that's probably not bad advice since this is Ray's situation not mine. Howie and I go inside, grab two creamsicles from the freezer, and stand in line. Howie is mildly concerned for his friend, but he's not about to miss out on a creamsicle opportunity solely on Light Bulb's behalf. This is one smart boy with his priorities straight.

When Howie and I come outside with our frozen treats, we're just in time to see an angry-looking old man in a white short-sleeve shirt and tan fedora crossing Wennington Avenue heading in our general direction. It's Light Bulb's grandfather, and he's got Ray marching behind him, still holding his red face and crooked specs. I whisper for Howie to watch, pay attention, this should be fun, and now maybe Fat Angelo is going to get his and it's about time.

There he is, that's the kid who smacked me, says Ray, still walking behind his grandfather for protection. The mad-looking old man in the Bogart hat struts across the corner, heads for Fat Angelo, and then to my surprise, passes by Jello and comes right up to my face. Before I can say anything he's shaking a finger in front of *my* nose and shouting.

You four-eyed, cockeyed, smart-mouthed little mick SOB. I oughhta slap the livin' snot outta you, you potato-eating good for nothin' pint-sized piece of garbage. . . .

Gramps, says Raymond, That's the wrong kid. He was tryin' to help me. It's the other one that slapped me, the big fat one.

Light Bulb's grandfather glances back at him, momentarily puzzled, then turns to me and tips his fedora. Excuse me, son. Excuse me. Then before you know it, he's over in Fat Angelo's face all mean and nasty and giving Jello the what for.

You fat, disgusting, sleazy-looking, garlic-eating, Dago tub of lard, you. I oughhta smack you silly. . . . Howie's grandfather talks like this nonstop for at least three minutes, all the while Jello just stands there with his big, ugly kisser hanging open and his stupid, glazed eyes bulging out. Not a bad imitation of Light Bulb, if I may say so myself. It ends when the old man finishes with, If you ever so much as lay another finger on this boy, I swear to God, it'll be the last plate of linguini you ever shove down your fat paisan face. With that, Ray and his grandfather march back across Wennington and down 57th Street where they disappear onto our Littlefield Street.

Fat Angelo still stands there against the wall in a state of shock. Most of the cherry popsicle has melted in his hand, and large red splotches of juice decorate his ample white T-shirt. I tell Jello that cherry is his flavor and really looks good on him, he should buy it more often. With that, Howie and I take what's left of our creamsicles and laugh all the way home to Littlefield about Fat Angelo and the bulging eyes and the cherry popsicle juice all over his flabby, miserable belly. All we wanted was something cold and sweet on a hot summer night, but we sure got a bonus in the bargain. You just never know what you're gonna get in ol' Southwest Philly.

One thing bothers me, though, the crack about me being cockeyed. I am very sensitive about the crossed eyes. And since there's nothing I can do to Light Bulb's grandfather because he's an adult and I'm only a kid, I decide to take this up the next day with Raymond. Ray says he's sorry, that his grandfather made a mistake, and it could happen to anybody. I inform Light Bulb that this is not good enough, somebody has got to pay for me being called cockeyed. Ray says his grandfather didn't mean it, and I say if he didn't mean it, then why did he say it? Light Bulb just shrugs a goofy shrug and so I give him a smack across the face, just like Fat Angelo did. Now Raymond is crying again, his glasses are crooked, and I feel a little better, although probably not as good as Jello does when he terrorizes a kid, since this is what he lives for and how he gets his jollies.

Another thing that bothers me is how I never met this old man before, never opened my mouth, yet Light Bulb's grandfather knew I was a smart-mouthed, potato-eating little mick, although he neglected to mention the limey half. Either this man has extraordinary powers of perception, or he is a psychic. My mother reads books about psychic powers, and I decide that maybe I should borrow some of them, since it would be handy to know about all kinds of stuff before it even happens. Maybe Ray should also read the books on psychic powers, since it might help him in the future to avoid corners where Fat Angelo may be eating cherry popsicles and looking for little twerps to torture. But I figure this is Light Bulb's business and he'll have to find his own books to read on psychic powers if he knows what's good for him.

So Raymond "Light Bulb" Watts, you are on your own. Good luck. You're definitely going to need it, pal.

Fan Club

Grandmom drives Howie and me to North Philly for our annual outing to Connie Mack Stadium, home of the Fightin' Phillies. The Phils are playing the lowly Houston Astros, formerly the Colt 45s, a struggling expansion team. But the Phils aren't what they used to be in '64, either. Most of the old names are still there: Callison, Dalyrimple, Covington, Gonzales, Short, Bunning, Rojas, Taylor. But the stars are getting older, and Philadelphia is no longer challenging for the National League Pennant. Today, the stands are barely half-full. Seems we had our one chance in '64, seven-and-a-half game lead with only ten to go, greatest collapse ever in professional sports. One for the history books. Oh, well.

This hot Sunday afternoon doesn't start out any differently, the Phils look sure to disappoint. The Astros jump on Phillies' pitching early, grab a several-run lead. The natives grow restless, and the scattered booing begins . . . a well-loved Philadelphia tradition. The worst treatment is reserved for Dick Allen, the controversial slugger who's been a focal point of hostility almost since the day he put on our hometown uniform. Allen is black, outspoken, cocky, feuds with management, and gets a lot of bad press.

In Philly, this is predictably a less-than-well-received combination.

Allen strides to the batter's box and the catcalls begin. Loud, vociferous, often obnoxious. He's already gone down swinging with runners in scoring position. The slugger stands in, taps home plate, coils for his patented buggy-whip swing.

Go back to the minors, Allen.

Try gettin' a real job, Big Mouth.

Whatever they're payin' ya, it's too much, Richie.

Grandmom turns to me, asks, Why are they booing this guy every time up?

I shrug. 'Cause he's a bum, Grandmom. Everybody knows that.

The Phils' cleanup hitter works the pitcher into a deep count. Now the Astros' hurler peers in, figuring this fastball hitter will be looking for the heater—all the way. Decides to trip the batter up, slip in the old deuce. Only problem is he hangs it in Allen's wheelhouse, and Richie doesn't miss it.

Crack! The ball leaps off the bat, shoots out toward left field. Climbing, climbing. Higher and higher. Fans jump to their feet, yelling and jostling to get a better view. The ball levels off and rockets straight past the **Coca-Cola** sign high atop the left-field bleachers, disappearing somewhere out into the streets of North Philadelphia. A monstrous, titanic blast of truly Ruthian proportions.

Slowly, Dick Allen circles the bases in his deliberate, nonchalant home-run trot. The booing has ceased. . . . Replaced by cheering, which grows and grows.

Grandmom claps, too. She looks at me, smiles. That's pretty good for a bum, she says.

He got lucky, I shrug. The pitcher made a bad pitch. Anyone coulda hit that lollipop.

The Fightin' Phils continue their rally, scratching and clawing their way back. My favorite player comes to bat, Cookie Rojas. Nobody on. The Cookie Man is a singles hitter, so he's just looking to get aboard, get another rally started. But to everyone's surprise, Rojas ties into a high pitch and sends one deep to left. Way back, way back. The Astros' left fielder runs out of room, and the ball falls into the bleacher fans' outstretched arms just above the **ALPO** sign painted on the left-field wall. The stands are going wild, it's a rare homer for the popular Rojas, and the comeback is in full swing.

Now it's the bottom of the ninth, and the Phils are only one run down. The first batter smacks a single, the second draws a walk. Tie run and winning run both aboard, looks like another surefire rally in the making. But a ground out and a pop fly suddenly bring the Phils to within one out of defeat.

Connie Mack Stadium grows eerily calm. The batter works the count to 3-2, says so right up there on the giant right-field Ballantine Beer scoreboard. Fouls one pitch off. Then another. Tension fills the stadium air, the game's outcome riding on every pitch. Fans take a deep breath, hold. . . .

Crack! A line drive to the gap in left, bouncing all the way to the wall. One run in, tie game. The fielders track down the bouncing ball. Here comes the throw from the outfield to the cutoff man. The third-base coach is waving around the winning run, it's sure to be close. In comes the relay throw. Everyone is shouting, going crazy.

The throw goes wild, sails over the catcher's head. The run scores, the Phils' bench empties, they're going bananas in the stands at Connie Mack, our hometown team has won, and suddenly it seems like the old early '60s magic is back.

Outside we guide Grandmom to the parking lot where the players park their cars near the clubhouse entrance. The best spot in town for Phillies' autographs. The afternoon sun is high, the macadam bakes, but we wait. Patiently. We are not alone. Dozens and dozens of other starry-eyed kids and accompanying adults mill about, waiting for the hometown heroes.

After what seems like an eternity a door swings open, and out pops aging Wes Covington, the hulking left fielder with the homerun swing, great arm, and gimpy knees. In short-sleeved sport shirt and dress slacks, Covington strolls slowly to his Caddy, engulfed by a legion of adoring fans. He signs programs, tickets, scraps of paper. His black softball-sized biceps bulge in the sunlight as he writes, and for the first time I realize maybe our neighbor Sal Cusumano doesn't have the biggest muscles in town, or Hammerin' Tommy O'Hanlon the quickest bat.

Covington keeps walking, keeps talking, keeps signing. I hold out my scrap of paper, but can't get close enough. The big man reaches his car, opens the door, waves, and climbs in. No more autographs from him, gotta try the next guy.

A commotion has already broken out back by the clubhouse door. We spot Johnny Callison, right fielder, 1964 All Star Game MVP. Not nearly so big as Covington, but talented and movie-star good-looking to boot. However, Callison waves off all the pleading autograph seekers. Dashes to his car and drives off the lot, no time for us.

Suddenly, there he is! The Cookie Man. Mild-mannered, bespectacled, maybe 5' 9" or 5' 10" tops. Crisp white shirt, shiny black shoes. Looks more like an accountant than the most versatile player in all of baseball, who plays all nine positions. But Rojas is mobbed instantly, and is already making his way to his vehicle by the time Howie and I reach his entourage.

Rojas signs a few autographs, then hops into an older ministation wagon that's already seen some miles. Surprisingly modest wheels for a growing celebrity. A utility vehicle for the league's number-one utility player.

The driver window rolls down. Then the rear window too, it's hot. Rojas pokes his head out, says in a funny accent, Okay, all you boys line up, I sign one-at-a-time.

Kids scramble for position, and we form a line just like at the ticket booth at The Parkland Movies. Two chumps directly in front of us get into a shouting match about who arrived first, but their argument quickly settles down as other kids tell 'em to shussshh it. Howie and I are maybe tenth and eleventh, not bad. Rojas must be in a good mood after hitting that home run. He takes his time, signs the programs, talks a little with each child. The line moves slowly, the sun gets brighter, hotter. This North Philly parking lot is now an oven, not a patch of green in sight. Nine, eight, seven . . . we're getting closer, closer.

I think about what I want to tell Mr. Rojas. How he's my very favorite player. How I've got all his baseball cards, at least one for every year since he became a Phillie. How the kids on my street named me Cookie, in honor of him. How I started the Cookie Rojas Fan Club, just me, Howie, and Barry Craig. How my mom made us all Cookie Rojas T-shirts, #16. But then Barry drowned in Dobbs Creek—while wearing his Cookie Rojas shirt. So this autograph is really for poor Barry.

Six, five, four. He's so close now, sitting behind the wheel of his car, I can almost reach out and touch him. Funny, Rojas looks just like a regular guy, you'd never give him a second glance on the street. . . .

The bad blood between kids Number Three and Number Two suddenly erupts again, and the shoving commences. One hostile push sends a bag of buttered popcorn flying against the rear door of Rojas' car. Dozens of oily kernels go sailing through the open window, drop to the floor, or go bouncing around in the back seat of the ballplayer's well-used utility wagon.

I ask you, what kind of demented person eats buttered popcorn at the ballpark for nine innings? Like when it's 94° already?

The Cookie Man's head swivels around. He sees the scattered popcorn on the back seat, the empty bag lying on the ground near his car door. Quickly, his moon face reddens, the Latin temper coming fast to the surface.

That's it! Rojas exclaims in his clipped Cuban tongue. That's it! No more autographs. I've had enough of you *leettle* smart asses for one day!

With that, the Phillies' jack-of-all-trades rolls up both windows, puts his little utility car in gear, and pulls off the stadium lot, leaving dozens of dejected little faces in his wake.

Ah, jeez!!

Our disappointment turns rapidly to frustration, and we begin to heckle the two goobers involved with the buttered popcorn and the idiotic shoving match. What a pair of morons.

It wasn't me, it was him!

Was not.

Was too.

Was not.

Hey, what do you suppose it is with the food at Connie Mack Stadium, anyway? Is it jinxed? Did somebody put the whammy on it? Maybe a hex? The Evil Eye? First we had Donnie's hot dog that Jackie knocked into Cincinnati Man's man's fedora, a one-in-a-million shot, and now this. Unbelievable.

The crowd soon disperses. Sans autograph, we climb into Grandmom's early 1950s clunker, which is every bit as hot as the sun-bleached parking lot—probably hotter. But it sure was a great game, great finish, and as we return to familiar Kings Cross, we're already in better spirits. Can't wait to go again next year.

Yep, the Phillies are still my team, and the Cookie Man's still their number-one player in my book. Does every job, plays every position.

But things will never be the same again. Not like they were back in '64.

Eventually, the Kings Cross chapter of the Cookie Rojas Fan Club passes quietly out of existence.

There will never be another season like '64. At least not in Philadelphia. Makes me wonder if the Phillies will *ever* wind up in the World Series. Sadly, my guess is probably not—it's just not in the cards, not in the cosmic scheme of things.

After all, what it boils down to is we're still in second-fiddle Philly—ain't like we're talkin' about the New York Yankees here in their magical pinstripes with the ghosts of Ruth and Gehrig patrolling the dugout. . . .

In the Big Pretzel, losing sports teams are fast becoming a time-honored tradition.

CHAPTER 14

The Trouble with Mickey

Little Mickey Mantle Farrell could pass for a choirboy, an angel, or both. He's got big blue eyes, curly black hair, porcelain-white skin, and wears a perpetual expression of innocence. His dad wants him to be a Big League baseball star, which is why they named him after Mickey Mantle of The Yankees.

People say you can't judge a book by its cover. And if they had Mickey Farrell in mind when they coined the phrase, they were right. Mickey may be the worst liar, cheat, kleptomaniac, and firebug in the entire neighborhood. Mickey is also my friend and Howie's friend . . . until, of course, our backs are turned. Mickey will steal anything you don't nail down, then steal a hammer so he can remove the nails from whatever it was you did nail down. Mickey has a problem. And so does the rest of our neighborhood—Mickey.

In short, Mickey is the kind of person your mother warns you about. Literally. One day, Mom takes me aside and advises me to "get away" from Mickey if he ever does anything that doesn't seem quite right.

Are you saying Mickey is *bad,* Mom? I inquire, knowing I'm backing my mother into an uncomfortable corner. It's the kind of question kids love to ask parents.

Well, no, my mother lies. It's just that sometimes Mickey doesn't think before he acts, she explains diplomatically. Problem is, Mickey does think before he acts. His actions are carefully plotted, the results coldly calculated. Grandmom Kane, who rarely has a bad thing to say about anybody, once told my mother that, in her opinion, Mickey is a bad seed. It's just the way he is. Some people are born bad.

Seven-year-old Billy Deemer from around the corner on Wennington Avenue is a Batman fanatic. He watches every episode. He's got the cape. And the bat mask. All he needs to complete his collection is a Batmobile. So when Billy's birthday rolls around, his parents throw him a little party with cake and ice cream, then present their son with his very own Batmobile. Sleek, black, and shiny. Sports the famous bat logo. Has a steering wheel just like the real thing, and a set of hidden pedals for locomotion. Billy is now in seventh heaven. Rides that Batmobile every single day. Same bat time, same bat channel. Problem is, young Billy also has a bad habit of leaving his toy parked in the driveway behind his house at lunchtime.

Ever since I lost my Schwinn bicycle I'm more careful about leaving things lying around. But that's me—not Billy. Seems Billy's going to have to learn the hard way, too.

Inevitably, birthday boy's Batmobile doesn't last the month. One day, after Billy has stopped in for lunchtime bowl of Spaghetti-Os, he returns to the driveway only to discover that his Batmobile is nowhere in sight. Curses! What diabolical villain, what evil mind could conceive of a plot so heinous? The Joker? The Riddler? The Mad Hatter? Perhaps the wicked Penguin?? None are ever seriously suspected. The only Southwest Philly archvillain capable of masterminding such a colossal heist in broad daylight has to be none other than the infamous Mickey Farrell.

Batman, alias Billy Deemer, in the company of an aspiring Robin and an Alfred the Butler, proceeds to stake out Mickey's house in hopes of glimpsing the stolen superhero's wheels. But Mickey and the Batmobile are lying low. Emboldened, Batman and his sidekicks approach the basement window of the Farrell home and peer in through the curtains. Gadzooks! There it is! Tucked into a far corner by the washing machine is the neighborhood's only genuine Batmobile—now painted a sickening shade of pea green. Great Scot! Is there no limit to the evil that lurks in Mickey's twisted mind?

Armed with concrete evidence, our superhero embarks on his next course of decisive action. He dashes home to tell his mother. Mrs. Deemer drops everything, rushes over to the Farrell household, and makes her accusation to Mickey's mother. Mickey's mother promptly dismisses the charges. Surely her little angel is incapable of such criminality. Does Mickey have a Batmobile in the Farrell basement? He most certainly does. And where did Little Mickey get his Batmobile? He found it. And since Billy's Batmobile was black, and Mickey's is green, surely they couldn't be the same one, now could they?

Holy Twisted Logic!! They don't make *green* Batmobiles. Even the Green Hornet's car is called Black Beauty! But don't try explaining this to Mrs. Farrell.

I once happened to glimpse Mickey's amazing stash down in the Farrell basement. It looked like the discount aisle at the Lester Avenue Woolworth's. Several Radio Flyer wagons painted pea green. Bikes and tricycles painted pea green. Baseball gloves, baseball bats, roller skates, box carts, sleds, water pistols, whiffle balls, air rifles, frisbees, basketballs, footballs, walkie-talkies, transistor radios. You name it and Mickey has it. Often in large quantities, various sizes, shapes, colors, and brand names.

And where does Mickey get all this stuff? He finds it. Just ask Mickey's mother, she'll tell you.

One hot summer afternoon the guys are all playing halfball in the street near 57th and Beaufort, just outside Jerry's Steaks. Jackie O'Hanlon is pitching. Diet Donnie Fahey is playing the infield. I'm playing the outfield. Frankie Pellegrino is at bat with a mop handle. Scotty Morgan is on deck, Johnny Deemer behind him. Just as Tutti Frutti whiffs on a half-moon floater, Mickey Farrell comes sauntering down 57th Street, bold as you please.

Hey, guys.

Yo, Mickey. Wanna play?

Nah. I'm gonna get me a cheesesteak. You guys want some?

Yeah, right, Jackie O'Hanlon snickers.

No, it's OK, Mickey Mantle Farrell assures him. I've got the money.

With that Mickey reaches into his jeans and pulls out a roll of fives, tens, and even a rarely seen twenty. Jaws drop. This new development brings the old halfball game to a very sudden stop.

Mickey motions everybody into Jerry's Steaks. C'mon, guys. Once inside, Mickey steps up and orders a cheesesteak with onions and mushrooms.

Anybody else hungry?

Diet Donnie, the neighborhood junk-food aficionado, eyes Mickey's flash roll hungrily. Um, um, I'd like a pizza steak with extra cheese—and a diet Coke.

Johnny Deemer, remembering his brother Billy's stolen Batmobile, volunteers next by ordering a hoagie and an Italian water ice. Frankie the Fruit puts in for a tuna melt and strawberry milkshake. It's suddenly party time, and Tricky Mickey is the life of the party.

Jackie O'Hanlon looks at me. I look at Bugs. Jackie calls me aside, speaks first.

Listen, my mom told me if Mickey Farrell ever starts doin' anything weird, that I should get away from him. I don't know what Mickey's up to, or where he got the money, but this looks kinda strange to me.

My jaw drops for the second time in less than five minutes. Wow! Jackie has gotten the very same lecture from his mom that I had gotten from mine. I stand there, mouth watering, practically tasting the hamburger with fried onions and ketchup washed down with a thick, creamy black & white milkshake. But, to my credit, and Jackie's timely reminder, I decide to pass. Mickey Farrell means trouble, pure and simple, and that flash roll of fives, tens, and an eye-popping twenty has danger written all over it with a capital D. Better safe than sorry, Charlie.

Jackie has a pimple ball, even though it's a little flat, so we decide to go to DD's paved, empty lot beside the Hebrew school on 57th and Beaufort. Just the two of us. There, in the sweltering sun, we played sock it out, trying to punch the ball over the fence and into the narrow walkway behind the Jewish building. Time and time again we try. Inning after inning, three swings, three fly balls, and three outs. Once I have to reach over the chain-link fence and knock the ball back into the lot to prevent an O'Hanlon homer. But the ball is just too soft and won't carry, so we decide to leave it at a 0-0 tie. Besides, we're both hungry, thirsty, and it's getting closer to supper time. So we leave the lot and head east up Beaufort Street for home.

We have long since forgotten all about shady Mickey Farrell and his fistful of lovely green magic.

Bugs and I turn the corner at Beaufort and start crossing 57th, angling our way toward the bottom of Littlefield.

Hey, what's goin' on? Jackie points. He pulls up short and motions toward the bottom of our little street. A police van blocks the way, sealing off cars from entering. Next to the boxy van stands a very tall, very gruff-looking cop. Jackie and I play it cool, pretend not to see the cop, whom you couldn't hardly miss, and start to make the turn onto Littlefield. Oblivious, just another day, not a care in the world.

Hey, you two, where youse think you're goin'?

Um, um … us, officer?

Yeah, *you*, he growls.

Well, well . . . we live here. This is our street.

Yeah? What addresses?

5611.

5619.

All right, he waves us on. Youse kids go right up the street and onto your porches. Don't stop 'til youse get home, and mind yer own business.

We do a fast walk up the block. 5659, 5657, 5655, 5653. . . . There are more police near Jackie's house. Lots more. But they're looking up at one of the houses on the even numbered side. Surrounding it. Waiting for orders.

I blurt out, Hey—it's Mickey's house!

No, the cops aren't there to retrieve Billy Deemer's stolen Batmobile painted that awful pea green. Something big here is goin' down. Jackie and I pick it up the last couple of yards, Converse high-tops springing off the concrete squares, and sprint up Jackie's stoop onto the O'Hanlon's awning-covered front porch. Quickly we duck down behind the strategically located chaise lounge, giving us the best vantage point on the block.

One cop has climbed up and gained access to the continuous porch roof on Mickey's side of the row house street. Others huddle behind a squad car. Guns are drawn and ready. Some of the cops wear flak vests. On command, the officers approach, heading for the porch, the doors, and the windows. The cop up on the porch roof slides open a second-story bedroom window and crawls inside. The other cops push open the front door and duck in, weapons drawn, disappearing into the darkness. Directly across the street, Jackie and I wait excitedly for the gunfire that never comes. A few moments later a burly sergeant leads Mickey out of the Farrell house. We are close enough on our narrow street to eavesdrop on the conversation.

All right, son, now what did this man look like?

Um, um, stammers Mickey, well, to tell you the truth, I really didn't see the man. I just, you know, sort of heard him kinda movin' around.

But when you called 911, you said he had a gun, presses the sergeant. How did you know the man had a gun if you didn't see him?

The blood drains from Mickey's cherubic face. Um, um, I don't know. I just kinda figured he was a robber and, you know, had one.

The sergeant looks at his lieutenant. The lieutenant smirks. The cops now knew the score. A few more questions, and Mickey is busted. They put Mrs. Farrell's little angel into the back of the squad car and give him a free ride to the station, today's guest of honor accompanied by the siren and flashing lights.

Mickey gets sent off to a special school for "special children" as we are told. Mickey is special all right. Eventually we learn that Mrs. Farrell had cashed her paycheck, left all her money in her pocketbook, then left her pocketbook at home while she went to work. Tricky Mickey found the pocketbook, and the flash roll, and decided to hold a neighborhood party. Problem was, when four-thirty rolled around, he needed a convenient story. That's when he decided to dial the cops.

Billy Deemer never does get back his beloved Batmobile, whether in green or in black. Mrs. Farrell keeps it in safe storage in the Farrell basement. After all, Mickey has *found* it, right? And in Kings Cross it's finders keepers, losers weepers. Where Mickey Farrell is one very lucky, very special child.

Misguided Communication

Mom and Dad have a big fight. No big deal, nothing new. The Orange and the Green have been mixing it up for 800 years now, give or take a few decades. From the looks of things, I see no reason for hostilities to cease any time in the near future.

Next morning, Mom prepares Dad's lunch, same as usual, but she's still plenty steamed. So Mom decides to include a little culinary surprise to get the Old Man's attention.

It's now lunchtime at the auto repair shop and Dad has taken his seat beside the other Brimstone mechanics. Sets down his thermos, opens his lunch box, takes out the wrapped sandwiches, gives them a cursory inspection. Wow, big surprise.

Meatloaf . . . again.

Dad announces, I got meatloaf sandwiches today—third time this week. Anybody want to trade?

The tire mechanic says, Yeah sure, I'll swap you my ham and cheese for one of them meatloafs.

Deal, Pop agrees. The exchange is made.

Dad is enjoying the ham and cheese. Glances over to the tire mechanic. Hey, Chuck . . . how's the meatloaf?

Chuck doesn't say a word, but he's wearing an awfully funny expression. Something's definitely not right. The tire mechanic stops chewing.

Chuck?

Chuck carefully peeks between the slices of Wonder bread, extracts what appears to be a folded piece of notebook paper. Dad's face turns purple.

The Old Man says, Here—give me that! Swipes the slip of paper away from the befuddled tire mechanic. Checks the other meatloaf sandwich, hands it to Chuck, then inspects the mystery object. It's a note, obviously not intended for Chuck, addressed to none other than dear old Dad. . . .

From his loving wife:

YOU'RE STILL A MORON, JAMES MORRIS.

Karate Dan

He's a stocky kid. Moon face. Freshly scrubbed, clean behind the ears. Sporty new plaid shirt, Boy Scout looks. Just sitting there up on the porch. Mrs. Baumgartner's front porch on Wennington Avenue. Day after day, just sitting. Watching us hanging out, playing boxball, goofing around. Who's this mystery kid and where'd he come from? And what's he doing taking up space on this old lady's porch?

Diet Donnie, always the nosy one, finally asks Larry Litman, the older Jewish teenager and wannabe rock 'n' roll star. Litman lives next door to Mrs. Baumgartner and a few doors up from Donnie. Say, what's up with this new boy, Larry? Oh, he's just Mrs. Baumgartner's grandson, says Litman. From some suburb God knows where, way up in Bucks County. He's spending the summer with grandma. Believe his name's Dan, but he's pretty quiet . . . doesn't say much.

Suburban kid, huh? Sitting alone up on the porch. Afraid to venture off. Probably heard stories about the city. About the neighborhood. About us. Betcha he doesn't much like the way we look.

Slowly, eventually, Suburban Boy inches down from the porch onto the stoop. Still watching, still saying nothing. Me, Jackie, Donnie, Howie, Frankie, Bobby, Scotty, Johnny, and the rest of our gang are starting a new game of halfball. We need one more person for even sides.

Hey, kid . . . you wanna play? We got room for one more.

With some effort we coax Suburban Dan off Mrs. Baumgartner's steps and into the game. It's obviously he doesn't know diddly about halfball, so we teach him. Soon we discover he hasn't played boxball, wireball, stepball, stickball, sock-it-out, or just about any of our everyday street games. Like this boy's from another planet instead of Bucks County, which is supposed to be just across the city line up north. But we take our time and "learn" him.

Yo, the Water Ice truck comes making its rounds, and we line up to buy Italian ice with soft pretzels & mustard on the side. The vendor guy has tutti frutti, lemon, cherry, cherry vanilla. . . .

Sorry, kid. No root beer today.

What a drag. Betcha he wouldn't dare show his face without tutti frutti. Or cherry vanilla, for that matter. These two flavors rule.

Soon we've got All-American Dan eating water ice and soft pretzel like a pro. As if he were born here in Southwest Philly. No sweat.

Yo, Danny! Not too bad . . . pretty good, huh?

Dan's still a bit shy, a little hesitant. But he's making strides. Maybe Danny won't want to go home to Bucks County by the time the school year rolls around.

Hey, Danny, inquires Diet Donnie one afternoon. What kinds of stuff do youse guys like to do for fun back home?

Oh . . . lots of things, says apple-cheeked Dan. Make model airplanes, take guitar lessons, swim over at the swim-club pool, hang out at the mall, play records, practice my karate. . . .

Karate—for real? You do karate?

Sure, I know karate. My Uncle Mitch was in The War . . . stationed in Japan during the Occupation. Learned karate and all kinds of martial-arts stuff from the Japanese. Now he's a black belt, and he gives me private lessons on the weekends. We're in this secret military martial arts club together. I'm studying so I can be a grand master some day, just like my uncle.

Wow, cool. Why they keep this club secret, Dan?

Well, 'cause it's some pretty dangerous stuff we do. You can kill people with the kind of stuff I'm learning. The Government doesn't want knowledge like that getting spread around. You know, like falling into the wrong hands and all. They want it kept real quiet, real low-profile. That's why our club's gotta stay, well, sorta *underground.*

Boss, Donnie observes.

Can you maybe show us some karate moves, Dan?

We all nod in agreement. Yeah, can ya, Dan? Can ya? Huh??

Dan frowns. I'm really not supposed to. It could get me into some serious trouble.

Aw, c'mon Danny. Just one move, huh? Maybe a little one. We ain't gonna tell nobody.

With apparent reluctance, Danny Boy relents. Okay, he needs a volunteer. Picks one of the scrawnier onlookers who've gathered around.

Showtime.

Now look, you guys, Dan makes us swear. You gotta promise never, *never* to tell anyone you saw this. All right?

Hey, you got it, Big Guy. Our lips are sealed.

I'm trusting you guys, says Suburban Dan, picking up a stray popsicle stick from the stoop. Here . . . take this. Pretend it's a knife. Hold it up like so.

Like a director in a Hollywood movie, Dangerous Dan positions the scrawny, would-be attacker.

Now, when I say "GO" you come at me . . . in slow motion . . . with the knife.

Handy Dan readies himself. Barks, Okay . . . GO!

The boy advances, clutching his popsicle weapon.

Slower! Dan instructs him. Inch by inch.

Now we're in super slo-mo.

Dan says, The basic idea in this situation is to deflect the attack . . . turn your opponent's momentum against him. You do that with what we call "leverage."

The skinny boy's popsicle "knife" creeps toward Dan's babyish face. Like so, he demonstrates, sidestepping the make-believe switchblade, sliding a cupped hand under his attacker's elbow, stepping around and forward to hook his right leg behind the sacrificial lamb's left calf muscle.

And now for the leverage!

In a split second Danny juts his right hip out, turns, twists, and flips Skinny Boy to the sidewalk.

SMACK!

Ooowwwwwwl screeches the bony, undersized street urchin.

Sorry, Dan apologizes.

Skinny Boy starts to sit up.

Stay put for just a minute, Karate Man commands the boy.

Then to us, If you'll notice, my left hand is still clutching the wrist that holds the knife . . . and with my right hand I'm still controlling my attacker's left elbow. With my opponent still on the ground, momentarily subdued, this gives me a few options.

The crowd steps even closer, leans forward to get a better look.

With my thumb I apply pressure, then rotate.

Ooowwwwl, shouts Skinny Boy. He instantly submits, dropping the Popsicle stick.

Master Dan continues. . . . If I were to rotate with full force— turn, turn, and keep on turning using all my weight and leverage— I could snap the radial bone in his wrist just like it's this popsicle stick.

Dan reaches over, picks up the "knife" and snap it in two for effect.

Boss! exclaims Jackie.

Now *that's* cool, agrees Donnie.

Also, continues Karate Man, I can choose to pull his arm tight, turn it in the *other* direction, and, in one motion, come down and jam my knee into my opponent's rib cage.

Danny demonstrates, but stops short as he lightly touches his kneecap to Stick Boy's chest. This looks quite slick, not to mention painful.

Again, using full speed and leverage, I can easily break a rib. Maybe even puncture his lung. With all the internal bleeding, this would leave my opponent helpless.

Solid, observes Scotty Morgan, all the while chewing baseball-card bubblegum and blowing a pink bubble.

Karate Dan stands tall, faces the gang, and gives us a solemn, Asian-style bow. Demonstration over.

We are duly impressed. A couple of the boys even clap. Guess you can't judge a book by its cover, because Dan just looks like your typical, average kid. Even kind of square and nonthreatening in that wholesome, suburban way of his. But it's only a disguise. For beneath that mundane, everyday exterior, Dan is a trained killer. Truly frightening. Say the wrong thing to this boy and you could be history . . . finito.

Our boy is now revealing he knows forty-three—yep count 'em—forty-three different ways to take someone out. Permanently. And he's learning new and more deadly tricks all the time from his uncle and their underground club. Soon Dan will have earned his fifth-degree orange belt.

Hey, wait a minute, Bugs O'Hanlon questions him. I've heard of black belts, brown belts, and even white belts in karate. But never an orange one.

No kidding, says Our Man Dan. This is a *secret* branch of karate.

Oh yeah, right. We forgot.

So every night, right after we've finished playing stickball, boxball, stepball, wireball, wallball, sock-it-out, or whatever, our little group gathers around. With dusk approaching, it's time for the Karate Dan Show. Every episode is a thriller. You don't want to miss it.

Danny Boy's got a special headlock . . . one that'll cut off a person's air supply and put 'em in a coma in less than thirty seconds.

A little up-and-under technique with his thumb and index finger that can pop a guy's eye right outta the socket.

A sidewinder karate chop that'll bust a windpipe from the front or break the spinal cord if thrown from behind.

A lightening-quick double chop capable of perforating both ear drums simultaneously.

Not to mention a vicious sidekick that can sever a knee, and the handy, surprise drop kick that'll turn any adversary into a soprano.

Yep, he's Karate Dan, and everyone gives him plenty of room. You play nice with Killer Dan. Stay on Danny's good side.

Hey, Dan . . . you thirsty? How 'bout I get you a soda?

Before too long our man Dan is strolling around bold as a peacock, all cocky and sassy. Ordering kids around. Playing bully on occasion. Earning something of a cult status.

One day we're all playing sock-it-out on Littlefield Street. I'm up, and I punch the ball into the outfield for a hit. Dan takes off from first, running the chalk-colored bases. Tries to go from second to third base. Throw comes in. Frankie tries to make the catch for the put-out on Dan. White pimple ball and Karate Dan arrive at the same time.

Dan runs into Frankie. BLAM! Knocks Tutti Frutti to the ground. Hard. Momentarily stunned, hot-blooded Frankie shakes it off and jumps to his feet, looking for a fight. His voice vibrates with rage, his lip quivering.

Hey, kid! Frankie screams at Dan. You did that on purpose!

Fruit is on the thin side but muscular, one of the toughest kids our age in the entire neighborhood. Frankie's looking for an apology. But he's now trying to stare down the one and only Karate Dan. Uh oh.

Forget it, man, says Dan flippantly. You're not hurt—just walk it off.

Dan's cavalier attitude only serves to further enrage our volatile Frankie. Hey, I'm talkin' to *you*, kid! Nobody pushes me like that.

We try giving Frankie the high sign. Quit it, Fruit. *Back off, buddy*—before you get yourself hurt. Or maybe even seriously killed. But Frankie pays us no mind. Steps forward, gets right in Karate Dan's face.

Fair one . . . right now! Frankie barks. We look on, unbelieving. Frankie has called out Dangerous Dan. His anger has truly runneth over, obliterating all good sense.

Oh, well . . . I guess Italians are just like that, don't you know.

Karate Dan flinches for the briefest of moments, then turns to his audience. Tell him to back off, guys, Mr. Martial Arts implores us. I don't wanna have to hurt this kid.

Our eyes beg Frankie. *Cool it, man. Are you crazy?* But it's too late for that now. Frankie is past the point of no return. There's gonna be a showdown at the OK Corral. We just pray that our poor Frankie hasn't brought a knife to a gunfight.

Frankie pushes Dan's shoulder. I said fair one!

Dan jumps back, assumes a karate pose. Curled knuckles at the ready for a series of deadly chops.

I'm warning you, Dan threatens. These hands are registered as lethal weapons!

With that Frankie hauls off and slugs Danny square in the mouth. The Suburban Wonder grabs his mug in pain and tries to step away. But Frankie jumps right on him. Bam! A shot to the cheekbone. Wham! A punch to the stomach that doubles Dan over. Thump! An uppercut to the jaw finishes him off. In barely five seconds our summer guest lies blubbering in the middle of the street.

Naturally, we're all stunned. But in an instant we realize the sad truth: Dan's entire karate act has been a gigantic fake. One big fraud, con job, snow job. And we all fell for it. What a bunch of morons.

He's no orange belt, black belt, or any other kind of belt. He's just a wiseacre. Probably checked out a do-it-yourself martial arts book at the library, if that. Danny Boy's just a slick suburban punk with a fast mouth in sore need of a little attitude adjustment. . . .

. . . Or, just a scared boy trying to fit in with the rough-and-tumble kids in a strange neighborhood.

Either way, the damage has been done. In the immortal words of Yankee great Yogi Berra, Dan has made "the wrong mistake."

Next day, Karate Dan comes around, all quite and humble, trying to act as if nothing ever happened. Wishful amnesia. Dan's ruffled way too many local feathers with his mouthy tough-guy routine, and now it's payback time . . . Kings Cross style.

Within half an hour Jackie O'Hanlon purposely picks a fight with Karate Dan. The suburban kid immediately tries to punk out, but Bugs just laughs in his face and pops him one. Say, what's up, Doc? Wham, wham, wham! Again, Danny goes down with basically no resistance.

Later in the week comes Diet Donnie's turn.

C'mon, Karate Man! Show me what you got! Let's see some of them fancy moves.

But Danny is out of both fancy talk and fancy moves. One shot from hefty Donnie and Dan's running home to Grandma Baumgartner's house, holding his nose. This time he's got the good sense to stay with Grandma.

I think a summer vacation in Kings Cross might do Fred Talbot from Langford–Alton a world of good. It would definitely enlighten his pushy buddy Ernie Imhoff. Teach both of them some valuable insights. Like not messing with people you shouldn't be messing with.

For weeks Karate Dan sits forlornly on the old lady's front porch, rarely wandering off. A pathetic figure. Neighborhood kids taunt Danny from the street, calling him all sorts of names. Sissy, Grandma's boy, worse. . . .

Dan just looks away, pretends not to hear, and stays close by Grandma's door. Eventually, he goes home to Bucks County two, maybe three weeks early. The boy never shows his face in our neighborhood again. No surprise.

I feel sorry for Dan, but that's life. What can you do? Chalk one up to experience. Just one more lesson learned the old-fashioned way. You take your lumps and move on.

So long, Karate Dan . . . it sure was fun while it lasted.

Summer of Love

Uncle Joe is married now. He and his wife have a new baby daughter. They've sold the Studebaker, bought a Volkswagen Beetle, and are heading to California. The world of Fortran, COBOL, and computer databases will have to wait. It is 1967 . . . the Summer of Love is upon us. Time to leave Philadelphia behind for the Promised Land. Head out for the Left Coast. Pitch a tent, live on the beach, sleep under the stars, wake up with the sea breeze and the morning sun.

♫   ♫   ♫   ♫

Are you goin' to San Francisco?

Better wear a flower in your hair.

Back in Philadelphia, we wonder about Uncle Joe. Goldwater campaign manager who listened to The Beatles, wouldn't go hunting, or take in a Phillies game. Dad and Uncle Hank's little brother Joe. College boy. The Morris family member who always marched to a different drummer.

Yes, the times they are a changin'.

Gram is all alone now in her house on 61st Street by the Baltimore & Ohio freight tracks. Mom and Dad have me stay there for a week. Away from Littlefield and the endless summer street games of boxball, wireball, stepball, halfball, sock-it-out, buck-buck, and hide-the-belt. A minivacation away from vacation.

It's quiet at Gram's house, but I find plenty to do. Read all of Uncle Joe's *Mad* magazines. Copy faces out of comic books using Silly Putty from a plastic egg. Walk my Slinky up and down the stairs. Build a fort on the living room floor with my resident erector set and Lincoln Logs.

There aren't many chores. My biggest job is the daily run to Philly Fruit supermarket just down the block on Parkland Avenue. My grandmother always lets me throw in a bag of "Gauchos" peanut butter and oatmeal cookies, and, of course, a bottle of root beer. Gram's bribing me to stay longer, knowing school is still weeks and weeks away.

At night we stay up, watch the late shows. The news, Johnny Carson, old black & white movies. No set bedtime. I fall asleep to the grinding sound of endless boxcars from the railroad, and passing trolley cars on Parkland, which doppler in the distance. Sparking electrical wires over the railroad bridge as they disappear past the lighted billboards into the darkness. Giving off that hollow, faraway ocean sound a seashell makes when it's pressed firmly against the ear.

Some mornings I go exploring with Brian McLaughlin, the neighbor boy. Behind Philly Fruit, the land of empty, trash-strewn lots and closed factories down by the commuter tracks. Brian's favorite place is sprawling, windswept Buell's, the once-giant manufacturer, now abandoned, that used to make the city's trolleys and later buses. Turned out hundreds of tanks for the war. Employed thousands in its heyday. Now a ghostly, stripped-down skeleton of its former self . . . like a bombed-out airplane hangar in a war zone. Empty tracks roll right through the plant where the flatcars, now long gone, used to be loaded for shipment. One look at Buell's and you might think maybe the Japs and the Jerries had won the war. But it's a fabulous playground for two twelve-year-olds all alone with nothing but hours to kill. Cops and robbers. Treasure hunting. Throwing rocks. Surveying our acres and acres of weed-covered domain.

Later Brian and I find a bulky cardboard box that once held a large appliance. We flatten it out, toboggan down the B&O railroad embankment. Again and again. Magic carpet ride in the graveyard of American industry. The momentary thrill of gravity, while the slower pull of gravity on these surroundings largely escapes us.

Pop says a lot of the big companies have moved away for cheaper labor. Down South to escape the unions, and overseas where people will work for pennies and aren't protected by labor laws. The rich executives think they're smart, says Dad, but how clever will they be when there's nobody left who can buy their products? Where's the profit then?

Now Buell's is an industrial graveyard, and the old steel plant down by 58th is gone too. Ditto for the refrigerator factory, the cigar factory, the pencil factory, the chocolate factory, the paint factory, the ball-bearings factory, and a dozen other smaller plants and shops. Who knows when the ice cream factory or the giant light bulb factory will be next? Everything's going in one direction.

Down and out.

I'm back at the house on 61st in time for lunch. Tuna on toast with raisins and celery. More peanut-butter Gauchos, more root beer. Then Gram and I watch the soaps. *General Hospital*, her favorite. *The Edge of Night*. *Dark Shadows* with Barnabas the Vampire, my favorite.

Some tea in the late afternoon. Hot tea with condensed milk for Gram, cold tea with sugar and lemon for me. Sitting on the enclosed porch, former Goldwater campaign headquarters, watching the world go by. Windows up, screens down, hoping for a breeze. Cats stretched to full length, trying to radiate the heat from their matted fur.

Spaghetti for dinner. Then more Gauchos, more root beer for dessert. Gram misses Uncle Joe. He'd usually be coming home from work about this time, walking through the side yard, coming in the back door. Always through the back door, it's the old-fashioned way. Company comes in the front.

Gram talks on about her family. Generations long dead. Her mother's family, the Fishers and Durangs. Theatre people, used to perform on stage in downtown Philadelphia. Once performed for George Washington. Came up with the music for the *Star-Spangled Banner*, the first persons to sing the anthem in public. Her father's people, the Roses from merry old England, the Blackburns, and the Orems. One of the Roses had to escape back to England . . . he was promoting bare-knuckle fights when a man got killed and the police came looking, asking questions. The Blackburns were lawyers, always looking to turn a buck. One liked the green stuff too much, got himself caught embezzling funds from a client. The judge sentenced him to Moyamessing Prison, but the family paid off some officials to look the other way. At night they'd let the well-heeled convict take a carriage ride home, then he'd be back at the prison gates before sunup. No one ever got wise. Grandpop Orem had been the money man and family patriarch. Made his fortune in Ireland, then retired to France, married a Frenchwoman. But the French wife had other plans . . . America, the storied Land of Dreams. So they resettled in Philadelphia, had a daughter. The mother became a super-patriot, loved her adopted country. The daughter became a Francophile, loved everything French. The father became an eccentric, always banging on people and furniture with his ever-present cane, spoiling his beloved dog.

And then there's Gram's husband, my father's father. His name was Bill, but she doesn't call him that. Gram has a special pet name for this man . . . The Rat. Couldn't trust him as far as I could throw him, Gram says. Which wasn't very far, since Gram is under five feet and The Rat was over six feet. The Rat worked as a long-haul truck driver, and when he wasn't driving he was out walking. He'd walk from one end of Philadelphia and back again, forget the trolley. Marched in the St. Patrick's Day parade each and every year, too, the bum.

St. Patrick's Day Parade? The Rat, Dad's father, was an Irisher?

His mother came from County Cork, says Gram. Her family's name was O'Donnell.

Dad's father the Irishman . . . you learn something new every day. Perhaps Ray Watts' grandfather, the one who called me a cockeyed, smart-mouthed, potato-eating little mick, was even more psychic than I realized. This gets me thinking, and I so I ask Gram another question.

Gram, how did The Rat die?

My grandmother's face turns ashen, and it's obvious I've struck a nerve.

Don't ask foolish questions, says Gram. But instinct tells me I've stumbled upon some great secret here, and curiosity gets the better of me. So I keep after Gram, bring the subject up at meals. What happened to The Rat, Gram? How'd he die?

Obviously, I figure, since he's never been around, the man must be long dead.

Again and again and again, I push for an answer. Finally, Gram loses her cool. All right, all right, since you *must* know, The Rat fell down the stairs and hit his head. That's what happened to him, I'm not saying any more, so don't ever ask me again.

I don't. But for months after Gram's revelation, whenever I'm at the house on 61st Street, I can't help but to stare at the landing at the bottom of the stairs. In my mind's eye I can see an old man, white hair and eyeglasses all askew, lying crumpled and unconscious. An ugly knot swelling up on his wrinkled forehead.

389

Now it's time for me to leave. Back to Littlefield with all the endless summer street games of boxball, wireball, stepball, halfball, sock-it-out, buck-buck, and hide-the-belt. I miss my friends . . . it's time to head home. But I spend one last evening with Gram. Hoagies with sweet peppers from the deli on Parkland. The last of the Gaucho cookies and root beer. Watch *The Fugitive*, Dr. Kimble always on the run. The news, The Late Show with Johnny Carson, and an old black & white movie. Late in the night, I go to bed in Uncle Joe's room, Burnham letter sweater in the closet and textbooks on the shelves. Listen to the Baltimore & Ohio freight trains as they thunder by, and the late-night trolleys as they doppler over the 60th Street bridge, sounding like giant moving seashells. Sparking their way along the low-hanging wires . . . sailing through the hot, humid, urban night.

None of the cats come in to stay with me tonight. Top Cat, Toes, Blackie, Golly, Grey . . . they're all OK. But not like my old Herman. Half cat, half raccoon, one ear torn to shreds, burrs clinging to his fur. In the blackness, just before I fall asleep, I can almost hear his distinctive purr. *My* cat, my special buddy. It's been five years since he disappeared. Never did get to say goodbye.

Too smart, too streetwise to have ever gotten lost. But I guess I'll never know.

The legendary, mythical Rat, my grandfather, sprawled unconscious at the bottom of the stairs. Giant-sized knot growing fast on his thick Irisher's skull.

Comes the roar of another diesel engine, the blast of the horn, followed by the thunder of another hundred boxcars rolling past. Clickety-clack, clickety-clack. By the time the caboose passes under the bridge and the world fades into deafening quietness, I am fast asleep.

The Legend of Crazy Sam

Nobody seems to know this Crazy Sam—don't even know his last name. But just about everyone in Kings Cross knows *about* him. Caretaker for the old Mt. Lebanon Cemetery that straddles the lower part of Dobbs Creek. That's the Protestant place where all Gram's people are buried—my mother's family and all the

Catholics have their own separate deal out in the suburbs. This Crazy Sam lives by himself in the only house on Mt. Lebanon's grounds. Just Sam, his hound dogs, and a couple of thousand dead Protestant people . . . nice and quiet. Drinks rotgut whiskey, they say—makes him meaner than hell. Talk is old Sam caught a piece of shrapnel in the head during the Battle of the Bulge. Never really been the same since . . . the nearby Hayden Police Department tried to bring Sam aboard years ago, him being a veteran and all. But the borough had to let him go. Wasn't working out, the man was too unpredictable. Nothing specific, just gossip. That's the way it's always been with Crazy Sam. Lots of rumors, nothing solid.

One thing's for sure, Crazy Sam hates kids. Don't ever let him catch you on his turf, especially after sundown. The man takes things personally. He'll come after you in his beat-up pickup truck, sic the dogs on you. Has a gun rack in the truck, keeps a gun loaded. Shotgun, double-barreled. The scoop is he takes out the lead shot, pours rock salt in the shells in place of the lead pellets. Won't kill you at a distance, but it burns like a son-of-a-gun. Make you wish you were dead.

The cemetery looms as a partial barrier between Kings Cross and hardscrabble Haskell, the next neighborhood over. Or, if you're Catholic, between Our Lady of Perpetual Peace and Holy Epiphany Parish. It's such a big piece of real estate that naturally Mt. Lebanon's going to serve as a boundary, whether official or not. Even the Lester Avenue trolley car takes a detour around Mt. Lebanon. Turns south to Kings Cross Avenue at 60th, then west past the cemetery, and finally back north to Lester Avenue along 63rd where Lester picks up again on the other side of the sprawling graveyard.

The cemetery's also a natural spot for kids to explore. All those trees, hills, open fields, looping cemetery roads, mausoleums, row after row of tombstones. Problem is, some of the hardcore juvenile delinquents from Haskell like to throw the occasional beer blast in a few of the more remote areas. Go crazy, party hard, knock over some headstones, do more than a little damage. If I were in Sam's shoes, I might get a little steamed myself. But shooting at kids? Like we were so many rats down at one of Haskell's many auto junkyards? Seems a bit over the top to me. Maybe somebody oughtta pull this Sam fella off the track before he hits the wall. Not every kid in Kings Cross or even Haskell is a delinquent.

And you shouldn't get shot at just for being a kid in the cemetery.

But that's not the way ol' Crazy Sam sees it.

If you took a poll in Kings Cross, I'd say maybe half the kids would claim they'd gotten a dose of Crazy Sam's rock salt. Most of the remaining half would tell you they were shot at but missed.

Myself, I'm too scared to get close enough for either. Once me, Howie, Jackie, Dave, Scotty, and some of the others sneak in to find the gravesite of Betsy Ross, the lady who designed the first Stars and Stripes. You know, the colonial one with the stars all in a circle. Davey Cutler has been to see the Ross tomb, but has trouble remembering the way. Just as we make a wrong turn, then try to double back, someone shouts, Here comes Crazy Sam! Look out!!

In two seconds flat, kids are scurrying left and right, ducking down behind the headstones. Sure enough I hear this engine coming fast, peek out from behind a slab of granite to see the infamous red pickup bouncing down the gravel road in our direction. Trailed by a moving cloud of dust and dirt, pebbles flying every which way.

I duck back down, close my eyes. Start to pray.

Please, God. I'll won't ever play in the cemetery again. I swear.

Crazy Sam never sees us. The truck keeps going, up, up, and over the next hill until it drops out of sight. The dust settles, the cemetery grows quiet again. Forget Betsy Ross, she ain't goin' nowhere. We all hightail it outta there, through the woods toward the creek and Dobbs Creek Parkway, hearts beating a mile-a-minute. Take the long way home along the Parkway to Venice, nobody minds. No one has the stomach for daring the shortcut—a mad dash across open fields to the cemetery's eastern exit. What if Crazy Sam comes back around and spots us? Out in the open? All by ourselves? What then?

Ducks on the pond, rats in the junkyard.

Besides the Betsy Ross gravesite expedition, there's the time Howie and friend Johnny Deemer come back to Littlefield Street all excited and out-of-breath. Ran all the way home from the infamous Mt. Lebanon. The back of Howie's dungarees look all torn and disheveled. Johnny has a nasty red mark on his forearm.

I ask, What happened?

It was Crazy Sam! says Howie. He caught us and let us have it with the rock salt. My legs feel like they're on fire!

I look to Johnny, who nods earnestly, emphatically. His eyes are saying, It's true, Jimmy. We ain't lyin'. We swear.

Whatever Howie and Johnny say, you gotta take with a grain of salt, ha ha. This is the same Howie who conned Bertie the Bunyip for birthday presents on local TV. The same Howie who painted food coloring on gumballs to cheat Mr. Nolan out of dozens of chocolate bars. The same Howie who tormented the poor kosher Fish Man into a homicidal rage. The same Howie whose big mouth is always getting me into scrapes, getting Big Brother Jimmy to fight his battles. The same Howie who climbed up on Grandmom's porch rocker as a toddler and plunged through the glass window, turning his thick little skull into a terrifying, glass-slivered, God-awful bloody mess.

He's been adding to those scars ever since that day. Howie *never* does anything the easy way.

So I have to wonder, is this another one of Howie's tall tales? The overactive imagination of two suggestion-prone preteens? Mass hysteria Kings Cross style?

Adults don't shoot at kids, right? Not even with rock salt, for God's sake.

I hustle Howie up to our bedroom so Mom doesn't see. Get a washcloth and some water, make Howie strip off the jeans. Sure enough, ugly little red welts up the back of one leg and down the other. Then I look closer at the pants . . . see the faint white markings against the dark blue denim.

Salt.

These aren't mosquito bites on Howie's skin, or scratches from thorny bushes. This is the real deal, Howie and Johnny are on the level.

Yep, Crazy Sam really is crazy.

Which explains why the story going around this summer is so entirely believable. Kids swear by it, and now even some of the grown-ups are buying in, too. It's the talk of the neighborhood, the talk all around Southwest.

They say Crazy Sam killed a kid back in July. The kid's got a name, too—Russ Mahoney. He's a run-of-the-mill Haskell punk who's been missing for weeks. No clues, no nothing. Got grounded by his folks, slipped out of the house, was last seen in the vicinity of Mt. Lebanon Cemetery. Crazy Sam's cemetery.

Now, *voila*—no more Russ Mahoney.

Word is Crazy Sam caught Russ, chased the teenager behind one of those big mausoleums. Cornered him. Shot the kid point blank in the face with the rock salt. Even loaded with salt, that twelve gauge is a mighty powerful weapon. Must be deadly at close range. Very deadly.

Hid the poor kid's body in the mausoleum. Waited for the next convenient, underattended burial. Told the guys with the back hoe to take a break from the heat, go get some lemonade. When no one was around, dragged Russ Mahoney's body from the mausoleum over to the freshly dug gravesite.

Now Russ is bunking with some old geezer in a lime-green polyester suit and a bad hairpiece. Six feet under. For all eternity.

This all starts as rumor, grows into rampant speculation. Pretty soon it's become a done deal. Crazy Sam killed the boy, no doubt, case closed. After all, this is *Crazy Sam* we're talking about. Right?

Great theory. The only problem is, two weeks before Labor Day, Russ Mahoney turns up alive and reasonably well down in sunny Florida. Seems he got tired of his parents' nagging requests to stop flunking school, quit getting into trouble with the cops, and cut out drinking beer with all the other lowlifes under the B&O railroad bridge. So he hitchhikes all the way down to Ft. Lauderdale. Bums around, hangs out at the beach, goes dumpster-diving for half-eaten ham-and-cheese sandwiches. Now tired and hungry and bored, he calls Philadelphia, has his parents arrange for a seat on the next Greyhound bus going north.

One way.

So much for the speculation about our man Sam. The entire "He Murdered Mahoney" story is full of baloney, so much hot air.

Doesn't matter, say Sam's critics. It's just a question of time. He's gonna kill somebody someday with that shotgun. After all, he's Crazy Sam, isn't he? Whaddaya expect? The man's more than a few bricks short of a full load. A walking time bomb.

But kids like Howie and Johnny keep going back for the thrills. For them hiding out from Crazy Sam in Mt. Lebanon is even more fun than running behind the mosquito truck when the city is spraying the streets of Southwest in thick, misty clouds of DDT.

As for me, I'm still playing it cool, keeping my distance from the cemetery. Crazy Sam's not going any place. Neither is his shotgun. And rock salt is cheap, they haul it in by the truckload every winter for Mt. Lebanon's roads.

Besides, even if Crazy Sam doesn't getcha, maybe Disappearing Diana will.

Disappearing Diana doesn't need a gun. Unlike Russ Mahoney, Diana is not alive and reasonably well. Disappearing Diana is a ghost.

Mt. Lebanon Cemetery, you see, is haunted. Or at least that's the word in old Kings Cross. Ever since that fatal, late-night, one-car wreck on winding Dobbs Creek Parkway back in the fabulous '50s. The mysterious tragedy that cut short Diana's brief, promising young life.

The accident that gave Southwest our very own honest-to-goodness spirit-in-residence.

Disappearing Diana

It happens just about every May, sometimes early June. Usually during prom season. Dressed up high-schoolers out in tuxes and gowns, enjoying their big night on the town. Too much to drink, too far to drive. Boys trying to impress the girls. Teens, parties, alcohol, automobiles, adolescent hormones—not the best of combinations.

Nervous parents wait up anxiously for the sound of a car pulling up out front. Most kids don't have a problem, most make it home okay.

Meanwhile, out on dark, lonely Dobbs Creek Parkway, a solitary car negotiates the tricky twists, the dangerous curves. It's late, the driver's probably fighting back a yawn. Suddenly, in the beam of the headlights, seemingly out of nowhere, materializes a young woman.

Hello, what's this?

Startled, the driver slams on the brakes, barely stops short of the young lady. She wears a beautiful white prom dress, carries a bouquet of flowers, seems strangely disoriented.

Even though it's a crystal-clear night, stars shining brightly and not a cloud in the sky, the girl is thoroughly soaked from head to toe. Sloshing, dripping. . . .

Still shaken, the driver pulls off to the road's shoulder. Opens the door, hops out.

Miss? Miss, are you all right?

Dazed and confused, the young lady replies, Yes. Yes, I think so.

The motorist looks around. Doesn't see any other cars. That's odd. Where did this person come from? Why is she wandering all alone in the park so late at night? So oddly out-of-place. Dressed like *that*?

Miss, do you need some help? Is there anything I can do?

Again, a look of bewilderment crosses her young face. Then she answers, hesitatingly.

Yes, thank you. I'm trying to get home. My boyfriend's car broke down, and I promised my parents I'd be home before one o'clock. Can you drop me off?

Sure, no problem. Get in. Where do you live?

Hayden, she replies. Adjoining suburb, other side of the park, just a few minutes drive. She gives him the address. He's a local, knows right where it is.

The teenager sits in the passenger seat. Water runs down her hair, her face, her expensive dress. She stares straight ahead, shivers despite the warmth of the evening.

How'd you get so wet, Miss?

I don't know, the girl whispers. Continues looking straight ahead. A very sad, very faraway look.

The two make some small talk. The ride doesn't last very long. Soon they've arrived at the address in Hayden. Our Good Samaritan hops out, goes around to open the passenger door for the young lady. When he does, he gets the surprise of a lifetime.

Nobody is there. There's nothing but a damp seat and a puddle of water on the rubberized floor mat. The man looks up the street, down the street. Even under his car. Gone! Nothing, nobody, empty. . .

Impossible. Yet she was there not a minute ago—he saw her with his own two eyes. And now there's this puddle, sure to befuddle.

Despite the late hour, the man decides to ring the doorbell. He's angry, wants to get to the bottom of it all. Must be some sort of teen prank. But how'd they manage to pull it off? Like magic?

A few moments later the light goes on. A grey-haired woman answers the door in her bathrobe. Fearful and suspicious. Can't blame her, strange man at the door this hour of the evening. What's the matter?

The driver explains his predicament. Describes the young lady, the dress, the bouquet of flowers. The old lady's eyes grow big. She covers her mouth, turns, retreats into the house. Soon the husband appears. But when the driver begins to retell his tale, the old man breaks down. Sobs uncontrollably. The wife coaxes everyone inside. No use disturbing the neighbors so late at this late hour.

There, on the mantelpiece in the living room, is a school yearbook picture of the same young woman the driver had been sitting with in his car not ten minutes before. Same blonde hair, same blue eyes, same dimpled chin. In an expensive white prom dress, carrying a bouquet of flowers, carrying on a two-way conversation. Anxious to get home before the dreaded one a.m. deadline.

In the flesh and blood, very much alive.

Only problem is, Diana Whitby has been dead for most of a decade now. It happened on prom night. Her careless boyfriend driving too fast, taking the curves on Dobbs Creek Parkway just a little too wide. Some bourbon on the rocks, too much centrifugal force. Lost control right by the little bridge that spans the creek. Ran his father's Buick clear off the road, down the short embankment, glanced off a tree. Flipped those shiny new wheels with the sporty tail fins right smack into the muddy water. Roof face down, spinning wheels face up.

The boyfriend climbed his way out with a only broken wrist, some minor scratches and bruises.

Poor, pretty Diana never made it home. Rescue personnel pulled her from the partially submerged wreck nearly an hour later.

They buried Diana right there in nearby old Mt. Lebanon Cemetery. Just a stone's throw from the scene of the accident. Just Miss Whitby, a few thousand other departed souls, and Crazy Sam bouncing up and down the cemetery roads, looking for juvenile trespassers to plug their backsides full of his signature rock salt.

The man who visited the Whitby house that night wasn't the first, probably won't be the last. Every year, about the same time, around the same place, the ghost of Diana Whitby tries to hitch a ride home. Succeeds . . . then disappears.

That's prom season in old Kings Cross.

Legend has it that if you lie down on Diana's grave at night and look up at the stars, you'll get a big surprise. They say at the stroke of midnight her ghostly arms will poke straight out of the ground and wrap around you in this great big spirit-world bear hug. Ghostly white arms. Slender, icy, bone-chilling fingers.

All you gotta do is say the magic words. Three times. . . .

Diana, please come home.

Diana, please come home.

Diana, please . . . come . . . HOME!

Gives little Jimmy Morris the willies just thinking about it.

Me, I'm taking their word for it. Fat chance you're gonna catch me out in the middle of Mt. Lebanon Cemetery at the stroke of midnight. No way. Not with Crazy Sam around.

And certainly not with Disappearing Diana on the loose.

Down the Shore

Dad likes the mountains, Mom likes it "down the shore." So, we almost always split our summer vacation. Spend one week at the extended Morris family's hunting cabin, where Dad walks in the woods looking to photograph the deer and black bear. Meanwhile, Mom watches us kids, cooks, cleans, and washes the clothes. Then the following week we're "down the shore" at Fleetwood, New Jersey, where Mom doesn't have to cook or clean, and we can all lie on the beach, swim in the surf, and stroll the boardwalk.

My father's sister, Aunt Marilyn, and her husband Pat rent a place on a cozy, sandy little street by the back bay. We bring blankets and sleeping bags and us kids all camp in the living room, wall-to-wall, which is great fun. The corner there store carries all my favorite comics, as well as both glazed and chocolate-covered donuts, so I get a chance to catch up on Iron Man, Captain America, Spiderman, and the Fantastic Four while swinging in a canvas hammock on the front porch and stuffing my face with frosted goodies.

Days are spent on the dazzling, white-hot sands at the famous Fleetwood beach. In the early evenings, we kids prowl the boards, munch on pizza, and frequent the popular amusement rides out on Iron Pier.

Daytime at the beach Mom tries her best to keep me all covered, since I look like a glass of milk and can get sunburned in just five minutes under an electric street lamp. Seems I'm nearly as white as the infamous Disappearing Diana, wonder if she does the burn and peel, too. It's not fair how Dad and Howie and other people can get all tanned and bronzed while people such as Mom and me wind up looking like cooked lobsters. Mom makes me wear a baseball cap, sunglasses, T-shirt, long shorts, and knee-high white socks when I'm not in the water. It makes me look like a miniature version of Claude Rains as the Invisible Man. Or maybe Lon Chaney Jr. as Kharis, the murderous Egyptian mummy I once played on Halloween Night going door-to-door in Kings Cross while in a progressive state of unravelment.

Howie and I go wading in the relentless Atlantic surf, and we have lots of fun until I get stung by a passing jellyfish, and then I don't see a wave coming which knocks me down and drags me under where I swallow about a half-gallon of salty, foamy, polluted seawater. So much for communing with Nature.

I go back to our beach blanket amidst a sea of baking bodies that stretches to the horizon in either direction up and down the coast. Grab a cupful of soda pop from our plastic jug, then remove my weighty T-shirt which is now all salty and soaking wet and sticking to my goose-bump skin. About a hundred or more transistor radios are all tuned to the same rock-and-roll station, playing the Doors' smash hit *Light My Fire*. Over and over and over again, there's no escaping the song this August.

♪♫♪♫♪♫

C'mon baby, light my fire

C'mon baby, light my fire

Try to set the night on fire, yeah. . . .

I try to ignore the driving beat, instead put my head down on the blanket and let the sun dry out the moisture. The rhythmic churning of the surf, the gentle sea breeze, the distant cries of the seagulls. A person could get used to this . . . I'm feeling better already.

♪♫♪♫♪♫

The time to hesitate is through.

No time to wallow in the mire

Try now, we can only lose

And our love become a funeral pyre.

400

I soon fall fast asleep, and by the time Mom and Dad come back from their swim, the sun has already done its damage. My white skin is turning red, and I'm starting to do the boiled, radioactive lobster thing like in some B-horror movie at The Parkland. Mom wakes me, reads me the riot act, has me put on my soaking T-shirt again, but there's little she can do after-the-fact. It's sure a drag being the one who has to be all Grade A, pasteurized, and homogenized just like Casper the Friendly Ghost. Never a bronzed tan, it's always the peel-and-burn scene for me. Bummer, as they say now.

Later that afternoon, back at the rental near the bay, Mom lathers my back in white, soothing Noxzema cream to cool the flame. I feel hot and achy so I take a nap on the couch before supper and wake up somewhat hungry and in better spirits. We have a special dinner which includes a feast of shrimp that does wonders for my appetite, despite my itchy skin. Shrimp is a special treat, and beats the dreaded ham and cabbage every time. Italians eat lots of shrimp—and when it comes to fine grub, these Mediterranean types sure know their stuff. *Abondanza!*

After the sun goes down me, Howie, and cousins Kevin and Maureen hoof it over to the famous Fleetwood boardwalk, where we walk the boards and take in the dazzling concoction of sights, smells, and sounds. We all buy some ice cream—I have a root-beer float, then we stop in an arcade to play a little skeetball. Skeetball's a cross between bowling and baseball where you have to underhand these dense tennis ball–sized rubber spheres down a raised alleyway into a series of concentric circles with cutout holes as your targets. I get the hang of skeetball quickly and soon win enough points to earn a stuffed animal.

Naturally, I take the orange tiger with the bold black stripes.

Then it's off to ride the bumper cars, me and my prize grrr tiger at the wheel, where I catch Howie not paying attention and slam him sideways a real good one, hope he has insurance. But when we hop out of the bumper cars, I notice that my stomach is starting to do the flip-flop, no doubt a result of the jellyfish, the swallowed salt water, the sunburn, all those little shrimps, topped off by with a generously large root-beer float and a little topsy-turvy bumper-car action. Definitely not what the doctor ordered, Mr. Jimmy.

So when it comes time to ride the "Cannonball" roller coaster out on Iron Pier, I take a rain check and sit on a bench overlooking the water and the waves, watching all the lights from passing boats. The nighttime ocean air has a calming effect, and I do my best to ignore the screams from the rocketing coaster as it twists and turns, rises and falls, I never did much like heights to tell you the truth. This bench is comfy and suits me just fine. Besides, I blew most of my night's budget on the root-beer float and the skeetball.

Next we visit the Seaside Pool where my eldest cousin Kathleen works as a lifeguard so we all get in free every night. Have you ever heard of anything so silly as having this pool on the boardwalk right next to the world's second biggest ocean? But the place is surprisingly crowded, especially after dark, with kids doing high dives and low dives and just horsing around in general. It is here at Seaside Pool that I am finally, this week—at last—learning how to swim.

If only Mr. Tanaka from the downtown Big Brothers could see me now—sorry, Charlie. No longer am I afraid to come into the deep water. What a difference a year makes. No sweat, I can't believe I behaved like such a baby.

Before we make the long trek back to the rental under the fat summer moon there's one more ride we all want to try. It's the infamous and legendary Black Hole, where they spin you around so fast, flatten you against the wall, then drop the floor out from under your feet. Look, Mom—no hands. Sounds great, we've saved the best for last. I'm definitely psyched.

We buy our tickets, stand in line, wait to be herded inside. People on the ride before us come out of the Black Hole all dizzy and disoriented but I pay this no mind. Just your regular tourist wimps, I figure. Hey, I'm not afraid of the Black Hole, me being almost an eighth-grader who can hold his own, even knows how to swim. If you go, then I'll go too . . . so count me in.

Sure enough they march us into this big, creepy, circular room with strong lights shining down from on high. Stand us all against the curving wall, facing toward the center of the circle, people staring back at one another. Then the big steel door shuts and the engines start their whining, revving into action. We're moving— slowly at first. Then faster and faster, gaining speed. The engines grow louder and louder. Spinning clockwise, the weight of gravity pressing your shoulders against the turning metal wall. Tighter and tighter.

My sunburn starts itching again, annoying at first, then maddening, and finally, escalating to downright painful. I try to pick out Howie's face against the moving wall, or cousin Kevin, or his sister Maureen, but everything is just a blur of motion, can't focus.

My skin is burning, stinging, screaming. My stuffed orange-and-black striped tiger lies trapped beside me, another prisoner of gravity. Somewhere, probably inside my head but can't tell for sure, that awful song starts to play. Loud, louder, the pounding volume growing. . . .

♪♫♪♫♪♫

C'mon baby, light my fire

C'mon baby, light my fire

Try to set the night on fire.

I want the ride to slow down, to stop. Just let me off, please. No refunds, you can keep the money. My stomach's doing the wigglies like a sport fish on a fisherman's hook, there's no escape, I'm caught.

Suddenly the entire floor drops away, my aching belly lurches, and it feels as if we're in some runaway elevator plunging about twenty floors. I'm suspended in midair against the smooth metal wall, my poor back and shoulders all ablaze from the radioactive cooked-lobster effect. Only centrifugal force holds me in place, same as the water in a bucket you swing over your head that doesn't spill.

Nice trick—so long as you do it with the bucket. I put my hand over my aching, temperamental belly, close my eyes tight, and start praying. I'm feeling the volcano fast welling up from within. As stomach upsets go this is a potential Vesuvius, could erupt at any moment . . . hey, look out below!

Please, God. Not here, not now. Upchucking in public has to pretty much top the list of the most supremely humiliating experiences. But here, in the Black Hole, the results could be disastrously unthinkable. Instead of falling harmlessly to the floor, the vile stuff would spew out and around at everybody and everything. Sticking to the cold metal walls, flying onto to unsuspecting, immobilized people who've got no possibility of escape. Undoubtedly starting a volatile chain reaction of mutually assured destruction. Critical mass, if you will—hysterical, involuntary, gut-wrenching group upchucking. First me, then someone else, then a whole series of other people as the sudden emergency reaches critical mass. Gross me out, a true catastrophe of epic proportions. The poor helpers would slide open the metal door only to find what looked like the results of a first-strike germ warfare by them Ruskies. Then they'd probably be forced to close the Black Hole for the rest of the summer just to get the stink out.

All because of me, Radioactive Lobster Boy, a.k.a. little ol' Dizzy Jimmy Morris. What a way to make the national news, I'd be the laughing stock of Southwest Philly.

But somehow, through the power of prayer and pure fear, I manage to hold my insides together long enough to weather the ride. After what seems like an hour or longer, the giant engines cut back, the weighty pressure eases, the spinning slows, and the very welcome floor comes rising up to greet my suspended sandals. Solid ground at last.

The spinning slows further, then ceases. The metal door slides open. Funny, but it almost feels like we're still spinning. Somebody please stop the world and let me off, much obliged.

Everyone shuffles toward the exit with me following behind, leaning on the sloping metal wall for support, clutching my striped companion, the little trophy skeetball tiger.

Nice ride. Who knows, maybe by next summer I might feel well enough to try it again.

Once outside, I savor the fresh salt air and seek the temporary comfort of my familiar bench.

C'mon, Jimmy . . . it's gettin' late. We've gotta be headin' back. You can sleep back at the house.

In a minute. I'm comin'. Just gimme a minute. Me and the grr tiger need a break.

Maybe Dad is right. Perhaps we should spend both vacation weeks up in the cool, clean, shady mountains. Not down the shore. . . .

Sorry, Mom. It was just a thought.

Do You Renounce the Devil?

With only days to spare, Mom and Dad have finally come to a much-debated decision. I'm not going to Sanders for eighth grade, instead I'm going to Catholic school, it's a done deal. Maybe I should be happy, since I'm finally going to be going to school with most of my neighborhood friends—Jackie O'Hanlon, Bobby Schaeffer, Frankie Pellegrino, Donnie Fahey, and most of the Littlefield/Wennington crowd. But this also means I won't be seeing many of my former Longstreet classmates ever again. No more Sherman Sykes, no more Rachel Moskowitz, no more Chuckie Long, no more Sara Webber, no more Coleman James, no more Physical Phil Buckley and briefcase, and no more Claire Miller. . . .

Old Horse Face Claire Miller? How could I possibly be missing *her* already?

Of course Dré Barnett will be in Sanders, but then he's black. Sanders is why Dré's here in the first place. And Davey Cutler from down the block is going into ninth grade at Sanders, but that's because he's Jewish. The Jewish kids have gotta go to public school, no choice in the matter, since they don't have a private school of their own. The Hebrew school on 57th and Beaufort doesn't count—all they teach there is Hebrew with the squiggly funny lines that don't look anything like the alphabet. Hebrew doesn't exactly cover the state requirements for the Three Rs, except maybe over in Israel where they just had this little shooting match called the Six Days War. Seems Southwest Philly ain't the only place where the action's gettin' hot and heavy.

Anyway, Davey can't very well be going to Catholic school, where you make the sign of the cross, recite the Lord's Prayer, and get beat up by the nuns and all that. It wouldn't be kosher. Besides, all the Catholic magic words are in Latin, and David only knows the Hebrew and perhaps a smattering of Yiddish, so it really wouldn't ever work out.

Which brings us to another problem . . . I'm not exactly Catholic either. Mom's a Catholic, but Dad's a Protestant, so us kids are sort of in the middle being pulled on from both ends. We're not really anything—yet. I think the Catholics call this being in a state of Limbo, or so I've heard. Seems I've been in this Limbo place going on thirteen years now, trapped as a prisoner of the forever war between The Orange and The Green, English versus Irish.

But that's all about to change. The Catholic school has decided to accept all us mixed-up half-limey, half-mick Morris kids, but only under one condition. We've got to be baptized Catholic, become *made* members of The Church. Uncle Patrick and Aunt Marilyn are going to be our godparents, since Uncle Pat's an Irisher and Aunt Marilyn converted to Catholicism way back when she and Uncle Pat got married down in Derby at Most Blessed Pius IX.

So on the appointed day we meet Uncle Pat and Aunt Marilyn in front of the OLPP Church at the start of a very wicked rainstorm. We can see the angry thunderheads rolling toward Kings Cross and both the church's twin green domes moodily silhouetted against the darkening sky. There's only little snafu, Dad's decided at the last minute he's not coming inside. Seems he can't bear to watch, this wasn't his plan, and under normal circumstances we'd probably never be converting to Catholicism. Our current predicament has all the trappings of another diabolical Papist plot, surely The Vatican must be behind all this busing madness. Mom is angry, Dad won't budge from behind the wheel, time's a wasting, and the priest is waiting. So we leave Dad to stew in the family car and enter the massive front doors of OLPP with our Uncle Pat and Aunt Marilyn at our sides.

The big church is cavernously empty, with only minimal light filtering though the panes of stained glass high up on the shadowy walls. Our new shoes scuffle across the marble floor and make intrusive sounds that echo through rows of empty hardwood pews, only to dissipate in some far corner of this vast expanse. The smell of faded incense lingers, and I'm awestruck by the grandeur of this special, magnificent place. I now see the familiar statue of the Blessed Mother with her sweet smile, and the ancient box of candles with a small number of flames still flickering. After all these years, I still must resist the urge to run over and blow them out birthday style, just a huff and a puff, the horror and shock on Grandmom Kane's face still fresh in my memory.

We reach the front of the church, stand stiffly by the altar, and in a few minutes a ruddy-cheeked priest in a long white robe and dark shoes comes out from a room tucked away behind and off to one side of the altar. The priest smiles graciously, introduces himself as Father McNulty, and ushers us over to this beautifully carved, white marble font atop a heavy stone pedestal.

It's all over in a few relatively painless moments. Father McNulty leans each of us children over the gleaming marble basin all filled with holy water, sprinkles us, performs the sacred baptismal rites. Anoints our foreheads with his sacred oil, makes the sign of the cross. Reads something from the Bible and says some magic Latin words for good measure. Everyone is very serious, but I catch a quick look at Mom's face and detect the hint of a smile.

The big part comes when Father McNulty asks me if I, James Morris, do renounce the Devil. I say, Yes, Father, I do. I'm pretty certain the priest is referring to the well-known, red-skinned troublemaker with horns, pointy tail, and sharpened pitchfork. But a nagging thought crosses my mind that he may instead be talking about my miffed Presbyterian father parked curbside in this late-summer downpour, speaking of which, we can hear the increasing thunder and hard rapping of windswept raindrops against the massive church's high windows.

But it's too late now for any second thoughts, like spilled milk and so much water under the bridge. What's done is done, and there's nothing my father or anybody else can do about it. Today I'm a made member of the Roman Catholic Church, the One True Faith, the only way to Heaven and eternal salvation. A true little Irisher, no doubt to my mother's extreme satisfaction. Father McNulty gives Uncle Pat and Aunt Marilyn a quick refresher course on the duties and responsibilities of being godparents, then it's back outside for fast goodbyes to Uncle Pat and Aunt Marilyn with a hurried dash through the weather into the back of Dad's waiting 1956, two-toned Chevy Bel Air. Our stony-faced parents say little and avoid looking at each other, and us kids know to keep quiet in the backseat during the short ride home to Littlefield Street.

It may be September and not mid-March, but that night in the Morris household is like a repeat of St. Patty's Day only without the ham and cabbage. Missing also are the "Kiss Me I'm Irish" buttons with shamrocks and the food coloring Mom sneaks into Dad's beer to make it look all weird and foamy green. Dad drinks his beer plain like on most nights, then starts straightaway on a marathon filibuster about the Pope, the papal conspiracy to dominate world politics, and the cowardly IRA thugs who have mustered the guts to blow up statues of English heroes, but only long after they're long dead and buried and can't fight back.

Sometime well into his second beer, my father vows to purchase the largest Union Jack money will buy, and display it prominently on our front porch for all the world to see.

I wouldn't try that here, Mom advises him. Not in Kings Cross, for God's sake. Use your head just for once.

That's right, Land of the Free and Home of the Brave, Pop snorts. Well, if someone doesn't like it, then they can just kiss my royal English you-know-what.

Dad does go on to say one thing that's news, and I don't hear Mom denying it. Seems I was scheduled to have been baptized Catholic once before, back when I was just a little baby. Aunt Marilyn and Uncle Hank were supposed to have been my godparents. But when the Church found out that Uncle Hank was a Protestant, they instructed Mom to find someone else to be godfather. Dad told them that if Uncle Hank wasn't good enough for the Church, then just forget it, and Mom backed him up, so I didn't get baptized. Which is how Howie, Laura, and me, even though we haven't made a regular habit of eating meat on Fridays, have come to enter into this dreaded state of Limbo.

Until today. . . .

So I understand Mom's being upset at Dad for skipping our baptismal ceremony, but then again maybe Dad has a legitimate gripe against the Church for what happened long ago. After all, it's the same church where Mom and Dad got married, and Dad was willing to let me get baptized there as a Catholic years before, so long as they let Uncle Hank be my godfather. So it's not like the Old Man's been entirely against the place his whole life. I don't know, except it's a tough call for sure. Same as late last autumn when the Fahey truck got melted right across from Grandmom's back yard. Yeah, maybe Buck Fahey shouldn't have been hiring loads of nonunion roofers and breaking all the rules. But then the roofers had no business torching his truck, which caused the Fahey house to catch on fire with everyone sleeping inside unaware of the spreading danger.

So it looks like this Catholics versus Protestants problem has been going on for a while and is bound to keep on going on and on. It's not only a Mom and Dad thing, my parents have got lots of company.

I doubt there was any use trying to run Uncle Hank past the priest for a second time, just to keep Dad happy. Lately Uncle Hank's been in this group they call the Masons, and from what I can tell the Masons and the Catholics don't exactly see eye-to-eye. The way I figure it, if the Protestants are to Catholics what dogs are to cats, then I guess the Masons must be like huge English bulldogs with spiked collars, big sharp teeth, and menacing pushed-in faces.

Guess after today I can forget about ever being a Protestant like Gram, Dad, Uncle Joe, Uncle Hank, and the rest of the extended Morris clan. No more juicy hamburgers on Fridays at the Parkland Restaurant for this good little Catholic boy.

And then there's Lent. Saints preserve us, as Grandmom Kane would say.

That night I lie in bed wide awake and listen to the storm sounds as they fade away and are replaced by the normal street noises of a waning summer in steamy Kings Cross. In less than a week I'll be marching off to Catholic school in my starched white shirt, grown-up tie, and woolen pants. No wonder these people pray a lot.

Heaven help us. In the name of the Father, and of the Son, and of the Holy Ghost. . . .

Heck, I don't even know how to tie a real necktie yet. I'm scared and growing more nervous with each passing day. I've heard all the rumors, listened to all the stories. A hundred kids in every classroom, nuns beating kids with yardsticks just for chewing gum or talking out of turn, making them do awful punishments like write 500 times *I will not forget to bring my notebook to class*. It's an insane asylum, all the toughest cases and JDs in Kings Cross go there, and now I'm to begin serving my sentence as the Catholics' newest inmate.

That's what Dad calls the all girls' school where Mom lived as a teenager, just like Hayley Mills in that movie *The Trouble with Angels*. Dad calls it the Catholic Slammer.

I still don't get it—what's all the big fuss? Why can't I just go to public school same as before? How come they have to bus all these colored kids here, and how come they're all starting to move into our neighborhood, too? Nobody I know really wants them here. Mom says even most of the colored parents are against having their kids bused here, have been all along. So who's shaking things up and changing all the rules?

I stare at the ceiling and my body refuses to fall asleep. My stomach is doing the flipping and the flopping, and those same terrible words keep running through my brain, like a mesmerizing mantra. . . .

O-L-P-P, Our Lady of Perpetual Peace.

O-L-P-P, Our Lady of Perpetual Peace.

O-L-P-P, Our Lady of Perpetual Peace. . . .

Dad just scoffs at the Church down at 56th and Lester, calls the place *Our Lady of Perpetual Bingo*. But Dad never had to put up with the nuns, or a hundred nutty kids to a classroom, or wearing a silly, starched white shirt, grown-up necktie, and woolen pants when you're only twelve years old.

Guess Dad lucked out. He's a Protestant. Got to go to Sanders back when they weren't sending colored kids to the school by the busload. The country had way more important things to worry about in those years—like paying back those rotten Japs big time for bombing Pearl Harbor.

Yep, now *those* were the good old days.

Now I'm just wondering if the sisters are *really* as bad as Jackie, Diet Donnie, Frankie, Bobby, Larry, Johnny, Scotty, and all the rest of them say.

I really do miss Longstreet Elementary, but there's no going back. So it's OLPP here I come, ready or not. . . .

Jesus, Mary, and good St Joseph. Pray for us sinners now and at the hour of our death, Amen. I can only hope Grandmom Kane has remembered to light a candle with my name on it under the statue of the Blessed Mother. Otherwise these crazy nuns I keep hearing about might decide to nail this poor little public school boy up on the cross, thumbs down and no mercy.

Hail Caesar! We that are about to die salute you.

Just before sleep finally comes, I hear the soft pop of another bottle being opened downstairs. Mom has already come upstairs to bed, leaving Dad alone in the living room settled into his favorite easy chair by the reading lamp. Now comes the Old Man's voice, humming and singing softly to himself in an empty room. . . .

♪♫♫♪♪♫♫

They'll always be an England,

And England will be free.

If England means as much to you,

As England means to me.

Guess you've just got to give The Devil his due. The Old Man may have lost a major battle today in the forever war between The Orange and The Green, English versus Irish, but he's not about to raise the white flag. No sir, not after nearly 800 years of blood, sweat, and tears. If his beloved Britannia can rule the waves of the world's seven seas, then surely merry old England can once again come to hold sway in the Morris household, where the sun never sets on the British Empire. Cream, as Gram Morris is so fond of saying, always rises to the top.

So us Morris kids better get ready for some home lessons, pop quizzes, and extended supper table filibusters about the great Charles Dickens, Rudyard Kipling, Lord Nelson, Winston Churchill, Queen Victoria, Queen Elizabeth, Thomas Jefferson, George Washington, and the entire cast of esteemed Anglo-Saxon heroes doing wonderful and miraculous deeds down through the centuries.

After all, this is our heritage, too—lest we forget.

God save the Queen.

Yep, that's my dad. Blue blood from the wrong side of the tracks. But I'm guessing this wrong side of the tracks thing must just be an expression, 'cause in Southwest Philly there for sure ain't no right side.

411

Meanwhile, upstairs at 5611 Littlefield, Mom and her newly minted little Irishers, her three converts to the One True Faith, the only way to eternal salvation, lie fast asleep in the Kings Cross sweltering summer heat.

Oh well, tomorrow promises to be yet another day, and the start of a brand new chapter in the never-ending war between the Morrises and the Kanes, The Orange and The Green, the proud and once-mighty English—and the long-suffering, ever-enduring Irish.

How it will all turn out I have nary a clue. All I care to think about is surviving the eighth grade in one relatively intact piece.

Saints preserve us.

To be continued in the upcoming book

=> *Row House Blues* <=

Tales from the Destruction of America's Largest Catholic Parish

For information, please visit *www.rowhousedays.com*

Oh, by the way . . . has anyone seen my Herman?

Printed in the United States
41328LVS00010B/13